SOUL MATES

With surprise, Eve stared at the man, seeing dark hair, almost as long as her own, swaying above tanned shoulders. When her searching eyes dropped to the bare chest, down to his moccasins, she flushed hotly at his virile manliness.

He was staring right at her. *Right through her.*

A plaintive sound echoed across the land and brushed Eve's mind. It was primitive, haunting, and so very, very beautiful she could have swooned from the stirring in her soul.

She looked at the painted face again and blinked out of her trance. "My name is Evelyn Michaels."

"And mine is Steven McCloud."

WHAT'S LOVE GOT TO DO WITH IT?

Everything . . . Just ask Kathleen Drymon . . . and Zebra Books

HEAVENSENT

SONYA T. PELTON

ZEBRA BOOKS
KENSINGTON PUBLISHING CORP.

ZEBRA BOOKS are published by

Kensington Publishing Corp.
850 Third Avenue
New York, NY 10022

Zebra and the Z logo Reg. U.S. Pat. & TM Off.

First Printing: March, 1995

Printed in the United States of America

For my daughter Lisa's children—Jennifer and Jeffrey LeBeau—who have the blood of the Cheyenne River Sioux

. . . And God saw
all the things
that he had made,
and they were
very good.

—Genesis 1:31

Prologue

They had taken the dresses, the bright ones, several yards of yellow cloth, and some blue beads.

At the headwaters of the Colorado River, in one of the settlements in the heart of the wilderness, Evelyn Michaels's brothers, John and Derek, along with Maggie Dexter's brother, Hank, had fashioned a log cabin.

From midsummer until Christmas they hunted and trapped, then gathered at the trading posts, where they spent the proceeds of their season's work. The mules' packs were filled with pelts, catches to trade at the Rendezvous. At the post convened a medley of traders, trappers, and hunters. The white men, the Mexicans, the Indians—and the half-breeds—known as Amerindians—would amuse themselves gambling, dancing, drinking, and with wrestling or shooting matches. All this was frequently interrupted by bloody fisticuffs. These contests were nearly always over horses or women, both of which were considered very valuable.

More often than not, Eve's and Maggie's brothers would get into a row with a few of the Amerindians. Usually, nothing more serious than a few blackened eyes and a bloody lip would result.

For John, Derek, and Hank, the brawling and gambling eased the long days and nights between midwinter and early summer, when there was not much to amuse themselves with in their leisure hours. As for Eve and Maggie, they spent their days in the little cabin hard at work at their many tasks.

In the flickering light of a tallow candle they spent their spare time—which there was so little of—reading, stitching upon crude samplers, mending, washing, and cooking. Commodities of all kinds were bitterly scarce. Once in a while a ragged volume or bits of fabric turned up in the saddlebags or rucksacks of one of the white traders and the women persuaded their brothers to swap small pelts for these highly valuable items. Derek had promised to bring back some yellow cloth, blue beads, and sewing needles from the trading post. Eve wanted to make a yellow dress; all she could think of these days was the pretty dress she would stitch.

The wilderness dwelling was no place for well-bred women of Maggie's and Evelyn's ilk, but fate would have it no other way. The crude life would be their lot until something better came along, for Eve knew her brothers would not want to take her and Maggie back to St. Louis.

Eve longed for something better, more exciting. She thought it was long overdue. And yet, this was the way she believed her life was going to be for a long time. Simple and uneventful . . . her dreams were just that: dreams.

* * *

Late one Sunday, a dewy blue morn, when the brothers were long overdue from the trading post, Eve and Maggie ventured out to investigate. Hours later, after being informed at the trading post that their brothers had not been seen among the others gambling away precious coin, Maggie and Eve continued the lengthy search, tired and desolate at the end of the day.

"It's just no good, Maggie," Eve said, sitting down on a log, her chin in her hands.

"They must have gotten lost," Maggie said, looking worried and frightened.

"Big men don't get lost," Eve told Maggie. She stood up then. "We'll go back to the cabin and see if they've returned."

"I'm afraid they won't be there, Eve."

"What do you want to do? Keep looking until we drop?"

"No. You're right. We'll go back."

On the way back to the little mist-shrouded cabin, Eve and Maggie found their brothers at last.

Lying in pools of congealed blood, they had all three been unmercifully slain. Both of Eve's brothers had slit-open throats and Maggie's brother, Hank, had been viciously stabbed to death. Lying beside Eve's brother, Derek, was the empty beaver pack, no pretty yellow cloth or blue beads within. The bright material he'd promised her and Maggie were nowhere to be seen. But Derek Michaels always brought back what he promised. She had seen the yellow cloth just the week before, where it had been for months. No one could have bought or traded it . . . it had to have still been there.

"I can't tell if Indians did this or . . . I just don't know." Eve would have flung herself weeping to the bloodied earth if not for Maggie, who was standing dry-eyed with shock, her face the shade of limestone, her hands twisted together in a knot.

Eve had to remain strong for Maggie, the younger of the two. It was up to Eve now as to what the future would hold for them. She was twenty. Maggie was nineteen. If they made a disturbance and complained at the trading post, no doubt the word would be passed around and their fate would be the same as their brothers'. They were too young and tender to fight big burly trappers or savage Indians. They might get raped if they complained too much or too loud.

After Eve gently laid out the bodies in a crudely dug grave and covered them, she said prayers while Maggie clutched the old Bible. Maggie could not even glance one last time at the dearly departed as she and Eve left the grave site.

Back at the cabin, Maggie continued to sob uncontrollably, softly. Eve thought this must be better than having Maggie stare into space, as she'd done at first. She handed her friend a tin cup containing hot broth and, at last, Maggie started coming back to the world.

But it was a lonely, bleak world she returned to.

The early summer months turned sultry, the very air laden with a platinum mist. The sky and the land drew forth a hot brilliance like a pearl-gray sea. Not a leaf or a pine needle stirred above the cabin as the young women made preparations to leave.

They could not stay the winter. It would be too dangerous with trappers and Indians passing the cabin on their way to Sam's Trading Post. The well-beaten path curved out front, and two young women living alone unprotected . . . What was Eve thinking? Maggie wondered.

Softly Maggie complained, "We'll be out in the open, Eve. How are we going to protect ourselves? At least here we have a cabin to hide in. We could get a rifle. Maybe our brothers did not take all the weapons and they were not all stolen from the—you know."

The bodies, Maggie did not say.

Eve kept packing, not looking at Maggie. "The murderers left us not one single weapon, Maggie. They killed our brothers and took all they'd been carrying—guns, ammo, even the hunting knives strapped to their legs. How will we purchase a rifle? We have no money. Nothing to trade. No bright cloths or beads that the trappers or miners would need to lure squaws to their beds. We surely won't be giving *our* bodies. That'd be a sin. Besides, I never would let a man touch me. At least on the trail we can find a bush or rock to hide behind. In the cabin they would surely find us. There would be no safe place to hide or run to. Outside we can see them coming, that is, if we're careful and alert."

It was time to depart.

Eve heard Maggie sigh. The sound was small, almost inaudible, but Eve heard the soft lament. She looked up from their meager baggage as Maggie murmured, "We are going to make it, aren't we, Eve?"

Eve nodded soberly, her misty eyes grave. "We are. I promise. We'll find someone to take us in and we'll work for our living. We're strong, Maggie, and young. We have that going for us," she said gently, hoping to God she was right.

Maggie was quiet a moment before she sighed

again and said to her friend, "Eve, I'm going to die missing Hank. He was so good, so kind. I don't think I can go—I really don't—"

"Yes. You can go on, Maggie. The past is gone. And our brothers have gone to a better place; just think of it that way."

"Have they, Eve?" Maggie was looking at Eve intently, as if Eve's reply would answer some deep, unsolved question plaguing her.

"Yes!" Eve turned from the bag of food she was packing. "Do you not know of God, Maggie?"

"I used to think so," Maggie answered harshly.

"I don't believe you. God is on our side, Maggie. Just believe and it shall come to pass."

Maggie asked, "How will we do it without them?"

"I know as much about trapping as any man. I studied the procedure of the winter hunt while our brothers were . . . still . . . alive. They taught both of us how to set traps, to skin and care for the furs, how to build a bridge by dragging quaking-asp poles across a creek with a horse."

"I don't remember, Eve."

"Well, watch and remember."

Eve placed one end of a rope around a pole, the other around the saddle horn. They had four old mares to pull the wagon, and on the bed Eve laid wickiup poles, sacks of clothes and bedding, a bag of flour, hard beans, and other grub, little that was left. Shovels and hatchets came next, and finally the blackened cooking utensils followed.

Maggie reached for the hatchet and held it up. "Weapon," she said with a rare smile.

"Right. You sound like a squaw." Eve smiled

back, reaching for the shovel. She grimaced as she tossed it back, hoping she'd never have to use it.

They were off before dark that night, naively deciding it would be better to leave when dusk was settling down, their passage near the trading post possibly going unnoticed.

Starting down the trail, they were two specks moving alone in vast green reaches of hills and valleys.

Maggie's face shadowed. "Darn it—I'm afraid. I don't want to be, but I am."

"Well, I am too," Eve confessed with a shrug. "That does not mean we are dead, does it?"

Maggie's shoulders leapt with an embarrassed gesture. "I guess not." She shook her dark blond braids, adding, "We are alive and healthy." She smiled at her own wisdom and muttered softly under her breath, "And *sort* of afraid."

Feeling safer the farther they rode, Eve and Maggie did not make camp until the following morning, when the sun was hidden behind a platinum mist.

The country was open, visibility good for miles around when the two young women stopped their tired horses on a lookout point high above a creek. Silence sluiced the air, and there was no movement anywhere, not behind, not below. Eve and Maggie exchanged glances and then stared out to the infinite unknown.

The two of them. So alone.

Before darkness fell again, the two followed the Spanish Trail which had many branches. One of the most frequently used crossed the Green River just north of the Colorado border.

It was there, at the heart of the Green River, long the hunting grounds of the Ute and Shoshoni Indians, that Eve and Maggie finally fell into the clutches of Pierre Dessine and his brutal followers.

Among them was a wicked and dangerous man named Scar-Face.

Dreams of Thunder

Part I

Chapter One

Eve ran, the old blanket under her arm. She was wearing a beaded Indian dress and beneath it she had wrapped a band of cotton cloth about her chest to keep away unwanted male attention.

Shading her eyes with one hand, Eve kept running as she stole a quick glance at the fiery ball of sun; already it was a blindingly bright glare as it shone against her dark hair and once-creamy features. Now she was as dark as the Indian girl Many Stars.

No breeze blew over the tall spiked fence of the fort. Her eyes ached as she looked around at the hellish surroundings: cluttered yards, dirty one-room cabins. Enclosed by a long palisade built on a rock foundation, the fort had several large storage rooms for pelts dug into its dirt grounds. A number of log cabins lined the inside walls, while outside the fence, other cabins and wickiups served the trappers and their squaws.

Fort Robidoux was alive with the creaking of wagon wheels, the bite of the Spanish slavers' whips, and the harsh whoops of drunken revelry. Robidoux's new fort had quickly grown into Utah's first permanent white settlement, serving as the trading center of the Rocky Mountain and Great Basin fur trade for more than a decade. Ute Indian legends held that Fort Robidoux was built on the ruins of an even earlier fort, the work of a mountain man, Jim Reed, who had loved an Indian girl and lost her at the Whiterocks Fork of the Uinta River, where she'd drowned.

Still hurrying with her bundle, Eve made her way to the one-room cabin, where no pretty curtains blew from open windows and no small children could be seen playing outside. Older Indian girls and boys, dirty and sad, walked about with sunken eyes, sweating and toiling for the Spanish slavers and miners.

Evelyn Michaels was just twenty, but the bloom of youth had recently disappeared, leaving a haggardly appearance; the strain of the past weeks had taken its toll. Even her beaver-brown hair, which had been hastily braided down to her slim waist, looked dull and badly in need of washing.

In the still, sultry surroundings, Eve now hurried to sit with her friends, Maggie Dexter and Many Stars. The nights were cold and they would need the extra blanket that Eve had stolen. The other two women sagged wearily against a low-roofed adobe shelter inside the walls of the old fort; the rest of the buildings were log cabins.

Again the three women cringed inwardly at the wickedness and debauchery of the slavers with the Indian women. Many Stars's huge black eyes looked very sad. She was wearing a standing collar of turquoise-and-blue beads which the slaver, when he came by, would yank on, almost choking her. A black-tipped white feather hung upside down in Many Stars's hair.

Eve had helped Many Stars and saved her many times from the slavers. She had tricked the slavers when they'd been drunk, slipped Many Stars out the back door before they could have molested or killed her.

But Eve had not been able to rescue Many Stars before one of the Spanish slavers had cut her finger off for trying to escape. Many Stars had almost bled to death, and she had shivered so much the night before that Eve thought she'd lost her friend.

"Move along there!"

Again the crack of the whip on some hapless soul's back, the material covering it rent to the waist and the victim left bare to blister in the relentless sun. Many Stars shivered when she saw this, and Eve gritted her teeth, wishing she were a man. Maggie sagged closer to the building, fearing and watching the foul men with big dark eyes.

"Bastards," Eve hissed, watching the men out of the corner of her eye. How would they like to be treated in such an inhumane way, she asked herself angrily.

The slavers were buying and selling the Indian women—some half-breeds, some barely older than children—selling them to one another and using them over and over. Exhausted and bruised, the Indian women could hardly stand after the detestable bastards had taken their turns on them and tossed them out the door, all fight gone. If lucky— and this made Eve smirk with bitterness—the women would sometimes be purchased as wives.

"Can you believe these men?" Eve asked Maggie.

"They are filthy pigs," Maggie whispered softly, head down, afraid of being overheard.

Soon Eve's and Maggie's turn would come. But now they had to worry about Many Stars.

Two men sauntered over to where they sat. Eve recognized the Frenchman, Pierre Dessine, the one who'd brought them to this fate and so far left them unharmed, except for Many Stars's loss of her fingertip.

Eve, understanding French, English, and a little Spanish, listened intently to the conversation he carried on with a Spanish slaver nearby.

"À bon marché," Pierre Dessine was saying, "good bargain."

Eve and Maggie exchanged wary looks as the dark Spaniard feasted his eyes on Eve, his lecherous gaze coming to rest on the beaded bodice of her Indian dress. Pierre had told Scar-Face of her trickery, how she'd wrapped a band of cotton cloth about her chest after he'd gotten the Indian dress for her.

"Her chest is—" Pierre had begun, demonstrating to Scar-Face with coarse movements and gestures. Scar-Face got the picture.

Scar-Face stared hungrily, aware that pressed beneath the cloth Eve Michaels had beautiful breasts. Ah, yes, she would be a good bargain, as Pierre said. Once all the dirt and grime had been washed away, she would prove a comely wench, apparently of French or even Spanish descent. Perhaps some Indian blood? This did not matter. He knew she could be a beautiful whore when cleaned up and gowned properly. Many Stars had served him well, but he was tired of her.

Once the copper coloring from months in the sun

wore off Eve's face and arms, they would be creamy as ivory, soft as a dove, as pale as her rounded breasts, Pierre Dessine thought.

Eve was clutching the remnants of an old blanket, when a door behind them crashed open. This caused Eve and Maggie and the Indian girl to jump in alarm. Maggie cringed against the wall, fearing to lose a finger, as had Many Stars, that, or worse.

Had their time come? A drunken *engagé* leered from the rough-hewn portal. He unsuccessfully steadied himself against the jamb with his meaty, hairy arms.

Eve caught a whiff of his stench, his sour whiskey breath as he leaned from where he wavered a few feet from them.

"Get out. Go away. Be gone," Eve said all in one breath, hoping he would get the message and not stay where he wasn't wanted.

No such luck.

Eve grimaced as he waggled a grimy finger in a come-hither motion toward her. She immediately shrank back out of his reach.

"Do not touch me, you bastard!" Eve shouted, then was sorry for her outburst as a whimper was heard.

"Maggie," Eve whispered to her friend. "Don't cry out, or he'll come after you. He preys on the weak. Try to be strong, Maggie. He'll not look at you then."

The Indian girl with the white feather in her hair crept closer to Eve for comfort and security. Maggie now began to cry uncontrollably, and Eve cradled the younger woman in her arms, her eyes flashing a warning to the ravager to come no closer.

"Ha," the *engagé* snarled, reaching for a whip that hung from a nail on a door frame.

Eve looked up as he wiped his mouth of slimy drool with the back of his hairy arm and lurched forward. He tilted his head back so far that he almost fell, pulling deeply from a bottle of fiery liquid. Tottering, he wiped his mouth again in the same fashion, eyeing the young women closely while he spoke a warning.

"I don't want her, I want you." He pointed directly at Eve. "Dammit, come 'ere, you dark-haired wench!"

"Never! Go away, filthy pig!" Eve shouted defiantly, and hugged Maggie closer. "Don't come any nearer, or I will kick you between the legs!" she dared to shout, feeling Many Stars hovering at her back.

"Ey, what'sa matter, sweetheart, don' you like old Will?"

The Indian girl blinked in horror as she looked at him, at the huge lust evident between his legs. Many Stars was repulsed by this man, praying he would come no closer to her and the woman she'd come to think of as her "white" friend.

Will laughed harshly and then his bloodshot eyes lit up at the display of spirit he'd witnessed in Eve. He liked that; there was little spirit in the women at the fort.

Eve saw it too. Read his lust. She changed her mind about Maggie's lack of courage and whispered, "Maggie, keep crying. He hates it."

"But he will want *you* then," Maggie said in a frightened whisper.

"So be it. Better me than you," Eve shot back in

a low voice, aware that Pierre and Scar-Face were watching from the palisade.

As Pierre Dessine came over, Eve grabbed him boldly by the arm as she stood to face him.

"You have brought us here. Now please take us away from this place. I will promise you anything, *monsieur*. We do not belong here." And then for the first time in her life she lied. "You will be paid handsomely if you heed my wishes. Our people wait for us."

"Why did you not tell me this before?" Pierre said, glaring at her hotly.

Eve fumbled. "I—I was afraid."

He looked into her eyes for a moment, then turned to Will. "Go away, Will. You've had enough of wenching for one day. Besides, these two are mine. I never gave orders for them to be brought to this side." His eyes glinted over Eve and again saw her worth. He spat out to Eve, "You better not be lying to me, *mademoiselle.*"

She looked up at him. "You can believe me." Her tongue flicked her lips as she spoke in French. "I do not lie." She looked across Pierre's shoulder to see the scar-faced man watching; the Spaniard's eyes glittered.

Many Stars and Maggie looked at each other as Eve faced the Frenchman like a bold soldier would. Pierre walked away and Eve's smile was sly as she turned to Maggie and Many Stars.

"I know him now," was all she said.

With a little smile Many Stars revealed, "I know a little French."

"Good," Eve said as they settled down to await the next event.

"What now?" Maggie asked in a trembling voice, huddling close.

Eve answered, "We get some rest."

"We can only hope," Many Stars said in ragged French.

In French again, Many Stars added, "I also know some from each of the Shoshonean tribes. The languages of these tribes are related. I can also speak some of the Dakota language—very little."

"Good enough," Eve said. "When and if the time comes, we might need your knowledge."

Eve looked closely at Many Stars, seeing the pain in her eyes. The Indian girl would be hurting for some time, and although Eve had treated the wound according to Many Stars's medicine, all she could do now was pray that infection would not set in.

"Will you be all right?" Eve asked Many Stars.

"I will," said Many Stars. "I have suffered worse from the hands of man." Her eyes would have rested on Scar-Face had he been present at the moment.

Eve would hate to see Many Stars die. She was very gentle and warm-hearted. And even though she'd never believed an Indian could be loving or trustworthy, Eve knew she could trust Many Stars with her life. Already she was like a sister to her.

Later that afternoon a very strange thing happened to Eve. She stood to ask the guard for water—after having sat for a long time with her legs tucked under her—and she wavered, having to clutch the wall for support. Her eyes dimmed, and in that gloomy mist she saw a strange object, now two, and one seemed to be riding upon the back of the other. If she had not felt so weak, it would have been funny.

A turtle and a butterfly. *What did this mean?*

Am I losing my mind, Eve asked herself, watching the sky grow dark blue as she rested again at the entrance to the shelter.

Chapter Two

Midnight came, and after Eve and her friends had been fed some greasy slop, they tried to sleep in the crude shelter that had been set up for the "extras."

"Maggie?" Eve whispered. "Many Stars?"

When Eve was certain Maggie and Many Stars finally slept, she slipped outside for air. The coolness of deepest night made itself felt. She filled her chest slowly, many times, then expelled the breaths, one by one, finally becoming relaxed.

She saw that the guard was asleep, a bottle lying empty beside his languid arm. Now she looked around for a place to sit and be at peace, careful not to wake the snoring guard.

"I might as well stay close," she told herself. "No telling what might happen in this awful place."

Seated on the hard-packed earth beside the hut, Eve gazed up at the huge stars scattered across the Uinta Mountains. Silent tears burned her eyes as she prayed to God that the morning ahead would be better for Maggie, Many Stars, and herself.

This nightmare must end sooner or later.

Eve clasped her hands in her lap, feeling the grime between her fingers, knowing her face must be smudged with the same dirt. She was not allowed to bathe, and doubted if even a tub were available. The women had used up the remainder of their drinking water to wipe away some of the filth with pieces of torn petticoats and blanket remnants. Mostly the material had to be used for washing away the blood from cuts and to soothe bruises.

"What a way to exist," Eve said to the night air. If there was a hell, Maggie, Many Stars, and herself were in it.

She had fought like a tigress when they'd been brought to this hellhole. Knocked down so many times, Eve had become dizzy with pain, but Maggie, Many Stars, and she herself had had no idea where they'd been brought. Not at first. They had been forced to trudge with a motley garrison of Canadian and Spanish *engagés* and hunters. A few Indian women along the way, like Many Stars, had been captured also, and trekked behind Eve and Maggie as they followed the Uinta upstream.

She had seen the dark-eyed man, a Spaniard, as he angrily joined them, giving Eve to believe that Many Stars had been his captive and had just lately run away. He had watched her with the eyes of a hawk, as if plotting evil plans for Many Stars's future.

Mercilessly slain and left unburied along the trail were those too sick or too old to keep up. Then they had come upon a group of children laughing and playing; right before the Indian mothers' eyes they had been whisked off and away by the Spanish slavers. Emerging from the woods, Eve had glanced up to see a huge cloud passing across the sunset, giving the puffy white substance a silver lining. She would never forget the beautiful sight or the golden mo-

ment. That was when she had felt Many Stars slip
her hand shyly into hers, and Eve had felt that she
had gained another "sister," for Maggie was like
one also.

The moon had made an appearance by now as
Eve stood up to stretch the stiffness from her muscles. Grief and many trials had exhausted her at last,
along with the painful memories she tried to hold
back, like thoughts of her parents and her brothers.
She could not dwell upon those, or else she'd not be
able to function at all.

She faltered again, holding her hand to her forehead.

A vague memory sifted through Eve's brain. It
was almost as if she could hear the sound of drums.
Like thunder. Then the sound grew dim, receding
into the fleeting images from her past.

"I must not lose my mind," Eve whispered as she
looked around, then picked up the hem of her skirts
to step back inside the gloomy, musty interior.

She must keep going, Eve told herself, be strong,
keep busy for herself and the others.

Hours later Eve was still worrying. She had never
felt so dirty and cold and miserable. Now she lay in
the beaded Indian dress, wondering about the slain
Indian woman who had owned it before, and slept.

Early in the morning, while it was still dark outside, Eve dreamed. . . .

An Indian woman, slightly older than Many
Stars, was wearing Eve's mysterious Indian dress.
The woman was not very pretty, but her bright,
dark eyes were kindly, her smile curious and open.
She beckoned to Eve, holding out both arms, still

smiling, and Eve walked right through the woman, coming out on the other side wearing the beaded dress.

The woman had vanished like mist-smoke.

Morning dawned. Suspense and tension hung in the air like a torch waiting to be ignited in the dark of a cellar. As Eve bent over Maggie's straw pallet, she looked up to see Many Stars already awake and staring at her.

"What is it?" Eve asked Many Stars, noting alarm and renewed fear.

In French Many Stars answered, "Blood. I saw much blood in my dreams. And many warriors in the hills."

"What does this mean?" Eve asked, looking down into Maggie's awakening and worried eyes.

"They are coming."

"Who is?" Eve held Maggie's hand as she got up.

Many Stars's eyes were beautiful and liquid black with a touch of blue in them. *"Ute Indians.* We will run and hide now, to wait out the attack and ensuing battle."

Calmly, Many Stars stood and gathered the blanket, waiting for Maggie and Eve. "Come," she said. The urgency was in her voice, not her movements.

"Yes," Eve said, whirling with Maggie as if in slow motion. "At once."

Every careless movement would cost them. They moved cautiously and fluidly, without panic, without hysteria, like soaring hawks making shadows across the land.

Maggie was learning.

Chapter Three

It was not the Utes, but the Shoshoni.

The hills above Fort Robidoux were full of war-riors.

The rebellion had exploded!

"Them Injuns ain't all Utes; they's mostly the Shoshoni!"

"What's the difference. They's all bloody red-skins. Keep the gate closed! Keep your eyes on the walls!"

Watching his back, getting his rifle ready, Scar-Face, thinking himself well read, arrogantly mum-bled, "The Uto-Aztecan family, this includes the Shoshoni, Comanche, Ute, Paiute, Hopi. There are even more branches. The one I'd like to kill is Sun-cloud, before he gets me, as I hear he would like to slay me even though he does not know me." Scar-Face shrugged and kept getting ready for battle. "Holy Mother, what did I ever do to him, will some-one please tell me?"

Scar-Face received no answer and sneered down at his rifle, wishing he were putting it to Suncloud's face.

Turning from Scar-Face, Will and the mountain-man Jim Reed shrugged, grabbing rifles from the storage rooms as outside the palisade, trappers and their squaws were running from cabins and wicki-ups. The squaws were screaming and running with their arms thrown in the air.

The Shoshoni were already attacking, coming down from the hills. Will and his motley garrison of *engagés* cussed all the while they worked to prime the weapons. First the weapons exchanged hands at the tailgate of a clumsy buckboard groaning with the weight, and then they were distributed.

Will turned just in time to catch Eve and Maggie and Many Stars sneaking out of the shelter, knotted scarves holding mysterious loads.

"Ha! I see you *ladieees,*" Will taunted.

Will would have laughed at the astonishment written on their alert faces if the situation had not been so serious.

"Injuns are attackin' and they'll be climbin' over those walls in no time!" Will snorted at the suddenly dispirited faces. "You ain't goin' nowheres, ladies."

Arrows began to fly from the wall. Will ducked, thrusting two heavy rifles into the cabin. "Here! Use them! Them Injuns has already got over the walls."

Wildly, Eve looked down at the weapons, then back up at Will. Was he crazy? Giving women firepower?

Indians over the walls? How?

"Use them," he repeated. "If you don't, you and your little friends might find yerselves scalped. But first them redskins'll rape you and take turns on you three. If the Utes don't get you, the Shoshoni or the Paiutes will. They been seen in the hills too, wearin' them fancy beaded breastplates 'n feathers 'n color-ful tight-assed leggin's. The Shoshoni are worse than the Utes when it comes to 'taking' a woman. So use them rifles if you want to stay alive."

Eve grunted and spat out with irony, "Ah, *Dieu,* what would be the difference if it be redskins or you filthy pigs."

Maggie leaned to Eve. "Maybe we should use these weapons on them, not on the Indians."

Many Stars grinned at that idea.

"Very good," Eve said to Maggie. All motion now, she began to prime the weapon. "We'll use them on whoever tries forcing us to his will. Whoever even thinks it."

Maggie and Many Stars nodded.

"They are coming in," Maggie exclaimed. "Look. They've killed the guards and opened the doors to the others." Her eyes widened as the ponies and paints exploded into the fort in a tumultuous display of savage color and sound.

Eve stared at the Indians—strange Indians— wearing furry hats with horns and feathers, skin hats, leggings with various colorful designs. Some even wore beaded hair ornaments and skimpy cloths covering their backsides. Eve swallowed, thinking that some of these warriors were very good-looking!

Bullets ricocheted off rocks and whined like wild bees through the sultry morning. One bullet hit its mark and unhorsed a bloodthirsty warrior trying to zigzag his way inside the fort.

"Ha!" Will called to his partner. "Got me another of them blasted redskins, Jim! See, them Utes're riding with their Shoshoni brothers. They's comin' in first and then some more of them nasty Shoshonis will follow."

"Just lookee that—Arapaho!" Jim returned.

"They got together and there's too damn many of 'em Injuns for us!"

Will and Jim and the others estimated the band to consist of slightly more than three hundred well-armed, rebellious Utes, Shoshonis, Arapaho, and breeds.

"Them handsome bucks hate whites," Will snorted.

"Yeah," returned Jim, " 'specially cruel slavers like us." He chortled and spat brown juice. "We'll run and hide when the fightin' gets goin' good, just like them wimmen plan to do. Then we can celebrate later, when there's only us and the wimmen."

"Can't wait to get my hands on that woman."

"Which one?"

"The one they call Eve."

"Naw. I'll take the little blonde. The Dark Hair don't have any jugs."

High on a hill, Suncloud was seated proudly on his painted war horse, Wind. Suncloud did not hate all whites or Spanish, but turned hard and uncaring on those at the fort who were cruel and wicked, like the Spanish slavers. Shoshoni men, women, and children had been captured many times; they were either branded by the slavers with hot irons, the women beaten, bruised, and sexually assaulted, or forced to work long days in the hot sun or freezing cold. All this with little rest or food. Often those captured had escaped, only to return to the village with a hand or a foot hacked off. This, after they had taken more than their meager share of food at the fort. Some were hungrier and more energetic than others, was all.

Suncloud did not like to think of what he was most angry about. He would find the ones who had raped and slain his beloved Morning Moon. She had been left naked, her beaded dress nowhere in sight, her body pecked unmercifully by buzzards.

Yes, truly today Suncloud hated those most cruel slavers and wanted to punish them accordingly.

This was not all. He had been compelled to join the uprising for other reasons.

Suncloud looked into the sky, watched a soaring hawk making shadows across the land.

The image of the turtle and butterfly had come to him once again. The same pictures he had seen when he'd gone on a vision quest. Some older men laughed because his vision had been of a turtle, and then, when he looked back at the elders, they turned somber faces upon him. But Suncloud knew they were still chuckling about his "important" vision.

For some reason, Suncloud had a feeling that today was—he shook his head and winced—the beginning of his "turtle quest."

On a lower bump in the hill a young Indian with blue-black hair stood barefoot on his horse, staring down on the fort. He was handsome but for the knife scar above his right eye.

Tames Wild Horses had again seen the vision of his love to come and feared in his heart that she had been harmed in some way, or, worse, already slain.

This could not be, he told himself. Great Father had given him a vision and he could only pray now that Shining Eyes—his name for her—would know him also. He prayed that she had dreamed of him as he had of her countless times.

Shining Eyes would be with the slavers this time. Tames Wild Horses had dreamed of this young woman, of her soft lips, delicate features, enormous eyes, moon-dark hair, and gently swaying form. She would be so happy to see him that her eyes would shine. She would hold out her arms and run to him. Then he would take her far from the Indian settlement to be alone with her.

Tames Wild Horses looked to his cousin, Suncloud, on the higher rise. He, too, bided his time. Not for love. No. Suncloud sought revenge for the cruel treatment of his wife, Morning Moon. He had been informed that the Spanish slaver Scar-Face who had bought his wife and brutally used her had shown up at Fort Robidoux.

Suncloud of the Shoshoni. He was white man; he was Indian. He was a combination of the white man's cleverness and savvy and the Indian's keen understanding of nature. He was as close as a brother to Tames Wild Horses. He was loved by women and children, though sometimes he was too busy for them. He had never hated with savage fury or revenge in his heart. Not even when his sister had been taken by the Comanches when he'd been very young; at least he'd thought Honna would have a chance with Indians of the Shoshonean branch. But when the recent messenger had come by with the news that for years Honna had been so brutally used by a Spanish slaver it had caused her to lose her mind, Suncloud had been like a different man. Honna had been out there wandering all these years, or dead in an unmarked grave. No one knew which it was. If she'd survived, she would be a young woman now.

This news, upon the tail of his recent loss of

Morning Moon, was too much for Suncloud. He was on the warpath as bent for revenge as he'd be if he were a full-blooded Indian.

Tames Wild Horses hated to think what would happen to those on the receiving end of Suncloud's wrath. Tames Wild Horses knew only that he would have to save Shining Eyes and keep her from harm. What Suncloud did with his captives once they brought them back to the tiny Indian town of Wild Thunder was Suncloud's business.

Shining Eyes was his.

Chapter Four

The torrid morning wore on, erratic fire from the Indians that had stormed the gate punctuating the heat. Those at Fort Robidoux did not observe or even suspect that many braves were moving stealthily and with customary stratagem around to make their attack from the rear.

Even now rope ladders slapped the tall spiked fence with hushed stealth, and lean bodies moved with cunning.

"Them cussed Injuns is awfully quiet," Will said, watching his back. "They know we ain't got many men left, betcha."

Their gunpowder was in short supply, and Eve knew most of it had been dampened when the boxes had slid off into the Green River. Payment for their cruelty and corruption, she thought now as she watched them struggle with the wet and ruined ammunition.

Eve looked at Many Stars. The Indian girl had not shot her rifle off. Eve herself had not used hers. She saw no reason to. Not yet.

Just as she was thinking this, two of the Spaniards came by to snatch their weapons away. They were now defenseless. Although she'd never fired a rifle before, she did know how to use one and felt more secure with one.

Will was sweating it. Bad business it was, in this tight situation, losing that gunpowder. He told himself uneasily that the gunpowder didn't matter that much after all. The Indians were hell-bent on revenge, and there was nothing goin' to stand in the way of McCloud. He was the leader of the Wind River Shoshoni and a smaller band of Great Basin Utes. He was called Suncloud by the Wind and Basin Indians. He led their community in a small town called Wild Thunder. Will had no idea where that town was; he'd never been there. McCloud was an odd sort. Will believed he had some white blood in him, and rumor had it that his great-grandmother had been Teton Dakota Sioux, his grandfather of Sioux blood also. No one knew about Suncloud's father. Or what had happened to the rest of his family, like his wife, Morning Moon.

Will knew about Honna though. He'd never seen her, but he knew Scar-Face had used her until he'd tired of her. His eyes went to the women over in the log cabin. Honna would be about the same age as Many Stars. He had heard that that was not the girl's real name, that in the past she had been hit so hard she had seen many stars, and this is how she got her new name. Maybe she was Honna, he thought slyly.

Will spat onto the ground. Yup, McCloud—or Suncloud—was just too damn sly for his own moccasins.

Will was right, for suddenly there came an all-out charge from the rear. Many more braves had reached the interior of the fort by using ropes slung over the wooden palisade.

To avoid bullets, Will started running crookedly out into the open space. But like the fool he was, Will never got to see or tell how many braves were firing on them.

Rifles blasted as mounted Indians spilled through the now-wide-open gate. Eve, with Maggie and Many Stars tucked behind her, saw the bright-red spurt of gunfire going off every which way.

Indians and slavers alike exploded like bits of china fallen from a shelf.

Many Stars saw a man run out, trying to make it to another cabin.

Arrows sped, and Jim staggered a few steps before collapsing to meet his death instantly with an arrow piercing his evil heart.

Thirteen Spanish slavers, all of them having wallowed in debauchery the night long, were next to perish as they tried in vain to make it through the flying dust swirls to their nervous mounts.

Eve grabbed for Maggie's hand and crawled low with her behind wagons. Many Stars scampered right along with them.

Upon reaching a wild-eyed horse, Eve snatched at the dragging reins of the frightened animal. "Come on," she yelled to her friends. "We have to hurry!"

Finally Eve managed to shove Maggie up and then hoist herself into the saddle before her dazed friend. Many Stars ran to find her own horse and soon returned, leading a black and white paint away from a fallen Indian.

"We have no weapons," Eve yelled, her voice faint above the crazy din of thunder.

"I know this," said Many Stars, searching around but seeing none with her hurried gaze.

Maggie shouted, "Lord help us."

"If he can even hear us!" Eve shouted.

Eve whirled the prancing mare with wild eyes bulging nearly out of its head.

Gunfire slammed through the air.

Eve had to bite down to keep from screaming out her rage and fear.

There was no way out. Both exits were full of fighting whites and Indians!

She tasted blood, it was so thick in the air. This was a nightmare come true. Many Stars had dreamed of this.

Next, Eve knew, it would be their virgin blood, hers and Maggie's. . . . Their fate would be the same as Many Stars. From an earlier conversation, Eve had a strong impression that the Indian girl had been passed around—or kept solely for Scar-Face's pleasure!

For a long time Eve and Maggie, still mounted on the shying, dancing horse, hid behind the walls of a cabin, listening, while the fighting crashed, bullets whined, Indians screeched.

A wild tumult of sound all around them.

"When will this hellish nightmare end!" Eve vented, whirling her mount in a cloud of whirling dust and wind.

Long dark hair was in Eve's eyes, her cheeks were reddened, her eyes moist and burning.

Three women on two wildly frightened and screaming horses. The animals bumped against each other, then spun away, almost rearing to the smudged and fiery sky.

Black and orange, all mixed together with dust and blood and sound.

"When!" Eve shouted her fury to the sky once again.

It didn't take much longer, for soon the hated trappers, slavers, and *engagés* had been massacred or driven from the fort.

And at last, as the sun touched the horizon of the western slopes with bloodred hues, the Shoshonis and Arapaho whooped their last cry of victory and some began to withdraw.

The remaining Shoshoni formed into a double line of riders. Ten bodies of women and five children were roped across saddle blankets, their own among the young breeds who had perished earlier from hunger and usage.

A tall, strong warrior astride a prancing mount held a feathered lance and advanced before the line. Tames Wild Horses's face was like copper sun. He was sad. He was frustrated. He had been unwise and foolish. There was no woman with shining eyes.

Suncloud rode into the carnage slowly, his face with black and white and red war paint still shiny and smooth. His mouth was tight, his expression stern as his dark gray gaze flicked over the cruelly slain Shoshoni and breeds.

Suncloud's head lifted to the horizon. Those that had managed to escape, those slavers, they would not get far: The Utes were going after them even now.

Tames Wild Horses returned after investigating the grounds. "No sign of this man you seek."

Suncloud's eyes lifted to Tames Wild Horses's scar. "Did you look for the scar that is said to be on the lower part of his face, dragging his, uh, handsome mouth downward?"

"Ai. I pushed bodies over and saw no such markings." He smiled grimly. "And no handsome men. All ugly." He would have chuckled, but now was not the time for levity.

"Pawnee Joe has said this Scar-Face wears a blue coat with a red sash, a real dandy," Suncloud added, and Tames again shook his head with the corner of his mouth quirking in a near-grin.

"There was no one. He must have escaped," Tames Wild Horses said. "You will keep looking?"

"I will," was all Suncloud said.

Eve peeped out from behind the building, shocked at the carnage before her weary, blistering eyes. She was so tired. "I need a home to go to," she murmured in a moment's weakness, forgetting that she was not alone.

She couldn't take much more. She was only one woman with two hands, cracked and old-looking ones at that.

Many Stars caught Eve's eyes. The girl was saying something. But it was in the Indian tongue and Eve couldn't understand it.

Her heart thudding, Eve waited for the Indians to depart. She jumped then upon hearing a deep voice as it rang out coldly to issue a command. The voice was powerful and obviously the leader's. The reverberation of it was close, much too close.

Eve gulped down hard and found no saliva to swallow in her dry throat. Please God, make them *nice* Indians.

"Oh . . . my . . . God," Maggie whispered, her eyes rolling after hearing the strangely deep voice.

"There are some who are hiding here," Suncloud said in Shoshoni to the warriors. "Maybe Scar-Face and the Frenchman are with whoever hides. Like women."

Eve and Maggie tensed collectively, grabbing for each other's arms, wondering what the man had said. Had he discovered there to be more alive at the fort, namely Maggie, Many Stars, and herself? That was impossible, for he could not see them.

Could he sense them, then? Who was this man with the deep, stirring voice?

"I think they are leaving," Eve said to Maggie. She looked to Many Stars as she said in a whisper to Many Stars, "What did you say? I don't know what—"

Putting a finger to her lips, Many Stars frowned and shushed them as she listened from behind the building, watching, waiting, listening to the Shoshoni language.

Mincing his mount's steps, Suncloud let his gaze scan the horizon, and all at once his lean face grew alert and his wide back went ramrod straight.

To the puzzlement of the other warriors, Suncloud whirled the painted stallion and urged him to where his instincts led him.

Tames Wild Horses watched and wondered what was going on. He felt something too, and his face began to break into a grin. Looking down, checking the ground for hoofprints—they were many—he almost slid from his horse with excitement.

Tames looked up and grinned hugely. He had spotted a bit of white doeskin and beads.

Now Eve knew he was coming, for every nerve in

her body told her so, and she willed herself not to appear frightened. She backed the mare a few paces with hands that shook to betray her confidence.

Eve was astonished and awed at the look of the man when he at last rounded the corner of the building and the red dust had settled.

Suncloud's hard, flinty eyes flicked over them at once as he drew near.

Eve held her breath, but Maggie sobbed once, gulped, and buried her face behind Eve's greasy brown hair.

With surprise, Eve stared at the man, seeing dark hair almost as long as her own swaying above tanned shoulders. When her searching eyes dropped to the bare chest, down to his high-topped moccasins, then up again, she flushed hotly at his virility.

My Lord, she almost breathed aloud.

He was staring right at her. *Right through her.*

A plaintive sound echoed across the land and brushed Eve's mind. It was primitive, haunting, and so very beautiful, she could have swooned from the stirring in her soul.

She looked at the painted face again and blinked out of her trance.

"My name is Evelyn Michaels," Eve said in a rush. She gulped, her face hot, and looked quickly aside.

"My name is Steven McCloud," he shot back, watching for her reaction.

Eve looked up.

"What?"

"You look very surprised," Suncloud said, noting the younger woman hiding behind Eve and dismissing her as an innocent female. "Why is that?"

Eve could hardly believe what she'd heard. He

spoke English well, his words precise and melodic. My God. His slight accent suggested that he might have hailed from Devon, an island in the Northwest Territory of Canada. Eve frowned. She must be mistaken. But there were lots of Indians in Canada. Why not him?

"You said McCloud?" Eve ventured to ask the tall stranger.

"I did."

"You're an Indian," she argued, unaware that Maggie was peeping over Eve's shoulder in curiosity.

Suncloud said nothing, just rode away from the frowning woman. He stopped at Tames Wild Horses.

"Take them." Suncloud gestured to a group of warriors standing their horses nearby. "They can help, just in case the Dark Hair tries to escape. It would be just like that one to get them all into trouble."

"Did you see a woman with moon-dark hair?" Tames Wild Horses asked, trying to keep his excitement to a low roar.

"Go see for yourself." Suncloud began wiping the paint from his face. He stopped. "Why are you grinning so stupidly, Tames?"

"The red paint is smeared all over your mouth now and the black stuff rings your eyes; you look like a woman." Tames Wild Horses grinned wider.

McCloud wiped harder with the rag before stuffing it into his stained buckskins. "*Ah-ah!* I sure wouldn't want to look like a woman. How am I now?"

"Better."

* * *

"He is arrogant," Eve hissed over her shoulder at Many Stars.

"He is handsome," Many Stars said. "And nice. I can tell a good Indian when I see one. I should know. I am Indian myself."

"What kind of Indian?" Maggie asked, trying to keep her shivering knees still against the sides of the horse. She'd wondered this since she met Many Stars.

"I have no idea. I was stolen from my people as a child, and so I will never know where I belong."

"How sad," Maggie said. "What will they do with us now?" She gasped then as she saw the second Indian coming around, followed by a group of strong-looking braves. He was handsome, and also of a strong build. He had very long, very black hair.

Maggie swallowed. But she hadn't blinked once since seeing the young, strong brave.

Maggie hid behind Eve's shoulders as this second Indian with a scar on his temple walked his mount closer.

Tames Wild Horses felt his heart pound. *Aii!*

She will know me. She will see me and her eyes will shine. Then she will come running to me. Down off the horse and into my arms.

She did not come. Tames smiled warmly and reached for Shining Eyes to come onto his own horse. He flicked his wrist with a come-hither motion.

Maggie screamed and fell off the horse.

What is this? thought Tames.

She was up and running, glancing over her shoulder, tripping, steadying herself again, until she reached the other side of the cabin.

He was coming! Maggie screamed and ducked, wondering when the arrows would come flying.

Many Stars smiled as she watched Maggie Dexter run and the handsome young brave go after her.

With a kick to her horse, Eve made to go after Maggie, but Many Stars put her own mount in front of Eve's.

"Let them go. She is safe with that one. I know a kindly face when I see one. He is harmless," Many Stars said in French.

"He means to rape her!" Eve shouted, spinning her horse away from the obstruction of Many Stars's mount.

With war paint smeared all over his face, McCloud rode up to Eve's horse. "Let her go. The maiden is correct. She has nothing to fear from Tames Wild Horses. He's not a bear; he's a gentle young pup."

"And do I also have nothing to fear from you?" Eve spat out. She blinked. "Oh. You spoke French."

"Certainement. I speak many languages. Now, come with me. I see that the braves are more interested in what we have captured and have ridden off to escort them." He smiled. "As usual, the young breeds and Wolves don't listen to my commands. Unless, of course, it is of a more serious nature."

"We are your captives, then?" Eve asked, bewildered when he spun his horse and began riding away from her. "Answer me!" she shouted at his back, her face red, her heart pounding madly.

"Come with me or be buzzard bait like the rest of the carnage. Maybe you would enjoy waiting around until the cowards return to imprison you once again."

What? Just like that? He was riding away? What sort of man was he?

Many Stars was following him. Eve couldn't believe that her friend would desert her. They had been through so much together. She gritted her teeth.

"Many Stars." Eve tried to speak to her friend but saw that she was soon left alone. She could hear laughter as the braves pointed at her and then trotted their horses away, leaving her to her own choice as to what to do.

Making her decision, Eve spun her horse and went to look for Maggie.

"What?"

Eve stood her horse still.

When she had rounded the cabin, she had found that Maggie and the young Indian brave were nowhere to be seen.

Chapter Five

Ragged thunder of horses' hooves sounded as braves rode off to scout the area up ahead and then returned. Utah George was among them, as was Frog Catcher; there were even a few who spoke the Nez Perce, Arapaho, and Ute tongues.

Eve watched them from her position at the edge of the camp, where she sat near the fire, chewing pemmican, the food of the busy Indians. They had pushed so fast, there had been no time to hunt along the trail. She listened to the cadence of the harsh Nez Perce tongue, wondering what they were saying as they looked at her and gestured. She had some knowledge of the different bands that had frequented the trading post on the Green River; her brothers had pointed out all the different nations and "Shoshonean branches" of the widespread area as they spoke: Ute, Shoshone, Bannock, Snake, Arapaho, Crow, Nez Perce, Blackfoot, and many more.

She dearly missed her brothers and she constantly worried over Maggie's fate with that gentle-faced Indian she had disappeared with back at the fort.

They had ridden for days on end. The sun had

come up over the mountains. Then the moon. The sun again, with cloudless blue skies. Day after day, night after night. By the ghostly light of the moon they rode. At times beneath the sweet golden sun they rode.

Mountains loomed. Narrow trails wound through hills and rock, along creek beds as they rode across the wild land.

At night braves grinned at each other, jesting and poking at the campfire, casting peeks over their shoulders at Eve.

Sometimes Eve wondered what the braves had in mind for her. In St. Louis she had seen men give her the eye; these braves did not look at her with craving. They were just laughing and curious. What about this man called McCloud? He hardly looked her way, so she couldn't tell much about what he was thinking.

Fragrant smoke filled the air. Eve's mouth watered. The scent that wafted on the smoke stream smelled deliciously of roasted meat. At last, she thought with growling belly, someone must have brought back a deer.

Again McCloud was nowhere to be seen. They would pitch camp and then he would make himself scarce. Maggie and the handsome brave who'd taken her had not caught up with them. Many Stars was the only one who would talk to Eve. The others kept their distance, even McCloud. But she saw Many Stars going to talk with him and not return for hours.

Eve was almost on her own at these times. This was when she really grew lonely and longed for her old home in St. Louis. She had thought it strange that people sometimes talked to themselves when she'd been a little girl. Now she was growing tired of the sound of her own voice.

McCloud had realized almost at once that Many Stars could very well be his lost sister, Honna. His intention was to discover if this was the truth.

Now Many Stars saw him coming again, to join her at the river's edge, where she was searching for watercress. They would talk for hours each and every time they made camp. She would look into his deep gray eyes and feel a strange emotion she could not name. Was it like kindred spirits? she wondered.

"Honna," he said softly as he leaned his Hawken rifle against a tree and approached on tall moccasins, smiling down at her.

She rose slowly to her feet. "What did you say? I do not know that Shoshoni word. At first I thought I imagined this. You did call me that name, Honna, two nights ago. What does this mean, this name?"

"Grace, in English. The Hopi Indian word is *honovi,* gracious strong deer. I named you Honna."

"I see." Many Stars nodded. "This is your name for me?" Now she shook her head, giving him a curious peek, saying, "No. I do not understand. Are you courting me, Suncloud?"

He threw his head back and laughed. She looked up at him; he was several inches taller than her. Tall and strong and lean. His dark brown hair hung long and loose, past his shoulders. At one wrist he wore a leather band with multicolored beads.

"What is it you find so funny?" she asked, apparently greatly irritated.

"First, I could not court you, Honna. Second, I named you Honna when you were a little girl, not now." He smiled and tilted his head, amused at her curiosity and total bafflement.

Mystified if not frightened by his words, Many Stars took her knife and walked away from him, along the riverbank, knowing he would follow. She whirled when he came too close.

"Do you always gather the herbs and wild onions? Are they good for you?"

Despite herself, Many Stars laughed. "You know they are, Suncloud. How long have you been with Indians?"

"What?"

She stared up at him for a moment. "I knew you had white blood, but did not like talking about it. You think yourself more Indian inside than white, do you not?"

"That is true." He sat on his heels, reached for her ankle, and lifted the hem of her skirt. "Ah. It's as I thought. The ghost mark."

Many Stars jumped back. "What are you doing? After what has happened to me, I despise the touch of a man."

Heavily he said, "I'm sorry about that. I could not find you after my Comanche cousins took you away."

"How did you know?" She studied his face closely now. "Who are you, Suncloud, that you speak to me thus?"

McCloud reached for her and pulled her shaking frame into the loose circle of his arms. "I am your brother. Don't you know me, Honna?"

"What?" She pushed back. "Get away. I do not wish to speak to you anymore. You say strange things that frighten me, Suncloud."

"McCloud. Steven McCloud. Suncloud to the Indians. Do you know who your father was?"

Torn by curiosity, Many Stars asked, "Why did you look at my leg a few minutes ago? And how did you know I had a mark there?"

"Do you remember One-Arm?"

Many Stars shook her head. "No. I know of no one by that name."

"He is our grandfather, of the Cheyenne River Sioux. He lost his arm many years ago, before you were ever born. He almost lost his life when he tried to save you. The Comanche who took you warned him away with a knife to your throat. He survived an arrow to his own throat."

Dazed, Many Stars went to sit upon a huge rock. She held her aching forehead. "I believe you speak the truth, Suncloud. It is too much for me to take in, but I know that I must. McCloud, McCloud. Your name is familiar, and from the first I heard it, I knew this."

McCloud was silent for a while, then looked up to the pinpoints of stars, then back to her. "Why does she wear the beaded dress of my dead wife?"

"Your mind is too fast for me, Suncloud. Do you speak of Eve Michaels?"

He had decided a switch in topic would clear her mind somewhat and free her from the burden of hearing too much at once. She was remembering some things, but this woman had been a child of only six summers that long-ago day when she'd been captured by Comanches over a long-lasting dispute with One-Arm. She would find these memories hard to summon.

"She wears the dress of my dead wife," he repeated.

"She does?" Many Stars looked toward the camp and then back to this man proclaiming to be her brother. "How can this be possible?"

Suncloud looked toward the camp, as she had, then back to Many Stars. "It is the same. I have an excellent memory, Honna."

"The woman who wore the dress first . . . *was your wife?*"

McCloud nodded slowly, then stood motionless, waiting for her next words.

Looking sad over her remembrances, Many Stars explained. "Scar-Face sold the dress to the Frenchman Pierre . . . Pierre Dessine. He had given the dress to Eve Michaels after her dress became torn."

"How do you know about the dress? Did you see my wife?"

Many Stars looked down and away. "I cannot speak of it now."

"Maybe later," he gently said.

"Yes. Later."

"Something else: How did you come to know this Eve Michaels and be with her?"

Many Stars told how Eve and Maggie had been snatched off the trail and made to join her and other Indian women who were being brought to Fort Robidoux.

"Scar-Face was tired of my being his slave since I fought him tooth and nail at every turn. He was planning to sell me, when he met up with Pierre Dessine. Scar-Face was looking for a woman with white blood and she had to be not only beautiful but intelligent. He's a book . . . uhm, reader." She smiled contemptuously at the words she had just spoken.

"Then he saw Eve Michaels. The Dark Hair."

"Yes. He saw her and wanted her. He was biding his time."

"That is what I thought," added Many Stars.

McCloud's mouth curled. "For the right price."

As they walked up the bank together, Many Stars saw the homely but strong-muscled Frog Catcher waiting for her. "I must set Frog Catcher straight at once. I have had my fill of men. He must not pursue me in this."

"You have become hard, Honna McCloud."

She whirled on him. "Please. Do not call me that. I am Many Stars. And she is who I will remain."

"As long as you wish to, you carry excess baggage around with you," he murmured.

"What did you say?"

"Nothing. I understand. Go tell him who you are."

"Yes," Many Stars said, happy he could fathom a woman's feelings. "There are many things we have to discuss, Suncloud, sometime soon—again."

"You have taken the words from my mouth, ah, Many Stars."

She looked up at him as they walked, noting how handsome and wiry he was. "Why do you seem more Indian than white, Suncloud?"

"I wish you would not have said that. It bothers me that I'm part white."

"Do we have so much white blood, then?"

"Much mixed blood. Even some traces of Spanish." He looked across to where Eve Michaels sat before the glowing campfire, chin in her hands. "Even the Dark Hair has Spanish blood. You can see it was in her ancestry."

Many Stars looked across to Eve, then back to McCloud. "I did not know," she said, thinking to herself that Eve might very well have some Indian blood herself.

"We'll talk later, Honna."

She tossed her head. "If you prefer to call me that, that is your choice."

McCloud took hold of her hand, looking down at the mutilated forefinger. "A fresh wound. It is healing. And who did this to you?"

Many Stars stared up into the dark, steely eyes of her brother. "It is not who you think. Not Scar-Face, but one of the Spaniards at the fort. He is dead now. I saw one of the Shoshoni warriors slay him."

"Good. Otherwise I would go looking and kill him myself."

He hugged her again. This time she did not draw back. "Go. Set Frog Catcher straight." He grinned. "Before he thinks you are his captive prize."

"I will be no man's prize, ever again."

"This I do believe, Honna—Many Stars."

Eve saw Many Stars talking and laughing with McCloud as they came up the riverbank. What a strange man. *He looks to be falling in love with Many Stars. That happened quickly. She would have thought Many Stars sick to death of men after having been Scar-Face's captive and slave.*

"Many Stars!" Eve called as the woman was walking toward a young brave. She came over to her friend and Eve looked up from her position beneath a tree. "What is happening? Why have you become so distant? I am worried about Maggie and need someone to talk to. Please, come and sit down, won't you?"

"Yes." Many Stars sighed, seeing that Frog Catcher had his attention elsewhere now. "I am sorry I have ignored you, Eve. I did not mean to. It is just that so much has happened. Listen— McCloud is my brother."

"What?"

"Yes. We talked and discovered this is true. Your eyes ask: How did we know? McCloud is a great talker. He asks many questions. He wants to know everything."

Thoughtfully, Eve regarded Many Stars. "You are amazing and truly brave."

"I am?" Many Stars asked.

"Of course. Look, you have been ill used by Indians and trappers alike and still you are in one piece. You are very strong and enduring. I wish I could say the same."

"I have been abused by only one man, Eve. True, that man was like many. He is the one my brother hates most. He took me from the Comanches when I was about to become wife to a man who already had two wives."

"How old were you when the Comanches took you from your brother?" Eve asked, trying to discover more about Many Stars and McCloud at the same time.

"I was a child of six summers. They were not as bad as Scar-Face; he is the one who made me a slave and harlot. He also murdered Suncloud's wife."

"How awful for him," Eve murmured, her eyes searching out that tall, wiry frame but not seeing him in camp.

"It is true." Many Stars looked away and then back to her friend. "You wear her dress."

Eve looked down, touched the soft white doeskin.

Her eyes misted as she looked up to the mountains. "She was in my dream the other night. I walked right through her, coming out on the other side of her wearing this dress on my own person."

"Nothing surprises me anymore, Eve. And this revealing dream of yours means something. You will maybe replace his wife."

"Never! I think men are disgusting creatures, animals, devourers of women. The only men I cared for were my brothers, and even they were half-brothers I sometimes had thought . . . because . . . because they were lighter-skinned than I am. There's no one left." She sniffed and sighed deeply. "Even Maggie is gone."

"Not gone, Eve. Just in the company of that handsome and kind-faced young brave."

"Kind. I pray." Eve's gaze fell on McCloud, where he was at the moment kneeling and working with the iron contraption of trappers. She couldn't drag her eyes away from the muscles bulging along his bare arms, and the smooth hills and valleys of his chest, just like an Indian's.

"Yes," Many Stars said. "A kind and gentle warrior I believe Tames Wild Horses to be."

"Tames Wild Horses? Warrior?" Eve kept her eyes on McCloud, unable to look away. "These men are trapper Indians. I know of them. If they are so peaceful, why, then, did they join the Utes and Arapahos and attack the fort?"

"See, Suncloud sets traps for the beaver. And all the while he thinks to trap the evil Scar-Face, the one who escaped from Fort Robidoux."

With a frown Eve asked, "He thinks this while he's trapping? I don't understand, you must tell me what you mean, Many Stars. And why do you call him Suncloud?"

"The killer of his wife and the murderer of my soul will not escape my brother. The Indian's call him Suncloud. He not only is Indian but has white blood also."

"But his hair is not yellow. It is as dark as my own."

"I do not know, Eve. Maybe they call him Cloud because of his name *McCloud*. Where the sun comes from, I have no idea. Maybe he is very bright"—she grinned—"like the sun. His first name is Steven. Mine is Honna."

"Then you are not all Indian," Eve said, looking her friend over as if seeing her with different eyes. "I thought I detected blue shadows moving in your dark eyes. When you are in the brightest rays, like now, I can detect this shade."

Many Stars said nothing to this.

Eve knew this conversation was coming to a close.

"Don't stay away so long, Many Stars. I miss your company. I'm lonely and, I must confess, frightened in the company of so many virile Indians. Especially McCloud. His eyes stray my way often, and I can't help looking his way also. I admire him as a handsome man. No more."

Many Stars narrowed her huge eyes. "Have no worry, Eve. McCloud still mourns the death of his wife. He touches no woman."

"A few more questions: When did she, this Indian wife, die?" Eve asked, once again her eyes drawn to McCloud's manly frame, his long, dark hair, the mysterious side glances he sent her way.

"Not very long ago." Many Stars thought for a

moment. "Almost a year now that I think back. The time passes so swiftly, Eve." She saw her white friend nod.

Many Stars knew what the next question would be.

"How did Scar-Face . . . do it?" Eve bit her lip. "And why?"

"She tried killing the evil Spanish with a knife she'd stolen. Scar-Face caught her, but in the process she cut him. He said she dared come close to his face with the blade. He had enough scars to mar his handsome features, he'd growled into her face."

"What was her name?" Eve softly asked, looking to the man who mourned his Indian wife.

"Morning Moon."

As Many Stars walked to find Frog Catcher, Eve looked down at the beaded Indian dress she wore.

When she glanced up and across, she found those mysterious eyes on her. He was gazing into her soul and she did not think she liked it. He seemingly discerned what was within.

Well, Eve thought, squirming as the cotton cloth bit into her chest, *what do I have to hide anyway?*

McCloud looked away. When he did, she glanced down at her chest. Ha. So that was it. He'd no doubt never seen a full-grown woman as flat-chested as she!

Word spread throughout the camp that Many Stars was McCloud's long-lost sister, Honna. Apparently, she had not lost her mind and soul, was not left to wander, but had been slave to Scar-Face, as long as he, this bastard Spaniard, saw fit. Many Stars had talked long and hard to Frog Catcher, and now he understood her revulsion and why he could not pursue her. She was Honna McCloud, Steven McCloud's sister, a white woman's daughter, One-Arm's granddaughter.

Frog Catcher told this to Utah George, who did not understand or sympathize as easily as Frog Catcher.

"Though Many Stars has been with another man, I would still take her as my woman, my bride," Frog Catcher told the breed.

"You will have to wait until her heart is in the right place. Her soul is burdened by what has happened to her," Utah said. "I hope it was my arrow that pierced the heart of the Spanish devil who took Many Stars's finger."

Frog Catcher sighed, his pockmarked face giving a painful twist. "She is beautiful, is she not?"

"Beautiful," Utah agreed. "And brave. So is the Dark Hair."

Frog Catcher looked across camp to the white woman who had come along even though McCloud gave her the choice of her own path. "What will he do with the beautiful Dark Hair?"

"Whatever he wishes," Utah said, then shrugged with a grin. "Your guess is as good as mine, my friend." He flipped the long braid he wore over his shoulder. "When the trapping is done, I wonder if he will allow the Dark Hair to accompany us to Wild Thunder. The way he looks at her . . . I do not know."

"Yes. She is a temptation for Suncloud, all can see this." Frog Catcher chuckled. "She has no meat on her bones. Morning Moon had more curves and a round, handsome face. This Dark Hair has the high-class European looks." Frog Catcher grinned.

"Many Stars is skinny too. Lovely she is, but needs more fat to survive the winter winds."

Utah finished with the trap he'd been setting, looked up, and said, "We will fatten them up."

"Ooooh, ahhhh," Frog Catcher hooted long and hard. "Not the way you are thinking, my friend. You must slake your lust with Red Beads, in her lodge, set up just for that purpose." He spoke of Wild Thunder's most infamous harlot.

Utah shook his head, the single braid swaying. "Sometimes there is a need for change."

Frog Catcher did not see Utah's bright brown gaze trail Many Stars as she went to join the Dark Hair beneath the cottonwood trees near the river's edge.

With hair falling in her eyes, Eve smiled when Many Stars came over to join her. Many Stars tossed her arms high and whirled in a circle, then dropped slowly to her knees before Eve, who was grimacing as she plucked a sage hen one of the men had dropped at her feet.

Wiping her hands on the grass, Eve asked, "What is it, Many Stars? You look so happy, so free."

"That is because I am. Once again I feel like a child. I did not wish to think about my childhood before. But now I find the freedom to do so, to remember all things happy and lovely." Many Stars laughed with abandon. "It feels so good not having to heed a man's wishes. I never want to be a slave again. Not to any man!"

"McCloud makes you feel this new secure position among his kind. I know what you mean. A man like him is—"

"Yes?" Many Stars waited, looking at her friend curiously. "A man like him?"

"Oh, it's nothing. I was just entertaining foolish thoughts." Eve shot to her feet after skewering the bird over the fire. "Ugh. I hate plucking hens. It seems so cruel even though they're dead and feel nothing. Let's walk. I'd like to see what the men are doing with those traps over there."

Many Stars smiled to herself, wondering what the future held in store for the Dark Hair . . . and Suncloud.

Chapter Six

"It's horrible," Eve said, walking away from the beaver trap. "I know, it's a way to make a living and I know as much about trapping as any man. My brothers became trappers after we left St. Louis and struck for the wilderness." She glanced over her shoulder at the traps, then kept walking. "The poor little beaver. Why do we have to do this to them just to keep warm and trade for other things we need?"

Many Stars laughed. "Sounds like you are brother to the beaver. Maybe you have had a vision."

I have already had my share of visions, Eve almost said. And one of them had been about a turtle. Eve thought that perhaps Many Stars would laugh at that one.

Coming to a halt, Many Stars took a long, hard look at Eve. "Are you lonesome for your home? It seems to me this is the way it is for you. You miss your old path, the way you used to live among the civilized whites. Did your family have a very nice house?"

"Have you ever seen a real wood house?" Eve asked Many Stars. "A home with people who work for you, a dining room with pretty silverware, nice clothes to wear, dresses that float around your ankles like silver clouds? No? I suspected you hadn't."

"Scar-Face showed me pictures," Many Stars said. "They were very pretty. Just like you say. Pretty dresses. Silver things to eat with. Jewels." Many Stars's eyes were large and luminous. "Did you have many jewels, Eve? Did you wear sky-color dresses and wear sparkling things around your neck and wrists?"

"Diamonds," Eve said. "They would sparkle like thousands of stars in the sky. After a party I would place them back into a gold case lined with black velvet. Thousands of lights would twinkle up at me from the case. Some rainbow colors."

"Thousands? I do not know this word, Eve."

Eve smiled. "It means many many *many*. Like your name—Many Stars. Is that your real name? Now that you've been reunited with your brother Suncloud, does he say?"

"I told you: He says my real name is Honna. He says we will talk more about when I was a little girl and he was my big brother. A *boy* he was, of course."

"Very tall and lanky, I would think," Eve said, trying to picture him that way.

Eve and Many Stars walked back to the trees beside the riverbank. McCloud was standing there, waiting for them. His gray eyes took in Eve's slender form in the once-pale doeskin dress, her feminine features with gentle cheekbones, the smooth grace of her shining sable hair.

"We are going to the Rendezvous," he was saying. "Many Indians and trappers will be there. Do you know about the Rendezvous?" he asked Eve, staring down at her flat chest, eyes piercing, boldly studying.

Her eyes flicked to his and held him. "Of course I know about the Rendezvous. My . . . brothers, John and Derek, were trappers."

She had said that with hesitation. He asked, "Were?"

"They were killed, murdered by Indians, I think, but I don't know"—she shrugged, looking away and biting her lip for control—"for sure."

Many Stars exchanged a look with McCloud.

After she'd recovered somewhat, Eve looked back at Many Stars and her brother. "Maggie's brother was with them. We were left alone to care for ourselves after they were slain, and we followed the Spanish Trail. That was when the miserable bastard Frenchman and the Spanish slavers found us, at the heart of the Green River. One of them . . . he tried to . . . he ripped my clothes."

Eve looked into McCloud's eyes. Her heart jumped and began to pound heavily at the look in them. "He gave me a—this Indian dress to wear."

He snapped softly, "Who?"

"Pierre Dessine." Her chin lifted as she struggled to look at his eyes now, not at his bare chest peeping out from the leather vest. "You wife's dress . . . I'm sorry."

"Don't be," McCloud told her, bending to a pile of beaver skins, again looking up at her flat chest. "My Indian wife was and is none of your concern. You didn't know her."

I had a dream about her.

Eve's eyes felt like burning embers as she turned away, walking to water her black and white spotted mare, leaving McCloud and his sister by themselves.

Returning the horse she'd named Zeena to its tether, she lovingly rubbed the velvet nose and leaned against the gentle mare.

What do I want? Eve asked herself. *Where do I wish to make my home?* She'd never thought much about who she was or what she wanted to accomplish. She'd only drifted through life, taking things as they came: Sew and clean and cook. Sleep and wake up. Eat and eat again.

In St. Louis it was: Dress as pretty as you can for a party. Make sure the cakes have plenty of white icing. Go to worship on Sunday with Mama and Papa. Tea time and laughter and sewing with her friends. Flirt with a beau. Perhaps think and dream about falling in love someday. But not now.

Romance had been only a fantasy for her and her girlfriends, but somehow more so for her friends than for her.

Eve remembered her neighbor, a fluffy-headed creature named Theresa, used to talk about who it was that she would marry. It was always someone tall and beautiful as a god, someone young and swift, and this magical being would look into her eyes—so Terri had said—and the whole world would turn inside out, the way things happen in stories. "Don't you know, Evelyn? Where lovers die for each other, and they go into some sort of spirit world in search of each other." Evelyn, as the fluffy little neighbor had called her, had screwed up her face. It had been full of freckles back then, and she'd looked at the fluffy one as if she'd been crazy.

That seemed so long ago. No more fantasies; she'd never had many anyway.

Now her struggle was to exist. Eat and stay alive. Make sure she found Maggie and helped her survive also. To get away from the Indians and back to civilization—even if it was to be a small cabin on the outskirts of a tiny town.

Eve hugged Zeena's neck and face. "Now I have you." Her gaze drifted across to encounter the smoldering eyes of Steven McCloud. "Yes, now there is you."

Turning to Zeena, Eve put her back to the tall, wiry man, telling herself that this was all that mattered now: to survive.

Falling in love had never occurred to her. Not until then. And she was horribly frightened, more than she had been for her life at the hands of slavers and Indians.

Weary and lonely for Maggie, Eve lay down for a nap inside the tent. Late-afternoon sun slanted across the tent, bringing pale sunshine and shadow to play within the hide walls where Eve took her rest.

Watching the shifting patterns, Eve soon felt her eyes drooping, and then she slept. At once the dream vision came to her.

She was in the dark embrace of the night. Again she wore the simple yellow dress, and the blue beads were around her neck, drooping heavily to her skinny chest. The dress was much smaller in this dream. Her dark hair was long and she was wearing it loose in back with a slim sable-brown braid on either side of her head.

"Come here, Mist Smoke," someone called, and

Eve saw the little girl in the yellow dress run to a woman who was holding out her arms to her.

This cannot be me, Eve told herself. *The child's skin is copper-hued and her eyes . . . I can't see her eyes. And that is not my mother who is playing with . . . whoever that little girl is.* Ah, yes. Mist Smoke, the woman said.

Now another woman was coming toward them. Mother! Eve looked at her and shouted. Narcissa did not seem to know she was there; she did not even look at her. She was talking to the little girl and the woman. It came to Eve that the elder person was named Winter Woman.

"Mist Smoke," said Winter Woman. "Go and play. Your mother and I wish to talk of when you will go on this journey."

How do I know what she is saying? Eve asked herself. *She is an Indian woman. Her mouth moves but it does not move exactly with the words. Yet I know what she speaks.*

And I know what the little girl is thinking. She now looks to the women and she is very sad. She, this Mist Smoke, does not want to leave this place.

What is this place? Eve looked around in her dream and saw the smoke from many tipis rising in the air. She was surprised by the clarity of her dream vision. Glancing down, she saw a scrawny dog yipping and scratching at her heels as if he wanted her to run and play with him. . . .

I cannot do this. I am . . . now I am running through the trees, now the tall grass, in the direction of a creek that cuts across the camp.

And suddenly she was the child of her vision.

Eve lay down in the grass, and when she awoke she was wearing a buckskin dress.

But I am still in the tall grass. How can this be? A man is coming toward me. A white man! He is my father.

"Remove that dress at once, Eve. We are going home. Go put on your yellow dress."

"But my name is Mist Smoke. I belong here."

Eve felt a profound sadness moving within her. *I do not want to leave here. This is my home. There is no other. Oh. Look! Over there. Winter Woman is crying.*

"Do not cry, Winter Woman. I will come back. Father wants to go to that town far far away on a wide river. Will I ever see you again, Winter Woman?"

The woman had only a few gray strands in her hair, and Mist Smoke was afraid that by the time she returned, Winter Woman would be very old and white-haired. Just like her name: Winter Woman.

She was crying as she looked back at the Indian encampment, the tears rolling all the way to her chin. Winter Woman said *wohitika;* she wanted her to be brave.

"Huka." The little girl said that she was not afraid to her elder.

A huge man with a hooked nose walked over to Mist Smoke, and for the first time took her hand in his large, dry palms. He said *"hunhunhe,"* and Eve knew this was a man's expression for sorrow.

He, the chief of this band of Dakota, was sad to see her go. She waved to them as Narcissa took her hand and they set off for the hills. . . .

"Tuwe miye he?" Who am I? Her dream faded to black.

Eve awakened to the sound of someone moving outside her tent. She looked around to see only the lavender twilight.

Chapter Seven

"He hates me," Eve said to Many Stars as she stroked the piebald horse. "I can feel it. I can see it."

They had reached the Rendezvous on the wide flats of the Green River. Half the camp had already become inebriated on company whiskey and were stumbling about and shouting. The annual Rendezvous, where both fur companies, the French and American, rivaled one another for the attention of and bidding with the trappers, Indians and whites alike.

Many Stars was listening as she worked over a weathered stump of pine, preparing the leaves of a streamside sunflower for Eve's and her own lunch. Suncloud's party was housed in a temporary camp of skin tipis and lean-tos.

"Why? I don't know." Eve kept talking as if to herself. "You tell me, Many Stars. He's your brother. Why does he seem to dislike me so very much?"

"Yes, Suncloud's my brother. But I know him no more or less than you do. We have been apart for many years, many moons. I was a child, he was a boy. We have become like different people. Everything shifts, all things change, nothing stays the same. Tomorrow you and I will be different than we are today."

"I realize that, Many Stars." Her eyes had snagged on McCloud standing in a crowd of men. She returned her gaze to the Indian blanket she was folding, disgusted with herself for staring. "Do you think if I wore another dress he would not stare at me with killing eyes?"

Many Stars smiled at her friend as she pulled some of the meat from the streamflower leaves. "I will try to get you another dress. Look, Eve. There are many different kinds of Indian women here: Shosoni, Ute, Nez Perce, Bannock, Crow."

As they began to walk about, Eve noticed not much difference in the women's dress. Some were slimmer, some fatter. "Some of them are very young. Are they all . . . do they all sleep with men?"

"No. Some women with husbands. Many whores. White men call them squaws. And a few maidens come along with Mother to meet Father. All sorts of Indian women, especially the squaws, love trinkets. Bright beads. Shiny mirrors. Colorful materials. Trappers and braves give for their favors."

The bright dresses, a few yards of yellow cloth, and some blue beads.

"What is the matter, Eve? You look funny. You seem to have seen a ghost or something."

Eve recovered from the glaring memory of her dead brothers.

Shaking her head, her long dark hair falling in wavelets to her waist, Eve said, "It's no different than a civilized get-together at a neighbor's. Rendezvous." She laughed at the similarities. "Like a big family picnic where men get drunk and act stupid."

"You've never been to the Rendezvous. No family outing or visit to the trading post." Many Stars looked up and caught her brother glancing their way, then back to what he was doing. "You will be shocked, Eve Michaels."

"Not after Fort Robidoux, I shall not."

Smoke from Indian cooking fires drifted in the air lazily, fragrantly. Shouts, gunshots, and bawdy songs interspersed with loud laughter.

"It gets very crazy at this big trappers' 'picnic,' Eve. Fights. Indians sell wives and daughters for the firewater French trappers bring. Sometimes there are killings. Indians get drunk, set fire to white trappers as they sleep. Couples rut like animals in the open."

All of a sudden Many Stars felt Eve's hand on her arm. Many Stars turned to encounter a big, wide man, his leathery face creased from years in the mountains.

"Wagh! Them's some pretty sweet-lookin' skirts. Helluva deal. I'm gonna get me a piece of that." The burly trapper looked closer, punched his friend in the arm and pointed to Eve. "Huh! That one looks like she ain't got no tits." He spat tobacco juice near Eve's feet. "Must be just a little gal."

Many Stars leaned to Eve. "You wear the cloth bindings to keep brutes like him from finding you attractive?" she whispered in French.

Eve smiled. *"Certainement."*

"What'd she say? She talked low and whisperlike. Was that French, Frank?"

"Yup, Bob. The Indian gal and the flat one was

speakin' French. Hey, Frenchie, where's your tit-
ties?''

The trapper with the spittle all over his chin
moved closer to the women and touched Eve's
chest.

At the same moment that Eve hauled back and
smashed Bob in the nose, McCloud looked their
way. He excused himself from his company and
began running through the men.

He ran, straight and tall, eyes wild, like a sky full
of storm. He weaved his way, darting here, then
there, coming fast, his dark hair flying past his
buckskin-clad shoulders.

Bob didn't know what hit him. One minute he
was standing up, the next he was sailing through the
air. Bob rolled like a grizzly, full of padding and fat,
after coming out of hibernation.

As McCloud stood at the ready, waiting for the
trapper to gain his feet, he felt the presence of the
other man sneaking up behind. Just as Frank
grabbed McCloud by the shoulder to whip him
around, McCloud spun, catching Frank in the
throat with a hard blow from the side of his hand.

"Wagh!"

Frank gasped for air and dropped to his knees.
McCloud turned in an instant to catch the full force
of Bob as he slammed into him, knocking all three
of them to the ground with Bob's momentum.

McCloud pushed to free himself of the weight,
heard the soft thud as the trapper went limp. Rolling his weight to the left, McCloud glanced up and
saw Eve looking at him with a glare in her eyes.

Eve held a rifle above McCloud.

What is this?

"Dark Hair—" McCloud warned.

Eve now shoved the barrel into the chest of Bob, pulling back the hammer. McCloud kicked at the barrel as the shot rang out and a cloud of dirt exploded on the ground near Bob's feet.

Angry rage showed in Eve's face. "I will kill the next man who tries that."

"*Aaah!*" he exclaimed.

Quickly, McCloud sprang to his feet, snatching the rifle from Eve's hands with such force that it pulled her into him as she still hung on. McCloud clamped his hand around her waist to keep them both from toppling, and the anger in her face subsided and grew soft as she felt the strength in his virile body.

Eve was pierced by a deep and pervading sense of wonder even as a chill traveled her spine and limbs.

McCloud stared, his eyes a deep, unfathomable gray, looking at her with raw desire.

Loose and free, Eve's hair flowed down her back like a dark river. Of a deep brown color, the sun caught and held its true brilliance, brought out streaks of a lighter shade, even a hint of red.

Carefully and cautiously, Eve pushed away from McCloud, saying, "Not to worry, *Suncloud*. I'd not use it on you. You protect us—that is plain for all to see. What would we do without you?"

After his gaze coolly swept her chest and face, McCloud turned his attention to the men on the ground. Just then Utah George pushed through the crowd. Frank was finally getting his breath and Bob was beginning to stir.

As the two lumbered to their feet, McCloud looked at them with a side glance. "Move on. And don't touch the women again."

They both ambled painfully away, licking their
wounds like a pair of whipped dogs.

Utah George sauntered over to McCloud. "I see
you have everything under control. I suggest, if I
might, that we complete our business and move on.
Those two will be very drunk and very angry by the
night's dark moon, and back with their friends."

McCloud nodded, watching Eve and Many Stars
leave the area. "All in good time," he said in Shoshoni, dropping his gaze to the gentle sway of the
Dark Hair's doeskin-covered hips. "I don't intend
to run from the likes of those."

As McCloud shouldered his rifle and began to
walk away, Utah lingered over those words, rubbing his chin.

Utah saw the feminine sway too, but his gaze was
not resting on Eve Michaels's back.

Later that night, as Eve and Many Stars crawled
into buffalo robes inside the cozy tipi they had set
up, Many Stars saw that her friend did not sleep yet.

"What is it that keeps you awake?" Many Stars
asked, trying to see her friend in the semidark.

"Will you do something for me?" Eve reached
out her hand.

Many Stars touched the tips of Eve's cool fingers.
"Anything you ask, dear friend. You were there
when I needed help treating my wound. Without
you I would have lost my hand, perhaps my life.
You were the bravest warrior woman back at Fort
Robidoux."

Eve sighed and looked back up at the smoke hole.
"Thank you, Many Stars. This very kind of you to
say so. I do feel like I'm in a war at times, mostly

with myself, I guess." She glanced over at Many Stars's dark face.

"What is it you wish me to do, Eve Michaels?"

"Teach me Indian sign language," Eve said, lying on her back, looking up at the stars through the tiny hole.

"Is that all?" Many Stars heard her friend's murmured answer. "I will do better than that. I shall teach you Shoshoni and whatever other Indian language you wish to know. I even know some Dakota."

"Good," Eve said, frowning thoughtfully over the word *Dakota*. "I might need to know these things someday. And as long as I'm out here in the wilderness—for now—I would like to learn everything I can about the Indians and their cultures."

"Yes, Eve," Many Stars mumbled sleepily. *"For now."*

After Many Stars had gone to sleep, Eve still stared up at the night sky. *Everything changes, nothing stays the same as it was the day before. Tomorrow we will be different than we were today.* Many Stars had said this.

Eve blinked sleepily, finally shutting out the night with her falling lashes.

For now. Or, perhaps . . . forever.

Eve was dreaming again. She was walking in the Land of the Tallgrasses. A child again. Scattered over the range was every hue of yellow, purple, blue, white, pink, brown. Amid the flowers, acres of wolfberry were interspersed with shining thickets of silverberry that flashed a wave of white as the wind blew across them, turning their hoary leaves to the sun.

She was in her bed in St. Louis, dreaming of the Land of the Tallgrasses. It was a sad time. She wished to return to the land of the Dakota, her friends. Narcissa said her people were here now, in *St. Lewey.*

Evelyn still had her memories . . . of buffalo summer.

Tatanka: buffalo. She could see him browse woody plants on forest edges, and where grassland joins stands of lodgepole or ponderosa pine at the foot of the hills. With great enjoyment, watching an old bull feed in a stand of four-foot ponderosas on a lower slope. Occasionally he turns aside from his grazing to rub his head vigorously against the branched stem of a young pine.

"Look, Winter Woman, Look!"

Starry-eyed and stupid-looking, the buffalo stood and scrubbed away—in turn, on one side and then the other, he hooked a horn around the base of the tree and stripped upward.

Winter Woman frowned. "It is a great job of head scratching, but the tree is ruined, as you can see," she said to Mist Smoke.

"Ah, yes, Winter Woman. But is he not the largest and most impressive creature of the grasslands. He is majestic, the *tatanka.*"

"Ai," Winter Woman agreed. "Come, child, it is summer and we must pick berries. We will make color, dye, of them for your beads."

"Blue berries, for the beads," she begged Winter Woman. "Oh, look! Is it *susweca?*"

"Yes, little one. It is the dragonfly."

* * *

Drenched in sweat, Eve awoke and looked around, catching sight of Many Stars in the dimness. She drew in her breath sharply. *I am not in St. Louis. Not in the cabin in the wilderness. Not with Maggie.* She blinked, rubbing the nape of her neck, feeling confused and disoriented.

And who is Winter Woman?

Lowering herself back upon the sleeping robes, Eve looked up at the dark velvet with stars like tiny diamonds twinkling down through the small smoke hole.

Now I know where I am. I am with Many Stars. At the Rendezvous. Maggie is gone, vanished with a Shoshoni brave.

Where are you, Winter Woman? Who are you? Do you have something to do with the yellow dress, the turtle, blue beads, and—

"Tuwe miye he?" Eve blinked after she'd said this.

Many Stars lay awake, her back to Eve Michaels. She had heard the white woman speak the Dakota words: Who am I?

Now Many Stars was confused. Who is she, this Eve Michaels?

I will keep this to myself, thought Many Stars as she closed her eyes and returned to the Land of the Night Walkers.

Chapter Eight

McCloud stepped into the Rocky Mountain Fur Company tent. One-Eye Charlie Donovan, a patch over his left eye, gave the younger man a cheerful greeting as he appeared at the opening.

Charlie stepped outside with McCloud to examine the parfleche bags stuffed with beaver skins. Charlie looked them over and nodded, taking his time.

McCloud explained that he'd had to dress the skins himself because Morning Moon—who usually took on the task—was gone.

"Gone?" Charlie asked, handing McCloud a strip of dried bison meat. "Where'd she go?"

Looking away and across camp, not eating the meat, McCloud squinted and then looked back at Charlie. "Where do many women go after they've been with Scar-Face?" he asked Charlie.

The man stopped chewing suddenly.

"Gawd. Don't tell me he—" Charlie sliced across his throat with the finger holding the strip of bison meat.

"That's just what he did, Charlie."

"I'm real sorry, Suncloud."

"Don't be." McCloud leaned his rifle against a pile of logs as Charlie inspected and priced the plews. "I suppose you'd like getting some goods, like tobacco and pretty stuff, for your own trading post."

"Yup."

While One-Eye Charlie continued to examine the plews, chew his meat, and scratch his head, McCloud looked across the camp to see his sister bringing more wood to the cooking fire. The Dark Hair glanced idly up at the two braves approaching their hide tent.

McCloud had never felt as he was feeling now. The Dark Hair was affecting him as no woman ever had. He didn't like the feeling. He was angry over this unaccustomed passion. His body ached and burned as with a strange fever.

She is like an Indian woman, McCloud thought. *She is tough.* She reminded him of a sweet warrior woman when she'd held that rifle at Trapper Bob's head. He found himself admiring her as she helped Many Stars with the cooking. Her slender ankles caught his eye, as did the gentle swell of her buttocks beneath the doeskin dress.

McCloud's jaw clenched. He was too preoccupied with this woman. *She has bewitched me. I must not let this happen. It's happening just the same!*

Feeling McCloud's presence, Eve looked over to the Rocky Mountain Fur Company tent, and watched him watch her. She heard the snort of horses. Looking aside, struggling to appear unaffected by McCloud's gaze, Eve walked toward the staked horses and scratched the ears of the piebald Zeena.

Done with Charlie, McCloud shouldered his rifle

and walked away, meaning to send back braves to load the stuff he'd just bargained for in order to stock his trading post a bit tighter for winter.

The Moon of Popping Trees, winter, he knew, was a long way off yet. Still, a soul never could tell when the snows would come in the high country, sometimes as early as the Moon When the Plums Are Scarlet, September. For now it was still the Moon of Making Fat, June.

With a smile and a sudden determined lift to her chin, Eve walked back to the cooking fire, hoping that McCloud was not looking her way. Her own gaze would not then be drawn to where he was. He could turn up anywhere, surprising her, making her jump. And she did that just then as Many Stars came up from behind unexpectedly.

"Eve, I must show you the herbs I have gathered. Good medicine. These plants, pounded by stone or crushed between fingers, will help cure many aching heads in the morning. Look at Frog Catcher; he is becoming inebriated. He looks sick and lost as he wanders about the encampment."

"I see," said Eve.

Many Stars giggled softly. "Like a sick calf is Frog Catcher."

"He pines for you," said Eve, blinking because she was beginning to sound like Many Stars.

I must not lose my identity among these people, Eve told herself. I have to find a way back to . . . my home. Where was home? St. Louis? Canada? Where? She shook her head.

Eve suddenly said, "Frog Catcher is falling in love. You are very lovely, it's no wonder. I've even caught the other young Indians with him watching you, Many Stars."

"Who?" Many Stars asked. "You mean Utah George? I have noticed. I am not interested in Utah or Frog Catcher."

"Yes," Eve said. "Both of them have a hard time keeping their eyes off you."

"And so," Many Stars said with a jerk of her head, "I see my brother Suncloud looking at you, Eve. He has lost his wife. You wear her dress."

"Is it the dress or the woman he stares at?" Eve put the question to Many Stars.

"He cannot lust after a dress," Many Stars said with a laugh.

Eve's chin hardened.

"What is it?" Many Stars asked Eve. "Why do you look that way?"

"Get me another dress, Many Stars. I don't care who you get it from. I don't want McCloud to continue to see me in his wife's dress. He thinks of her and I'd rather not be a reminder of another man's wife. First he looked at me with anger, now he looks with lust. Next he will be coming to rip it off me."

"He is a man, Eve. And you are a beautiful woman. He would look at you."

"Teach me your medicine, Many Stars. And the languages."

"First I will have Utah George help me get you a dress. Stay here. I will not be long. I saw some pretty squaws in nice clothes among the Nez Perce."

Eve shrugged. "I'm not planning on going anywhere. Just please don't take too long. These rowdy bucks make me nervous."

"I know what you mean. But look"—firelight

reflected in the soft, luminous eyes of Many Stars as she lifted her head—"Suncloud's men are watching over us. Over there, by that company tent. All Shoshoni warriors. You have nothing to fear or be nervous about."

Watching Many Stars walk away, Eve murmured, "I am not so convinced. Not after Trapper Bob's itchy fingers and lustful actions."

Finishing with the deer meat he was cutting into strips, Utah George froze into stillness as he saw Many Stars coming toward him, dark hair falling about her shoulders. She had combed it loose from the braids, and jet-blue lights danced in the strands. All day long he'd thought of her, wanting her. She was that rare creature among Indian women, and had almost a white look about her. He knew she was Suncloud's sister. They both had the same father. But Suncloud's stepmother had been white, Brian "Spotted Horse" McCloud having married her long after Honna had been abducted by Comanches. He knew more about the McClouds than anyone realized.

Many Stars was not a virgin, this he knew. It did not matter. He had fallen for her instantly and irrevocably.

Many Stars walked up to Utah. "I need your help in locating some things, Utah."

"I know, Many Stars. You really want to say you need someone to go with you. To help you keep the bucks away. Do not look that way. You are beautiful and desirable. What man would not want you." He swallowed the hard lump in his throat.

"Thank you, Utah. I do need your help. And you are right; there are many whose eyes I don't need trailing me right now. I cannot keep them from looking. I just do not want hands reaching out and grabbing. That I could not stand."

"I understand." Utah walked with her, and Many Stars fell silent. He wanted to talk with her more, but he could see there were important matters on her mind. There would be plenty of time later for them to become good friends. This was what she needed, a friend, a male friend, only she did not realize this. He would make her see this in time.

Eve cringed at the loud voices of the gamblers playing a hand game around a campfire. Sparks crackled and tossed their hot shapes upward, dying out in an orange flare before reaching the treetops. She looked up to see the rising moon traveling across the vast bowl of dark sky.

"Where is my sister?"

Eve drew in her breath sharply at the deep male voice beside her. It was him, and a warm sensation tingled along her spine. McCloud.

He was there beside her. But how? When? How had he come so quickly and quietly, like a dark panther on padded paws.

She looked back over her shoulder, answering him. "She went to find Utah George."

"Why?"

Rubbing her palms on stained doeskin, Eve stood and turned in a half-circle. She looked at him once, then away, into the blaze. Swallowing, she finally got her voice.

"She went . . . to get something."

"What?"

A man of few words.

Now Eve faced McCloud. Again that strange

shock that sent currents racing through her. His arms hung down his sides, but his face, copper from the blazing warmth, was intense.

He looked hot, as if on fire. Even his dark hair, long and loose, was lit with flames.

The bowl of dark sky arched above them and the Wind River Mountains stood out black against the northern sky. He took one step toward her. Eve automatically inhaled his pleasantly musky odor. Her heart jumped and began to pound anxiously.

"What is it you want?" Eve asked, feeling trepidation at his nearness.

"This."

McCloud pulled her close, his mouth taking hers in a long, deep kiss. Eve felt his hardness urgently press against her body. Hot desire, rivers of it, coursed through her as she leaned toward him. She ached with this new need.

His mouth still claimed hers, and the hot, smoky taste of him was inside her own mouth. She moaned.

They were lost in each other's embrace.

Suddenly, breathlessly, they broke apart.

"Take the dress off," he said, eyes hot and steely-dark.

"What?"

"You heard me. Go into the tent and take the dress off. It's my wife's, it belonged to her, Morning Moon. Do you not hear me?"

Eve's eyes narrowed. "I know her name; I've heard it before." She stood her ground. "Why do you hate me? You have no reason."

"Why do you believe I dislike you?"

"Hate—or dislike?"

He shrugged. "The same."

"What have I done to you? Did you think that I stole this dress from your . . . dead wife's body? I was not part of the killing, if that is what you think."

Eve was sorry as soon as the words came out.

He gripped her hard. "Were you there?"

"You know I was not."

He turned his head sharply to the side. "How would I know?"

"Many Stars must have told you. She was there. Ask her. She saw them as they . . . they did . . . that to Morning Moon."

"You already said it once." His hard fingers bit in. "Why not say 'kill' and 'body.' You must know much about being another man's whore, his—"

Crack!

As McCloud held Eve's wrist in his tight grip—after she'd slapped him—he glared into her face, his mouth tight, his jawline hard.

"You need someone to blame. But I am no whore. Nor was I ever. Her hand clamped into a fist. "I know what it is, Indian McCloud. You hate anyone who is all white, especially women. You are a half-breed, not all Indian after all." Her voice was deep, husky, womanly. "Yet you act as if those who have white blood are beneath you and your people. Even the man you call friend at the Rocky Mountain tent has more love for you than you do for him. Because someone may be white, you turn their affections aside?"

"One-Eye has Ute blood."

Eve looked defeated, but only for a moment.

"White whore," he said, his voice angry and deep.

"There. You said it. You hate me. I haven't a

drop of Shoshoni, Sioux, Bannock, Ute, Snake, Crow, or whichever—therefore I am an outcast and you—"

He snatched her hand. "I will make you my slave, just as Scar-Face made my sister his slave."

Eve stared at McCloud in shock.

"But not your whore," she finally muttered.

"My slave, Dark Hair."

"You are insane, just like all men in these mountains. I should have never left with my brothers to come here from St. Louis."

"I will take you back there in time. You'll be my slave for a year."

"Why?"

"Because I need one to do the work of a squaw. Is that not a good enough answer?"

She glowered at him. "No. And you do not need a slave. You need someone to torment, McCloud, someone to pass your hatred to. You are so full of hate for the whites and Spanish slavers."

"You have Spanish blood. I can see it in you."

"If I do, it is very little, only a drop. The rest is English. White, as you say. I believe it is the Europeans you hate mostly. You must have drunk too much firewater, your brain has to be pickled, McCloud. That is what's wrong with all the men here. They can't think straight, their minds are clouded, so they kill, rape, steal, and do all sorts of ungodly things against one another and especially against the women."

Just then another bawdy song was being sung, punctuating Eve's tirade with raucous hoots and hollers.

"You see," Eve said. "Drunk on evil spirit water. Makes men crazy in the head."

McCloud laughed once, his head flung way back. He looked into her face again. "You almost sound like an Indian, Eve Michaels. Almost."

She stared back at him defiantly, unmoved, eyes hot, lips pursed, jaw clenched. Inside, however, she was a mass of jangled nerves and mixed emotions. Eve began to think he was playing a game with her, toying with her to see how far she could bend and stretch.

Suddenly McCloud was quiet, still, intense.

"You lived in St. Louis, near the river?" he asked.

"Yes, I did." Eve wondered what was coming.

"I knew your father."

Again she stared back at him in shock.

"My father?"

"He was a trapper for a time, *non?*"

"Yes. I believe he was. I don't understand."

"I was a seventeen-year-old trapper. I learned the ways of the beavers, mountain men, and all Indians of the Basin and Plains. Not only Shoshoni. I also learned to defend myself with a knife and bare fists, like the whites, not only bows and arrows. I was contracted to trek up the Missouri with goods for the Rendezvous. I came upon a man, another trapper, who was rutting over an Indian girl. Her name was Evening Song, a beautiful Ute. He passed her to his friends."

"Who was he?" Eve's eyes were bloodshot and wild.

"You sound angry, Eve Michaels. You are not? You shake your head, but you are angry and confused. Waiting? I will tell you, Dark Hair: Everett Michaels . . . close to your name, Eve, went whistling up the Missouri, never looking back at the Indian girl he and his companions had left on the riverbank. I see you flinch. Yes. Evening Song had bled to death. They called this man Rhett; does this ring a bell?"

Eve slanted her eyes away, then back up at him. "You know what, McCloud?"

He shrugged nonchalantly.

"My father's name was not Everett Michaels. It was Blake, McCloud. Blake Michaels. They called him Blackie."

Chapter Nine

McCloud looked disgusted.

"So I made a foolish mistake." He shook his head, then looked up to the summer sky. "Blake Michaels," he said with a grunt. "They called him Blackie."

Many Stars looked at her brother, who sat with chin in hands before the campfire. "Tell me that whole thing again, brother. I want to laugh a little more."

"What? So that I look a bit more each time like a stupid jackass?"

"Oh, Suncloud." She ruffled his thick, dark hair. "You look so sad. You are not as fierce as they say you are. You are soft and cuddly inside, like a big, funny bear."

"Bears are not funny, Honna. They are fuzzy perhaps, and ferocious."

"Did you go to school when you grew up?" Many Stars asked her brother as she continued to bead a bodice.

"Yes. In Cheyenne. Not a real school, only an old boardinghouse where he saw his 'pupils' and taught them what he knew because he was lonely and wanted something to do with his life. His wife had passed away."

"Who do you speak of?" Many Stars asked.

"Ah. I am sorry. There was a man there in Cheyenne by the name of Fitzsimmons—he had a mother who was Dakota—who taught me many languages, history, geography, showed me ancient maps and manuscripts, among other things. Many women wanted me. I always wanted to be free and wild, to marry a beautiful Indian maiden, just like my father had. She was your mother. She . . . something happened to Slender Arrow."

"My mother was called Slender Arrow?" Something tickled at the edges of her fuzzy memory—a pretty woman with slim hips and dainty feet.

"Yes." He looked serious, sober.

"I do not wish to know at this time." She changed the topic. "What about your second mother, this one you call 'step'? She was the European white. It is obvious you did not love your stepmother. What was her name?"

"I do not remember." He looked at her. "Truly, after Spotted Horse took her for his wife, I did not look at her when I saw how white she was. I put their marriage and her image from my mind."

Many Stars strung a bead, looking down at her work again. "I realize you hardly ever think of yourself as a half-caste, but you have this: You are a red and white apple."

McCloud scoffed, "Never, I am not white on the outside, red on the inside."

"You are. Even though your flesh boasts a coppery color. You are torn between the two. And you want Evelyn Michaels. I know you do. But it's too soon after Morning Moon's departure to the Indian paradise for you to court Eve. You kissed her, I know, and this only served your anger and frustration more fuel."

"Get the Dark Hair ready," he ordered, picking up his Hawken rifle, slinging it over one shoulder by its strap.

"Eve can get ready herself." Many Stars stood as dazzling sunlight streamed through tall pines. "She is a big girl, Suncloud."

McCloud only stomped away, his moccasins kicking up clouds of dust, his fringed buckskins swaying in rhythm to his long stride.

Kicking Wolf watched from the cover of brush near the riverbank, then he went sneaking off to join his friends.

What a man, Eve thought as she watched Suncloud ride through camp making last-minute inspections before their departure.

Then she caught herself before her thoughts went any further and led her into dangerous waters. She had enough just thinking about where all her crazy dreams were going to lead her. She had always wanted to forget the past. Why? she asked herself. Because, she answered, it's just too painful remembering and . . . and being parted from loved ones all these years.

She knew, however, that all those long-ago years were just beginning to haunt her.

The sun was only beginning to rise above the Wind River Mountains as the party of Indians and the Dark Hair wound their way through the hills where the sky pilot and yellow cinquefoil bloomed; the wildflowers occupied alpine meadows, boulder-fields, and open rocky ridges. The lupine carpeted low-elevation prairies and open forests.

Many Stars had gone to the Nez Perce camp the night before. Eve now wore a different Indian dress, one of a fawn color and slightly longer. It was clean and soft, and Eve felt confident and comfortable mounted on Zeena. Her gaze often strayed to McCloud, who would ride back to the end of the line, then pause to ride beside her and Many Stars in the middle of the Indians that were strung out like beads on a necklace.

As the returning war party—and the women—rode up from the river into the foothills of the Wind River Mountains, a breeze stirred the pine trees into a faint whispering and sighing sound that threaded through the monkeyflowers.

McCloud was checking the sturdy pack horse when he asked himself: What is different about this woman? He had never encountered this strange feeling before, that he wanted only one woman for himself alone for the rest of his life. His feelings for Morning Moon, even though he'd loved the handsome woman fiercely, had not been of such a possessive nature. What was it about the Dark Hair, he mused again. Was it that she was a white woman? That made him irritated and angry. He'd never been attracted to a white female before. He remembered a pair of soft lips kissing his most responsively and convincingly. He had been curious about the vibrant woman he'd held loosely in his arms. Her elusive fragrance titilated his nostrils as no woman's scent had ever done before, inflaming his senses and his desire. This feeling was like an itch he couldn't scratch.

They turned their horses toward the faint sound

of water dancing over stones. They stopped to rest beside a small stream where the alpine aster and primrose bloomed, and then farther along they made camp for the night.

McCloud was talking with one of his men when Eve looked up from her position beside Many Stars as they pitched their small tent on dry grassland beside a moist meadow. Her breath caught as she listened to the rich sound of laughter and stared at McCloud's face. The harshness banished into startling youthfulness as he laughed. Fine lines etched around McCloud's deep gray eyes creased with humor. He looked over to her as he was laughing with Utah, and there was no cynicism or hostility now in the smile that widened his mouth, showing the gleaming whiteness of his teeth.

Then he realized something and froze. He was being too friendly, but he could not help being good-natured when she was this pleasant.

Boldly, his eyes found her. McCloud had never met anyone like this Eve Michaels with her coy, maidenly demeanor, and she fascinated him. He felt like laughing into the wind for joy as she kept feasting on him with that amused and surprised look.

She was putting up the tent with Many Stars. It was a conical lodge of specially tanned elk stretched over a framework. Stones were placed at the bottom of the tipi to hold it down. Within the circular interior there would soon be a smoldering fire and a simmering kettle. Many Stars was making berry-watercress soup for her and Eve with the bit of meat she had left. The dog soldiers, along with McCloud, would eat something else.

Eve was like a happy little child as she helped Many Stars pitch their tent. She was enjoying herself, and she laughed as Many Stars made jokes and said, "You will make some man a fine squaw, Dark Hair." Her gaze flicked over McCloud and came back to her friend. "Umm-hmm."

Eve laughed as she looked over her shoulder. "I thought 'squaw' was a derogatory term, Many Stars."

"Some call their women squaw with adoration and affection." Many Stars saw Utah George look over and smile; she was amazed to feel her face flush with heat. In a lower tone Many Stars added, "They make eyes, have fun, make squaw laugh."

McCloud wanted to be laughing with Eve Michaels, sharing the humor with her, but he had the distinct impression that she was now laughing *at* him. It stung him to the bone as only a few things in life could. He felt apart from her, like the outsider he was and always had been in the white world.

Had been. Not now. Still, she was in a different "place of mind" than he was. Then why did he hear the words *He is waiting for you* when he was near her? What did they mean? Nothing, he told himself.

Ai. Loving Eve would only cause them both pain and strife.

The dark was like a night creature as it deepened and surrounded the camp. Eve was alive to every sound and sensation. The low campfire, flanked by moss-covered rocks, with the Indians moving back and forth talking softly in Shoshoni. Chewing jerked meat as horses cropped grass quietly at the edge of camp. High in the hills a coyote's howl shivered, a lonesome sound in the dark as Eve paused in her labors to experience everything this wild Indian paradise had to offer.

McCloud leaned back against the tallest of pines as he stared into the blaze of the campfire. Across the clearing, through the slit opening of the tent, he saw Many Stars settling down in her bed robes. Utah and the others still hung idly but with senses alert around the cooking fire.

McCloud's eyes became sleepy, and drooped.

A twig snapped.

Eve stood at the edge of firelight as he grabbed for the loaded rifle that had been leaning against the tree.

Eve asked, "Would you shoot me in your hate for all whites?"

His hand fell languidly to his side as he kept his eyes trained on her but said nothing. One part of him didn't want to frighten her away, and the other wanted to shout at her to leave him.

From the edge of firelight, Eve walked toward him. His body was already hard with desire as he watched her. McCloud felt as if he were taking a sweat bath, the ceremonial vapor bath given under a skin-covered hut. Steam was produced by heating stones and pouring water over them. Thoroughly sweated out, the participants ended the ritual bath by diving into a nearby creek to cool down—just what McCloud needed at the moment!

Eve asked, "When will I see Maggie again?"

"Don't worry. You've been told Tames Wild Horses would be the last Indian in the land to rape a woman or mistreat her."

"So Many Stars has said." She looked up into the star-spangled sky. "This is a beautiful wilderness." Her voice was soft, evocative. "Don't you believe that the first white men who entered the West found most Indians friendly and helpful? And hasn't it been the other way around also?"

McCloud relaxed, warming to her easy way of conversing as she gazed up at the night sky. "True," he said. "The mountain men had many partners among the tribes." His jaw hardened. "It was after the whites became serious rivals for the game, furs, and the land itself that the red man became alarmed."

"And angry," she said, noting his long legs and tall moccasins.

"That too," he said easily, stretching languidly.

"And battles took place when they could not drive out the white men by other means."

"More so than ever, and more battles are coming," McCloud told Eve. "Life for the Indians is simple, for they make everything they need. Free to move about as they wish, they follow the buffalo and elk herds, trap beaver, hunt game, and hold tribal dances and worship the Great Spirit. Horses are some Indians' only wealth, and they prize them. In winter they gather in villages made snug against storms and eat meat cured during the summer hunts."

"What about children?" Her eyes looked soft and misty.

He looked surprised that she had asked that question. "The children are cared for tenderly and their days are happy and busy. As soon as they can shoot a bow and arrow, the boys practice to become skilled hunters—and trappers as in our town of Wild Thunder—or dog soldiers. They spend hours on Indian ponies and become expert riders. The girls learn how to dress game, cook, and sew. They marry quite young and join the other women in doing all the camp work."

She would not ask if Morning Moon had given him a child, but she could see a tender light moving in his gray eyes, giving her to believe there might be a child waiting for his return in this town of Wild Thunder.

He continued to relate the Indian way to her. "When white traders appeared among them, the Indians trapped animals and sold their skins for beads and bright material, looking-glasses and other trinkets. As it is now. But they want little more than that from the whites. Most of all, we wish to be left alone."

We . . .

Eve turned and left him. McCloud sat, feeling tense, staring in her direction long after she'd gone back to her bed robe inside the tent.

Eve could not find sleep and drifted out of the tent, walking beneath the stars. She felt the need to be alone in the dark, to think. She needed the night silence, where she could not hear Many Stars's breathing. She went beyond the low embers of the camp, glancing over her shoulder, checking to see if everyone was asleep.

She felt a presence behind her, knowing who had followed her into the dark beyond the camp. She felt trapped, certain some dreadful blow would fall on her. Instead, Eve felt warm hands stroking her soft hair as it cascaded over her body.

"McCloud," she whispered. "I will go back. I was only getting some fresh—"

"No," he said. He pulled some of her hair to his

face, inhaled its fragrance while Eve stiffened and turned her body away.

"Come here, Eve Michaels. Stay with me."

He touches my soul.

Again Eve felt McCloud's hands on her. Pushing wisps of soft hair from her face, he gently ran a finger over her profile, lingering at her mouth, whose soft fullness he slowly outlined. Pink, like dusty roses, so soft, he thought. He touched her shoulder and caressed her slowly, moving a hand down her back, over her buttocks and thighs.

"What are you—"

"I want to see what it is you hide," McCloud said, still touching.

She had removed the cloth binding her breasts. Now he would know—if she did not move away.

Eve stood rooted to the spot. She couldn't move, couldn't breathe. But her heart was surely hammering hard and fast—she could hear and feel it in her ears and throat.

Like sunshine, warmth flooded her.

He touched his mouth to her throat and wouldn't let her move away. She wanted only to escape—or did she?

His breaths became slow and heavy, warm against her face, and he drew her against him. He reached for her breasts, rubbing their fullness in his hands.

Ai, yes.

He put his mouth against her ear and sighed deeply, eagerly kissing and nibbling the curve of her neck. "I thought so," he said, his hands moving down her body, pressing her urgently to him. "I knew there was more to you, Eve Michaels."

"Wait—" she said.

"No," he said.

He began to caress her cheek, kissing her mouth to find her yielding softly to him. Then he kissed her deeply, gathering her urgently into his arms, his desire for her obvious and unrelenting. And Eve met his warm mouth as if she were coming in from the cold. She was unable to deny the warmth that surged in her body or her desire to respond to him.

No, she thought suddenly, *no.* Still, she could not break and run from him.

He stroked her thighs, which she only pressed more tightly together, and he pulled her gown toward her waist, pushing his hands against her belly.

Eve arched her back and stiffened even more. "No," she murmured hoarsely. "I ask you not to touch me. How can you when you hate so much." It wasn't a question.

McCloud was still for a moment, then pressed his body heavily against her. His breathing was hard, his body taut and eager for hers. "There is us and only the dark, Eve Michaels."

"The dark has eyes, brave Suncloud."

"Not this night. My men rest heavy."

Ebony fire.

He clutched her to him in an almost crushing grip, and nestled his mouth below her ear, gently stroking the slender column of her throat with his tongue.

"Please," Eve said even as she flung back her head and arched toward him.

"I'll not rape you, Eve. But I will have you one day. I will, I promise you that. And soon."

Eve stood very still, barely breathing. He moved back, stepping away from her, his dark hand still holding hers, stretching until he parted with her. At first Eve thought her body and its limbs would snap under the tension she felt. Then, very slowly, she let herself go, and relaxed under his loose hold.

"Go to bed, Eve Michaels."

She looked at his face, which was like carved walnut in the night.

His fingers barely touched hers at the tips, and then let go.

She ran.

He watched.

McCloud knew their coming together was inevitable.

Kicking Wolf scattered the ashes of the dead campfire. The dog soldier was a big man, strong, and a little on the heavy side.

Eve glanced at Kicking Wolf and felt her face flush with heat. Sometime during the night an Indian woman had made camp beside Eve and Many Stars's tent. Eve didn't know how the Indian woman had gotten through the guard, but she had. She and Kicking Wolf had been lying in the robes all night, making love. Eve had hardly slept at all from all the moanings and ecstatic shouts.

Now McCloud saw her red face as he walked his stallion over to her. "She is Taz, Kicking Wolf's woman."

"His wife?" Eve looked over at the heavyset woman packing the animals.

"Of course. What else could I have meant?" McCloud tested the sharpness of the Green River knife at his belt, then swiftly checked and cleaned his pistol and Hawken rifle.

"She might have been a—" Eve flushed again, letting the subject drop.

"I'll leave you with your red face now, Eve; I go to join my men."

Good, Eve thought. *I am glad I can go to join Many Stars.*

Eve did not know what she would have said or done had he brought up the night before and their intimate moments beneath the starry sky.

Eve could feel McCloud's eyes on her as they quickly ate their meal of jerky and hardtack. She glanced his way, then swiftly aside. His eyes had a dark, unfathomable look she'd come to know in her few days with him and his men . . . perhaps it had already been a week. She couldn't be sure. Time had swift wings.

Throughout the day, as they rode on, stopped to drink from a stream and eat sparingly, and then mount up again, Eve's body became flushed when she thought about McCloud. Even now she thought she could still experience the heat of McCloud's body, his tantalizing mouth seeking every part of her face and throat. She had been surprised at the warmth that flowed from her, and the eagerness with which she accepted his body pressed against her breasts and thighs.

Eve blushed to think that McCloud had discovered she was not flat-chested without her cloth bindings.

Night was upon them and Eve was staring into the blaze of the campfire as she thought back to how she'd lost her mother.

The fire.

It had been accidental. A servant had failed to tend a cooking fire properly. The flames had traveled fast in the wind that had been up that night. Her family had lost the main part of their house. Worst of all, her mother had perished in the fire. John and Derek had never been close to their mother, so it had not been as much a loss as it had been to Blake Michaels and the daughter he also had never come to know. Theirs had been a malfunctioning family. Blake had begun drinking heavily, and then he had gone away, never to return.

While she'd been alive, Narcissa Roussillon Le-Bleau—she'd never called or even thought of herself as Michaels—had lived up to the name Narcissa. She had glittered at parties and balls. Eve recalled Narcissa's gorgeous clothes, her jewels, perfumes, gay manner. She had also taught Eve to be wary and fearful of men. Only pretty things mattered, Narcissa had instructed Eve. If you did not watch out, men would have their hands all over you.

Eve and her older brothers had made a curious trio—one imp of a girl whose nerve went unchallenged, and two handsome boys, similar in character and alike in appearance, both blond and fair of skin. Eve loved them, and was desperately drawn to them following Narcissa's death and as her nightmares grew worse. Often, one of the boys, or both, would spend time comforting Eve in the timeless way of sheltering a frightened, quivering animal in one's arms. She missed them terribly.

The nightmares had not returned for years. She hoped they never would. She would always see Narcissa dressed in one of her glittering ball gowns, her body, hair, jewelry, all going up in flames. The diamonds would flare in Eve's eyes and she would awaken to sob and cry her heart out, clutching, not a doll, but an old yellow dress. . . .

"Eve!"

"Oh . . . what?" Eve started from her reverie and looked up as Many Stars came running up the riverbank and fell to her knees beside Eve.

"Look! All these fish, I caught them myself." Many Stars held up a long slender spear made of wood.

Eve watched as Many Stars put them all together on a string and got to her feet. She was so proud and happy that Eve could not bring herself to worry the Indian girl about her bad dreams. Besides, she had not had the nightmares in so long, she thought perhaps she might not ever be bothered by them again.

Now there were the other dreams. Dreams of the turtle and the butterfly, the yellow dress, and blue beads. The death of her brothers.

"Would you like help cooking them?" Eve called, finishing the braid she'd been putting in her hair.

"No. You take down the tipi, Eve. Soon we will be on our way to Wild Thunder. Suncloud says it is not so far now. First"—Many Stars grinned holding up her catch—"we eat good!"

The fish had been delicious and Eve laughed as she watched McCloud lick his fingers one by one. When he was in a good mood, it reminded Eve of the wonderful times she'd shared with her brothers.

He seemed so vulnerable and boyish as he stared into her eyes, and in that brief moment, as she looked back at him through a dark curl that had fallen across her cheek, Eve knew that she held the power to hurt him.

Chapter Ten

Many Stars rode an Appaloosa ahead of Eve's piebald horse. The trail they were riding was a precipitous one: a rocky canyon so narrow they had to guide the animals down the creek bed between overhanging willows and huge boulders.

The smell of many-flowered phlox was sweet and tickled Eve's nostrils. Also there was the primrose growing in rock crevices, talus slopes, meadows, and on stream banks.

Eve and Many Stars rode between McCloud and Utah George at the head of the group, with Frog Catcher and the dog soldiers behind; the pack horses brought up the rear. She had never ridden so high in the air. At times she believed they passed through clouds, and she smiled when she beheld the monkeyflowers; the blooms were so beautiful, she believed she had entered paradise.

Eve suddenly felt the urge to paint, to learn, to grow as a human, as a woman. To fashion things from nature, to create something from out of the wild. To be a warrior woman. To heal. To know a man.

She had never desired a man, never wished to

know one deeply and intimately. What was happening to her now? Suddenly everything looked and felt so different. All the flowers, the sun, the rocks, everything was so beautiful. And she was alive, so alive, especially when her eyes came into contact with McCloud's.

An outcropping of rock held up by tall pines and brush could be seen up ahead through the willows, and as they rode below it, she looked onto a wide green valley, wondering what the coming days held in store for her.

The small town of Wild Thunder was nestled in the foothills of the Wind River range. The line of dog soldiers and women entered weary and hungry just as twilight descended. Eve and Many Stars remained mounted; the Indian woman looked as foggy and bewildered as Eve felt.

"I am too tired to move a muscle," said Eve, looking around at the stares of the villagers.

She was so hungry and weakened from fatigue that she wouldn't have cared if the copper-skinned strangers walked over and stripped off her clothes. But she perked up a bit as she recalled the story of a captive girl who had really been stripped of all her clothing and her body painted in various colors.

What am I thinking? I am not a captive. I have friends—well, at least one. She shuddered despite the warmth of the bloodred sundown and the careless mood she was in.

Here, there was plenty of room for lodges, wicki-ups, and tipis, wood for cooking fires, and plenty of forage for the animals. Drifting lazily in the air was the lovely, inviting scent of cooking meat and smoke from the fires.

The smell of wood smoke tickled her nostrils. The tipis and wood dwellings were a welcome sight.

Her stomach growled in hunger.

Eve looked again at her surroundings. Small children—half-breed and full Indian—were everywhere. There was even a trading post, a large log house, and other buildings. Eve wondered how people could come here to trade, since the town was secluded in the wilderness so far from civilization. This was the way they must want it to be, she thought, and kept riding.

The trading post where they stood was the largest of four rough log buildings that made up Wild Thunder. They were separated by a little distance, and outside the dusty street of buildings squatted the Indian dwellings.

Trailed by children, Eve and Many Stars put their horses away in the corral, and as soon as Eve began to walk away, Zeena whinnied and followed her to the end of the log fence.

"You have found a friend," Many Stars said, watching as Eve rubbed her face on Zeena's velvety nose.

"Yes, she's a beauty," Eve said as they walked toward the store, where several men had gathered outside to see what McCloud had brought home to Wild Thunder.

Eve was surprised at the looks of the half-breeds. Old men. Young men. Long hair, army-issue hats and boots, civilized shirts and pants, moccasins. And all the men, even the youngest, wore knives and pistols strapped to their waists, thighs, or ankles. Some stood near the post, rifles in hand, as if they'd been glued there.

"Do you see anyone you know or recognize?" Eve asked Many Stars.

"No one." Many Stars felt as much a stranger there as did Eve Michaels.

"Do you not know me, Honna?"

An older man with long, thin gray hair, a leathery face, and one gnarled hand came walking toward her. He smiled, and Many Stars could see that most of his teeth were absent. But it was the missing left arm that caught her eye.

"I am One-Arm."

Obviously, Eve thought as she watched the man take Many Stars into his one-armed embrace. Eve looked around again. After hearing that, it was easy to name some of the other Indians: Black Beads, Patch, Wounded Leg, Scarred Hand, Greasy Face. Most looked as if they'd been in battle.

As One-Arm led Many Stars away, Eve found herself standing alone in front of the trading post. Everything was twilight gray now. The wood buildings. The grass growing at the sides of them. The horses. The men.

Unreal. Voices were fading. Curious eyes. Looks exchanged.

Something did not feel right inside Eve's head. Everything was growing dimmer. Beginning to whirl. The gray turned black. . . .

When Eve woke up she was lying in the back room of the trading post. There was a damp rag on her forehead. A child's voice came out of the twilight. Eve frowned, disoriented, as dark images became people. The faces blurred and took shape.

The child was speaking a mixture of English and Shoshoni, and Eve recognized the word *father;* someone had taught her the English language.

Eve opened her eyes to behold the prettiest little girl she'd ever seen, with the palest shade of brown hair she could imagine, so beautiful and sleek. Shining hazel eyes peered into Eve's face. The child looked worried as she took Eve in from head to foot.

"Will you be feeling better soon?"

My God, she speaks English.

"I hope so," Eve said, holding her head. "Who has taught you English?" She looked at the lovely child wearing a faded calico dress beneath a buckskin vest. Why, she almost looked civilized.

"One-Arm. He knows many languages and speaks almost all Indian tongues."

How bright, Eve thought, looking above the child to see McCloud standing there. Wonder filled her gaze as she studied McCloud for answers.

"Whispering Bells is my daughter," he said like a proud father.

"My second mother, Morning Moon, went away and she has not come back yet. But I think she will pretty soon." Whispering Bells looked up at her father.

"I have to go now, Whispering Bells." He stooped to hug her. "I have to see to—"

"I know. You don't have to tell me. You have to see to the men and the horses and the hunting and the store."

Without another word to the lonely child he went into the other room, at once talking with the men gathered there with things to trade and gossip to share.

"He's always busy," Whispering Bells told Eve. "Do you want to know how old I am? Everyone asks me that question. So I will tell you: I am eight summers. I am known as Whispering Bells." She giggled. "That is Indian talk."

"I know," said Eve. "Do you have another name? I mean, besides your Indian one?"

"Yes. My French name is Fantin. Father doesn't like to call me Fantin McCloud, even though that is my real civilized name."

Eve blinked, knowing she had found another intelligent female besides Many Stars to converse with.

"Come," Whispering Bells said. "That is, if you can get up now?"

"Oh, yes." Eve sat up on the crude bench. The child at once took Eve's hand in her small, smooth one.

"It gets dark here in Wild Thunder pretty early, but I will show you around anyway. There are lots of smoke lights." She looked up at Eve. "Are you hungry?"

"Yes. In fact, I am starved." Eve pushed the cloth aside, held her head, and smiled.

"I prepared some really good stew. It's got lots of meat in it. Deer meat. And vegetables. I love to cook. You will come to my place. It is not far from Great-Grandfather's."

The child's hand felt warm and wonderful in Eve's and she couldn't wait to taste this stew that Whispering Bells had prepared. Her growling stomach attested to how hungry she really was.

* * *

"That was wonderful stew," Eve told the child as she helped her clean the wooden bowls and put things away in the chest in the small one-room cabin. Eve looked at the child's golden chestnut hair in the light from the cooking fire. "Where did you get your pale hair from?" she asked Whispering Bells.

"My mother." She shrugged. "Not Morning Moon. She wasn't my real mother. She was my second mother. My real mother went away. She always goes away, and then she comes back when you don't think she will." Whispering Bells shrugged as if this were not all that bad.

Softly, Eve gasped. She tried to hide her surprise from the child. "Your . . . real mother?"

"You look surprised," Whispering Bells said. "You shouldn't be. I think I really look more Indian than white, but I have only a little blood of that race, like my father."

"Your mother was white." It was not a question, but a statement. Eve knew it was true. "A French woman?"

"Well, not really. She gave me a French name, but McCloud doesn't like it. He prefers Whispering Bells. My mother is . . . was Spanish. That's what McCloud tells me."

"McCloud?" Eve looked astounded. "I thought I heard you call him Father earlier."

"I did. But he doesn't like it when I do. He really likes to be called Suncloud."

"Who stays here with you?" Eve asked the child, growing angrier by the minute.

"Red Beads. She sleeps with *all* the men over at the Cheer Lodge."

That did it. Eve was up off the floor mats and heading for the door.

Whispering Bells looked sad and worried at the same time. "Where are you going?" All the people she'd really cared for always went away, like both her "mothers." One-Arm was the only one who stayed. But he was a man, her great-grandfather. She needed a woman—besides busy Red Beads—to talk to.

"I will be back." Eve spoke each word emphatically.

Eve found McCloud outside the post, talking to some men. "I have to talk to you," she told him in a tone that lifted his eyebrows.

The men turned away, talking among themselves as the Dark Hair almost pulled McCloud along the dirt street. The moon was high over the mountains and the night air had grown considerably chilled, the smell of the yellow pea flowers in the air.

He stopped far down the street, where it turned into a beaten grass path. "What is it, Dark Hair? Why do you look as if the mountains are falling down around us?"

"They are." Eve rubbed her chilled arms. She paced back and forth, finally coming to stand before him, glaring up into his night-darkened eyes. "How can you leave a child with a woman like Red Beads to care for her? Whispering Bells is practically all alone in that one-room cabin. She cooks for herself while Red Beads is out . . . servicing all the men in this . . . town. Whispering Bells is only a child."

He glowered down at her. "She did just fine before you came here." He saw her mouth drop into a sardonic slant. "And how do you know about Red Beads and what she does?"

"I heard about her at the Rendezvous. She's . . . my God . . . she's a whore."

"Morning Moon has not been gone all that long." He lit a cigar, puffed, looking down his nose at her astonished face. "It is only temporary. Do you care if I smoke? I smoke outside only."

"Go ahead." Eve turned away from the stream of smoke he blew out. "I didn't know you smoked."

He grinned. "I smoke anything I can get my hands on: peace pipe. Cigars. Cheroots." He inhaled, blew out, delighting in the smoke that curled around his head. "What is your problem, Eve Michaels? Do you need a man to bed you? Is that what all your frustration is about?"

"I don't know what you mean. I . . . I've never . . ." She let it hang, knowing not what to say next.

"And I do not believe you."

"What are you—"

Tossing his cigar aside, he grabbed her, taking her in his arms. Eve struggled, wanting to get away from him, but he was too strong and she was too vulnerable to his advances. His lips came down on hers, and her face was flushed, her knees wobbly, her heart pounding a rapid rhythm.

He felt so good and she did not want the ecstasy to stop, and yet she knew she must bring it to an end before it got any fiercer. But her struggles served only to join her hips more intimately against his. Her hair tangled with his, dark melding with dark.

Strands of her hair fell between their lips, but he kept on kissing her until she was nearly swooning.

The night sky yawned above with shining constellations, and inky-black lodgepoles silhouetted against the orange cooking fires.

As he kissed her, she thought of something very strange: Him atop his horse, Wind, as he rode by, hard buttocks, sinewy thighs and flanks . . .

Why, she wanted to scream at his head, did he bear such hostility and suspicion for her sex? And why was he kissing her if he did?

"Stop, damn you, stop," she breathed between kisses. He was making her feel out of control and crazy inside.

"You don't want me to, Eve. Say it—you do not." His mouth was hot against her ear—

"I—oh, you are taking my breath, please—"

"Say it."

"We have to talk," she said with quick nibbles to his throat, her fingers clutched about his shoulders, opening and closing like butterfly wings.

He filled her vision with his tan face, cruelly handsome at times, but softer now, like a boy who badly wants something he cannot have.

He cupped her breasts in his big hands, astonished afresh at their soft weightiness. When he still would not release her, she bit his chest and pulled at his fringed leather vest.

"Ouch," he said in a velvety voice. "You little she-cat."

He pushed her away to look at her.

Her hands were on her hips as she said, "You asked for it. You wouldn't keep your hands and mouth off me." She looked down at his fingers examining his chest for wounds. "I didn't draw blood, if that's what you are looking for."

"Come here," he ordered, reaching for her. He added in a lower voice, "I'm not finished with you."

"Oh, yes, you are."

"No—I am not."

She looked up at the sculpted cheekbones under taut flesh. Would there be any hope for mercy or understanding from him if he really got her alone? She could hear voices and the faint scuffling of feet in the dust not far off, so she knew she was safe.

"It is time to eat," Many Stars said, making both Eve and McCloud jump at the sound of her voice.

"I already ate," the couple said almost at the same time.

"Come, Eve. It is time to talk with Whispering Bells. She is lonely. One-Arm has gone back to his cedar house."

McCloud put in, "She's been lonely before. Come here, Eve, I want to talk to you."

"Oh, so now you want to talk." She narrowed her eyes at him. "I thought you had other ideas, like—"

Many Stars intruded again. "Eve, when a man is in a mood like he is, it is better to leave him alone."

McCloud's eyebrows rose. "Oh? And what sort of mood is that?" he asked Many Stars.

"Bad," Many Stars came back, tugging on Eve's arm.

"Too late, McCloud," Eve said, looking at Many Stars. "You should have talked when you had the chance. Instead, you had to go and—"

"Come," was all Many Stars said, turning with Eve. "Do you not know when a woman wants to be left alone."

Eve walked away with Many Stars, but she could not stop herself from looking over her shoulder.

Warrior women, McCloud thought. Do they always scratch and hiss and kick to get what they want? He snorted as Utah George came over to join him.

Intense, sudden desire for Eve Michaels lanced through McCloud so strongly, he had to struggle to hold back from going after her, taking her then and there.

"Utah, where do the warrior women, the good ones like Many Stars and Eve Michaels, keep their weapons?"

"I can't answer that, McCloud. It just wouldn't be right."

Warrior woman, Utah thought. Very appropriate. For the both of them.

Chapter Eleven

Eve was glad that Many Stars had come to find her before anything had happened between her and McCloud.

When they returned to the cedar dwelling of Red Beads and Whispering Bells, Eve saw something very strange. The old man with one arm was throwing someone out of the house. The exchange of angry Indian words filled the air like rapid-fire bullets. The woman stuck out her huge chest and bumped it into One-Arm, and that was when Whispering Bells stepped between them.

"We should help," Eve said to Many Stars, starting to walk from the edge of the cottonwoods.

"No. One-Arm and Whispering Bells can take care of this matter themselves."

Eve looked at Many Stars. "But how could you know this? You have been here for only one night."

"I know how everyone thinks and acts in Wild Thunder. I get around fast, Eve Michaels." She touched Eve's mouth and drew away. "Shh. Watch. Be still."

"You must go, Red Beads," said Whispering Bells. "I have someone else to stay with me." She spoke in Shoshoni, then in English as she turned toward the cottonwoods. "Eve Michaels will live with me for a time. You may come back if you wish." She had switched back to Shoshoni. "For now I have company."

Red Beads chattered away and waved her hands in the air.

Whispering Bells shrugged and turned to the old man with the long gray-white hair; she spoke in English again. "This is the way it is, right, Great-Grandfather?"

"R-right," One-Arm said in halting English. He was very tired from throwing Red Beads out of the cedar house. In Shoshoni he told Red Beads to go stay at the Cheer Lodge now.

Eve turned to Many Stars. "How did she know we were here? She said my name and turned toward us."

"For having the white blood, Whispering Bells's senses are very much like an Indian's. She knows things when no one else can see. The old man sensed our presence also. I saw his eyes shift our way, saw his cheek twitch before he put his attention back on Red Beads and her argument."

Strange people, Eve thought as she followed Many Stars to the cedar lodge. *Very strange. Then, am I not also strange for dreaming the things that I dream about—turtles and yellow dresses and such?*

In the morning Eve and Many Stars walked to Whispering Bells's little garden in back of the cedar dwelling. Eve was wearing a soft buckskin dress, amber colored with a row of worked beads that formed a pattern across the bodice and back; fringe ran along the hemline and arms. An Indian boy by the name of Arrow Maker joined them.

"Do you make arrows?" Eve asked after Many Stars had whispered to Eve what she wanted to ask the little boy in Shoshoni.

"Why else would my name be Arrow Maker?" he shot back to Eve, screwing up his mouth at her funny-sounding speech.

"What did he say?" Eve asked Many Stars as she smiled at the boy.

Many Stars told Eve.

"I should have known," Eve muttered to herself.

"Come," Arrow Maker told Eve, taking her hand. "I will show you."

Eve shrugged as she was tugged along by the little boy. Whispering Bells held back her laughter behind her hand. Eve looked at Many Stars as they walked by her.

"What did he say? Where is he taking me?" Eve looked over her shoulder at Many Stars, who was wearing a big grin.

"You will see," Whispering Bells said in English, and now Many Stars had to ask the girl what she'd said.

To Many Stars Whispering Bells also said in Shoshoni, "You will see."

"The Indian arrow has six parts: the head, shaft, foreshaft, shaftment, the feathering, and the nock."

"What did he say?" Eve asked Many Stars, and she translated.

"The head is the point of the arrow. The shaft is the main, rodlike part, which sometimes has a piece of a harder material attached to it at the front end, called the foreshaft."

"What?"

Whispering Bells translated.

"Very interesting," Eve said, watching the boy handle the arrow as he showed them how it was made.

"The shaftment is the other end of the shaft, and the nock the end that is grooved for the bowstring. The feathering is the feathers attached at the end. Length varies with the individual and materials at hand. Usually the shaft is plain.

"The West Coast area arrows are painted with stripes for identification. The Plains Indians put grooves lengthwise, these are sometimes called lightning marks or blood grooves. Some arrows have no feathers, other have either two or three. The feathers are from a great variety of birds."

A deep male voice added: "And an arrowpoint is used on the end of an arrowshaft." They all looked at McCloud with a frown as he went on. "The point is usually made of flint. However, many other materials can be used, such as bone, antlers, wood, shell, and copper—"

"Say . . . quit stealing his show," Eve said to McCloud of Arrow Maker, who'd been doing just fine. "Go on, Arrow Maker. I would like to hear the rest." She shot McCloud a you-better-not-dare look.

"Copper is used by the tribes in the region of the . . ." Here Arrow Maker faltered and looked to his teacher.

"Great Lakes and up into Canada."

"That's enough," Arrow Maker told McCloud in Shoshoni. "I know the rest."

Eve stuck her chin in the air at McCloud and gave the boy her undivided attention once again.

"With the coming of the whites, arrowpoints began to be made of iron. An arrowhead is usually smaller than two inches in length."

Eve found McCloud watching her. He must be remembering last night, she told herself, feeling how hot her cheeks were becoming.

"Spearheads, for fishing, are longer. The shapes are different sometimes, but they are usually made in the shapes of leaves, such as the willow. Some points have no barbs and are made for easy—"

"Withdrawal," McCloud said, seeing Eve shudder as he translated.

"Other points are barbed and are used in warfare." Again Eve shuddered, even harder, and the boy went on to press his point while trying not to grin. "They are made to inflict a jagged wound and are difficult to remove."

As Arrow Maker kept gesturing and speaking, McCloud moved closer to Eve on the bench made of sawn logs.

"The points are usually fastened to the shaft with sinew, rawhide. War points are sometimes fastened loosely so that they can come off when they stick in an enemy—"

McCloud held up his hand for Arrow Maker to halt. "I see your friend Brown Sparrow over there. Why don't you go play with him now." He looked at his daughter. "And you too, Fantin, why don't you run along and play."

"I don't like to play war games, Father. You know that." Whispering Bells blinked. He had called her Fantin. "Do you know what you just said, Father?"

"No." He was looking at Eve and how pretty she was with her hair in dark braids, fawn-colored strips holding the ends together, and a deep amber-colored dress that was too tight for her and showed all her beautiful curves. "What, Fantin, what is it?"

She gave a little tug at each corner of her lips, looking at him as if he were the most helpless male in the world.

"See you later, Father. I think I will go and play." She smiled at Eve, waving as she went. Her look said He needs some help bad. You should give it to him.

Eve blinked at that silent message and pulled her eyes away from the willowy back of Whispering Bells.

"What an utterly delightful child," Eve said in an old lady's quavery voice, reminiscent of her aunt Ida back in St. Louis.

"Say, that was very good. You sound just like— well, I am not sure. Someone I used to know." McCloud frowned. He had more important things to think about at the moment.

As she turned to face McCloud, she met his unrelenting stare. They were so close they could have touched noses. And lips.

His eyes. Untamed. Beautiful.

Eve looked down and was surprised to find her hand in his. She took in the expanse of copper-hued flesh staring out at her from between the folds of his hide shirt.

Bulging pectorals greeted her quick glance. Her heart picked up a faster beat. Her breathing grew more rapid, more erratic.

"You know about arrow making and just about everything else having to do with this wilderness, don't you?'' She watched as he nodded slowly, his eyes still trained on her carmine mouth. "Now, what did you want to talk to me about.''

All of a sudden a shout came: *"Ashkanena!"*

McCloud shot to his feet. Eve followed, still feeling the warmth of his hand folded over hers, now gone. She had been losing herself in the pinwheels of his eyes, the colors arranged there so perfectly— dark brown, light brown, flinty gray, a bit of green . . . why, his eyes were hazel, and not all gray, as she'd first thought.

Dark hazel. Why had she not noticed before? She'd thought they were just dark Indian eyes.

Now she too came alert to the repeated cry. Eve spun about. "What does *Ashkanena* mean?''

He slowly turned to gape at her. "You said that very well, Eve Michaels—there just might be some touch of Indian in you somewhere. The *Ashkanena* are a band of the Crow Indians.''

"I understand that now. But what does the word mean?'' Eve still wanted to know as she straightened her tunic.

"It means Blackfoot lodges.''

"That is a strange name for a band of Indians.''

He grabbed her hand to pull her along. "You think *that* is strange. Wait until you meet them.''

"Wait!'' she hollered, trying to yank her wrist from his grasp. "Are they friendly, or nasty and mean? I'm just not up to meeting any ugly, cruel Indians today.''

"You'll see.''

It turned out to be a false alarm. There were no Ashkanenas, and so everyone went back to whatever they'd been doing before the alarm was called. Just a small band of friendly Nez Perce and a few

Bannock half-breeds and a few squaws coming with beads and blankets to trade for heavy pelts.

In minutes Eve found herself standing in the back of the store with McCloud. "Who is minding the store?" she asked him as he stood very close, looking into her eyes as if he couldn't get enough of them.

"Utah George and One-Arm. No one will come back here."

"What do you want?" She backed away from him.

"Come, I will show you."

Once again he grabbed her by the hand.

Eve took one last look at the tiny room in the back of the store. How she would love to decorate the place with lace curtains and some nice pieces of furniture, maybe even some furry pelts to cover chairs and plump pillows for the floor. It could be very cozy and livable.

What am I thinking? This is not my home, and I'm going back to St. Louis as soon as I can find some friendly white people to take me back there.

Eve was looking over her shoulder at the trading post, unaware he was already far ahead of her. "I saw some nice furniture in your store, lovely pieces of beautiful mahogany, pale oak, all very nice," Eve told McCloud as she caught up and walked with him. "Where did they come from?"

"You should know, Eve. Bits of furniture are to be found on the trail from the east to the west, all due to the westward movement. The loads become so heavy that those moving have to shed some pieces along the way." He shrugged, looking down at her lifted face. "A Native American finds the 'thing' and puts it in his tipi or little cedar house.

Or"—he looked at her with a grin and a shrug—"it ends up in my store."

"I notice chairs are pieces of logs around here. Why don't they use the furniture you've got in your store?" She watched where she was stepping, as the wild trail was becoming littered with pine needles and old branches. "And why a turkey wing when they can use a broom? You have lots of brooms in your store."

"Indians prefer turkey wings, I guess."

Eve laughed, beginning to feel there was lots of fun and humor in McCloud after all. And he was not a fierce Indian named Suncloud after all. To her he was just Steven McCloud, a man with some Indian blood. Mixed blood. Why, she had mixed blood herself, even a drop of Spanish; at least this was what people had been telling her, something her mother never cared to discuss.

Eve glanced up at the wildly handsome man walking beside her.

McCloud just had to find out who he was, that was all, because to her way of thinking, he was just like a little boy.

Eve looked straight ahead and nodded to herself.

A lost little boy needing some direction in life. Maybe she could give it. She could lead and he could follow.

Yes. She liked that idea very much. As long as he kept his hands to himself . . . well, part of the time, at least, she told herself with a smile.

He kept his hand in hers as they walked toward the enclosing woods.

And she was beginning to feel much warmer than she had been before. What woman would not, with such a bold and adventurous and vital brave walking beside her.

He also made her feel strong and secure . . . then again, she did have some power over him herself.

Chapter Twelve

Eve and McCloud were having lunch together, a delectable stew made with lots of wild vegetables and a thick gravy that Eve thought tasted strange but delicious. They were seated outside Quiet Doe's tipi, situated in a clearing in the surrounding woods where wildflowers grew all around.

It was a beautiful and peaceful summer day, a perfect setting for a lunch outdoors and some restful conversation—and the company was very good, Eve reminded herself.

Eve stopped chewing after Quiet Doe had gone back inside. She looked into her bowl and then up into McCloud's face. "There is no meat in here," she said, poking around with the utensil she'd been given to eat with. "No meat at all. Just berries and vegetables."

Eve resumed chewing the crunchy and delicious fare.

"Quiet Doe knows that I do not always eat meat. Only when it is the only food available."

Eve swallowed a well-chewed carrot. "Otherwise you eat only fruits and vegetables? And hardtack?"

He nodded to her questions. What would you call this kind of person? Eve asked herself.

"Does Whispering Bells eat only vegetables and berries?"

"Mostly, yes. She usually puts very little meat in her stew and prefers birds if she can get them."

"So young to be cooking and caring for herself," Eve said, chewing the wild turnip and swallowing the taste of added wild herbs, so delicious.

"Well, it is good . . . *woyute,*" Eve said, surprising herself after having said the Indian word. She shrugged and went back to eating.

"What did you say?" McCloud turned to ask her. That word was the Dakota word for food. How did she . . . Ah, Many Stars must have taught her some of the Dakota language.

"I asked about the children," Eve said, looking away for a moment.

"Most of the children of Wild Thunder have work they love to do. Arrow Maker is . . . well, you have seen for yourself."

Eve frowned. "How did Whispering Bells get her name?"

All of a sudden McCloud was up on his feet. "We will go now." He dipped his head into the tipi and spoke in Shoshoni. Whatever he'd said, Quiet Doe answered in a singsong voice.

"What did she say?" Eve asked, catching up to him and asking herself what was eating away at him; what had she said? She repeated when he did not answer, "What did Quiet Doe say to you?"

"She said to thank you for coming along with me. Next time she hopes that her husband will be out hunting in the woods with the children so that she can visit with you."

"What could we say?" Eve shrugged. "I really don't know that many Shoshoni words."

"You'll learn."

It sounds like he believes I'll be staying here for the rest of my life. I really do not think so.

Following lunch outside Quiet Doe's tipi, they walked until they reached the beautiful lake Eve had seen when they'd been up much higher, when the place had appeared to be like a clear blue jewel as they were coming into Wild Thunder.

At the height of the western slope, a vivid green hollow nestled in an alpine setting, a clear blue lake in its center. Around it, tall, slimly tapered firs stood like candles. The shooting stars, alpine daisy, alpine laurel, were growing there, bestowing beautiful color to the area. In the higher background loomed snow-crested peaks and in the lower mountains the starlike stonecrop grew in the rocky areas.

Eve's shoulders lifted and she sighed, looking around. "What are we doing here?"

"Talk."

Again she studied their surroundings after catching her breath at the setting's magnificence. She felt like an Indian now, and the feeling was not bad.

"Here?" Oh, sure, of course, Eve thought. What better spot for a scene of total ravishment.

He sat on a fallen log and pulled her down next to him.

"Sit down and listen. Now, don't look at me that way. I do not have it in mind to ravish you. I could do that just about anywhere in Wild Thunder."

She held up a stick. "Just try," she warned with a glitter in her eyes.

Grabbing the stick, he tossed it aside. "Listen.

Whispering Bells needs a mother and . . . and I would like you to fill that position."

"Does this mean you have to make me your wife?"

He nodded. "If you like. That would be the most natural way of it. For you to become Whispering Bells's mother, you should first become my woman."

Wait a minute here, Eve told herself. *His woman?*

"What do I have to do in order to . . . be your woman? And I thought you wanted a slave."

"You're correct. My wife. My slave. My woman. You will be all. Like a squaw."

Eve began chewing on a thumbnail, then stopped. "Am I your captive? You know, like in captive woman . . . captive bride?" She shuddered violently, hating that word *captive* with all her being.

"No. You've never been my captive. I take captives only when they've done something wrong and hurt one of the people of Wild Thunder and need punishing." His face grew as dark as fury unleashed. "Especially the children. No one touches the children of Wild Thunder. They are totally safe and sound in the circle of Wild Thunder's embrace."

Tilting her head, Eve looked up at him, thoughtful. "It seems to me you think of yourself as this Wild Thunder."

He looked up at the patch of sky surrounding the lake, making the water even bluer. "Yes. In a way. I came and conquered, chasing all the bad Spaniards out of this area. Even the bad French, who took more scalps than the Indians themselves did. I hate slavers. They seem to never leave. They are like poison."

"You named this town below us Wild Thunder, didn't you?" She slid a glance at him.

"I did."

Suddenly she lifted his wrist and gripped it manacle-hard. "You hate slavers? Then why would you like me for your slave?" She tossed down his arm in contempt for his simple philosophy.

For the second time that day he turned away from her questioning.

"Wait, McCloud. Come back here." She watched him walk back to the entrance to the wooded trail that led to Quiet Doe's and then the town of Wild Thunder itself. "We are not finished talking." She kicked the grass and stones with her tall moccasins. "Where is Maggie? I want her here with me, not gallivanting with your pretty-faced young warrior . . . what's his name? Tames something?"

"Tames Wild Horses," he yelled back. Now he stood with his hands on his lean hips. "He will come here with her soon. Perhaps they've married."

Eve screeched, "Married! To a full-blooded Indian?"

"He's not."

"Not what?" Her blood ran hot, then cold.

"Not full-blooded. He's—"

"Even so . . . you cannot do that without a preacher. That's—" Waving into the air, she paused with her hand in mid-stroke.

"Would you like to see how?" he called back to her from along the trail. "A bet?"

A bet?

Eve cast one last longing look at the blue pool, then ran after him. Such a beautiful day. Such a beautiful lake. *I shall return.*

Oh, yes, I shall. Someday in the near future.

She hung behind when she'd caught up, worrying a strand of fringe between her fingers. "No. No bet. No wedding, not for either of us. Not Maggie. Not . . . I."

Later that week Many Stars was helping Eve plan for her marriage to McCloud. She'd finally given in. Actually, she'd made up her mind at that beautiful blue lake.

As Eve worked on a white dress, she thought of her friend. How she wished Maggie could be there. And just when she thought she might never see her friend again—on the tail of the wish and the dreadful thought—Maggie came riding into Wild Thunder with Tames Wild Horses.

She was smiling too.

Chapter Thirteen

"Are you married to him?" was Eve's question as soon as Maggie came down off the pinto she'd been riding. Tames Wild Horses had already ridden off to find McCloud. Tames wore a big grin on his face as he looked down at Eve, his strong boyish features friendly and peaceful.

Eve asked again, "Are you, Maggie?" and merely glanced at the string of horses going by.

"No, Eve." She hugged her friend. "We are not married, but I am—" Maggie wasn't allowed to finish.

"Then why are you grinning like that?" Eve asked. "What did he do to you? He did not . . . did he?"

"Oh, Eve. He is the most wonderful man. At first we did not get along—then . . ."

Eve shook her head. All she wanted to know was if Maggie was in one piece—and all Maggie did was smile in a daze past Eve's shoulder.

"One thing led to another," Maggie said. "I even helped tame a few horses in that string you just saw."

"You could have gotten yourself killed, Maggie.

You've been with him for over a week. Are you sure you are all right? Sure you and he did not—"

"Would it be so bad?"

Eve blinked.

"Oh, Eve." Maggie hugged her again. "You should be this happy. Then you would not ask me all these questions. You would leave what is already well and good alone. I don't mean to preach, Eve. But you are asking me questions that can't be answered at this time."

"You look to be all right." In fact, better than all right, Eve thought, wishing she could look as good. "You really do look great, Maggie."

"I am." Maggie took Eve's hand after a little Indian boy ran up to care for Maggie's horse. She stopped to look Eve over. "You have changed. Even your speech is different."

Eve laughed lightly, saying, *"You* are telling *me* that?"

"Let us go and share some food."

She's beginning to sound like an Indian; Eve wanted to sigh in exasperation. But she only walked straight and tall. . . .

Like a squaw.

A part-time preacher-lawman arrived in Wild Thunder to perform the ceremony. Eve was ecstatic to hear her message had gotten out for a preacher to come, and then her spirits dropped. McCloud had sent the preacher-lawman away.

McCloud wished to get married Indian-style. Didn't what she want count for anything? She did love Whispering Bells very much and wanted the best for her. No other woman should be her mother.

The girl needed a mother to cook and clean for her so that she could go out to make mud pies and play with her dolls and have fun before she found herself a grown woman without a childhood.

Like herself.

A band of Shuckers arrived, the ragged cousins of the Shoshonis, a people without horses or rifles. They usually kept far away from whites, but when they came to Wild Thunder to visit or to trade, they spoke to their cousins and invariably shunned the half-breeds. On foot, the half-naked Shuckers were coming from Les Trois Tetons and planned to return to the desert lands when their visit was over.

"What will they think of their friend Suncloud marrying a white woman?" Eve asked Many Stars.

"Nothing," Many Stars said with a shrug. "One-Arm has said that Suncloud has had two wives already. The first one was a Spanish. Whispering Bells's mother. Her name was Chara."

"Lovely name," Eve said, puzzled over why she'd experienced instant jealousy. She had heard this, so why the stab of emotion coming stronger this time? And why would McCloud marry Spanish, didn't he despise them?

From north of the Snake River came the Flathead and Nez Perce with heavy loads on the backs of their horses. A few white trappers trickled in, angry-looking mountain men with constant scowls of discontent and vexation on their rugged faces.

"What are all these people coming in for?" Eve asked herself, nervous over the coming wedding. She didn't need more complications than she already had.

A deep utterance intruded on her voiced thoughts.

"Why does this bother you?"

Eve jumped as McCloud appeared in the doorway to the little cedar house. Her eyes fell to the beaded leather wristband he wore and then down farther, to his tall moccasins, and up again to his wide chest, long, wild hair, gorgeous face. . . . Her breathing quickened. Was he always going to make her body and nerves fly into agitation?

"Were you listening?" she asked, blushing. "You shouldn't, you know, listen to woman talk."

He laughed. "You sound like a squaw I used to know."

She flashed him a scorching look, but he only smiled wider and came into the room, filling it with his masculine presence.

Many Stars said, "I have to go."

"Oh, were you here?"

As if she'd not heard that question, Many Stars kept talking. "My friend Red Beads and I are having victuals together." She grinned. "Eve has taught me another English word. *It is good, yes?*"

"Yes," McCloud agreed. Then his brow darkened as he swung back to Many Stars. "Red Beads! Honna, what are you doing with her?"

Many Stars frowned back at her brother. "Suncloud—is Red Beads more lowly than I? And am I any better?"

She left her brother with these questions in order to contemplate their simple wisdom.

Choosing a fluffy mat in the corner to sit on cross-legged, McCloud mumbled to himself: "Why does everyone in Wild Thunder seem to be at my throat?"

"Ah, poor Suncloud." Eve went over to sit with him. She reached out to ruffle his dark hair, worn loose today in spirals falling down over his shoulders. "Indians have stick-straight hair. Why does yours run in wild rivulets when you let it loose?"

"Because," he said, snatching her to him and taking her in his passionate embrace, "I am a wild half-breed, if you remember."

She laughed lightly. "So I remember."

He kissed her mouth, and when they broke away, they were both breathing heavily. Eve was even hearing drums, drums of wild thunder. *Beating. Beating. Beating.* Wildly. In her blood. Lord, how they were pounding.

She swallowed and turned aside. She knew she was blushing all over.

Touching a strand of dark hair, he asked, "Will you make me a lunch of camas-cake bread, wild parsnips, berries, and—"

He started to rise from the mats.

She pushed him back down.

"Wait—what kind of berries?" she asked.

"Ripe serviceberries." His eyes gazed deeply into hers and his hands itched to climb her desirable body. All in good time, he thought.

"Where will we find them?"

He pulled her to her feet. "At the blue lake. We'll go there now to pick some and," he said, kissing her breathless again, "to be alone."

"I would like some smoked salmon," Eve said, licking her lips, remembering the delicious taste of when her brothers had brought some home to her and Maggie.

"You will have some. The Nez Perce are great salmon fishers. You'll be eating a fat fish by nightfall, one big one all to yourself."

"One for Maggie too. She loves smoked salmon."

"For Maggie." He nodded. "Tames Wild Horses might become jealous if a handsome Nez Perce fisherman brings her the gift of a delicious fat fish."

"Silly," Eve laughed. "Fish are not delicious raw. You must cook them. And why does not Tames Wild Horses catch her a fish?"

"He does not fish. He only tames wild horses."

They laughed together all the way to the blue lake, hand in hand, enjoying the gorgeous summer day, the blue sky above the firs and cottonwoods. They found much to joke about, many things that they both liked—and disliked. They stopped often to kiss and caress, not becoming overly familiar with their touches. Not yet, McCloud thought, and kept to himself. They laughed with gladness and pleasure, stopping to enjoy a scurrying creature on the ground or a perched bird on a limb above their heads.

A few times Eve heard McCloud whistle a chord or two from an old Quebecois tune and then take her hand and resume their walk to the blue lake.

Eve was afraid they were falling in love.

McCloud knew they were and that he had never felt this way before. He wondered if Eve, who'd never been married, did.

A misty veil of clouds drifted over Wind River Peak, but the sun still shone down into the clear waters of the small blue lake. As they walked hand in hand through the thick grass to a slightly elevated spot above the lake, McCloud pointed out the various mountain flowers.

"Primrose, paintbrush, columbine, balsam root, camas, and many others."

"How do you know them all by name?" She swept her arm wide, smiling when he reached up to snatch it to his lips, then press a gallant kiss there. "Hmm, that was exciting and nice."

"I have more for you, Eve Michaels. Much more entertaining recreation than simply kisses on the hands and lips. Shall I bite you?"

"Oh," Eve said, breaking away and stepping lightly through the grass. "Here is a lovely spot to sit." She looked up at him, her fingertips brushing his. "What did you bring to eat?"

Unfolding his tall frame, he sat cross-legged beside her. "Me," he said, showing her his empty leather pouch.

"What?"

"Taste me, Eve."

He pressed his lips to hers and slowly, gently, pushed her back into the grass. She felt the length of his body against hers and the strong arms folded on either side of her head, fingers cupping her cheeks. One finger pressed her chin downward, opening her mouth, his tongue going inside at once.

"Hmm, you do taste good," she murmured inside his mouth, licking, poking here and there.

"I need you," he whispered, "desperately."

He bent over her and shifted, nuzzling his hot mouth between the valley of her breasts, over the buckskin, wishing the dress would suddenly melt from her flesh.

She could feel his breath heating up, coursing through her body like a molten flame. It was sudden, vibrant, beautiful, primal. She clung to him, pressing upward to his iron-hard body, feeling his long, hard shape beneath the pliable buckskin.

His hoarse whisper broke the silence. "We'd better bring this to a halt now. Otherwise I won't have a virgin bride by the end of the week."

Eve looked aside from his passionately burning eyes and felt her face turn pinker than some of the wildflowers in the area. "How do you know?"

McCloud cleared his throat. *"Are you a virgin?"*

She smiled into his dark hazel-gray eyes. "Which would you prefer, Suncloud? One with her maidenhood intact or—"

He leaned back with his hands behind his head on the cushiony grass. "Tell me," he said.

A hot tear rolled down her cheek. "There was a young man in St. Louis. He was much older than I; now that I look back, I was really very young, just a girl in frilly pink dresses, white satin slippers. I'd never had a romantic thought until he came along. In fact, I'd already forgotten him after a few weeks, and to tell the truth, remembered him only now. I thought he was perfect: dark hair, blue eyes, sculpted mouth, tall, strong, and the most beautiful hands on a man ever, and—"

"That's enough," McCloud interrupted. "I don't wish to hear how pretty he was. Tell me what happened. And open your eyes," he said, seeing her lids fall, slumberous with passion.

Eve shook herself and looked wide-eyed at McCloud. Her heart started to pound even faster than when she'd been a schoolgirl in love with Nathan Adams. When she thought of Nathan now, compared to this man . . .

"I want to know what happened," McCloud pressed the issue in a surly, mountain-man voice. He folded his arms across his wide chest.

Eve's shoulders shrugged and then were still. "He was in love with another beautiful woman. She had red hair and was . . . voluptuous. She ran her own business."

McCloud's eyebrow rose dubiously. "What kind of business?"

"I have no idea, but the way she walked and talked made town gossips question her virtue. As for Nathan Adams, I threw myself at his feet and poured out my heart, begging him not to go. He walked off with my arms still wrapped around his legs."

"What happened then?" McCloud was close to laughter.

"He fell down the stone stairs outside our mansion and couldn't walk for two weeks. During that time, Miss Letitia found herself another beau, a much richer and more cunning one, and headed for California. Nathan suffered a broken heart. He came calling a few months after Letitia's departure and begged me to grow up a little and come to him. He'd marry me . . . as soon as I was ready."

McCloud's gaze fell to her chest. "What kind of growing did this puny Nathan want to be accomplished before setting a wedding date?"

Eve grinned after her eyes had followed his downward to her full-blown breasts. "Yes," she said. "Just that. He even reached out and touched me there, saying he could wait. I felt . . . all shivery and so very happy. After he left I spoke to Narcissa, my mother, and she discovered through the servants' grapevine that Nathan Adams had plans to join our lands once we were wed. And then we learned he had been found asleep, quite drunk, in a hotel room with . . ." she blushed. "Two women and another man."

"That quite did it for me," she continued. "As

you can understand. Never would I wait for such a man and become tainted by even walking down the street with him, everyone knowing what he did for enjoyment of a week's end."

"What happened to your mother when you were growing up? Where was she all this time?" McCloud asked, curling two fingers around her chin and stroking gently.

"I thought I told you already. I didn't? Well, after my father went to make more money for her, she ran off to California with her lover. That was hard for me to understand, when Narcissa couldn't stand the touch of man. She drummed this into my head, that nothing mattered but clothes and money and jewelry, to watch out when a man came my way with lust gleaming in his eyes."

McCloud chuckled wryly. "Did they come your way?"

"I didn't give them a chance. Usually I dressed like a boy—even wearing old buckskins"—Eve frowned over her own words for a moment—"and let my appearance go after Mother left for California. Then she returned—"

"This Narcissa?"

"Yes. She . . . died in a fire."

He could tell she did not wish to discuss her mother much longer.

"An old friend of my father's saw us off to the mountains, my brothers John and Derek and myself, because my father was long gone by then."

"Maggie and her brother too?" McCloud asked, kissing her hand again, making her feel better now. "Did they go along?"

"Yes, they joined us," she said sadly as she recalled their fate.

While she'd been talking, McCloud had gotten up and started picking the berries from the wild service trees. Eve trailed behind.

"They are also called the shadbush or the June-berry," he instructed her, picking the fruit from a tree resembling the mountain ash.

Resting her head on McCloud's arm for a moment, Eve sighed and looked up at him. Then she began picking the fruit along with him, to bring some back to town.

McCloud slung his filled pouch over his shoulder, asking, "What was that for?"

She stared up into his eyes fringed with thick black lashes. Something stirred within her breast; it was a savagely magical feeling, one that made her heart expand and her breathing quicken.

"You are a good man, McCloud. You are smart. You are handsome and I—"

Tossing the pouch aside, McCloud gathered her into his arms, kissing her mouth, chin, eyes, nose, and back to her mouth. Groaning, he said, "I wonder if we should wait—"

Breaking away, Eve gave her head a toss and said in a low, provocative voice over her shoulder, "I think we should."

Remember, she's a virgin. She hadn't had to say it in those exact words, he already knew that she was pure and spotless.

McCloud spun around, bent to gather the service-berries, and then ran in place for a few moments, grinning hugely, finally falling in with an Indian lope to catch up with her trail-blazing stride.

* * *

At midnight Eve began tossing and turning in the hide and fur bed situated across the room from where Whispering Bells slept. . . .

Eve's brother Derek had promised to bring back some yellow cloth and blue beads and sewing needles from the trading post. It was Sunday and they should have been back yesterday afternoon. She and Maggie searched and searched, but could not find them.

Eve lamented softly and flung a leg over her fur pallet, her foot trailing with it until her toes reached the puncheon floor. Whispering Bells heard the thump but rolled over and went back to sleep.

She and Maggie still could not find Derek, John, or Hank—what had happened to them? They were not at the trading post or in any other building nearby. They must have gotten lost. Big men don't get lost. There, up ahead, bodies, lying in pools of blood, sticky blood . . . their throats slashed from ear to ear . . . the empty beaver pack beside Derek's body.

"No pretty yellow cloth or blue beads," Eve kept saying in her sleep over and over. "Maggie—where are the bright dresses? No pretty yellow cloth . . . no blue beads. Whoever took them . . . must have murdered . . . brothers."

Oblivious of Eve's night thrashings and murmurings, Whispering Bells slept on, having spent a hard day cooking and cleaning and skinning hides. She was exhausted and slumbered like the dead.

Kicking Wolf slipped by near the wide cracks in the door, halted, hunkered down, and heard the words of the Dark Hair. He then slipped away into the moonless and starless night, leaving as stealthfully and silently as he'd come.

Chapter Fourteen

McCloud was in the back of his store, seeing a man who'd come from the American Fur Post at Fort Union. Half-breed Pawnee Joe was a friend he'd met a few years back. Joe had some new weapons for McCloud—new issue Mackinaw guns. Actually, the new issue was somewhat old by the time they came into McCloud's hands.

"Got some news for you, McCloud. You wanta hear it?" Pawnee Joe asked his friend. "I think you might like ta."

"Go ahead," McCloud said, sliding his butt onto a fine piece of ornately carved rosewood furniture that had made its way out west and been cast aside along the trail. "I'd like to hear what is no doubt going to mess up my plans for my wedding."

"You getting married again?" Joe grinned, showing a few blackened teeth, stick-straight graying-black hair hanging along his high cheekbones. Joe wore no feathers or symbols that might make him look more Indian than white.

"Who is the lucky woman this time, this second, no, third bride?" He chuckled and coughed. He reached for a cheroot from his pocket, but

McCloud shook his head. "That's right, you don't want anyone smoking 'round here in this back room. We can smoke some kinnikinnic outside later, huh, or over in Red Beads's Cheer Lodge? Smoke pipe?"

"Not today, Joe. I've got too many things going on."

"Wedding plans, huh?" Joe waited until after McCloud had nodded and said yes before he went on. "Some of your friends was on their way to do some trading with ya."

"Bannocks and Utes?"

"Yeah. They're afoot mostly now. Greasy Long Hairs and Crow took their horses and left women and children for dead."

"That band of renegades again?"

"Yeah. And your Arapaho friends, they're all banding up together to get into big trouble. They done some killing right back on those Crows."

"No . . ." McCloud pressed his mouth together in a taut line. He hardly ever swore, but a word slipped from between his lips. "Damn them. Just when I thought we'd be able to get along better and we might have some peace around here. They know I don't want any killing of folks coming to trade at my post."

Joe leaned closer to whisper, "If you ask me, I think Kicking Wolf is part of your trouble. Yeah, yeah. I know," Joe said, holding up his hand, "you trust Kicking Wolf. You better watch him. His brother was the one who killed my cousin and left him for dead beside the Little Sandy. One of my pals saw Kicking Wolf meeting up with a scar-faced man. Could just be the one you're hunting. And I

never fergits a face. Do you know of Scar-Face's
cousin Huivi?"

"Huivi?" asked McCloud, scratching the bridge
of his lean nose.

"Yeah. Means scarf in some language or 'nother.
Wagh! Scar-Face and Scarf. What a mix, huh? You
wanta get 'em? I'd like ta. That Spanish dresses gals
up in yella dresses and takes 'em to the Sioux camp.
Trying to get his hands on some gold. He's real
mean to them there Indian maidens he captures.
Still think Kicking Wolf is in with him on the nasty
schemes. You wanta get 'em?"

"Do I look like I'm out hunting?" McCloud
snapped at Pawnee Joe.

"Hey," Joe said, backing off. "I know you don't
wanta believe anything bad about Kicking Wolf
'cause he's done you some favors. I gotta go." Joe
picked up the pile of things he'd come trading for.
"Just watch your backside, friend. Keep an eye out
for those Long Greasy Hairs and Crows, and especially Scar-Face. I wouldn't worry too much about
the Arapaho."

Pawnee Joe returned in less than an hour, all
excited, shouting for McCloud to come and see the
Arapaho for himself, what he'd been talking about.

"They's being defiant," Joe said, tossing aside the
butt of a cheroot. "Look!" He pointed after they'd
walked a distance into the valley.

As Joe and McCloud watched, wondering what
they were up to, the Arapaho on the ridge formed
a double line of riders. They thought it might por-
tend the danger of an all-out charge; certainly the

hill slope was gradual and low enough for the Indians to reach them without much difficulty.

"We're dead if they decide to take us," Joe said, feeling stupid for having dragged his friend McCloud into danger.

Twelve bodies were roped across saddles. There was no determining how many had really been wounded or killed in the skirmish they'd had with the Greasy Long Hairs.

The Arapaho line came forward to the ridge at a walk, halting out of rifle range in case someone would care to shoot up at them. A big Indian holding a feathered lance advanced before the line. Shaking the lance at Joe and McCloud, he yelled something in a tone of defiance, then turned north along the ridge, the rest following in an irregular column at a trot.

McCloud stepped aside and looked down at the rocks that had broken loose and rolled down to their feet. Joe looked up at McCloud, noting the frown on the lean face and the glint of steel in his eyes.

"What did they say?" Joe asked, kicking aside a rock.

" 'Keep out of it,' " McCloud answered, telling him what the Wild Ones had said.

"They want you to mind your own business." Joe began to smile like a sly fox. "Will you?"

"No."

Joe ran a little to keep up with McCloud's long Indian strides. "What you gonna do, Suncloud?"

McCloud's mouth quirked at Joe calling him Suncloud, since he hardly ever did.

McCloud said, "I'm gonna take it easy. See some

friends. I don't like it when innocent people on their way to Wild Thunder to trade get cut down."

"It ain't right," Joe agreed, squinting upward.

"Nope."

"When are you gonna wanta to do something about it? I wanta go with ya."

McCloud looked into the deep blue eyes of the tall, slim breed. "First I am going to marry a woman by the name of Eve Michaels. After I make her my bride, I'll go meet some whites, and then some full-bloods."

"Full-bloods? Like Sioux Indians?"

Pawnee Joe was the nosiest man alive, but McCloud had always put up with him because he liked him. The big man meant no harm. The only problem with Joe was he'd always wanted to be white, all white. Sometimes Joe was dense too; he forgot things easily. That's why McCloud never trusted the man with important information.

That afternoon, when Joe met Eve Michaels, he fell instantly in love. Anything she wanted of him she had only to ask for.

"Should I fetch ya some water?" Joe asked, a twinkle in his eye. Or was that a wink?

Eve was laughing.

"Why . . . Joe Palomino, don't you remember me?"

He gulped, looked first to the left, then to the right, and blinked, craning his neck to get a closer look at her. He pointed to his chest. "I know . . . you from somewhere?"

"Ah, Joe Palomino, huh?" McCloud was chuck-

ling as they sat on the floor around Whispering
Bells's stew pot.

"You sure do get around, Joe," Eve said, seeing
Maggie as she stepped inside and smiled, looking
from one to the other, wondering what was going
on. "Joe," Eve kept on, "does the name Blake Michaels ring a bell?"

Joe scratched the top of his head where the hair
was a little thinner and stood up, making his face
appear longer than it really was. He blinked, his
hand falling to his lap with a loud smack.

"Yoweee! Are you Blackie's daughter? The
skinny one in pigtails that was always bugging me
with questions and wanting some of my Pawnee
cake down on the keelboat?"

"That's me. I still love to eat johnnycake." Eve
smiled and touched his hand, remembering this
kindly man. "What name do you go by now?" She
saw the man blush; he'd always blushed under his
copper skin, making his complexion even darker.
"Are you still Joe Palomino?" She looked at
McCloud, with his hand over his mouth to keep
from laughing out loud.

That hand came away from McCloud's mouth at
last. "Pawnee Joe," he said to Eve. "You must be
mistaken. This isn't Joe Palomino."

Whispering Bells and Maggie were talking softly
in the corner, where a crude table was set up for
preparing food. They were fixing some camas-cake
bread to go with the savory stew, this time with tiny
pieces of succulent game hen mixed with the wild
herbs and vegetables.

Maggie brought some food to be distributed
among them, and then she turned to Joe and gasped
dramatically, dropping a piece of bread.

"Oh, Lord, it can't be—Joe Dexter." She threw her arms around his neck, but was instantly sorry, for she recoiled at the odors from a man who hadn't washed in many moons. "Uncle Joe Dexter."

After she'd caught the piece of camas-cake bread in her hand, Eve looked up at Maggie. "I didn't know you had an uncle named Joe."

With a giggle and a hidden wink to Whispering Bells, Maggie said to Eve, "You never asked."

"Waal, I ain't no Joe Dexter, that's for sure," Joe said, scratching his head again. "I know that for sure," he said again, and chuckled. "I never fergits a face and I know my own." Then he saw Maggie's and Whispering Bells's smiling exchange. "Awww, you girls was funning me. You just wanta have a few laughs at my expense."

"You sure don't sound like an Indian, Joe Palomino," Maggie said, serving him a dish of stew. He smiled at her and licked his lips at the sight of such a beautiful stew.

"Pawnee Joe," McCloud said, but fell short of convincing anyone.

"Waal, I really don't have all that much Injun blood. Just got what they call Injun skin."

"Sure, sure," mocked McCloud.

"You are a nice man," Eve said, "that's all I know. My father respected you and wasn't afraid to leave me alone with you down on the keelboat."

As soon as Tames Wild Horses walked in, looking around the room for Maggie, everyone grew silent, watching the pair move back to the door and go out together into the star-filled night.

"That couple looks to me to be in love," Joe said. He gulped some stew, then looked over at McCloud and Eve staring into each other's eyes and holding hands. "Waal, when're you two lovebirds getting married?"

"Tomorrow."

"What?"

Eve had jumped up, spilling some of her stew onto her dress. McCloud at once began mopping her lap and her bodice, still smiling into her face and into her eyes. Joe just kept on eating, paying no attention to them. Whispering Bells heard a sound at the door and wondered who was coming.

Just then One-Arm walked in, yanked his great-granddaughter's braids, and sat down for some stew. In Shoshoni he announced, "My great-granddaughter makes the best stew in the land."

Joe kept right on devouring the food as McCloud and Eve went out into the night, not taking Maggie's and Tames Wild Horses's path, but creating their own lovers' promenade beneath the dark mountain sky. They kissed, held hands, walked, and talked a little more small talk, then they went to their separate sleeping places, Eve's in Whispering Bells's cedar house, McCloud's in the small lodge Eve had never stepped inside.

Eve was up before the sun, thinking this was to be her wedding day, when she received the message that the ceremony had been called off. Suncloud had ridden out of Wild Thunder in the night with several warriors and Pawnee Joe.

"When will he return?" Eve asked Whispering Bells to ask Frog Catcher, who had brought the message. She smiled when she saw the young man shrug, smile back at Eve and Whispering Bells, and then walk away. "Well," Eve said, "that's that. He

had no more idea when Suncloud would return than
we do. I wonder when the next date will be set."

Whispering Bells made a funny sound. "You can
sometimes wonder and wonder and wonder with a
man like Suncloud. Father is like that. He makes a
woman crazy. He makes plans one day and the next
he is riding off with a war party and doesn't return
for many days, sometimes weeks even. He often
goes to meet with the Teton Dakota; they're supposed to be our enemies, but we have Dakota blood
from Great-Grandfather, so I guess that's why we
don't get bothered so much. Lots of breeds here."

Whispering Bells went to sit with Eve on the pile
of fur robes, and Eve put her arm around the girl
and gave her a hug.

"You are too young too worry about such
things."

"Ah! Ah!" Whispering Bells exclaimed. "You
said that in perfect Shoshoni. How did you know
how to?" she asked in the same language.

"I have been listening and learning. Many Stars
is a good teacher; I asked her several weeks ago how
to speak Shoshoni."

"You sound real good. Your Indian voice is
. . . *pretty?*" she asked. She said *pretty* in English.
"Is that what you would say of a voice?"

"Well, you could say *delightful.*" She hugged
Whispering Bells to her shoulder, stroking the girl's
long hair. "Or *enchanting.* Or *fascinating.* But that
last word is a little more tricky. Maybe you meant
my voice was *vibrant* and *strong.* Those two words
actually mean the same thing."

Whispering Bells looked up at Eve. "I know
strong. My father is strong, and so is Tames Wild
Horses. He *really* looks strong."

Whispering Bells rested her head on Eve's shoulder for several more moments, softly calling her Mother, then pulled her up with her to stand.

"Come, Dark Hair—that's what Father calls you—we will . . . what did you call it before: break the . . . ?"

"Break the fast. Honeychile," she said from her days in St. Louis. "Diz is de best time to *eat* good food. In de mawnin'."

Suncloud did not return that afternoon, nor the next day, nor the next. Eve was beginning to worry, wondering what could be keeping him.

"Oh, perhaps something has happened to him." Eve said this out loud to herself as she hung some washed clothes on ropes she'd strung from building to tree.

"To whom has something happened—*perhaps?*"

The deep voice thrilled her, and she turned to find McCloud—no, Suncloud—standing there, his chest bare, wearing high-topped moccasins, leggings, and he was carrying a skin shirt. He wore a turquoise-blue headband and his hair was loose and spiraling down his back.

Eve lowered her eyes to his chest. "Oh—you're bleeding. Are you hurt bad?" She dropped the piece of laundry onto the ground.

With a chuckle McCloud said, "You could have used that nice white piece of material to clean my wounds."

"You haven't had them cleaned out yet?" She gasped when his answer was in the negative. Then she saw his grin. "You did take a dip in a creek, I hope?"

"A little dip. I do need some help though." His grin was wider, showing her his beautiful white teeth after he'd straightened from picking up the wet white material.

"Oh, great chief, I am your humble slave." Eve bowed before his magnificent body and let out a little squeak when she was snatched to his chest. "Oh, wait. You will get blood all over my nice dress."

"A little red will give it color right there." McCloud put his hand on her bodice, pressed, then pushed her chin upward with two fingers so that he could kiss her deeply and thoroughly. "You will always remember where that dark smudge came from."

That is, if I take this deerskin dress with me when I return to St. Louis.

Eve walked with McCloud back to the cedar house, sat him down, and began to tend his wound. As she walked about, his eyes followed her, but her eyes asked silent questions.

Finally he spoke.

"The dog soldiers and I met up with some Utes I've been looking for. Had a long talk with them, smoked some kinnikinnic, and then went hunting for the Greasy Long Hairs. They're a nasty band of renegade Injuns—as Pawnee Joe would call them—"

"Joe Palomino?" Eve said, holding still when he jumped after the wound stung. He nodded and she smiled. "Did Joe go with you and the dog soldiers?"

"Yeah. Aaah!" he exclaimed as she removed dried blood, grinning at her concern and loving it. "The Greasy Long Hairs have got something to do with Scar-Face, Joe's thinking."

"What do you think?"

"I will know when I meet up with Scar-Face." He smiled at the top of her head. "Then I'll simply ask him."

"Oh, yes, of course." She put on a deep voice. "Uh, Scar-Face, do you have something to do with the Greasy Long Hairs?"

"Hush, woman." McCloud laughed.

Eve was enjoying this domestic role of nursing wife. She felt quite natural doing her task, and was at peace with him, herself, and the world.

"There, that is done," Eve said, holding up his shirt. "Now you can put it on."

"I think I will leave it off," he told her with a wink as she followed him out the door. "I like the way your eyes travel across my chest and look hot and pretty."

"You have a nice chest, Suncloud. Big and strong, lots of muscle. I will call you Suncloud when you are warring with your neighbors."

"Hey," he said, catching up with her after she'd ventured ahead of him to her makeshift clothesline. "You spoke perfect Dakota." He pulled her against him before she could lift and shake a piece of clothing from a huge wooden bowl. "You sound very nice, Dark Hair, your voice really excites me when you speak the language of the People. Say some more."

"No." She pushed at his arms. "You say we are getting married and then you leave me without a word." Pouting, she turned her back on him. "I don't know if I care to speak with you."

Taking her shoulder gently, he turned her to face him again. "I told Frog Catcher to tell you. Did he?"

"Yes. He told Whispering Bells and I listened." Eve grinned, flapping a piece of wet laundry in his face as she prepared to hang it. "I knew most of what he was saying. He thought I did not know. It was quite funny."

There was a golden glow shimmering around Eve, coming down from the sunny heavens above, and McCloud shivered in desire as he stood watching her. He wanted her very much. She was so young-looking today, seeming more innocent than her twenty years, and in her hair were two feathers, tips downturned.

He touched her hair and she turned, smiling up at him with a radiance that outshone the sun.

"Let's walk, Eve Michaels." Hearing her name, she realized she would be Eve Michaels McCloud as soon as the possibility of attack from the Greasy Long Hairs was a threat no longer.

"Where are we going?" Eve hung the last piece of laundry and then joined him at the path where he stood waiting.

"Come. You will see."

As he took her hand, Eve looked at his long fingers curling over hers. Crazy things were happening deep down inside her. She wanted to shout over the golden feelings flowing within her, the warm rivers of excitement flooding her being. She wanted to tell the world of his eyes, their provocative colors and tempting depths.

"Why are you looking at me that way?" he asked as they walked together down a small green hill.

Pulling her regard from his magnificent male physique, she exclaimed, "Oh, look, is that not Red Beads? What is she doing standing before that lodge?"

"That is Red Beads, yes, and she's standing at the entrance to the Cheer Lodge," he said bluntly.

"I see."

Unruffled, Eve looked around at all the wickiups, tipis, and lodges. There were many horses standing beyond in the field. The south-sloping hillside would provide cured bunch grass for horses all winter, she could see. Spirit voices seemed to float from out of the crevices and crannies of the rocks hauntingly. Across the creek, sheltered by hills and trees, stood a stout skin-lodge apart from other dwellings—Cheer Lodge.

"Are we going there?" Eve asked, waving at Red Beads. The other woman only glared back, Eve could see, as they approached the creek at a spot where they could walk on two stepping-stones and be on the other side. "Well, are we?"

"We will just walk by," he said, wondering at her strange mood.

"You should call this place Hidden Valley," she told him.

"I did not name this place. Red Beads and her friends named it. The name is—Thunder Creek."

"So this is *the* place," she said, looking up at him with a smile.

McCloud had to catch up then, for she'd walked away from him, going faster than the leisurely stride they'd been maintaining.

Eve paused to look up and down the creek, and the view was magnificent. On the other side she skirted the scrubby brush and walked over dead sticks.

As she neared the big, red-painted lodge, she saw that now there were three other women standing there with Red Beads. They were drinking something from big-handled cups.

"Who is their leader, their chief?" Eve asked as McCloud once again walked alongside her.

"I lead them all, but I prefer not to be called chief. My father was not a chief, so why should anyone call me by that title?"

He sounds defensive, Eve thought. "I don't know. I suppose they should just keep calling you Suncloud, as always.

"They look at me as if I were a stranger they knew was coming, not a white whom they would like to beat upon with sticks."

With a low grunt McCloud said, "None of my . . . *these* people take up sticks or stones. If they do, for any reason, it will be a first."

"That is nice of them . . . to be so . . . welcoming."

His face was pulled back to her. "What is wrong? You say that rather haltingly."

"Look, over there at the Cheer Lodge. Those women. They do not look at me with welcome in their eyes. No. Their eyes shoot knives and tell me that I am intruding and am not welcome."

"To them you are probably not all that welcome. The women of the Cheer Lodge see you as a threat."

McCloud glanced Red Beads's way. If looks could kill, Eve Michaels would already be lying dead on the other side of the creek.

"Why?" Eve asked, looking up at McCloud's handsome face.

"Because," he said, taking a strand of her shining hair, "the Dark Hair is very slender and beautiful. Healthy and young. Her skin is like dark peaches and cream. Her eyes have strange, lovely lights moving in them, like an autumn dawn moving swiftly ahead of a summer night. Her arms are slim but strong. Her breasts are full and high—not hanging down to there." He heard her warm chuckle as he indicated his waist.

"They are not that bad." Eve looked over to the lodge at the women. "Are they?"

"You should walk closer to see for yourself."

She stepped ahead of him. "Wait," he said, taking her arm and making her face him.

"What is it, Suncloud?" She looked up into the shining eyes.

"Before you came," he said, touching her hair, "the others were to me desirable. My women, the two wives I had, were desirable—"

"You had two wives at the same time?" She blinked up at him.

"Shh." He put his fingers across her lips. "Chara and Morning Moon were most desirable, and, yes, I had them both in one night many—"

"But that's—"

"Shh." Again his touch. "They all pale beside you, Dark Hair. Now I know they were *releases.*"

"Re—"

"Shh. Yes. There was affection, true. I needed them. I needed Red Beads. I wanted the others in the Cheer Lodge. As much as I could get, do you understand?"

"Yes." Eve's voice was very soft. She lowered her face, then he pulled her chin up for her eyes to meet his. "I understand."

He let her go and shrugged, kept walking. "You are different."

Eve blinked as he went ahead of her. *Wait a minute,* she wanted to yell. *You were about to say something very important.* Was she ready for it? she wondered as she caught up. She told herself she'd have to think about that when she was not with him. She felt too many tangled emotions when he came close.

First she wanted to go back home. Then she wanted to stay. She felt so torn.

How in the world am I ever going to leave this beautiful man? He's becoming very important to me. Like air. A woman had to breathe it. Maybe it was the same way when a woman needed a man.

Did he need her just as much?

Smiles were for Suncloud but not the Dark Hair. Red Beads's eyes were dark and malicious as they swept over the Dark Hair. Already she had a bone to pick with that one. She did not like it that she'd been kicked out of Whispering Bells's house—and by that old man One-Arm. All because of this white woman, this Dark Hair.

"She is not a paleface," Red Beads told one of the others who had dyed-purple feathers in her hair.

"I see," was all Purple Feathers offered.

Tall One was watching Eve Michaels with envy, trying not to show it, but it was in her heart if not in her eyes. Sometimes that wormlike hostility could be keenly felt by one who was intelligent and sensitive, but Tall One did not know this.

"She has nice breasts," Eve said of the woman who was very strong-looking and handsome. "She also has lots of muscle. What does she do?"

McCloud seemed to be blushing. "Her name is Tall One. You know what she does," he said to Eve. "She is the only one besides Red Beads who has a fairly passable body."

Why are we talking about breasts and tall women? Eve let the subject drop, thinking that men sometimes found the oddest subjects to talk about. Not that the Cheer Lodge women were all that odd.

"And why are we here?" she asked him.

"I thought you wanted to know everything. If you are going to live here—in Wild Thunder—you should know about all of us," he said to her.

All of us. Eve thought about that. *I don't want to be part of these people. St. Louis is my home, and the only wilderness where I know my own people is*—Eve shrugged. Maggie was here, true, but she was becoming an Indian just like all the rest who come and never leave.

Eve felt growing excitement when she reminisced about her home in St. Louis. To go back there, to be part of civilization again. To walk the streets and nod at people while carrying a pretty parasol overhead. To be in a warm house—a big white wood frame house with furniture, pretty pillows and lace, and silver candlesticks. To eat delicious hot food and cakes, and then stroll outside in a fragrant garden under the moon.

There was only one thing missing in this delightful setting: She couldn't picture McCloud there. He was too wild and ruggedly handsome. What would he look like dressed for the evening? Eve licked her lips. What an exhilarating thought. McCloud in dark trousers and white linen, a long-sleeved shirt . . . maybe with one row of cuff lace?

Eve shook her head. No. Plain white sleeves would be better. What was she thinking? She'd never see McCloud in such fine attire, nor would she see him in St. Louis. She was only dreaming.

Coming back to the present, Eve asked McCloud, "Does it get very cold here in the winter?"

Her attention was drawn back over her shoulder to the staring women.

"Very." McCloud told the truth. His eyes shone down into hers. "We crawl beneath many big thick fur robes and blankets."

Eve looked back at the women again. Now she could picture McCloud! He was in bed with several of those Cheer Lodge women, all wrapped together, limbs tangled, bodies naked and . . .

"What do you mean *we?*" Eve asked McCloud, stumbling over a stone as she dragged her gaze back to the path.

"I thought I'd get your attention with that one. All of us. Each of us. Alone or with someone."

I will be with someone again this winter, McCloud thought happily. He'd been facing a winter alone, without one special woman. It was nice to have a woman to warm your backside all winter long. He'd thought he'd never have another white woman . . . not after Whispering Bells's mother. Actually, when a man sat down and thought about it, what was so exciting about taking a woman to bed? You crawl between the robes with them, make love, grunt, and then it's all over. You had your release. You have a child or you do not. Either way, you have more sex. Same. Same. A man always needed that release. You loved a woman during the day because of the help she could give you. She cooked. She cleaned. Waved to you when you returned from hunting or fighting or trapping. And you loved her at night for the release from tensions and worry she could give you. Always the same.

As he walked with her, McCloud glanced down at Eve and then away to the sky. For some reason, one he couldn't fathom, he had a feeling that Eve

Michaels would change all that. She had a certain power over him. She already made him feel emotions that were fiercely dangerous for a man.

Nothing was ever going to be the same again.

Chapter Fifteen

Every time McCloud was about to make Eve his bride, something came up.

Suncloud had to ride out on his horse, Wind, both wearing paint, taking a band of nude-chested warriors with him. And each time he had to send Eve back from her room in the trading post to stay with Whispering Bells.

Eve and Maggie were having a talk. "Do you ever dream about our brothers?"

"Oh!"

At that moment a horned owl had swooped by, low to the ground, a silver-gray blur of shining feathers; it was visible for no more than an instant and then was gone.

Maggie smiled at Eve and answered, "Yes. Sometimes they are in nightmares that I have."

"Do you dream about the yellow cloth and blue beads?"

Maggie looked troubled for a moment before she answered. "Yes. I've never seen that combination before you mentioned it to our brothers and asked Derek to bring them back for us. It would have made a pretty outfit just as you'd said. In my dream a lovely Indian girl was wearing the yellow dress and blue beads."

Eve's eyes flashed. "Do not mention those things we dream about to anyone else, like Tames Wild Horses. Please, Maggie. Promise you will not."

"I promise. But I don't see why—"

"Promise." Eve looked stern as she stood in front of sagebrush and gray rocks.

"Yes." Maggie picked a tall wildflower and twirled it in her fingers. "Eve, have you and Suncloud made love yet?"

With a soft smile Eve said, "I call him McCloud."

"Eve. You are not saying. Did you?"

"Of course not. I wouldn't let him if he tried. We have had 'moonlit moments.' " She turned to Maggie, and stopped walking. "What is it like for you and Tames Wild Horses?" She laughed. "Doesn't he have a shorter name?"

"I call him Tames. Almost sounds like that river in England? Yes. He doesn't know about exciting places in the world. I have taught him some. Tames is so eager to learn. He would like to read and write English. I never thought I would be . . ."

"Would be?" Eve coaxed Maggie to finish. She waited. "Have you made love, or would you rather not say?"

"We are both eager to know and learn about the 'sleeping robes' thing, aren't we?" Maggie smiled at the ground littered with moist wildflowers as Eve laughed aloud. "I was going to say—I would be falling in love."

"That is as far as it has gotten with me also, or, I mean, us." She shook her head. "Oh, wait a minute. How can I speak for him? He—I don't know what he is feeling."

"Do not worry," said Maggie. "Tames has told me that Suncloud has said he thinks he is falling for the Dark Hair."

"Who?" Eve laughed then. "Oh—me!"

"Listen, Eve. I have found new wisdom: What lies behind us and what lies before us are tiny matters compared to what lies within us."

With a sly smile, Eve asked, "Who was it that told you that?"

Maggie laughed, saying, "One-Arm. He's full of gentle wisdom. I love to sit and listen to him."

"Are you learning Shoshoni?"

"A little. One-Arm speaks the language of the Cheyenne River Sioux. The Teton Dakota speak much the same language with very little variation. I love to learn about the different Indian tribes. It's so much fun, and Tames is teaching me Shoshoni. I think Shoshoni is harder than the Dakota language."

"I think Whispering Bells has learned much of her gentle simple wisdom from her great-grandfather." Eve thought for a moment. "Listen to this one Whispering Bells has told me: A good place to find a helping hand is at the end of your arm."

Maggie laughed, saying, "How true."

Eve smiled at a Ute child, brown as a berry, and the child, a girl, smiled back, her dark eyes dancing with joy as a wrinkled old woman bounced her on her knee in front of an old ragged wickiup.

Maggie dragged her eyes from the happy child, said, "How about this pearl: In trying to get her own way, a woman should remember that kisses are sweeter than *whine*."

"Hmmm. I like it; I think I shall remember that

one when I want something from McCloud. What
do you think, Maggie?"

Maggie lifted one shoulder provocatively. "I
think you are much much too bold, madam. However"—her eyes twinkled merrily—"I believe you
just might get your way."

Suddenly Eve was serious. "Maggie?"

"Yes?"

"What are we doing here?"

Maggie looked away. "I do not wish to think
about it, Eve. As for tomorrow, I do not worry
about whether or not the sun will rise; I am going to
be prepared to enjoy it."

"Very good, Maggie." They kept walking to
Windmaker's lodge, where games were being played
that night. "Is that pearl one of your own?"

"Yup."

Tames Wild Horses and McCloud were having a
similar conversation at the other side of the encampment as they returned from the hills, McCloud
with a young buck slung across his back.

"When will you take her for wife?" Tames was
asking McCloud as he led Medicine Hat, a black-
speckled mustang, considered good luck by the Indians.

"Soon."

"How soon, man of few words?" Tames asked
with a smile.

"That soon."

"Whew. You must really have something important on your mind if I can't reach you. What is this
dense fog you walk in, friend?"

"Thinking."

"Deeply."

All at once McCloud stopped, unloaded his burden of deer onto the ground, groaned, and straightened.

"You are going to tell me what you have been thinking?" Tames asked McCloud, who was stooped over the deer. "It is something that troubles your mind, I can tell."

"Well," McCloud laughed a little, "not so much my mind. I've been thinking—"

"We already know that," Tames said with a grin. "What?"

McCloud blurted out across his shoulder, "I was going to visit the Cheer Lodge."

"Why? Did you leave something there?"

With a sly grin McCloud said, "I'd like to."

"Uh. Now I know." White teeth flashed in the encroaching dark. "I think about it all the time."

They hunkered down together beneath the darkening sky, orange glow swiftly fading to heliotrope black, the purple-misted mountain peak looming over them.

"You do?" McCloud asked.

"Naturally." Tames punched McCloud, laughing. "We are passionate men. I think about Shining Eyes. No other. She is my love; I have waited for her a very long time, and she has finally come."

"This is Maggie you speak of?"

"Her. Yes. I had a vision dream of her, knew she would come to me. I love her with all my heart."

"Does she know this?" McCloud asked, thinking of himself and Eve Michaels.

"I am afraid to tell her all that's in my heart. She ran away when I first saw her and called to her. I was devastated when she did not run to me with her arms thrown wide in welcome. Now I have tamed her, gentled her, and she is not afraid as she was at first."

McCloud snickered. "Now you are afraid of her. Afraid to take her, thinking she will not like it or you when you are finished?"

With a tender smile Tames looked away. When he turned back to find his cousin still staring, he asked, "To the Cheer Lodge we go?"

McCloud looked up at the new moon, a silver slice going up the black-green mountainside. Softly he said, "I wouldn't enjoy it. There is nothing there that interests me any longer. I saw Red Beads and the others and felt nothing, *nothing.*"

"I was just testing," said Tames, a smile touching the corners of his full mouth.

"Were you? You speak the truth?"

"You better believe this, cousin. There is no woman on the earth like Shining Eyes. I have not been with her on the sleeping robes. Yet this I know. She will be perfect, and one day she will run to me with arms wide."

With a stern look McCloud asked, "How do you know she will have you?"

"I know." He looked at Suncloud. "Do you know this of Eve Michaels?"

"Enough of this woman talk. We will go to Windmaker's lodge. There are games being played there this night."

"Who will gut that deer?"

McCloud laughed, and straightened. "Look. It's already done."

* * *

Carrying fresh meat to be roasted at Windmaker's lodge, McCloud brought up the subject of his upcoming marriage and why it was not accomplished yet.

"Many tribes band together so that they can get food and furs and form alliances that often last for years," McCloud said. "True?"

"True." Tames Wild Horses agreed and went on. "These tribes who live along the rivers and streams become powerful because they control these routes." He frowned at McCloud. "Uh. Who has become too powerful? Who is forming a large band to battle the Missouri Fur Company and others, the small towns like our Wild Thunder?"

"The Greasy Long Hairs." McCloud nodded.

"This is stupid! With the animal migrations and the extensive fur gathering, the Indian is forced to compromise. Do they not see this?"

"There is something worse," McCloud answered. "I have been trying to help the straying families to return to their people in Thunder Creek, those Arapaho who have been coming closer and making plans to come back and reunite. They have relatives here. Why do they turn like savages and fight the Greasy Long Hairs and Crow?

"You saw the band of Arapaho on the hill? They have been forced to turn to fighting us again? What have we done to them? Nothing," Tames answered his own question. "They should return. We have relatives among them. Babies who will grow up like the Greasy Long Hairs, who wear stupid clothes and learn to kill. The single trapper is to be feared, his idea is to work alone and exterminate the Indian. The Basin Ute and Arapaho will find much trouble amid those whites. They are being called the

Bad Faces and the Wild Ones. They will be killed off before they can ever return to our village."

"We need to band together, seek the Teton Sioux for more strength, more power. We will talk on this more later," McCloud said to Tames. "We are almost at Windmaker's lodge."

"What will you say to Eve Michaels now? You have said she is to be your wife. Why do you tarry? Why not take her to wife before anything else happens?"

"How about you?"

"I am not ready to force marriage on Shining Eyes. Maggie will not like it."

"How do you think the Dark Hair liked it?"

Tames laughed. "Not much."

Everyone sat around a blaze on stools of wood, stone, or clay in the big lodge, playing hand games. They could smell the delicious odor of venison wafting in from the outside cooking fires.

"Look," Eve said, nudging Maggie as she glanced up and saw McCloud and Tames Wild Horses just entering the wooden lodge.

Sometime during the game Maggie had changed places with Windmaker, and now she smiled, seeing that Eve had just poked Windmaker in the arm, mistaking him for Maggie. The older man was laughing with Eve now, pointing over to where Maggie was smiling back at them, thinking the joke was on Eve.

With one hand on his hip, the other arm hanging gracefully to the side, the ever-present rifle slung on the strap over his shoulder, McCloud sought and found Eve with his absorbing gaze.

Windmaker was engrossed in the hand game once again. But not Eve. Her eyes were all over McCloud as he stood there, looking relaxed—and yet there was a leashed tension about him. Maybe it was the eyes that appeared tense, Eve thought. She could see that he had just washed up in the rain barrel outside, for his hair glistened with the orange glow from the lights in the lodge.

Eve was filled with warmth and wonder as her gaze ate him up.

Tames Wild Horses had already gone over to join Maggie, where she was playing hand games with Frog Catcher, Quiet Doe, Whispering Bells, and a few others who were gathered in a noisy, laughing circle.

The visiting Indians mostly hung back—those that had ventured inside to watch. The other, more primitive Indians, the Naked Ones and the Walking Blankets, stayed outside, roasting rabbits and game hens. A few of the Nez Perce squaws were helping roast Suncloud's deer meat and bringing portions inside to the ones "playing sport."

Keeping his eyes on Eve, McCloud walked through the people milling about and came to stand above her. Silence was golden between them as she looked up, smiled, and patted the thick lap robes, where he joined her, sitting cross-legged, his rifle behind him on the floor.

On the other side of Eve, Windmaker unfolded his tall, lanky frame and went to join his wife, Slender Otter, after he had placed a hand on Eve's shoulder and then upon Suncloud's. As soon as Windmaker had gone to another "table," McCloud slipped his hand over Eve's, squeezed, and stared deeply into her eyes.

As the games continued all around them, McCloud and Eve moved into a passionate embrace and kiss. Only the two of them existed. All others melted away into the shadows of their peripheral vision and the lights swirled as Eve and McCloud kept kissing, holding hands tightly, and squeezing shoulders.

Everything else became insignificant. The players blurred and became fuzzy until all was blotted out but feeling. Their senses soared, only for each other. Slanting his mouth across Eve's, McCloud pulled her tighter and tighter still, and then he groaned deeply.

Pulling them both to their feet, McCloud fled the lodge with Eve flying out behind him, her hand clutched tightly in his so that she could not escape even if she wanted to. Which she did not.

She was his slave, and he could take her anywhere in Wild Thunder that he chose.

He chose his tipi, a place she'd never visited during her entire three weeks in his town.

It was dark in the tipi, and Eve asked, "Where are we? Who lives here?"

"I do—when I am not at the store."

"It is dark in here."

"This is the way I want it."

"For what?"

As an answer, Eve found herself lying on her back upon a pile of thick, fluffy robes and rugs. It was soft yet firm. Her arms were flung over her head as McCloud joined her on the comfortable pile.

Wordlessly, at once, he was kissing her. Surprisingly gentle and persuasive. Eve had never been kissed like this, not even had McCloud kissed her this tender, seductive way before. There was so much emotion put into the kiss, and the caresses were endless as he put his hands where he'd never put them.

"Wait, McCloud. What are you thinking to do?" She pulled away from his kiss and his overly bold hands.

"Explore virgin territory."

"How do you know that is what I am?"

"You smell and taste better than any other woman on earth. You are sweet, untouched."

"What are you doing now? That tickles, you know."

McCloud breathed against her throat. "I know. And you can touch me."

Breathlessly, she said, "I will save that for after we are married."

"Just touch a little, Eve." He brought her hand down to his hard shape.

She drew back from his male hardness.

"No. Later, I said. You are too much a man for me to take all in one night."

"I have not taken you yet. You will know when I have you all the way, Dark Hair." He lifted her and put his mouth to her chest.

Her breasts tingled as he left them to trail a hot path down her stomach, up to her waist, and then back down. He was reaching between her thighs, beneath her skirt.

Eve yelled, "Watch out!" but McCloud already had his fingers inside her—*chastity belt!*

"Horsehair!" McCloud yelled. "What is this?" He looked down at her with fury in his eyes. "Whose idea?"

Eve blinked at his furious look and smiled sweetly. "Many Stars's."

She got up as he released her and brushed her skirts down, still smiling, now coyly.

"I'll be damned," McCloud said, using the favorite phrase of many miners and trappers. "A chastity belt."

"I will see you at the 'fun' lodge," Eve said, straightening the waist of her skirt as she went out. "Later, McCloud."

Her voice had not changed one bit; it was still low, calm, and full of sweetest honey.

"Yeah," McCloud mumbled grumpily. "See you later."

Drums of Thunder

Part II

All that glitters is not gold. . . .

Chapter Sixteen

"What is God?" Whispering Bells asked Eve.

"What?"

"You said God takes care of everything and everyone." Whispering Bells reminded Eve. *"What is God?"* she asked again. "Is this a person? A place? A thing?"

Eve laughed, then turned on a serious note. "Well, you could call him all of those things. God is everything, that's how he can take care of all of us and do all things through us, if only we ask. The Good Book says we can move mountains if our faith is only the size of a mustard seed."

"The Good Book?" Whispering Bells sounded excited. "Is this a very big black book?"

"Yes. Do you have a Bible?"

"A—what?" Whispering Bells said. "That's a funny English word. Bible."

"It is a very powerful word, Whispering Bells. The Bible is full of strength, love, wisdom, and many other things. Stories."

Whispering Bells ran to a rickety trunk. "Stories? I love it when we sit around the fire and the story-teller comes out of his tipi and begins to talk and tells of Indian legends and powerful spirits. It is so much fun."

Lifting the heavy book out of the old trunk, Whispering Bells exclaimed, "Here it is." She stood up with the leather-bound book in her arms, cradling the many-paged tome as if it were a baby.

"Where did it come from?" Eve asked, taking the book as Whispering Bells handed it over to her.

"A, uh—mish . . . missionary," she explained slowly.

"He left it here?"

"No. It was his daughter. She was pretty, with long yellow hair, lighter in color than Shining Eyes's."

"Shining Eyes? Who is that?"

"Your white friend. Maggie Exter."

"Dexter, sweetheart. Maggie Dexter. She is Shining Eyes. Oh, yes. I have heard this, and I believe Maggie loves her Indian name because Tames Wild Horses gave it to her." Eve frowned at her own words and then shrugged.

Just then Many Stars walked into the cedar-log house. "What do you have there?" she asked, bending over the big black book. "It is very pretty." Her fingers touched the engraved design bordering the cover.

"Very old," Eve said, touching it carefully as she opened the pages. "it is a Bible. Whispering Bells said a missionary left it here."

"His pretty daughter did," Whispering Bells corrected Eve. "She said I could have it forever and ever. That's how long a Bible lasts, she said." She turned to Many Stars. "I forgot what it was called, and Eve told me again. It's a funny word, but Eve says it has lots of strength, love, wisdom."

Many Stars backed away from the Great Book. "I am afraid of its power. I do not wish to look at it or touch it again."

She had her head turned away, and Eve went over to touch her shoulder. "Do not be afraid," Eve said. "The Bible is called the Good Book, or the Word. Jesus is God's son; he is a man. Jesus is the Word."

"How can this be?" Many Stars said, scoffing. "How can a man be a word? I do not wish to hear more of this nonsense."

Many Stars walked out the door, running across the field as if frightened of what she'd heard.

"That does it," Eve said, handing the book back to Whispering Bells. "I want a preacher."

"The preacher does not come here very much, Eve." Eve watched out the door until Many Stars was a black speck over the hill. "Why do you want him?"

"If McCloud and I are going to be married—and that event seems to be taking a long time happening—I would like a preacher to unite us."

"Unite?" Whispering Bells said. "What is that word?"

"It means to join, link, marry. To bring together. This is what your father and I should be doing one day soon, unless he has forgotten what he has asked." Eve thought for a moment, then said, "How did your father and Morning Moon come together—unite?"

"There was a wedding ceremony—Indian-style. I was very little when Father made Morning Moon his woman. She was very good to me. Not as good as you are. You are more fun. Morning Moon made lots of work for me to do." She shrugged. "But I still loved her."

Eve hugged the young girl to her side. "No wonder you never had any fun. Do you want me to call you Fantin?"

"That means child."

"Well—we should call you child for a while. Your white mother named you?"

"Yes. Her name was . . . I mean, is Chara. If she's still alive."

Eve smoothed Whispering Bells's brow with her palm. "I have heard that she gets into a lot of trouble."

"Whew. Did she ever." Whispering Bells looked up into Eve's lovely, caring countenance. "Maybe she still does."

Whispering Bells laughed. And it was a joyful sound.

"That is good, Fantin. It is good to laugh, Whispering Bells."

"And to smile," Whispering Bells announced. "It makes your face pretty. Otherwise it sags down to the ground. Great-Grandfather has said this."

"One-Arm is very wise. Should we go see him and show him the Bible?"

"Yah," said Whispering Bells. "Let us go show him this book that is like a big, strong man."

"Samson."

"What?" Whispering Bells blinked.

"You'll see," said Eve, taking the book when Whispering Bells got tired of carrying it.

Softly Eve said as they walked away, "I have two names too, Whispering Bells, so you don't have to feel . . ." Eve's voice drifted and then faded as Kicking Wolf melted back into the shadows and disappeared.

* * *

The preacher arrived that weekend. Eve was nervous, and McCloud did a lot of pacing. The visiting Indians, like the Nez Perce, the Dirty Faces, and the ones Eve called the savages—half-naked savages— were still hanging around. They knew there was to be a big feast with lots of wild dancing and heaps of delicious meat and other foods. Everyone was waiting with anticipation for the festivities to begin. They wanted to get enough to eat before the big chill was upon the land, which was about a month away in the high country.

Many Stars had fashioned a beautiful gown for Eve, of whitened buckskin with turquoise long-beads and pieces of smaller pale-colored beads that were almost transparent. There were even tiny bells on her bodice that Pond Lily had given her as a wedding gift. Her moccasins matched the dress, and they were tall ones, disappearing beneath the hem.

The white fringe swayed when Eve walked and the tiny bells cried out in a delightful song as she moved even the slightest bit.

Drums were beating slowly and made a rejoicing, unearthly sound with the addition of Skunk Cabbage's Indian flute.

Now Eve was walking to the lawman-preacher, and McCloud was meeting her halfway. They joined hands.

The revelers fell silent.

Eve let her eyes scan the crowd. Everyone she knew at the post was there. It was a beautiful night. Even the "savages" were smiling at Eve and McCloud as they became man and wife.

"I take you to wife," McCloud said, holding her hand and gazing into her eyes.

Eve, staring right back, repeated the words, taking him to "husband."

When the wedding was over and all their friends and family had congratulated them, Eve handed the Bible that Preacher Dan had been holding to Utah George. He took it as if he didn't know what to do with it. He turned to Many Stars, but she backed away; she had withdrawn when the preacher had held the book, saying words from it.

Many Stars was afraid of the strange magic of the black book.

Finally, the book came back into the hands of the preacher. He carried it under his arm all through the festivities, the dancing—then looked up to see that the newly wedded couple was nowhere to be seen.

"I almost forgot; it's been so long," Preacher Dan said. "The married couple at once goes into a tipi at the edge of the camp to be by themselves?" He looked at Whispering Bells, thinking he'd not get an answer from this pretty child.

"Yes, Preacher Dan. That is correct." Whispering Bells nodded as she munched on a greasy leg of meat, her lips shiny from the food.

Many Stars kept staring at the big black book at Preacher Dan's side but would get no closer to it than she had before. After a long while Many Stars walked up to him, asking him to tell her about it. The lawman-preacher was only too happy to tell the pretty Indian maid the story he'd told over and over again.

Seated beside the preacher, it wasn't long before Many Stars's eyes were wide, then misty, then moist, and finally full of joy.

* * *

Eve looked at McCloud in the orange blaze as they stepped into the small lodge, stopped, and were still.

What McCloud had worn to the wedding finally registered with Eve. She had been in such a daze during the ceremony, wondering if she would faint, cry, or shout from all the nervous excitement that had been running through her blood and nerve ends, that she didn't notice his clothing.

"What do you stare at, wife?"

"You, husband," Eve said. "You are beautiful."

"Men aren't supposed to be beautiful. They are handsome and strong."

"You are still beautiful. I don't care what you say."

He wore a white shirt with full sleeves that reached to the palms of his hands. His black pants were very civilized, and his hair was brushed back, very civilized also. That's where it all stopped. He wore a double row of beads around his throat. His headband was of turquoise and white, with silver discs that shone dully in the fire's soft glow.

McCloud appeared just as he was: half-Indian, half-white.

The firelight poured over her like hot honey, and McCloud thought he'd never seen such a beautiful woman. The excitingly hot, magnetic current that passed between them left Eve all atingle and faint with expectation. She smiled at McCloud, exhibiting a dazzling façade of tiny white teeth. He returned the smile with a lopsided grin that curved his sensuous mouth, and his sparkling eyes hungrily devoured the sweet features.

"You are even more beautiful," McCloud said, a fingertip reaching her bodice, then retreating before he had actually touched the clear beading.

"If you say so. You are the man. I am the woman."

They stood, not touching yet, but only gazing at each other's face. At last he took her in his arms, holding her as if he would never let her go. She felt him trembling, not with cold but with heat.

Eve glanced at the bed and her throat closed. She thought of the wood frame house in St. Louis and of this crude tipi-lodge. Then she looked at him again, and as she saw his face, all doubt, all regret, vanished.

He came closer.

She put her arms around him, drawing his head down, and kissed him deeply, urgently, passionately, with the yearning of weeks, keeping her eyes open all the while.

McCloud slid his lean, dark fingers through her hair, creating a dark cloud to spread about them as he lowered his face to capture her lips in what began as a gently given kiss but soon became forceful and demanding as his desire grew. She splayed her hands against the hard mounds of his chest. He lifted his head to smile triumphantly into her face. Her eyes widened at the feral gleam in the multi-flecked eyes and the flat, taut planes of his face.

"McCloud, be careful with me."

"Why?" He laughed. "Are you dangerous?"

"I am. And—"

"And I am even more dangerous?"

She said only, "I am woman. You are man. *A big man.* More powerful, with bigger muscles."

Eve was reminded of the tales of savage Indians

that roamed the wilds in search of white victims to rape and maul, and McCloud looked no less frightful at that moment. His face was close and she could see the wildly dancing lights reflecting orange in his strangely darkened eyes.

"You are going too fast for me."

"Am I?" he drawled, pulling her even closer.

She arched her back to release his grip, but he imprisoned both her wrists and stretched them high and tautly over her head.

This time when his mouth covered the gasping lips he pressed her back onto the fluffy robes with his full weight, his free hand roaming over the mountains and valleys of ever-warming flesh. He came to rest between shivering thighs.

"McCloud, you are very overpowering, but I like it," she said with a nervous laugh that was smothered by his mouth.

"I mean to be." He kissed her sweet lips, feeling the talons of desire clawing ruthlessly at his loins.

"Be gentle. I've never had a man."

"I would never hurt you," he growled into her face. What is the matter? Did another man hurt you? Eve, this is our wedding night. Tell me."

"No. It is just that you called me virgin not too long ago and made me feel very nice that you had thought of me as unspoiled."

His kiss deepened, and she could do nothing but sigh with pleasure as he guided her into a world of trembling passion from which there was no returning.

She did like this. She did. What had been wrong with her mother's thinking? Why had she warned her about something so heavenly and exciting?

At last, every fiber and muscle afire, Eve lost

control of will in her awakening hunger. Feeling his mouth at her neck, she heard him moan deeply in her ear, a sound of bold victory.

McCloud's hot mouth moved to the pulsating spot at her throat, paused, and then slid down to the fabric covering an auburn tip of her lucious breast. Through the cloth he titillated the crest, felt the burning flesh.

"McCloud . . . my clothes . . . I have too many on."

In a frenzy they both undressed; she was as ready for him as he was for her.

"You are even more beautiful with your clothes off," he said, his eyes alight with passion's blaze.

"And you, my savage lord."

He took his time arousing her naked flesh, and when satisfied that she was filled with wanting, he released her arms and coaxed her with gentle words, tutoring her in the use of her hands.

Eve moaned and grasped tightly at his upper arms, urging him to fulfill the destiny he'd known was his. Her nails dug into his flesh and he groaned deeply in his throat as he moved to poise himself above her.

He kneed her thighs apart—and just then the shout came from without.

"Suncloud! Come quickly! There is trouble!"

He looked down at her and cussed in the white man's tongue. Then he said, "Damn you, woman, you are a curse on me. Every time I want to get closer to you, something like this happens!"

He dressed quickly, hopping about as he pulled his pants on, and Eve laughed up at him, saying, "You are stupid, McCloud, you know that? Real stupid. You will never know what a woman truly wants."

"Want to bet?" he spat out as he left the tipi, taking rifle and knife and ammunition.

Eve sighed and lay back. "What in the world have I gotten myself into, Lord?"

She did not expect an answer.

"Do I have to come too?" She yelled after him, starting to grab her clothes. "Are we in danger?"

"No!" he shouted from outside. "This concerns men, warriors, not women. You are safe. Go to sleep and dream of shining knights."

Oh, sure. I can get right to sleep after you aroused me into a steaming pickle.

She had never lain awake like this for half the night, praying for sleep while her eyes burned a hole through her lids in the dark.

Eve finally slept. She dreamed about a mounted warrior as fierce as any the Old World ever knew. He was a knight without armor, fierce, indomitable. A conqueror . . . a man with the Plains Indians' blood mingled with his own.

He was Suncloud.

The dream turned from her fierce warrior and took her to an Indian encampment she had never seen. Wait! There, over there. The same people who had occupied her dreams before.

What are you doing? she cried out to them, but they just kept moving about the encampment as if she weren't there. Couldn't they see her?

Over here. I am . . . oh, no, not the child again. I am wearing the dress and a man, that powerful-looking man with the hooked nose, is waving to me. He is riding off with a bunch of handsome braves.

"Winter Woman?" Eve tried. Frustrated, she tried again. "Winter Woman. Where are you?"

Her sleeping gaze focused on a woman emerging from the mist; something, a conical shape, appeared behind the woman's frame.

There she was, standing over by a tipi covered with pictures. Stick horses and stick figures of men. You look so familiar. Winter Woman could not hear her; the words floating from her did not reach her.

"Winter Woman!"

She heard a sneeze.

Eve awoke, sitting up suddenly in the buffalo robes, straight as an arrow and looking about the lodge expecting to see Winter Woman. But there was only thick darkness.

She was alone. There was no one there, not even McCloud. Eve lay back down, wondering what her next dreams would bring her. Her eyes closed and she smiled with a deliciously warm feeling. She was making love with her husband again, feeling his taut bronze skin. But he kept going away, running from her and jumping on his horse, Wind.

Over and over again McCloud kept leaving her. Finally she closed her eyes and fell into a deep, dreamless sleep.

Eve was sound asleep and did not hear the moccasined feet outside the tipi slip stealthfully away, melting into the shadows of the moon. Kicking Wolf sneezed, then moved on.

Chapter Seventeen

"He has been taken!"

Eve came out of the tipi, looked at Cries Wolf, and gasped. "McCloud? Where has he been taken? And why?"

She stared up into the lean, dark face of Cries Wolf, wondering for a moment where this full-blood Shoshoni learned such perfect English. Many Stars had pointed out the quiet man to her before, and Eve had not paid much attention until the next time she'd seen him. Cries Wolf's brown eyes missed nothing. He was not very big, yet muscle rippled under his bronze skin.

He was not very quiet at that moment.

"The Wolves took your husband!" Cries Wolf shouted excitedly. "You will not see Suncloud for many moons." He shrugged. "Maybe you never see."

Eve peered aslant at the young man, one eyebrow rising. "Wolves took my husband and I will not—that does not make sense, Cries Wolf."

"No. The renegade 'Wolves' took them. Indians, you know, named Wolves?"

Eve blinked. "Who are these Wolves, and why

would they want to take Suncloud?" She sniffed, leaning closer to Cries Wolf.

"What is it?" Cries Wolf asked, leaning back on precarious footing to look at her.

She sniffed again, then rubbed her nose briskly. "You have been drinking."

He laughed, weaving from side to side as he finally moved. "Much firewater," he said, peering into the tipi, then back at her.

"Too much," Eve said. She looked at him closer, his face catching the light from a night fire. "Your eyes are bloodshot terribly . . . but there is something else."

Humor? Were his eyes laughing back at her?

Cries Wolf was repeating himself over and over, quite stupidly.

Cries Wolf howled, "Suncloud . . . you will not see him . . . for many moons."

A groan . . . and then Cries Wolf crumpled to the ground.

Passed out, Eve thought, looking down at him. She gave him a little kick with her toe, noting that he did not move an inch or make another sound. She kept looking at him, wondering what she should do. She certainly could not put Cries Wolf in her and McCloud's tipi.

Suddenly her answer came out of the dark blue night.

Two warriors materialized from out of the shadows and, laughing, began to drag Cries Wolf away.

Hands on hips, Eve asked, "What is going on? I have a strong feeling that a joke is being played on someone here."

The warriors and the fallen man melted back into

the dark, still chuckling softly. Just then a tired voice came from the pitch-black area.

"You are right. They are . . . were playing a joke—on us."

She whirled to face McCloud.

"I don't see the humor."

"And do you think I do?" he snapped, looking irritated and dirty and badly in need of sleep.

She followed his lean buckskin-clad form into the tipi. Just then he spoke again.

"I fail to follow their white man's humor."

With a tiny squeak of a laugh, Eve said, "Of course. Taking the bridegroom away before the marriage can be consummated. It is a white man's custom, and goes all the way back to the days of knights and their ladies. How odd."

"What is?" McCloud asked, removing his clothes once again, this time wearily and disgustedly as he cast them aside.

"You said something about a knight before you were, ah, whisked off into the night by the Wolves. Then I had a dream about knights becoming Indians. Without armor, of course."

"Of course," he growled. "You had a dream of the great and noble warrior Suncloud. He is dragged off by a passel of his Indian buddies and left to shiver in a crevice along a creek in the mountains while his passionate bride awaits him in their marriage tipi." He snickered at himself.

Eve plopped down onto the fluffy robes and yanked up a colorful Indian blanket. She giggled beneath it, then popped up. "This marriage is not getting off to a good start. We should have never done it. Why, I don't even know if we are in love with each other. I think that is important."

She picked up a juicy berry and began sucking on it.

He rolled over, putting his chin in one big hand, watching her consume the red berry. "Should we start all over?"

"What do you mean?" she snapped over her shoulder as she again readied herself to sleep.

Busily, Eve shook a lap robe in his face, and when the dust settled, McCloud was rubbing his watery eyes.

Smiling now, running his hand along her chemise-clad hip, McCloud was not surprised when she slapped his hand away.

He sighed, dropping his arm.

"Just as I thought. Oh, well. You are tired, it is too late, and you don't want to be touched."

He stared at her back as she rolled over and put it in his face. She had a nice back. Just now, however, it was covered with too much cloth.

"Well?" he said, reaching toward her tentatively.

Pulling the robes and blankets beneath her chin, Eve snuggled down and said, "Right, McCloud. For once you are right."

"A knight in the night. That is a good one. I shall have to tell my Indian buddies the Wolves."

"Don't you dare tell the Wolves. It was my dream. And now I plan to drift off and dream some more."

"Pleasant ones, then." His deep voice floated into a contented sigh.

At his words, Eve almost turned angry. But she was too worn down.

A moment later she heard him snoring. Oh, my God, he snores!

For not the first time that night, Eve gritted her

teeth and adapted to the situation. After a day like she'd had, however, even her nerves were complaining about inhabiting her body.

Covering her head with the blanket, Eve settled down and tried to get to sleep. Her eyes blinked under the covers. Was that the sound of male laughter outside the tipi?

No, Eve. It must be just the restless wind. It is a little wild and wayward tonight.

"Good night, husband."

Eve rolled over to search his form in the darkness. "I said, good night, husband."

Nothing but the silence—even the male giggles had vacated the area.

Eve punched the buffalo robes, turned over, and gritted her teeth, praying that sleep would return to her and this time would not be as restless and dream-filled as before. If anyone woke her again, they'd better be prepared to face a spitting tigress.

Ah . . . blessed dark . . . beautiful nothingness. The savage sleeps. . . .

Chapter Eighteen

Dawn slowly began wiping stars from the sky as Eve walked to Whispering Bells's little house. She had left McCloud asleep on his mats. What would he think when he awoke to find she had risen for the day and already walked out to find his daughter?

Eve smiled. Of course, he wouldn't know she had gone to see Whispering Bells, he would just wonder where she went. Would he worry? Would he actually care that she had deserted her new husband the first morning?

Eve thought not.

When Eve arrived at Whispering Bells's little cedar house, it was only to find that she was not there. It was awfully early, but she hurried to One-Arm's lodge, hoping he would already be up and about.

One-Arm did not speak English well. Whispering Bells had taught him some, but the old fellow hadn't listened to instruction very much, since he thought that that would make him more white than Indian. He didn't want to conform to the white man's world, even though he felt that this was inevitable.

Eve tried conversing with him in the little Shoshoni she knew. Finally he was understanding what she was asking, and ironically, that came about when she said *Fantin,* not *Whispering Bells.*

"Oh, Many Stars!" Eve shouted when she saw her friend. "Come here. We need help in conversing."

When Many Stars reached them, looking first at One-Arm and then at Eve, she grew alarmed. "What is it?"

"Do you have any idea where Whispering Bells has gone?" Eve asked. "She is not in the little house; I looked there and all around outside. Has she gone to the garden, do you think?"

"I passed by the garden while it was still dark outside," Many Stars said. "I did not see her there. What is wrong?" She turned to speak to One-Arm in his language. "Do you not know where Whispering Bells is, Grandfather?"

"No. She should be still asleep. I spoke to her late last night. The wedding kept her up with her friends almost all night. Here, there is Sings Wolf, we will ask him."

The teenage boy came over to them as One-Arm waved him to his side. Sings Wolf looked worried, as he wondered what he had done the night before. Ah, then he thought he knew.

"I am sorry," he blurted out before they could speak, looking to the Dark Hair, and then of One-Arm. "The Wolves were out last night and they asked me to come along. They said I should be initiated into the Wolf Brotherhood. I didn't do anything to Suncloud. I just watched while the older boys, like Cries Wolf, did all the dir—I mean, had all the fun. I had no firewater like the others did, truly I did not."

One-Arm did not feel like laughing, though the situation was somewhat hilarious. His face was stern, and Sings Wolf incorrectly took this as anger for his going along with the mischief of the night before.

"Have you seen Whispering Bells?" One-Arm asked Sings Wolf, holding up his hand for Sings Wolf to halt his lengthy explanation.

"N-n-no."

Sings Wolf blinked fast, afraid of what One-Arm would say next. He gulped and looked around at the women watching him.

Eve looked at Many Stars as she asked what was going on, to please explain the interchange. Many Stars quickly filled Eve in on the lad's predicament. Eve told Many Stars to please tell Grandfather to let the boy off the hook.

"He looks so sad, I'm worried that he might cry," Eve said, wanting to touch his shiny dark hair. "He is such a nice-looking boy. He will be shamed if he does cry. Do something, Many Stars."

One-Arm smiled at the Dark Hair before Many Stars said a word, and put his hand on the boy's shoulder. "We are looking for Whispering Bells, lad. There is nothing I wish to scold you about. We are all friends and family here in Wild Thunder and Thunder Creek."

"Kicking Wolf," said Sings Wolf, speaking of the now-grown man who used to head the Wolf Order. "I saw Kicking near Whispering Bells's little house very late last night."

One-Arm looked at the women one at a time before he asked Sings Wolf his question. "Before you went to steal Suncloud away from his wife? Or after?"

Nervously biting his lip, Sings Wolf said, "I—I can't remember."

"That is all right," said One-Arm, patting the boy's head. "You may go now. If you see Kicking Wolf, send him to me. Oh, and, Sings, see if you can get Suncloud out of bed." One-Arm smiled slyly at the Dark Hair, telling her he knew Suncloud was still abed.

Eve heard McCloud's name "Suncloud" spoken in Shoshoni. She also knew that this "thinking" senior saw more than he was letting on. What would he think if he knew they had not yet consummated their marriage bed?

The whole town was searching for Whispering Bells. McCloud had been warned about Kicking Wolf, that he was not to be trusted. He could not be found anywhere, but when he returned later in the afternoon, Suncloud again would not believe anything bad about Kicking Wolf, so like a great warrior.

"Where did you go off to?" Suncloud asked Kicking Wolf, staring deeply into the man's eyes and seeing no distress or pretense there. The man was as cool as a mountain pass on a hot summer's day.

"I had to see a trader named McKinley. He had news about your Arapaho friends."

"What did this man say?" McCloud asked, beginning to feel the first signs of suspicion.

"He says they were seen down by South Pass. He believes they were heading toward the Green River."

McCloud's eyebrow rose. "Green River?"

"Rock Springs, I meant to say."

"I see." McCloud turned away to rub his chin. Something did not sound right to him.

"I will go and keep my men searching for Whispering Bells." Kicking Wolf made a move to walk away, but said, "We will find her."

McCloud faced Kicking Wolf again. "Whispering Bells never leaves town without her father or . . . her mother. At times she goes to search for the wild mountain flowers, but that is not often."

"Ah," was all Kicking Wolf muttered.

McCloud frowned as Kicking Wolf walked away to join the men on painted ponies. Why did I say *her mother?* Why did Kicking Wolf say ah? He knows as well as I that Whispering Bells has not seen her mother for . . . how long?

McCloud did not want to think about Chara and her wandering, disloyal ways. He cared not if the woman ever returned or not; but Whispering Bells would like to see the fickle woman at least once in a while. After all, Chara was the girl's mother.

"Dark Hair," McCloud growled at the kneeling woman at the water's edge. "Come here."

Her eyes opening wide with surprise, Eve turned slowly to face her husband. She dropped the water skins at his fierce look.

"What do you want?" she asked, lifting one of the skins over her shoulder. "You should be out searching for your daughter."

"Why are you so angry?" he asked, coming closer.

"Do I look as fierce as you?"

"How would I know?" he snapped. "How can I see my own face?"

She shook her head at him. "Look in the water and then you will know."

He watched her walk away, thinking that she was looking more like an Indian bride every day. She surely appeared haughty now with those water skins slung over her shoulders, her skirts swaying around her knees.

He sashayed up to her and pinched her behind. Eve screamed, dropping the water skins. Her hands on her hips, she ordered:

"Go! Find your daughter! You act as if you do not have a daughter to look for. What is wrong with you, Steven McCloud? Are you crazy?"

"Will I find her?"

"How do I know?" She took up the water skins again and began walking briskly, her nose in the air.

"Where are you bringing those?" He strode beside her, grinning foolishly.

"To your grandfather, One-Arm." Eve kept walking as fast as she could.

"We have unfinished business, Dark Hair. You don't remember that we did not put the seal on our marriage bed last night?"

"Oh." Eve groaned. "Your daughter's missing and all you can think of is fooling around. Is this like all men?"

"My daughter will be found." He appeared angry again, fierce.

"Really?" Eve said, looking up at him in front of One-Arm's lodge. "Who is going to find her? The man on the mountain?"

With that, Eve slammed the hide door shut in his face. McCloud stood there for a moment, then yelled.

"I just thought it might be good luck to seal the

marriage bed before I go out to search for Whispering Bells . . ."

Over her shoulder she watched the door, placing the water skins where One-Arm smilingly waved her to put them.

One-Arm said something in a low voice, in Cheyenne River Sioux, patting a silky head beside him.

"Why do you not go to him?" Whispering Bells translated for Great-Grandfather as she looked up at Eve.

"Don't speak too loud," Eve warned the girl. "He might hear you. Even though you have been found, I want to teach him a lesson he'll not soon forget."

"Go to him," One-Arm said in Sioux, and this time Eve recognized the familiar words.

"Before you go," said Whispering Bells, "I want to thank you for finding me outside of town."

"What were you doing away from home?" Eve asked Whispering Bells. "You should not have gone so far. Tell me. What? Why? Explain all before I go to meet your father."

"I could not sleep after the wedding party, so I did not go to my little house. I thought I would go to find the mountain moonflower that blooms before sunrise. But it was not blooming. I heard someone following me. Then I thought it must be the Golden One, the mountain cat. I heard the padded footsteps running beside me. I could feel the hot breath next to my neck."

"Was it the Golden One, this cat you speak of?" Eve asked, trying not to smile as she heard McCloud outside, not too far away, making a howling, keening Indian sound.

Whispering Bells at last decided what she did see. "No. I saw men. Two men."

"What did you do?"

"I hid. I did not see their faces very well. But I knew they were after me."

Eve thought for a moment. Kicking Wolf had gone out of the town early that morning. He had not returned until later in the afternoon, and after that Eve had gone in search for Whispering Bells herself. She had found her outside of town, where she had remained in her hiding place behind dense bushes, waiting for someone she knew to come looking for her.

One-Arm was waiting to hear the whole story, and when Eve walked out the door, Whispering Bells was already telling him all.

Eve began walking toward the tipi when she saw McCloud near a stand of trees, leaning against one of the tallest pines. He beckoned her with a wave of his hand, and as she walked toward him, she could see that he was eager for her company, and, coming closer, saw the hard desire outlined by his tight breeches.

"You have been waiting for me?" Eve asked, now becoming aware of Wind and her own Zeena standing behind him in the trees. On their backs she could see packs of food and light baggage, enough for several days away from the village.

"I have."

"What is it you want, McCloud?" she asked, looking up at him.

"I want you to get on your horse and come with me."

He said it so nicely and politely that she walked to her Indian pony.

"Where are we going?" Eve asked, mounting her pony.

"Come—you will see."

She followed him up the winding trail that led higher into the mountains. Eve breathed the wonderfully cooler air, delighting in the feeling of freedom.

"Come—Eve McCloud. You are lagging behind."

"Eve McCloud?" she asked, watching his lean behind in taut buckskins. "Or slave?"

"Eve. Dark Hair. The woman."

"Maiden," she corrected him.

"Soon to be woman. My woman. It is not far now. Just up around that copse of pines there's a small log cabin."

"I can hardly wait," she said haughtily.

He rode straight and tall, telling her over his shoulder, "You will never forget this time of ours together."

"Can hardly wait," she muttered tersely.

He laughed with a manly chuckle. "Your name will be Shooting Star this night."

Now, that sounds exciting, Eve told herself, spurring her horse to catch up.

"Why didn't you tell me that you knew about Whispering Bells? All this time I thought you were cruel and insensitive."

"I have told you, just now," he said. "You found Whispering Bells and I knew it. What more is there to tell?"

"But why didn't you tell me sooner?" Eve pressed, holding her reins high as Zeena stepped around a pile of boulders. "As soon as you came to me at the water's edge, where I was filling the skins."

"I could have. But I thought I would let you stew awhile in your own gravy, thinking that I was so evil." He glanced over his shoulder at her. "You are a brave woman, Eve. A warrior woman, as I have thought since meeting you."

Warrior woman? That has a nice ring to it, Eve thought, following McCloud and beginning to wonder how much longer it was going to take to get to the log cabin.

Eve stood below Wind River Peak, breathing in the cooler air, delighting in the crisp feel of the chilly mountain breeze as it stirred her hair and stung her cheeks into a healthy pink.

Coming up behind her, McCloud wrapped his arms around her waist, then, turning her to face him, he kissed her until she was breathless and spinning. Standing her in front of him, he began to kiss her throat. Undoing her laces, he lowered his head, his lips doing bold magic between the valley of her breasts.

"You are beautiful, Eve McCloud."

"Do you want me to say the same of you again?" Eve said with a shaky laugh. What was he doing to her . . .

"No. You are woman. I am man. I will soon put my man to your woman."

Her head was so far back that it almost touched the ground as she laughed. "You say the most wonderful things, Steven McCloud."

He laughed with her, for the sheer joy of living and loving.

Taking her bodice down to her waist, he first kissed one blushing peak, then the other. His mouth fastened around a pink bud, working wonders with making it stand as straight and as tall as a mountain peak.

He pushed her skirt up to meet the bodice folds at her waist, then came against her in a hard rush of eager man. Against a moss-covered rock he pressed her backward, still hard, bending her over like a bow. Tickling her ear, he moved closer, making her laugh at the things he was doing as he nibbled and sucked.

Just then, while she was still laughing, he entered her. There was one tiny pang, then Eve settled into the security of his arms as he lowered her gently to the spongy ground and went into her strongly now.

Eve could feel his release pounding in her loins, making a thumping deep inside her. She clung to a shivering precipice, knew she was so close to something herself, and then it was over before she could find what it was she was seeking.

"Eve—my woman."

Eve said nothing.

After that they climbed the small hill to the cabin, and still she remained silent. McCloud kept looking at her, knowing she was not happy: It had been her first time.

The cabin held one tiny table, a crude bench, and two fluffy, fur-piled beds. Eve claimed one, McCloud the other. They ate silently, each sitting on one of the beds. McCloud glanced at her often, beginning to perceive what it was that bothered her. Later, he knew, she would find fulfillment.

After they put away the remaining food into the parfleches, they washed up and climbed back into one bed. Eve lay awake for a long time after he slept, her body tightly clenched. It would be better when they got used to each other, Eve thought.

At last she slept, later waking to long fingers caressing her deeply, a mouth teasing her breasts until she moaned with eagerness.

Eve turned fiercely to McCloud. He wooed her until neither could bear it another second, entered her with one deep thrust, rested within her while she gasped and abandoned herself to him. Then he began to work his body, a slow rhythm at first. She was drawn into the circle of the great strength of his arms as he surrounded her, all of him inside her body. Her own excitement rose to heights she could never have imagined. She was on the verge of explosion as he rose and plunged again, and yet again.

She met the mounting cadence of his need, feeling him shudder with clean, brutal strength and cry out as a sparkling fountain spilled over within her.

"Steven, *oh,* McCloud," she breathed, sobbing laughter muffling her words.

"My woman," he said, murmuring against her moist throat.

"Yes—your woman."

The next day and the next were glorious. They lingered for four days at the beautiful site, laughing and shouting like happy children, fishing from the shining stream, taking picnic food into grassy nooks and rocky crannies where the alpine flowers bloomed and nodded up at them with happy faces.

It was over all too soon, but Eve truly felt they'd had a splendid honeymoon. They reached Wild

Thunder late on the fourth night, and at once fell exhausted into their fluffy beds inside the tipi.

She was sound asleep. She was dreaming of her brothers again. She saw them—Derek, John, and Maggie's brother, Hank—lying in pools of blood. There was no one there. Suddenly, moving into her dreamscape, she could see three men, one of them an Indian. The others were not clear of countenance to her, there was too much mist in the surrounding area. The men bent—and then she saw them take up the yellow cloth and the blue beads. It was a special kind of material, this yellow length of softness, and very fine, and she'd planned to make dresses, one for Maggie, one for herself. If there was to be some left over, she'd planned to make curtains for the cabin from that. Now she looked closer at the three men. One held a bloodied hunting knife—wait! He looks familiar. Who can he be? Where had she seen that face before?

He is coming . . . for me!

Flinging aside a heavy blanket, McCloud reached for Eve's shoulder and tried to wake her up. Her eyes squeezed shut, resisting his awakening her.

"Eve. Eve. Wake up."

"D-don't come near me with that knife . . . Indian knife . . . no . . . get away! You killed my brothers!"

"Eve!" McCloud demanded she awaken now. "If you open your eyes, your dream tormentor will vanish. Wake up now. See who is here to help you and hold you. I am not the one hurting you—"

"What?"

Eve's eyes opened slowly. Then they widened as she saw a man looming over her.

"No, go away. You vile creature. You killed—"

Snatching her flailing hands in a firm grip, McCloud pulled her close to his face. "It is I, Dark Hair, Steven McCloud." He grimaced at the name. "You love to hear me say that, to admit my white blood, don't you?"

He sounded serious, yet Eve thought he was joking with her.

"McCloud." Eve's breath was released in a long sigh. "Steven. What are your secrets?"

It was McCloud's turn to say what?

"Who are you really?"

"Eve. You are still having your nightmare. You haven't an idea of what you are saying. Do you want a sip of water? Here."

He held the water skin to her lips, poured, and it dripped off her chin as she drank thirstily.

"Ah," Eve sighed. "I needed that." She lay back down into the circle of his warm embrace. "Don't go away, Steven. Stay with me. Close to me, for the rest of the night. It is dark and I feel so lost and alone."

"I am here." He chuckled into her ear. "You do enjoy calling me that white name."

"Steven?"

"Yes—that is what I—"

"Steven—I would like to find the men who killed my brothers and Maggie's."

He pushed her back down and sat up straight in bed. "You ask the impossible."

She touched his shoulder. "Why?"

"How can I find your brothers' murderers? I cannot even find those who killed Morning Moon." He flinched away from her hand. "No. Not now."

"You know who killed her. It was Scar-Face.

Why don't you go looking for him in the name of revenge? He is the one who held your sister captive for so many years. Perhaps it is he who also murdered our brothers?"

He turned to look at her, and she could make out his fierce eyes in the semidark.

"I will find Scar-Face one day. And those who went along with him also to perform the dirty deeds, like mutilating one of Many Stars's fingers and torturing the innocent youngsters."

"The one who hurt Many Stars is dead," she told him. "He was killed by the Indians at Fort Robidoux."

"Yes. But there are others. If Scar-Face murdered your brothers, then that is all the more reason I should slay him. Maybe there were whites involved."

"I still hear contempt in your voice for all whites. You do not care who murdered our brothers."

"I did not know them, Eve. They were your relatives. How can I seek revenge for those I never rode with, laughed and joked with, or fought against other enemy braves with? My brothers here—I would fight for something they believed in. Within reason."

"That is just the point, McCloud. They were my relatives, my brothers. Are you not a part of me now that we are man and wife?"

Her voice was soft.

Suddenly he turned and put his hand on her cheek tenderly. "You know what, Dark Hair, you are burying yourself deeper and deeper in my soul. I would do anything for you. You are in my heart now. More so than any other woman has been there. You have planted words and things you do into my memory, your every movement, your walk, your talk, even your shy whisper. My eyes see you in every part of nature, in every part of my being when I am away from you."

"And yet?" She waited. "There is more."

"Your brothers mean nothing to me. I am sorry. True, they were white, which makes them less worthy of my care."

Eve lay back down, facing the tipi wall. "I did not ask you to kill, to seek vengeance for me. I ask only that you . . . feel something of my grief and loneliness."

"Do you feel something for Morning Moon, for my grief and loneliness at her passing? Do you not feel jealous, just a little?" When Eve was silent, he went on. "You want to say you did not know her, how could you feel for my mourning? Right?"

"No one knows what another feels for loved ones who pass on to heaven. I would guess when we mourn, we mourn alone." Apart from Maggie; she was there with Eve. Maggie had seen, shared the terrible grief.

McCloud moved closer to Eve's back. "I am here now, my love. I will never leave you or forsake you. Is this not what we said to each other, 'As long as we both shall live'?"

"You do love me?" Eve turned to face him in the tipi that was brightening with the dawn light.

"I do," he said fervently. "Come now. Either catch more sleep or open your arms to me, my sweet warrior woman."

McCloud smiled. "We will grieve together and find solace in each other's embrace."

With tears brimming up, she cried, "Steven McCloud, you are very kind and wise."

She opened her arms to him then, and he took her
to his heart while the glorious morning burst over
Wild Thunder in a brilliant display of orange, yellow, and pink.

Many Stars paused outside the tipi, ready to open
her mouth to announce her presence, when she
heard the shouts of ecstasy from within.

She fled from the entrance and ran past Utah
George. The handsome breed smiled at her bronze-
red face. He would go to her. He would catch her
and turn her in his arms so that he might kiss her
cheeks, her hair, her eyes, her mouth. He wanted to
caress her, embrace her, hold her forever close to his
breast.

It was not time for love. Not for Many Stars.
First, he told himself, she had to heal. Someday he
might try to kiss her, hold her, embrace her tenderly, but not now.

He watched her run away from the joyous loving
she'd heard coming from the marriage tipi of
McCloud and Eve. Utah smiled again. Many Stars
would run one day into his arms, and he would
never let her go.

Utah George, in his usual quiet and reserved way,
walked through the town, liking this time of morning when amber and pink colored the town, giving
it a mellow glow of peace and happiness. He was an
optimistic man, and looked forward to what he
would do that day.

Just then a little girl broke into his musings. She
signed to him as he did not know Flathead, the one
language she spoke. She clenched both hands and

crossed her forearms in front of her chest with a trembling motion.

Cold, Utah thought, and took a blanket from the pile a woman was carrying in her arms. He smiled, telling her in Shoshoni that the little orphan needed one. After he had carried the blanket to her, the woman gestured for the little girl to come over, she could have a bowl of warm food to fill her belly.

Utah smiled, happy to have done a good deed by finding food and warmth for the little Flathead girl.

Breaking Utah's contentment, an Arapaho woman, one who'd had her tongue cut out by an angry trader thinking she'd cheated him out of some goods, rushed up to him and in sign language told him he was needed at One-Arm's lodge immediately. She told him that she could not find Suncloud or his woman. She had seen them carrying drying towels and the soap the Dark Hair favored.

They'd probably gone to the store to wash up, Utah mused.

What is it? he asked, signing.

The child is missing again, she answered.

Child? She had said child with emphasis. Child. What was the French word for child?

Of course. *Fantin.* Whispering Bells. *Child* was easier to sign than Whispering Bells was.

Trying to decide which way to go first, Utah George was relieved to see Suncloud and Eve come out onto the wooden walkway and pause to look up at the blue sky. They smiled, hugged, and then grew silent as they became aware of being watched.

"Wait. Stay."

Saying this, Utah George walked briskly toward them, and when he caught Suncloud's gaze, Suncloud could see that something had happened that demanded his immediate attention.

"Sorry," McCloud said, looking at his wife.

With her eyes on Utah George, Eve said, "We will see what it is and decide if you needed to say that."

Chapter Nineteen

In the cool summer dawn, when only the first streaks of pink light colored the eastern sky, Whispering Bells followed her mother over rocky terrain and into a treeline of ash, pine, and spruce. A man watched from inside the thickest stand of pines, but he would not let his face be seen by the girl. He had warned Chara not to reveal his presence, otherwise all might be lost.

Huivi, cousin to Scar-Face, could not fail.

The Dark Hair was wanted by a very important man—an Indian named War Shirt—and Huivi had much to gain should he bring Eve to the Teton Dakota Sioux. Even the most remotely related clansfolk were morally obligated to help find someone who has been lost. This person could be Suncloud!

Huivi's mission was to bring Eve Michaels to War Shirt. If he failed, it was Suncloud's duty to bring her to Great Eagle. Suncloud, leader of the Wind River Shoshoni and Basin Utes, had also been seen in Great Eagle's dream. But Huivi wanted the pouch of Golden Tears he'd been promised; he could go far and wide with that much wealth.

It so happens that Eve Michaels, the Dark Hair, as a small child had been lost to her mother's people, the Oglalas, a band of the Teton Dakotas. Her father, a white man, wanted Eve and her mother to leave the Dakota people and go back to St. Louis. In the Indian Nation, both parents had a definite place with reference to the child. For certain specific purposes only one half of one's relatives counted, while in respect to other matters the half excluded from the Dakota clan might be quite as important—like Narcissa Roussillon LeBleau, the Dark Hair's mother!

War Shirt had informed Huivi that in the Dakota clans a person's uncles and cousins would be reckoned as "fathers" and/or "mothers."

Eve's mother, called Crazy One, was one-quarter Indian and had a female cousin in the Oglala clan who was the wife of the chief Great Eagle. This woman, Winter Woman, was childless, and when she passed away, her youngest "granddaughter," Eve Michaels, became the Oglala princess. It was Winter Woman's dying request that Eve be found, for she had been away from her people for too long.

"Find her, War Shirt," Winter Woman said. "If Mist Smoke is still alive, find her and bring her back to show her where she learned to love, laugh, walk as a child. She will not remember, she was taken away at too young an age. Her white father did not care that her people wanted her to stay until she was older. Her mother cares only for the white ways; we do not know if Narcissa and her child are yet alive. If the girl is alive, she must be told of her grandmother's passing and that her grandfather, Great

Eagle, is now passing. She, this Eve Michaels, Mist Smoke, has been in his dream."

How ironic and strange, Huivi thought as he watched his mistress, Chara, with the child of her and Suncloud's marriage. Then Suncloud divorced her, and Huivi waited for Chara. But he could foresee that she was going to be trouble. Chara was already getting restless, just as she had gotten restless with Suncloud.

The men Huivi had sent in to Wild Thunder to spy for him had come out saying that Dark Hair and Suncloud had been planning to wed. But Huivi was determined to take the Dark Hair to War Shirt even if they'd married. With the gold he had been promised, he could take Chara to California, and from there to an island in the Pacific. Perhaps in such a place Chara would again find romance and love with Huivi.

He had a mission to complete and no one must stand in his way. Chara would help him, but she did not know about War Shirt and the Oglalas. He would see that she helped without catching on to his mischief and deceit. She was curious and suspicious about what he was trying to do, yet he could not let her in on everything, especially Great Eagle's dream of Suncloud and Mist Smoke. He had begged her to trust in him in what he was struggling hard to accomplish. Greed for wealth and adventure had shone in Chara's eyes. She would help. She was good at mischief and was sneaky.

Another thing he must see for himself—or let War Shirt find—was the mark on the Dark Hair's nape that would claim her as Winter Woman's "granddaughter," the Oglala princess, Mist Smoke, named so because of her eyes, which were the color of violet mistflowers with their amber rays shooting from the smoky centers. The white man called these eyes hazel.

Huivi himself had no idea how it came to be that the Dark Hair had moved so far away with her Indian breed mother, Narcissa, whom many thought possessed Spanish blood. Not Spanish, but the blood of the Teton Dakota Sioux!

Huivi knew he would have to employ his Greasy Long Hairs and Kicking Wolf a bit longer. They had already been somewhat successful in taking Suncloud's attention from the Dark Hair, for the half-breed leader of Wild Thunder did not spend nearly as much time as he wanted to with Eve, as rumor had it, and that gave Huivi and his men a better chance to get at the woman.

Kicking Wolf would accomplish the dirty work with the yellow dress and blue beads, Huivi thought with a sly grin as he hunkered in the shadows of bushes and rock. He had met with Kicking Wolf and all was being set up for their sly and deceitful actions. Dark Hair would surely not want anything to do with Suncloud when she discovered for herself the "truth" about him.

From out of his pouch Huivi took the bead-covered amulet bag that had belonged to the Dark Hair as a child. It was beautiful and in the shape of a turtle and contained her umbilical cord, saved when she, Mist Smoke, was born in the Sioux camp.

Huivi didn't care if the whole town of Wild Thunder trekked to Dakota territory with them as long as he was successful in bringing Eve Michaels—the Dark Hair—to War Shirt and from there to Chief

Great Eagle of the Teton Dakota, where she belonged. And her precious Suncloud could not accompany her, for then he, Suncloud, might get the Golden Tears and Huivi would be left out in the cold.

Chara might even want to leave him and go back to Suncloud as his second wife.

He confessed to himself that, yes, it was more than the booty promised by War Shirt that involved him in this dangerous mission. He, too, was beginning to feel a desire to bring this woman back to where she had been born, daughter to a white Canadian trader and a selfish and greedy woman.

Then again, maybe it was for the Golden Tears and nothing else. Huivi could never make up his mind if he wanted to be nasty or good.

Whispering Bells felt that someone was watching them, spying on her and her mother. She spun about at a sound, her hearing acute and unusually accurate.

"Chara, Mother, someone is there. I have heard a noise; it sounded like a man laughing softly to himself."

"Where?" Chara asked, nervously rubbing her hands along her doeskin skirt. "Come, Fantin, we should take you back to Wild Thunder. You've been gone long enough."

Whispering Bells frowned into the bushes, then up at her mother. "Why did you have me come here twice now? Days past the Dark Hair came to get me. Why did you look so scared and nervous when she and I walked away?" the intelligent child asked. "I kept looking over my shoulder and saw you, what you were doing. You were peering into these bushes like you were looking for someone."

"Well—I," Chara began, then let it drop. What could she tell the child? That she was trying to trap the white woman Eve Michaels so that her lover could take her to someone far away from there and receive a great treasure, a reward for bringing her?

"Mother, who are you hiding there behind you?" Whispering Bells asked, trying to see around Chara's red blouse and rust-colored skirt. "Something is very strange here. I would like to fetch Father."

"No! Not Suncloud!" Chara said, smoothing the child's hair with the back of her hand. "Listen now, I will come into the town with you. Just do not say anything to Suncloud about this issue."

Whispering Bells whipped her chin up to look into her mother's eyes. Chara lied a lot. Father had said so. She listened to him talking to Utah George. He'd said her mother liked many men. And she had a lover, a Spanish man. Whispering Bells thought this did not sound very good. Why couldn't she have been as nice as Morning Moon, or the Dark Hair?

"Why do you not want Father to come here?" Whispering Bells asked her mother. "I got a feeling you want the Dark Hair to come and find me again. Just like she did several days ago."

"Oh-oh." Chara bent down. "That is not true." Her eyes scurried off to glance into the bushes, then came back to the child. "Please, you must not say this to your father. You know how he is. Like most men, he believes only what he wants to." Chara cleared her throat.

"Not Father."

Chara sighed with a word on her lips that sounded to Whispering Bells like one of those swear words the traders and trappers use when they're really angry.

"Then prove to me you do not want the Dark Hair. Take me back to Father. Stop sending me messages to come meet you out here. Be a brave mother and come to Wild Thunder with your chin up. And then Father will like you. But not more than his new wife."

"What?"

Whispering Bells announced over her shoulder as she looked back to see Chara following, "The Dark Hair and Suncloud are married. They were married many days ago."

"What?" Chara screeched, jealous that Suncloud would do such a thing. She'd always thought he would wait for her to come back, and that he'd be longing for her until he was old and gray. "But then, he did marry that moon-faced Morning Moon, didn't he?"

"Morning Moon is no more. Scar-Face has killed her."

Scar-Face? Just hearing the name almost caused her to swoon. That man. Oh! She could not wait to see him again; he sent tingles of pleasure up her back. Huivi's cousin, Scar-Face. Much more a man than Huivi ever could be.

"Scar-Face has killed no woman," Chara said vehemently. "He is a good man, a handsome man. He wouldn't do that."

"Well, he did."

* * *

By the time they reached the edge of Wild Thunder, Chara's eyes were shooting bitter green sparks.

Huivi watched them go, gritting his teeth over the child's insolent behavior. That child was going to be trouble. It was going to be no easy task getting the Dark Hair out of Wild Thunder.

Caught unawares, Huivi gasped in shock.

Yelping next, Huivi stormed out of the bushes with a huge golden wildcat scratching and tearing at his heels. He ran until he found his horse, then jumped on, frowning when he saw the laughing face of Kicking Wolf not far ahead.

The Greasy Long Hairs were with Kicking Wolf, one of them holding a length of yellow cloth.

Chapter Twenty

"Who is that coming with Whispering Bells?" Eve asked McCloud. "Is this someone you know?"

She saw his mouth open as if he were going to yell something.

"*Ai!*"

"What is it?" Now Eve stepped back from the black pot she'd been stirring.

McCloud looked at Chara as if she were a ghost.

"My wife," he said. "My old wife."

"She does not look very old to me," Eve said, watching the pretty woman approach with Whispering Bells.

All of a sudden Eve shouted, "Your wife!"

"Yes. Whispering Bells's mother. What is she doing here?"

McCloud took his rifle from his shoulder and balanced it on the ground in front of him, both hands wrapped around the cold barrel. He looked as if he were going to do battle, poised as he was.

With her hand on McCloud's arm, Eve said, "You could give her a warmer welcome than that. I am sure she heard what you said. That was not very nice of you to speak of her that way, McCloud.''

Looking Eve over, Chara walked up to McCloud and the woman with the dark hair, her eyes still emitting green sparks. She looked at McCloud, and he could swear he heard the mating call. Chara's swishing skirts had always been a trap. Maybe she was looking for a man again. He decided to keep his eyes away from her and tried to close his ears to the sound of her laughing voice. Chara could be trouble, and her voice had always caught him in its silvery web.

"I have brought Fantin back," Chara said to McCloud. "She was wandering outside of town. You should watch out for her better than you do; you always let her roam wild."

"I have to go to the store," McCloud said, adjusting the rifle strap over his shoulder. "You can all get acquainted. I am happy to see you are found, Fantin, Whispering Bells. I have work to do, men to meet at the store."

"Just like a man," Chara said with her Spanish accent, watching McCloud swiftly walk away. "They are such cowards." She looked Eve up and down again. "And you are his new wife, I take it, eh?"

"Yes." Eve smiled pleasantly. "And you are his old wife."

Chara curled her lip. "He put me away. I had nothing to do with it." Her eyes rolled and she stabbed the corner of her mouth with her tongue.

Eve decided at once that this woman must be lying. There was something about her that did not ring true. Everything about McCloud's old wife, she with the laughing voice, spoke of unfaithfulness and deceit. What was she up to?

"I have brought Fantin back," Chara said, still looking at Eve as if she were seeing something from another world.

"Should we go to the little house?" Eve asked Chara, rolling her eyes as the woman looked down at Eve's moccasined feet. "I'm sure this child can make us something to eat and we can get to know each other better over a full stomach."

Folding her hands, trying to remain calm, Eve rolled her eyes again, wishing she could make her voice sound sweet. She did not feel like being nice, but nice she must be, for Whispering Bells's sake.

"Child, yes. That is what I named her. Whispering Bells is *so* Indian," Chara said, laughing in Eve's face. "Fantin means—"

"Yes, I know. It means child in French, and fantine means childlike."

"You are very clever, Dark Hair," Chara said, glancing over her shoulder one last time as they walked to the little house.

"No," Eve said, "Just observant. Also, I am just becoming more informed as I go along, if you must know."

"Tell me more," Eve said, chewing the delicious food that Whispering Bells had made.

"I am beginning to like you," Chara said, swallowing a piece of whitefish that had been floating around in her bowl of stew. "You are different from all the other women McCloud has brought into Wild Thunder."

"Were there many?" Eve asked, watching the

woman closely, realizing she was trying to get under her skin.

"So many you could not count," Chara said. "He has had one woman after the other. When we were first married, he used to bring long-haired squaws to Wild Thunder. They were very beautiful, young, and drunk on firewater, and I was very jealous." She laughed. "He used to bring them up from Thunder Creek."

"Are you Spanish?" Eve asked, staring at Chara's puffy red mouth chewing the bit of pemmican Whispering Bells had laid down next to her plate. "You look like you could be."

"I am a little Spanish," was all Chara would offer. "Fantin is a great cook. I always enjoyed her food. She makes great pemmican too, just the right amount of berries in it."

Dear Lord, Eve thought, how long has this child been cooking for other people? Her mother should have stayed home and done the cooking, not gone gallavanting off into the wilderness with just any man who tickled her fancy.

As if reading Eve's mind, Chara spoke the next words.

"Fantin learned to cook at an early age. You do not know much about the children here in Wild Thunder, do you?"

"I am beginning to. Remember, Chara, I have not been here all that long."

"Oh, of course, you will come and then you will go."

Eve ruffled, then asked, "What is that supposed to mean?"

"Our people rarely complain, but this time I thought it was necessary."

"No. Wait a minute. You said I will come and then I will go. You are avoiding the issue and trying to confuse me. This I do not like."

"You are wise, Dark Hair."

Eve chewed for a moment, then said, "Well, thank you. What do you mean by 'our people'?"

"You should listen and learn how small children talk," Chara said.

"Oh, you are trying to confuse me again, and I wonder why." Eve watched Chara, wondering what clever ruse she was going to pull next.

Chara smirked at Eve.

Fury and frustration filled Eve, but she struggled to keep her expression blank. Finally she had to say something more.

"Why are you so hateful? What have I ever done to you? I thought we on earth were supposed to love one another and not try to get the best of people we meet. You should read the black book."

"Have I gotten the best of you?" Chara said as she lounged back onto the furry cushions, apparently getting ready to go to sleep right where she was. "If I have," Chara said sleepily, "I suppose I am sorry. But right now I am so tired and need rest. So, if you do not mind, I shall do just that."

"Go right ahead," Eve said, getting up to help Whispering Bells clean up the mess Chara had made around her plate.

Eve looked down at the sleeping woman, and then over at Whispering Bells, who had kept busy and had been quiet while the women had eaten.

Just who, Eve asked herself, was the real child here, Whispering Bells or this puffy-lipped Chara?

* * *

"A town means order, and order means law," McCloud was saying to a couple of traders who had found their way to Wild Thunder, "and without them there can be no civilization, no peace, and no relaxation."

One of the traders asked, "You mean to learn to domesticate animals and plant crops?"

"We have already done some of that," McCloud answered, wondering how they had gotten him started on this conversation; he had many other things to do but was now growing curious as to what else they had to say.

"Ah," the French trader put in, "but first culture and good living begins when man learns to share the work and so provide leisure for music, painting, writing, and study."

"Yeah," the American said, "as long as a man is scrabbling in the dust for food and fuel, looking over his shoulder for enemies, he can't be thinking of other things."

McCloud argued, "No one of us is ever safe. I can see that the more complex a civilization becomes, the more vulnerable it becomes. Many disasters can occur. There is no security this side of the grave."

"Right," said the Frenchman, "and you're living here on the brink of savagery."

"The more ill-prepared people are to face trouble, the more likely they are to revert to savagery against each other," said the first man, eyeing the half-breed leader of Wild Thunder up and down, watching closely, listening hard.

"Oui," the Frenchman said roughly, "you are nothing but savages here in Wild Thunder."

"What is wrong with a few savages?" McCloud

asked, stiffening his spine to stand taller, proud of his people and their ways.

"You have renegade Indians living here, and there are whores down in Thunder Creek," the Frenchman said with a sneer.

McCloud towered over the argumentative men and they started to back up. Then they heard a lovely voice begin to speak.

"Yes," Eve said as she walked in, looking beautiful in feathers and buckskins. The fringe on her dress was very long, running from her arms in a graceful flow. "What is wrong with savages? In fact, there are many Indians here in Wild Thunder. The men are strong and able. The women are beautiful and talented. The children are happy and healthy. Why, there is a girl of eight who can cook better than a grown woman, besides being able to speak many languages. Our town is an example of what other towns could become. The leaders of our community are the hunter and fighter." She looked at McCloud and smiled. "A builder of civilization stands here before you."

McCloud wore a huge grin as he looked back into Eve's shining eyes.

"What about the whores down in Thunder Creek?" the American asked, looking Eve up and down as if she could be one.

Eve squared her shoulders and her chin shot up. She appeared inches taller.

"I prefer to use the word *seductress,*" she shot back. "And—we are all somebody."

"A whore is a whore," snorted the American, snatching up his gear, preparing to depart.

Coming around a counter full of skins, Eve, with

flashing eyes, said, "What about those in the Bible? Have you ever read the Good Book?"

"Merde!" exclaimed the Frenchman. "A preacher woman."

Eve laughed shortly, saying, "I could be." She looked them up and down, tossing her head. "I could be an Indian, a squaw, for all you two know."

She turned to McCloud, saying in a businesslike tone, "Where's the black book? These two need to learn a thing or two about life."

The traders looked at her dark hair, feathers, and buckskin, then backed out, turned, and ran.

McCloud was still feeling great pride in his wife as the traders walked out, leaving nothing behind and carrying nothing from his store. They went like birds scattering from the brush.

Eve had so excited and enamored McCloud that later, when they could find some time to be alone, he spread his shirt and she her buckskin dress on the abundant summer grass. She was naked and trembling, sweeter than the honey the bees made in the trees, and he kissed and caressed and stroked her until he could contain himself no longer.

She looked at the wild mountains above them as he made tender, painstaking love to her. They were lying next to the blue lake amid wildflowers, and the day was sunny and warm.

As he entered her in one sweet, gentle move as slowly as he could—for she was still as tight as a drum—she cried out in passion and pleasure, meeting his need, and he possessed her like the storm driving him. Their coming together was beautiful, the infinitely nuanced movements allowing time to sing by.

She whispered in his ear, "It feels so good . . . so

very very good to have you inside me." She gasped then as he made a powerful move.

"And it feels so good to be inside you, beautiful Dark Hair."

Their time was all too brief as they made love in this gentle, lovely, lilting dance as old as time. Now McCloud knew love in a new way, resoundingly personal, precious, and for the first time the knowledge of life was truly his.

Before long they both cried out in ecstatic satisfaction as their spirits mounted on golden wings. They loved once more, not in a flaming eruption of glory, but in a quiet glow of silver light on scudding clouds, softly, like amber sunset on wet river rocks.

Eve snuggled against McCloud and wept quietly. For the joy of living, giving, taking, sharing.

He was her husband. She was his wife. Their new life was just beginning.

There were no slaves here or captives, only lovers.

Chapter Twenty-one

"Who brought you here?" McCloud was questioning Chara fiercely as she sat fluffing a pile of rabbit furs, intending to have Pond Lily make her a fine winter jacket.

Batting her long lashes, Chara looked up at her handsome former husband. He had put her away by saying, "I divorce this woman," before One-Arm and the elders of the Wind River Shoshoni tribe. And then it was done. She had never shared his blankets again.

"I have come by myself," Chara told him, not looking at McCloud now.

"That is impossible," he said. "Women do not travel alone in hostile country, especially women like you, who enjoy their luxury at a man's expense. You must have had someone come with you. And why were you hiding Whispering Bells outside town the first time?"

"I did not hide her," Chara said in her charming "laughing voice," one she knew could always get to McCloud. "She came to me."

"What?" snapped McCloud. "Did she hear your

laughing voice in the wind and come out to find you?"

"Something like that," Chara said in her most charming, winning way. "You always knew I had strange powers."

"Evil ones," remarked McCloud. "Where is your latest lover? Did you lose him in the wind? Or did you slay him after you tired of him?"

"I lost him near the Belle Fourche River. I want to find Huivi. Will you help me, Suncloud?"

She always called him by his Indian name when she wanted something special like trinkets, colorful material for dresses, and pretty colored beads.

"Listen," he said. "The storyteller has come out of his tipi and is sitting before the fire. I have to find Eve and tell her."

"The Dark Hair?" Chara asked, one hand on her hip, the other buried in her luxurious hair. When McCloud did not answer, she asked, "What is his story tonight?"

"Sacajawea," McCloud said as nonchalantly as possible, and walked away.

"Not that one again," Chara muttered to herself. "Wait! Suncloud, I wish to tell you about Huivi; I must find him."

"Later, Chara."

Chara let her breath out in a fast huff and sat back down, pouting, her pile of pretty furs beside her. "He hates the Spanish even though there are some of us here, like his own daughter; she has some of my ancestor's blood."

She glared the way he had gone. "He has always hated us." Now, Scar-Face, there was a man to love.

* * *

Eve smiled, settling close to her husband, hugging his arm. "What is he going to tell a story about?"

"Sacajawea."

"Oh," Eve exclaimed. "I have heard this before. My favorite."

"Listen. He is telling now," McCloud said as he rested his Hawken rifle across his thighs, adjusting his bullet pouch so Eve could sit closer.

She looked at Tallfeather as he walked slowly, and Eve began to wonder if he was feeling ill or was afflicted with some malady. He was a big man, lean, and hard as jerked buffalo meat, with hair and eyes the color of midnight during a storm. Many Stars looked at him too, wondering if there was something she could do for him, some herbs she could gather to make this huge and gentle man well.

Norman Tallfeather began his story—a true recounting of Sacajawea—just as Many Stars, Frog Catcher, Utah George, Whispering Bells, Maggie, Tames Wild Horses, and others came to sit in the wide circle. Under the stars they all listened intently and McCloud translated easily, for Norman spoke slowly and paused often to elaborate with his hands.

"Sacajawea, or Bird Woman, was born in a camp of Snake, or Shoshoni Indians." Norman made many gestures with his body now as he told of Sacajawea. "These Indians ranged the Country of the Mountains. She grew up like most Indian girls. She was pledged as the wife of a much older man. When she was fourteen summers, a Hidatsa war party from the Missouri River village attacked the camp of her people; they sought safety in flight.

Sacajawea and an older girl tried to escape across the river near their camp . . . ah, but were captured! The war party then set out for home with their captives. The older girl escaped one night, leaving the little girl, Sacajawea, a lonely captive.

"Sacajawea was carried to the Hidatsa village in Dakota-of-the-North, where resided a French-Canadian trapper and fur trader by the name of Tous-saint Char-bono. No one knows his reason, but this white man bought the little captive and placed her in the care of his wife. She was also a captive from the Shoshoni Indians. She was not of the same tribe and yet they spoke the same language. This was fortunate for the little captive girl. When Sacajawea was eighteen summers, Charbono took her for his second wife.

"Char-bono was engaged as an interpreter and guide to Captains Lewis and Clark. It was understood that Sacajawea would go with them. They set out up the Missouri in the Time of Many Rains. She was the only woman in this party of men. In the Time of New Leaves, she—"

"Wait!" the Dark Hair said. She turned to McCloud as everyone looked at her, frowning, wondering why she had interrupted the storyteller. "You have left something out," Eve went on, holding her husband's arm.

"Don't interrupt, Eve," McCloud warned. "How can you do this?"

Norman Tallfeather looked the Dark Hair in the eye while asking Suncloud, "She is not happy with my story?"

"Steven . . . McCloud," Eve said, still touching his arm. "He has left something out. Don't you know what it is that he has forgotten to say?"

"What?" he said, feeling embarrassed as everyone kept frowning Eve's way, and irritated that she had used his first name.

"The baby," Eve said to McCloud. "He forgot Sacajawea's baby."

"She had one?" McCloud asked, thinking perhaps she was right. "Can you add something to Tallfeather's story that he does not know?"

"Yes, I can. Sacajawea was eighteen or nineteen years old when she gave Charbonneau a baby boy."

In Shoshoni, Suncloud related this bit of news to Tallfeather. He was excited, asking the Dark Hair to please finish the story, he did not know this part, and he looked around the circle, ordering everyone to stop their stupid frowning at once. The Dark Hair had something important to add to his story.

Now all eyes were glued on Eve, and she looked to McCloud for support and a guide in translating, feeling shy now that she had gained the attention of the circle of smiling, listening people.

"In Lewis's journals he wrote about Sacajawea, who delivered a fine baby boy," Eve related with McCloud translating. "This was the first child Sacajawea had borne and her labor was very hard. In the Time of Many Rains"—Eve smiled over to Tallfeather in respect—"Sacajawea went with them with her baby on her back; she was the only woman in this party of men. In the Time of Ripening Leaves they camped near the Yellowstone River. Sacajawea's great courage and alertness saved parts of a boat's cargo, and there was much danger to herself."

Eve turned to her husband. "How do you say 'deep summer' in your language?"

He looked at her for several moments before he said, "The Teton say Moon of Black Cherries."

Eve nodded and went on.

"In the Moon of Black Cherries, the party was nearing Three Forks in Montana, when Sacajawea saw that they were in her home country, and they camped at the spot where she had been captured. Sacajawea became their guide and it was hard going through the mountains. She knew the way to her home tribe, and she marched ahead of the party, catching sight of some of her people on horseback."

Eve laughed ebulliently. "At once Sacajawea began to dance for joy. At last, supplied with horses, the expedition set out for the Columbia, then down that river to the seashore. She had traveled a long way to see the Great Waters and the monstrous fish, the whale."

Eve paused, as did Tallfeather, and they all looked at her, wanting to know what happened next. Excited faces were turned her way and the storyteller's. She blushed, looking at Tallfeather, then at McCloud.

"Tell him to relate the rest, my husband," Eve pleaded. "I'm afraid I have it all jumbled up and cannot tell it as well as Tallfeather."

Tallfeather shrugged, looked around, wondering who knew the rest, and McCloud cleared his throat. "Tallfeather is weary. I will tell the rest."

Norman Tallfeather, who seemed to be afflicted with an unidentified illness, smiled and took his leave of the engrossed and fascinated listeners.

"You know the story?" Eve asked McCloud. When he nodded, she punched his arm. "Why didn't you say so?"

"I did not know the parts that you knew. Now I

will tell the parts that I know." He inclined his handsome head graciously.

"Good. I am listening"—she smiled around at everybody—"as are the rest of us."

Eve felt so happy to be a part of all these people who spoke various Indian dialects and even Spanish. It was like paradise for her.

"The returning expedition reached the Mandan Indian villages on the Missouri. Lewis and Clark paid Charbonneau for his services and discharged him. His wife, Sacajawea, received nothing." Suncloud looked down into his wife's frowning eyes. "Charbonneau had bought Sacajawea, so she was his woman. Lewis and Clark were appreciative of Sacajawea's services, however, and wrote a very nice letter to Charbonneau."

"Yes?" Eve asked, smiling into McCloud's eyes. "What did this letter contain?"

"The letter said that Charbonneau had gained their friendship, Lewis's and Clark's. Sacajawea, who accompanied them on the long and dangerous trek to the Pacific Ocean and back, was deserving of a greater reward than they had in their power to give her. They were very fond of her little son also. Lewis and Clark had said, 'If you wish to live with the white people, and will come to me, I will give you a piece of land and furnish you with horses, cows and hogs.' "

McCloud shrugged, saying, "That is all."

"Well," Eve said, "I have a bit more to add to that. It seems that a man named Brackenridge wrote a journal."

"What did it say?" McCloud was desirous to know, for he loved to hear of stories that contained letters, journals, and manuscripts.

"In Brackenridge's journal, he wrote: 'We had on board a Frenchman named Charbonneau, with his wife, an Indian woman of the Snake Nation, both of whom accompanied Lewis and Clark to the Pacific, and were of great service. The woman, a good creature of a mild and gentle disposition, was greatly attached to the whites, whose manners and dress she tried to imitate, but she had become sickly and longed to revisit her native country; her husband, who had spent many years among the Indians, also had become weary of civilized life.'

"And then a fur trader wrote in his journal: 'This evening the wife of Charbonneau, a Snake squaw, died of a putrid fever aged abt. twenty-five years. She was the best woman in the fort. She left a fine infant girl.'

"This fur trader, Luttig, was appointed guardian of the two children, but later his name was crossed out and that of William Clark substituted. After Charbonneau passed away, the court appointed William Clark guardian to the infant children of Charbonneau, a boy of about the age of ten, and Lisette Charbonneau, a girl about one year old."

All of a sudden Many Stars stood up. "Sacajawea is not dead. She still lives."

Eve gasped, as did many of the other women in the group of rapt listeners. As she stared into the camp's blaze, a myriad of ghosts swarmed before Eve's eyes, ghosts of the wilderness, of many other places, heroes and cowards, honest men and scoundrels, Indians in war paint, heroines, all haunting and unforgettable—but in front of them all stood the one ghost she could never avoid:

The past. It always came up to meet you.

Eve shook her head and listened.

"How do you know this?" McCloud asked his sister as everyone began to speculate on this strange possibility.

"I have seen her." Many Stars awed everyone in the audience.

Now Many Stars had a story to tell of the vision she had had after meeting the legendary Sacajawea. "Tell us what you have seen?" they all wanted to know; even Tallfeather came out of his tipi upon hearing all the commotion.

"Yes," he said, sitting down once again. "Tell us of your vision."

"She still lives," said Many Stars. "And she will have a monument set up bearing her name. She will be greatly respected by the whites. She is a great woman and her name will go down in history. But this is a mystery and by the time she is recognized fully and given all the credit due her, we will be very old or dead, as will Sacajawea."

Utah George looked at Many Stars, and to his way of thinking and feeling, she too was a great woman, one who had seen a vision that would reach far into the future. The Shoshonis and Tetons knew well the great strength that comes of visions, and the *wakan witshasha,* the shamans, grew very powerful from seeing them.

They were all lucky to have heard this enchanting and informative story, Utah thought, and especially Many Stars's wonderful vision.

McCloud clapped his hands. "That is all for stories this night." He whispered into Eve's ear: "This has made me feel very romantic. Has this affected you the same way?"

"Oh, yes," Eve said, rising with her husband and disappearing with him into the dark of the moon.

They paused in their walk, and she held out her arms to him. McCloud slipped into her embrace, and they held each other closely. A couple came by and they broke apart, McCloud nodding to them while they had passed.

"Do you want a child?" he asked when they were alone and he was cupping his face in her hands.

She looked into his beautiful night-darkened eyes. "Someday . . . perhaps."

This was said so softly that McCloud almost did not hear the words.

He took her into his arms and she went willingly, pressing herself against his lean hardness. McCloud touched his forehead to hers and rubbed his straight nose against her smaller, slightly upturned one.

"Children would be nice," she murmured, smiling and kissing him gently at first, then with greater passion.

"There is no telling how many we might have," he said into her ear, running his hand over her ribs, cupping a breast.

She sighed with pleasure and moved against him. He turned her with a groan, dragging her to the grassy ground and fondling her sweet curves as he undressed her swiftly.

"Yes," she whispered after she got back her breath, putting her legs about his waist, savoring the sensation of his bare body. "No telling."

He chuckled softly, saying, "I think storytelling appeals to you."

"Of course. So do you." Rubbing him to her, she moved sensuously against him.

Smoothing her hands over his hips, Eve caressed his firm buttocks. "I have wanted to be with you for hours. The time has passed slowly," she whispered in his ear.

McCloud moaned deeply, passionately, as her tongue followed the curve where his dark hair waved around his ear.

"Perhaps a *few* children," she said tauntingly.

He chuckled into her ear, beginning to thrust. "Then let's get started and see what comes of it."

Their heat grew so strong, it could have melted the deepest snow. They were like wild creatures as they mated, the surging river in Eve's veins changing from blood to fire. A new, swelling fire flowed into her limbs, then all through her, pulsing. The storm inside her sent lightning and thunder to her lower region.

Eve and McCloud were giving themselves, each unto the other, in a way so wondrous that Eve never could have dreamed this. It was a way that truly meant they belonged to each other.

"Oh, my—children—" Eve said with a sigh as McCloud went deeper. "They do not matter just now. Only this does. Only your love, Big Chief McCloud."

She laughed. And he joined her laughter, rolling her over and over, her leg now lying over his hip. On their sides, he resumed the thrusting.

Eve closed her eyes as he gave her even more pleasure. Bending, he lowered his lips to her breast, tugging gently as the lithe movements of his hips, his tongue, his murmured endearments all brought her to her peak.

Ecstasy that was almost painful tore through her in throbbing beats and she buried her face in his shoulder to silence her cry so that anyone passing their lovers' sanctuary for an evening stroll would hear nothing.

Eve and McCloud half dozed in the grass, rousing to kiss or stroke each other, then drifting again into a light sleep wrapped in a misty languor as a dazzling array of millions of stars arched over them.

Kicking Wolf came sneaking out of McCloud's tipi, closing the flap, then, studying his surroundings to see if anyone was about, he pressed himself close to the shadows and became one with the darkness as he crept slowly, stealthfully, away.

Chapter Twenty-two

Campfires flickered before the first crack of dawn. They appeared one by one until a line of fire edged both sides of the Snake River at Henry's Fork for many miles.

Breakfasts were hurriedly prepared and eaten. Tent openings were tossed back, skin flaps flung over the slanting bark roofs of the lean-tos, and the weekly cleaning began. Slab or dirt floors were swept with broken branches. A few of the men had fashioned brooms from grass brushes traded from the Indians and these were swung in a wide, wasted motion by inept male hands. Blankets and skins were draped over nearby bushes to air and be rid of crawling bugs. Supplies were checked and the gold balanced to see if there was enough to pay for the following week's stores and the anticipated betting on the race, the race that Scar-Face was sure to attend on the approaching Sunday, accompanied by his best friend and gambling partner, Pierre Dessine.

This was also washday. Bodies glistened in the sun as men standing waist-deep in the river stripped off their clothes and scrubbed them on the rocks beside the river. They immediately put back on the faded shirts and pants and the warm wind dried them shortly thereafter.

Knives, always sharp, were honed again to trim ragged beards and hair. A few men even shaved. The more fortunate ones possessed extra clothing.

Up- and downriver the mountain men, like the trappers and traders, took to the trails that led to Teton Taggart's Saloon and Trading Post. Though some owned horses or mules, most of the men walked in congenial groups. They joked and pounded each other on the back as they bragged of last week's take.

The men shouted and asked one another how they were going to bet, mentioning that almost every man in the country must be there at Taggart's.

Pawnee Joe had his ears peeled, listening for what news Carl Hepler had about Scar-Face.

"Heard Scar-Face's not a very popular man right now," Hepler mused. "That mining scheme of his cost the boys a lot of labor and money. Well, they're going to hafta leave pretty soon. No more Indian trouble around here."

"Yeah?" said Joe, waiting to hear more, all ready to go and report this back to McCloud.

Carl Hepler looked at the half-breed Pawnee Joe with a hint of a smirk. "When did you come up from Wild Thunder?"

"About a week ago. McCloud got himself hitched up with a white woman."

Carl said, "I'll hafta get myself down that way and see what the woman looks like. I wanta get me some things at his post anyway."

"She's real pretty, McCloud's wife is," Pawnee said, moving away from Carl because he wanted to be alone now and didn't want to reveal to Carl any more about McCloud. He had learned all he was going to hear about Scar-Face as far as he could tell by Carl's closed-mouthed attitude.

Pawnee Joe's eyes wandered to the cleared area around the saloon. The Nez Perce outcasts from Oregon country were standing in a tight group near the outhouse. A new company of American Fur greenhorns came in with a full supply of goods. Pawnee Joe was thinking of going into the dangerous lands to the north of the Snake, controlled by the Blackfeet but rich in fur.

First, Joe told himself, he had to get back to report to McCloud the news he'd heard about Scar-Face.

The sun was high in the sky as a murmur from the restless crow told Joe that something was happening. He frowned when he saw Scar-Face ride in early, nosing his horse importantly through the men until he came to the door of the saloon.

Joe didn't like that demon Scar-Face. It was common knowledge that he was a cheat and a murderer and a woman defiler. He and his partner, Pierre Dessine, from Fort Robidoux, were not very well liked by most men, and still they slithered around like snakes; Joe wondered who would finally kill them. Maybe they'd do themselves in by their own greedy, murderin' hands.

Pawnee Joe's eyes widened then. What the hell was that greaser doin'!

Trotting beside the mounted Scar-Face was a young Indian girl. A rope was tied to her waist, and occasionally Scar-Face would yank the rope as if to prove he had her as well trained as the horse. Her head was bowed as the man pulled her along.

Joe sidled up to a trapper, asked him, "You know what's going on, man?"

The bearded trapper said, "Wagh! Few weeks back she had appeared at a camp and the men had fed her. No one knows how Scar-Face came to possess her, but she follows that nasty greaser from camp to camp on foot and does his bidding. Has ta, else he just might kill her."

Bart was one of the few white men who could communicate with the Indians in their own language. He had once asked her what she was called, but the girl wouldn't answer him.

"She never told any white man her true name," Bart told Pawnee Joe.

"Hey, Scar-Face!" a man yelled from the crowd. "That's some horse you got there!"

The girl wore a yellow dress that was many sizes too large for her, and the hem had been roughly cut with a knife. The waist was held with a bright red sash. Around her throat she wore a necklace of blue beads.

"*Oui*—you have got a yellow mare," shouted an accented voice which Pawnee Joe thought belonged to Pierre Dessine.

"Yellow mare! Yellow mare!" the men chanted, and that became the greaser's name for the silent young Indian girl, he decided at once.

Pawnee Joe mused to himself, "I remember the story of Many Stars back in Wild Thunder, how she got her name. Scar-Face hit her so hard one day that she saw many stars. And she kept the designation, still afraid of being called Honna, her real name."

Teton Taggart came out of his saloon when he heard the shouting. When he saw that Scar-Face had already arrived, he beckoned through the doorway. Another young Indian girl appeared. Sweet Water's family moved a little closer to the saloon and watched her with expressionless faces.

Since Taggart had taken Sweet Water as his woman, he also had to support the few remaining members of her family. As long as Sweet Water pleased him, they would be fed and even allowed to drink the dregs in the saloon glasses. These cast-out Cheyenne River Sioux had lost their former pride and natural gaiety. They survived by any means.

Teton Taggart pushed his girl to the starting line of the dirt track used each Sunday for horse racing. Sweet Water's lavender white-woman's dress made her easily distinguishable from the other Indian girl. Both were barely in their teens. They stood quietly and each avoided looking at the other while the gamblers made their wagers and swore and pushed to get a better view.

Another trader from the Teton Forks fired his pistol to start the race. For a short distance the two Indian girls paced each other; then Yellow Mare spurted. She ran as though the ground were afire and she was afraid to touch it. Sweet Water fell farther and farther back. As her steps became uneven, she almost fell. Men stomped and howled as they waved encouragement to their choices.

Yellow Mare was conditioned by miles of running behind Scar-Face's horse along the trails that wound through the foothills. Sweet Water's life in the confines of the saloon had weakened her, or perhaps she did not have the will to win.

Scar-Face boasted to his friend Pierre, "I will take her, Yellow Mare, to Great Eagle and receive the prize of the Golden Tears."

"Oui. Well and good. But you do not know her real name."

"That is even better, my friend. She, the nameless one, will be taken for the lost child, Mist Smoke, and I will get the pouch of gold for bringing her to Great Eagle before he passes on."

"You have told me how many times you have tried this trick in the past and it didn't work. What makes you believe it will work this time?" asked Pierre.

Scar-Face told him again, "She looks more like the woman Eve than the others."

"You know yourself that War Shirt has said Great Eagle will know her when he looks into her eyes. Why don't you just go and get Eve Michaels out of Wild Thunder?"

"And as I said before, Suncloud will kill us before we even ride down that hill into Wild Thunder. Why not try another fake? What have I to lose?"

"Your neck for lying so much, that's what," Pierre said. "How many times do you think Great Eagle will allow you to bring another Indian maiden to him before he catches on to what you are doing?"

Scar-Face raised a black eyebrow. "And just what am I doing? I only try to help Great Eagle to be reunited with his little granddaughter before he goes for the Deep Sleep. What harm can there be in trying to help an old man?" Scar-Face laughed, sounding sinister even to his own ears.

"If only we had met War Shirt before Eve Michaels got away that day at Fort Robidoux. Then we would have known what a prize she really is."

"War Shirt has told others to search for Eve Michaels. We have to get there first, before another man thinks of the same plan I've been devising. To use a fake princess."

"Oh, I do not know if there could be another man with the same devious ideas of yours," Pierre told Scar-Face.

"Look, my little Yellow Mare is winning. See, Pierre, she is a winner. How can we lose with such as her?"

Yellow Mare crossed the finish line far ahead of her opponent. Curses of disappointment and shouts of triumph echoed from the hillsides. Scar-Face had won his bet with Taggart, but since the winners treated the losers, a fine drunken time was had to the profit of the saloon keeper.

Pawnee Joe watched the whole sad affair and shook his head with disapproval at the scene. He realized that most of the men thought the Indians were less than human. He had come to Teton Taggart's on this day to make sure the girls were not harmed by mountain men with too much drink in their bellies. He could not believe how far this stupid event had gone, using women as horses.

And, too, he'd wanted to see if the rumors about Scar-Face and Pierre Dessine being in the area of the Teton Forks was true.

Joe looked one last time to the drunken revelers pawing the young Indian girls. If only he could—he shook his head. He would only get himself killed.

Unconscious men obstructed the trail as Pawnee Joe rode out, and he looked down without pity as one along the way would stagger to his feet with a sick moan and another stood vomiting out his guts.

"Wanta drink?" a man asked from the ground, holding a bottle up to Joe.

"Nope. I go to smoke the peace pipe with my friend."

"Yer an Injun too, a dirty half-breed . . . I jes' know it," he muttered. Then he passed out, his face pressed into the dirt of the trail.

As Joe rode on, he kept pausing to look over one shoulder at the saloon and when he turned to face his journey, tears blurred his vision.

He would not forget Yellow Mare and Sweet Water, the yellow dress and the blue beads. . . .

Chapter Twenty-three

McCloud could not understand what was keeping Pawnee Joe. He should have been back from his journey up into the Teton Forks. He stood watching the winding road, looking for the sabino that Joe rode.

His Arapaho brothers had not been sighted along the ridge, and he wondered about them too, hoping that the Wild Ones would not be planning war with the Greasy Long Hairs and the Crows.

He smiled as he thought of Eve. She was not far away, only in the back room of the trading post, where she was sewing curtains, bustling about doing various chores. She loved that part of the store, wanting to make it look pretty. He liked his tipi. She liked . . . houses.

He wore buckskin trousers and a homespun shirt, the shirt she had made for him. He smiled, feeling like a husband, a real husband, for the first time.

He would build Eve a nice cabin someday. Perhaps they would move to the one in the mountains. He could always have his tipi out back, move it there.

As he walked about the dusty paths of Wild

Thunder, speaking to children as they ran up to him, he found himself looking for Kicking Wolf. He had not seen him for two days. Talk went that Kicking Wolf had sent his woman back to her people, and he wondered about that too.

McCloud surveyed his surroundings with eyes accustomed to spotting dangers that others might miss. He was nearing Quiet Doe's tipi, smelling her good cooking, when one of the Wolves ran up to him. It was young Sings Wolf, and he was very excited.

"What is it, Sings Wolf?"

"Our Arapaho brothers . . . they come." He could hardly speak and his excited words were jumbled together. "They spoke to Skunk Cabbage and he says . . . says that the Bad Faces are after them."

"You mean the Greasy Long Hairs?" McCloud tried to correct Sings Wolf.

"No!"

"What, then?" He felt like shaking the lad. "Tell me what you mean?"

"The Bad Faces are"—he gulped—"are after them, the Arapaho. I try to tell you, but you do not listen. The Greasy Long Hairs have gone into the land of the Teton."

He calmed the lad with a pat on his back. "Go, Sings Wolf, go and find Utah George, Frog Catcher, and Tames Wild Horses—and alert the dog soldiers."

"They already know. The dogs, I mean!" Sings Wolf shouted, casting glances over his shoulder, afraid that the Bad Faces were going to attack them and surround Wild Thunder.

"You must calm yourself, Sings Wolf. You will

never become a great warrior of the Wolves if you are so afraid that you pee your buckskins.

"*Who* knows?" McCloud asked in a deep, gentle voice.

"The . . . dog soldiers."

"Good. You have done well this day, Sings Wolf. Now," McCloud said, laying his hands on the boy's shoulders, "go and do as I said."

"Yes. I will alert Frog Catcher and Utah George." He spun around to do as McCloud ordered. "Should I alert anyone else that . . . that just perhaps there might be trouble?"

"Yes. Go and tell the women." He grinned, easing the boy's excitement and tension. "They need to know in case there's to be any trouble."

"I will run as swiftly as the . . . the ground squirrel!"

After Sings Wolf had run off, McCloud checked his rifle, loaded it, and made sure he had plenty of powder in his pouch—in case of trouble. The band of wandering Arapaho would need help.

Eve had cleaned out the back room to the store, sewn the curtains, polished the old cherrywood furniture she cherished, scrubbed the rough plank flooring, put some dishes on the bent shelves—then stood back to survey her thorough housework.

Something was missing, she mused.

Ah. It needs a few Indian trinkets. McCloud's manly things to make it look not just pretty but . . . handsome? Was that the word? No. More . . . ah, masculine. Yes. That was it.

She rushed off to his tipi, wanting to get back in time for lunch, when he would join her.

Eve wondered what all the commotion was about as she saw the Wolves running about. Man stuff, she thought, and chuckled. Acting like . . . Indians. Yes. *Wild* Indians.

As she entered McCloud's tipi, Eve surveyed the interior of the conical dwelling again, remembering their wedding night, and her heart thudded.

She had never looked around as she was doing then. She giggled. She had had other matters on her mind that night.

Eve walked around, touching things that belonged to McCloud—Steven. Suncloud. She shivered with delight.

There, his quiver with arrows. The arrows were striped with colored paint to mark ownership.

She touched his medicine bag carefully. Ah. This was the special parfleche for sacred items that represented things seen in the owner's visions. She would not look inside. But had he experienced visions? He must have. She smiled again.

The shield. Some battle shields were painted with pictures from visions, which offered spiritual protection. She stared at the picture of a . . . turtle?

For a moment a door from the past opened up and then slammed shut on her memory.

It hurts so very much to remember.

She looked back at the highly decorated and very colorful shields. What did the turtle mean? Had he seen visions of this?

Eve felt strange vibrations and moved away from the shield with the turtle on it. Something about this object made her remember her dreams and her own past, something that had happened long before. But this could not be, she deduced, walking away from the shield, erasing the vivid and striking sensations.

It hurts to remember. Was there something about winter?

No. Do not try to think of long ago. *Cease!*

She centered her attention on the tipi itself and what it contained. The Indians had deep appreciation for the tipi. Secure, mobile, and comfortable, it was looked upon by nomadic hunters as a good mother who sheltered and protected her children when they were not off on their buffalo hunts.

Buffalo . . . buffalo . . . summer.

Here and now, think and dwell upon this.

Eve was learning about colors too. To a Crow, black was the color of victory, while to a Sioux it symbolized night. Red was the hue of sunset or thunder for the Dakota Sioux. To an Arapaho, red meant man, blood, or earth. The Plains Indians used a variety of natural substances. Blue, for example, could be derived from dried duck manure mixed with water, yellow from bullberries or buffalo gallstones, black from burnt wood, green from plants, and white from certain clays. These pigments were often mixed with water-thinned natural glues, which helped the colors adhere to the surfaces. Pigments were applied with various instruments—one "brush" per hue—made of chewed cottonwood, willow sticks, porous buffalo bone.

A scene whirled in Eve's head for seconds in time . . . a woman crushing bullberries to make yellow dye. She had a pleasant face. The scene blurred and Eve felt dizzy for a few seconds.

Do not think of it, Eve Michaels.

Look, look around you. You are here now, in Wild Thunder. . . . Ah, yes, let me see.

Was Steven McCloud a war leader, she asked herself as she stood in the middle of the tipi next to a beautifully crafted cradleboard, wondering what it was doing there. Perhaps it had belonged to Whispering Bells?

She looked up to the smoke flaps that could be adjusted to retain heat or to ventilate, then down to the buffalo-paunch cooking pot that might contain the day's soup of buffalo meat, wild turnips, and wild onions—and she thought instantly of Whispering Bells.

Whispering Bells . . . she had to visit the girl that day.

Now her eyes fell upon the tipi lining; it was an additional layer of skin, brightly painted in red, orange, purple, turquoise blue, and gold.

Gold . . . yellow . . . dye prepared from bullberries. Great . . . great . . . what?

Move around, Eve, keep moving. Don't stand still and allow your mind to wander too far.

Her interested gaze went down to the bedding that was rolled and stored during the day.

She felt it then. Someone knew she would be coming there today.

Everything suddenly began to whirl: the quiver with arrows, the medicine bag, parfleches, shield, buffalo paunch, wooden bow . . . and her eyes were snapped back to the tipi lining.

Eve felt quite dizzy.

Colors blurred and spun together.

She whirled with them and fell to the floor.

Holding her hand to her head, she looked up. Then over to the backrest . . . she had missed it . . . the Plains Indian's easy chair.

Her gaze caught instantly on a bit of yellow cloth
. . . blue beads.

Again she thought she might faint.

Get it. Touch it. What is it?

Pull it out; see what it is.

Now. Go ahead—*look!*

Steadying herself, she walked to the bright material and tugged.

Her dream, mixed with the reality of Maggie's
and her brothers' deaths, came to her.

She pulled out the yellow material, seeing that it
had been severed roughly, jaggedly, with a knife
. . . and then the blue beads fell across her arms.

Eve shivered like a person with marsh fever. A
hush as complete as the quietness of deep sleep
descended upon her.

Yellow cloth . . . blue beads . . .

No . . . not McCloud. He could not have been the
one to slay her brothers.

Chapter Twenty-four

Suncloud walked back to his tipi to fetch his weapons, tossed the flap open, and stepped inside.

At once he felt a presence that he thought at first was strange but was actually very familiar.

The scent.

Eve had been there, he told himself. He could feel her. Knew she had stepped in and out not long before.

But why? She had been at the store, she had come looking for him, he thought, and wondered why, why here?

Tangled emotions dwelled within him. He had no time to sort them out. Eve could not be far, and he knew something was not right.

He had to make a decision. Time was of the essence.

The Crow were chasing the Arapaho into Wild Thunder. There was going to be a battle—or else the Bad Faces were going to pit their strongest against Wild Thunder's!

All the women, children, and old men of Wild Thunder were running wildly about the encampment. Suncloud was gathering his forces; he appeared handsome and formidable with his bare chest, war paint, and buckskins.

The Crow were coming!

Wild Thunder's Arapaho brothers were in need of aid. Even though they had rejected the people of Wild Thunder and gone out on their own, they were coming back, their hearts and souls crying for help.

Suncloud stood at the front of the line, a stalwart warrior, his head proud, his rifle at his side, his feathered lance in the air. The horse Wind tossed his head, ready to do battle, his hooves dancing in the dust.

Eve saw Suncloud atop the hill, his dark hair loose and blowing away from his face, and turned away.

She was going.

First she had to find Maggie, knowing she would have to plead with her to leave. Once Maggie heard the truth, she would come willingly, thought Eve, hoping she wasn't mistaken.

"What is the problem?" Suncloud asked Skunk Cabbage. "What do you say? Are they friends or enemies?"

Skunk Cabbage smiled.

"When two tribes chase one herd of wapiti, Suncloud, they cannot be anything else but enemies."

"Ho! Surely there are elk enough here for all the Indians in these hills."

"They take from the Arapaho; their children are starving."

"Then we must fight the Bad Faces?"

"So it seems, brother. Perhaps only one against one."

"We shall see," answered Suncloud.

Suncloud and the men of Wild Thunder were equally convinced that there was but one way out of the difficulty—they advanced upon the opposing party at a run. The Bad Faces, of course, had seen Suncloud's party and their intent, and they made it their business to meet them halfway.

Both bands halted as though by command, a long bow-shot apart, and stood with weapons ready, eyeing the other warily.

Suncloud frowned. Here we are, he thought, relatively few, preparing to dispute with an equally insignificant body the right to slaughter some few units of their multitudes.

The renegade chief of the Bad Faces stood forward, a giant of a man, his arms and chest gashed by the ordeals of some ritual. The sun dance? Suncloud wondered.

"Why do the men of Wild Thunder interfere with the hunting of the Bad Faces?" Aching Feet asked. "Have they painted for war?"

Skunk Cabbage spoke for Suncloud. "The braves of Wild Thunder know best whether there is war; it is with those who interfere with the Wild Ones who would hunt and live free."

"There is war only if the Wild Ones make it," asserted Aching Feet. "The Bad Faces have pursued these elk for a day. Let the Wild Ones and the men of Wild Thunder retire to their own devices and await there the coming of the elk."

"Since when have the renegade Bad Faces said what the men of Wild Thunder shall do?" flashed Suncloud.

Aching Feet surveyed the young men of Wild Thunder before replying. "I see that you have one who is more white than the rest of you," remarked Aching Feet. "He wears a single braid and a white man's shirt the color of the sky."

Suncloud glanced around at the men of Wild Thunder. He turned back to Aching Feet, his voice cold. "There is not one more white than the rest of us. And many wear these blue shirts, as you call them." Suncloud's eyes narrowed with anger.

"Send him out here and let him show the warriors if he has strength in those wiry arms. Tell him to lay aside his weapons, all save his knife, and Mahtotopah will do the same."

Mahtotopah, Suncloud thought, Cheyenne for Two Bears. Among them were not only the Crow but the Cheyenne renegades, then.

Aching Feet continued. "If the Long Braid comes, Mahtotopah will tear out the man's heart with his fingers and eat it before the men of Wild Thunder. But the Long Braid will not come. He is afraid."

The braves who could understand Aching Feet's words looked at one another, trying to pick out the one the Bad Faces' leader had selected to fight. They shook their heads slowly with wonder, seeing no man of Wild Thunder more white than the other.

"We will all dismount," shouted Suncloud.

And they all did, even Aching Feet. He came around his horse and faced Suncloud once again.

"Two Bears is a strong warrior," Aching Feet added. "He has counted more coups than any man of his tribe."

"I am not more white, but I will fight," said Utah George, surprising the other braves. Putting down his rifle and shot-pouch, he pulled his blue shirt over his head.

Many of the men of Wild Thunder had worn blue shirts or leather shirts, so who could have guessed which man Aching Feet had been speaking of? They all shrugged.

Still, Suncloud hesitated. As it happened, the Bad Faces had never seen the big, wiry man Utah at hand's-grips with an enemy.

"Suncloud need not be concerned," Skunk Cabbage said, smiling. "Our brother Utah is the strongest warrior for this kind of fight. Perhaps Aching Feet saw this."

"Aching Feet waits," proclaimed the leader of the Bad Faces. "The Long Braid is not in a hurry to die."

Then Utah George walked forward as soon as his opponent had given up his weapons—except the knife. Utah's legs were strong. His belly was flat as he walked forward. Not one ounce of fat lay over his torso, nor lapped in creases on his flanks. Only those who had seen Utah in action knew that beneath the layer of taut, wiry skin were muscles of inhuman strength. His calm exterior was a mask for a will that'd never yielded to adversity.

The Bad Faces greeted Utah with guttural laughter, and the men of Wild Thunder pulled long faces. Who could blame them, after contrasting the outward appearance of the two warriors? Two Bears was the biggest Indian they'd ever seen, well over six feet in his moccasins, with the shoulders of an ox, clean-thewed, bronze-flanked, his legs like tree trunks. He crouched as Utah approached and drew his knife, circling on the balls of his feet, the keen blade poised across his stomach in position to strike or ward off, as need arose.

Utah, on the other hand, had not even drawn his

knife, and his hands hung straight beside him. He slouched along with no attempt at a fighting posture, his whole body exposed to Two Bears's knife. The Bad Faces passed from laughter to gibes and humorous remarks, and Aching Feet decided that they were right in their judgment, for his best fighter commenced a kind of dancing progress around Utah. But Two Bears never came to close quarters, only maintaining a constant menace with his knife.

Utah, affecting his customary manner of stolid indifference, turned swiftly on the balls of his feet as Two Bears circled him. But Utah made no effort to stay the quick rushes by which his opponent gradually drew nearer and nearer. This play went on for so long that Suncloud's men commenced to fume with rage and humiliation while the Bad Faces were convulsed with laughter. Suddenly Two Bears decided to end the play. He bounded at Utah with concentrated energy and struck so fast that the bystanders couldn't follow it.

But Utah could. He came awake as though by magic. His calm attitude vanished. His lanky frame became instinct, filled with a vitality that flowed inexhaustibly from depths that had never been plumbed.

Two Bears struck. Steel flashed again in a wide arc, and the knife soared high in the air and fell, point down, in the sod, twenty feet away. Now there were just two heaving bodies. Utah held the man by one wrist and a forearm. Two Bears was struggling with every ounce of strength to break one of the grips so that he might seize his foe by the throat. All at once Two Bears stooped his head and fastened his teeth in Utah's shoulder.

Blood spurted from the wound and a quiver con-

vulsed Utah's body. But he refused to be diverted
from his purpose. Slowly, inexorably, he applied his
pressure. And slowly, inevitably, Two Bears's
straining sinews yielded to him; his left arm was
forced back, back, back.

Now there was a loud crack. Two Bears yelped
like an animal in great pain. The arm fell limp, and
with the swift ferocity of a cat Utah pounced on the
man's throat.

The jaws still fastened in Utah's throbbing shoulder yielded to that awful pressure. A single gasping
cry reached the men of Wild Thunder. Two Bears's
head sank back, and by superhuman effort Utah
heaved the man's body at arm's length over his
head. He held it there a moment, his eyes on the Bad
Faces who had laughed at him. Then he flung it at
them as though it had been a sack of corn.

Two Bears's body twisted through the air, struck
the ground, and rolled over into a huddle of inani-
mate limbs.

Utah shook himself, turned on his heel, and
walked slowly back to Suncloud and the others.

"Ho," he remarked mildly. "That made me work
up a sweat."

The Bad Faces, now carried away by the spectacle of their greatest warrior's end, abandoned all
thought of restraint and charged Suncloud's men.
Bow strings twanged. But the men of Wild Thunder
were not unprepared. Suncloud had fetched a dozen
of Pawnee Joe's rifles, and taught his warriors how
to use them. They were able to meet the enemy with
a devastating discharge that brought the Bad Faces
up short. The enemy had no fight left in them and
fled across the hills, pursued by the fleetest young
men of Wild Thunder's band.

They were left with the pleasant task of reaping a full measure of elk-meat, and the Wild Ones went out to fetch the meat.

The Bad Faces turned one last time to give battle—and the chase was on.

Eve couldn't find Maggie. She had no idea where her friend had gone. Maggie was hard to locate sometimes, making Eve wonder what the girl could be up to. It must be Tames Wild Horses that Maggie spent so much of her time with. She had to find her, tell her that they were living with a murderer in their midst—perhaps more than one. Tames Wild Horses? Had he been with McCloud the day her brothers had been slain?

Unable to stop herself from looking back at the awesome spectacle of man and beast, Eve turned slowly, then more quickly as she felt the presence of many more.

Her jaw dropped.

There, along the ridge, a group of impressive-looking Arapaho seated on spotted ponies turned to glimpse something behind them.

Suddenly Eve heard whoops and yells, saw the Arapaho spill down over the ridge and ride toward town. Another line of Indians, right behind the Arapaho, were giving chase. These must be the Crow she'd heard about. Their faces were painted in wild colors, and they looked to Eve like evil masks. Some of the faces appeared savagely angry. Some had long, greasy hair and no paint.

The band of Arapaho scattered to the four corners of town. Suncloud and his men now spurred their mounts into action, charging into the attacking Crow and Greasy Long Hairs. They were being chased right back out of town, away from the threatened Arapaho. Suncloud rode at the lead, shouting in a shrill voice *Hai, Hai, Hai!* with rifle held arm's length above his head.

What a man, Eve thought, then—*what am I thinking?*

Having seen enough, Eve turned away. She had other matters on her mind, like finding a way to leave this town and Suncloud forever. She had the damaging evidence in her possession. Suncloud must not learn why she was leaving Wild Thunder. He might kill her too, just as he killed Hank and her brothers.

Eve hid the yellow material and the blue beads. She then made her way back to the store, where she usually slept. The tipi was too primitive for her; she didn't always sleep there. Now she never would again, not ever.

As Eve walked away from the noise of running people, she began to feel that something was very wrong.

She felt that someone was in trouble, someone was unable to fend for—she had no idea if the one in trouble was male or female, human or creature.

Frowning with concentration, she tried to pinpoint the area that the fear was coming from.

Then she heard the sound of a baby crying. *A baby is in great distress.* Her head turned this way and that. But where was the crying child?

The wailing did not sound contained, as if in a tipi. No. The sound was in the open, unprotected, vulnerable to whatever harm might come its way.

Eve's eyes flew wide.

There! A toddler wandering about, looking lost, crying his—or her—eyes out.

Eve turned her head a fraction of an inch and saw the runaway horse, the flying hooves thundering directly toward the confused, crying child.

She looked at the dangerous hooves. The child. She quickly made her decision.

Just as the horse was coming, and coming fast, she shot out, putting herself in grave danger. Grabbing the child, she spun with the precious bundle, hit the ground, rolled, her body protecting the toddler.

The sharp hoof struck her on her right shoulder, knocking her to the ground.

The danger passed, the thunder moving quickly away from them at an angle. She did not see a mounted figure going after the runaway horse.

Eve felt something warm and sticky flowing down her arm. But there was something even warmer, wonderfully warmer in her arms.

She had never held a small child before, and the feeling was wonderful. Her hand was cupped over the child's head, over hair, warm and silky. How good the clean hair smelled, a smell so foreign to Eve.

Suddenly Eve knew what she wanted in life—her own child.

She hugged the crying babe and cooed in a pretty voice, "You will do for a start. Who do you belong to, baby?" She saw that the toddler was naked.

At the sound of Eve's voice the baby stopped crying, but rubbed her face with her fist. She blinked shyly.

Eve gazed into the beautiful hazel-green eyes.

"You are a white child," Eve said, her voice soft and gentle.

The tiny tot smiled.

"You light up the town, baby," Eve murmured. That smile is worth a thousand jewels, Eve thought. And she looks so very familiar, something in those beautiful eyes.

Disregarding the blood and the pain in her shoulder, Eve held the child closer to her.

"Why, you're as light as a feather," Eve said, hefting the child an inch.

"That is her name," informed a voice behind her. "Is she not beautiful?"

Whispering Bells. And behind Whispering Bells stood Red Beads. The woman, slightly older than Eve, looked shy and embarrassed.

What a change from the eyes throwing darts at her several weeks ago, Eve thought.

"What is it?" Eve asked Whispering Bells. "What have I done?"

"Her child." Whispering Bells lifted her eyes to Red Beads, but she spoke to Eve. "You saved her child."

"Whose?" Eve blinked. *Surely she could not mean that she belongs to Red Beads?*

"Look to the hills," Whispering Bells said, drawing attention to where dust was settling. "The Arapaho are still and my father is speaking to them. The Bad Faces have fled. My father chased them away.

Eve blinked and looked over at Red Beads, eager to get back to the matter at hand.

Red Beads held out her arms. "You save Feather. Brave woman. You might have died. You need arm seen to. Give me child to hold."

Feather whined as if she didn't know Red Beads, and buried her face against Eve's throat.

"She no like." Red Beads pointed to herself, hung her head, looking very sad. "I her mother. No time to care for."

"I see." Eve then asked, "Who does care for Feather?"

"I go now. You take Feather to Pond Lily. She cares for her." Red Beads turned away, looked across her shoulder.

"Pond Lily cares for Feather?"

"Yes."

"Who is the—"

"I have much work must do now. Many want Red Beads now. Men excited from chase. Drink firewater. Eat much meat. Want women. Come to Red Beads and others."

"You are the—" She stopped herself. How could she say "bordello queen"?

Red Beads only nodded as she looked down at Eve's quickly moving hands.

Incredible, Eve thought. Red Beads had understood her. "Why are you so sad, Red Beads?"

"I know not sad. You have hurt arm. Go take care." Red Beads walked away. She stopped once to call back to Eve. *"Dark Hair brave woman!"*

Eve bit her lip and ducked her head. Everyone in the town must have heard that. Eve turned toward Pond Lily's tipi, Feather still in her arms.

She was right, for all eyes were fastened on her as she walked slowly with the beautiful child, blood all along her arm.

Looking down, Eve saw the blood all over her wrist; some of it was on the beaded wristband that had been a gift from *him,* the murderer!

She glanced up along her arm, saw more blood, and in her side vision noticed a blur moving toward her quickly as she passed out.

The last thing Eve heard was a baby crying.

Chapter Twenty-five

"Feather . . . falling . . . catch her."

Still wearing face paint, McCloud looked down at Eve as she murmured in her restless swoon. Many Stars had poured an herb potion between Eve's lips to relieve pain and the potion made her drowsy.

Whispering Bells hovered close. "Dark Hair is worried about Feather. Pond Lily caught Feather just as Eve was falling into a swoon."

McCloud placed a hand on Eve's brow, then glanced around the room Eve had fixed up in the back of the store.

"Who is Feather?" McCloud finally asked, his eyes searching faces.

"Child of Red Beads," said Many Stars.

Utah George's face was red as he looked at Suncloud and Many Stars looked at him. "Who is Feather's father?" asked Many Stars, blinking wide upon noticing the blood on Utah's shoulder as he favored it with his hand.

"You ask me?" McCloud said. "I have no idea who the father is. I don't even know who Feather is." He frowned at his own words.

Whispering Bells melted inconspicuously into the

back of the room, then silently turned to go purposefully out the door.

"Any one of you could be Feather's father," said Many Stars. "I have heard that she has been used by . . . by all of you men!"

"She knows who the father is."

McCloud's head whipped up. "Who said that?" He scanned the people in the room, coming to rest on Frog Catcher, then over to Utah George, on down several heads to Sings Wolf. "What are you all doing in here anyway?"

"Sound like a man from the south country." One-Arm chuckled as he moved to Eve's bed. Looking down upon her, he lovingly brushed the dark hair from her forehead.

"And who has taught you more English?" said McCloud to One-Arm.

The old man's eyes shifted and fell upon Eve.

"Ah"—murmured McCloud—"our good lady of the words."

"And Bible," chuckled One-Arm, nodding his head like an old woodpecker.

"She will be okay," said McCloud next as he turned to exit the stifling room holding too many people to be comfortable. "I have warriors to go and confer with."

"Of course, noble Suncloud," Many Stars said as she dipped low, a grin on her face.

"Where did you learn to curtsy like that?" McCloud snarled.

"Where do you think?" Many Stars snapped right back at her surly brother. "With *whom* do you think, *gata?*"

McCloud's brows came together angrily. She had called him "wildcat" in Spanish, Scar-Face's doing.

The devil greaser had taught Many Stars too much
when he had held her captive.

McCloud's voice held weight. "From now on you
are to be known only as Honna," he declared. "No
more Many Stars."

"Yes, my noble Indian lord." Many Stars did not
sweep him a bow this time.

From the back of the room came loud laughter.
As McCloud passed there on his way out, he glared
at Chara and ground out: "You, most of all, shut
your mouth."

"Ah." Chara shrugged as McCloud made his
angry exit. "He does not even know who Feather's
father is."

All eyes swung her way, facial expressions asking
the question of the day.

And one voiced it out loud as she sat up in her
sickbed. "Who is Feather's father?"

As the room cleared and Eve got a good look at
Chara's face, taking in the nasty grin, she knew who
Feather's father was.

He was the one who had murdered her brothers
in cold blood. Hers and Maggie's.

Eve's wound healed rapidly. During that time she
stayed in the back room of the trading post.
McCloud was too busy to come to see her, the
returning Arapaho who'd banished themselves
years earlier taking up most of his time.

Why was he staying away? Because he knew himself who Feather's father was?

Plenty of visitors came to Eve's lovely little room
to bring stew, soup, herbal concoctions, and foul-
tasting drinks, and Pond Lily brought Feather.

Feather played on Eve's bed, and Eve fashioned Feather a cornhusk doll and other toys she had learned how to make when she was just a little girl herself.

Eve frowned as she was beading a childlike creature onto a bag to hold some tiny toys.

I used to do this, long ago, when I was a child. But how could I have made Indian toys? I lived in St. Louis. Did an Indian woman or man live with my parents? Why do I have this strange feeling that I did not sit on a chair inside a room under a roof? I sat on a log outside with the sky for roof as I helped make toys.

"But no," Eve muttered to herself while Feather smiled up at her, "I lived in La Canadas with my parents and brothers . . . when I . . . when?" Who had told her this? Why had she gotten the impression that Narcissa had been fabricating the story of Eve's childhood in La Canadas?

Swinging her legs off the bunk, Eve sat up straight. Feather tilted her head to look up into Eve's eyes. Her smile was so enchanting, so very endearing, Eve gathered the babe into her arms and hugged her close to her breast.

"Ah, Feather, Feather, you are such a sweet child." She kissed the top of the silken head, felt the cheeks that were like dewy rose petals press close to her own. "I love you, darling, do you know that?"

Feather, beautiful, beautiful Feather, rounded her rosy lips and blew. With tears standing in her eyes, Eve said, "Oh, you are trying to speak. It will be some time before you can do that, my love."

Pond Lily entered just then, her shoulders hunched in a humble fashion. Eve did not know if it was so much an ingratiating attitude as it was a permanent stoop from entering tipis and bending over the craft the tall woman happened to be working on at the time. Pond Lily made rocks look like beautiful gemstones as she chipped tiny pieces away and polished until they resembled jewels.

"Why is your name not Tall Woman?" Eve asked Pond Lily.

"Used to be. Husband did not like. Changed name to Pond Lily. We like new name much better. Children like too."

"Many children," Eve said with a congenial laugh. All of a sudden Eve saw the woman's animated features grow still.

Pond Lily possessed other talents too. For one, she seemed to be seeing one's soul as she looked into one's eyes. Eve believed that Pond Lily could tell what was inside a person. Pond Lily knew things others did not.

Just then Feather began rubbing her eyes. Day in, day out, Pond Lily nourished her and put her to sleep. The Dark Hair had never done these things for Feather, but she gave Feather something far deeper and long-lasting. Pond Lily had time only for caring for Feather's welfare. She had many children of her own, so their wants and needs, like love, came first.

"You are going away," said Pond Lily. "The Dark Hair will return. First you will travel far away and back. You will not travel alone with your person."

Maggie, Eve thought.

"You will travel with not only a woman, but a man. Perhaps many people will come and go."

Eve blinked.

Pond Lily's hand rested on Eve's shoulder before

she picked Feather up and took her to her own tipi
for a nap.

Far away and back . . .

What had Pond Lily meant? It sounded like Eve
was going to take a journey back in time. In her
mind? To when she was a child? As the young Indian men saw visions? The old men dreamed?
Women too saw visions. Many Stars had had one
about Sacajawea.

The Indian wanted to "see with the eye in one's
heart rather than with the eyes in one's head."

A vision quest, during which a boy "cried for a
dream," was an initiation rite only in the sense that
it was usually first undertaken at puberty. Unlike a
girl's introduction to womanhood, which happened
only once in a lifetime, vision quests were repeated
again and again, as often as an individual felt the
need for help from the "spirit powers." Pond Lily
said this might come before a raid, or during a
child's illness, or at a time of personal doubt. While
women also went on vision quests, they did so less
often and under more comfortable conditions than
the men.

One-Arm had informed Eve of the Dakota ways.
Among the Dakota, to seek a vision meant having
to go naked except for a breechclout and moccasins
to a lonely hilltop and staying there for four days
and nights without food while crouched in a vision
pit. One-Arm had also told Eve that Suncloud had
done this when he was a very young man. One did
not face this ordeal without help and instruction
from a wakan wishasha, a medicine man, who in-
voked the spirits to bring the quest to a successful
conclusion. "All the powers of the world," the sha-
man from the Teton Dakota had intoned to Sun-

cloud, "the heavens and the star peoples, and the red and blue sacred days; all things that move in the universe, in the rivers. All waters, all trees that stand, all the grasses of our Great Spirit Wakantanka, Great Mystery Power without beginning or end, all the sacred branches of the Grandfather Spirit: Listen! A sacred relationship with you all will be asked by this young man, that his generations to come will increase and live peaceably and in a holy manner."

And One-Arm, with a huge grin, had secretly informed Eve: Suncloud's vision had been that of a turtle!

Chapter Twenty-six

The Dark Hair was walking out of town. Maggie was not far behind Eve; she was catching up, her arms full of baggage, but kept glancing over her shoulder. She tripped once in a while and then kept walking.

"Don't look for him; he won't be coming," Eve said of Tames Wild Horses.

"How do you know?" Maggie asked, running now, the heavy loads weighing down each arm, and the pack of food heavy on her back.

"They are all still busy celebrating the return of their Arapaho friends; they are excited over the booty of all that elk meat. They are busy with the many tasks—just as if they'd slaughtered a herd of buffalo. No one will be following."

"I'm not so sure," Maggie said, still worrying, looking back.

"Maggie, sit down there, on the rock, for a moment. I have something to tell you."

"At last. I was wondering when you were going to let me in on your secret."

Maggie sat on a rock overlooking the town, where they were partially hidden behind bushes and boulders. "Now, why is it so dangerous for us to stay in Wild Thunder?"

"First tell me why you came along so easily?" Eve asked, biting into a piece of pemmican. She felt weak, hungry, irritated.

"We really should keep going, like you said."

"I told you they would not be coming. Though you are right; we should make this rest short."

Abruptly, unexpectedly, Maggie shrugged the blanket off her shoulders and the thing slid down, revealing the tops of her lovely breasts.

Eve gasped. "Maggie, why haven't you dressed?" She had only just noticed that Maggie wore only a blanket. "Where are your clothes?" She began to get up, ready to fetch some clothes from her own packs.

"Sit down, Eve. Tames Wild Horses took them."

Eve sat back down slowly. "He took your clothes and left you naked?"

"No. He did leave this blanket for me. Well, to keep warm if nothing else. But it keeps falling off my shoulders." Maggie smiled wanly. "It does not make for a very good covering, like a dress would."

"You look covered to me, I mean, until you let the blanket fall."

Maggie pulled it up again and grinned.

"So," Eve said, "you and Tames argued and he took your clothes to punish you." Eve snorted. "Just like a man to do that."

"Has Suncloud ever done that to you, Eve?"

"Well"—Eve thought for a moment—"no. Nothing like that. He never took my clothes." He took something far more important—the scoundrel.

"Tames has been really nice up to now. We did

everything together"—she saw Eve's shocked look—"except that, what you're thinking. We are not wed, Eve. Though I do find we share a love for horses. He says there have always been horse people in his family. Let me tell you about the horses he caught—"

"Maggie, we have to get going soon. Just tell me the facts. I know now why you went along with my idea to leave. You and Tames had a little spat. Now I will tell you why it is imperative that we escape—"

"Escape?" Maggie asked, looking surprised. "Like in captives?"

"Yes. Really, we are captives, ones who need to escape or else get . . . murdered."

Maggie began to stand up, tripped on the blanket, and fell sideways. Then, using her hands, she pushed herself up to a sitting position again.

"Murdered?" Maggie was confused. She fumbled about and adjusted the Indian blanket.

"Sit back down. Yes. Murder. Just like our—" Eve swallowed.

Maggie looked at Eve as she thought back to that tragic day. "Does this have to do with our brothers' murders?"

Eve blurted out, "Suncloud—McCloud—killed them, and he must have had someone help him do the dirty work. How could he have murdered three big men all by himself, with only one knife?"

Maggie thought for a moment, then said, "He would have to be very strong and fast."

"Right, Maggie. And no man is that fast."

"You are saying he must have had help. And his best friend is Tames Wild Horses." Maggie sucked in her breath. "I knew Tames was keeping something from me. Just the way he looked at me would make me wonder what was going on inside that boyishly handsome head of his. He had something to hide, Eve, and it was as if this made him very sad."

"Of course. Tames Wild Horses is a nice man, much nicer than Suncloud, and this bothered his conscience, knowing what he'd done—or what he had gone along with. No secret, Maggie."

Maggie's countenance softened. "Tames is very gentle and kind, Eve."

Eve gaped. "Is he kind when he takes your clothes and hides them?"

Maggie just kept talking. "He gave me many pretty gifts. I could talk to him. He knew about our brothers before I . . . told . . . him." Maggie thought hard about what she'd just said and Eve looked at her with a light in her eyes.

Eve got up to pace back and forth. "And just how did he know? Did you ask him?" Eve looked at Maggie sharply.

"No." Maggie hung her head. "I just gathered that the news travels from post to post; this is their grapevine, all the trappers, traders, and Indians, among other folk, like the settlers coming in at an alarming rate."

Maggie gulped.

"Who said that about the settlers? Tames Wild Horses?" Eve asked, leaning forward, touching Maggie's arm.

"Yes, he did. Why, what's wrong? Why are you looking at me like that?"

"Don't you know?"

"Eve, please sit down. Your pacing is making me nervous."

"Oh, sorry." Eve sat back down on a rock and looked at Maggie. "Well?"

"That's better."

"Maggie. Think. Suncloud and a lot of the other Indians—perhaps even Tames—do not like the idea of all the white settlers moving in. So they kill off a few here and there. Who's to know out here in the wilderness? It's not like St. Louis, where we knew law and order."

Eve saw Maggie's frown.

"Well, a little more than the people out here know," Eve said.

Eve was silent for a few moments, just looked as if she were thinking very hard.

Maggie started to pull the blanket back onto her shoulders. "What, Eve? I thought our discussion was over. Don't we have to get going and *escape* if they're so dangerous?"

"You do not strike me as concerned about what we've just talked about. Why?"

"I don't know, Eve. It's . . . well, it's just that Tames is such a good man. I know him better than I do Suncloud, who seems to have a dual personality, and I'm not so sure Tames had anything to do with our brothers' death. Maybe he's innocent; he sure looks that way." Her face turned from contemplative to pure softness.

Eve grunted.

"Look in this bag I've been carrying," Eve told Maggie as she pulled the thing open. "See for yourself."

Maggie looked into the buckskin bag. "What? I see yellow material, raggedly cut, and blue beads."

"What do you feel," asked Eve, watching her friend closely.

Something stirred inside Maggie. "Oh. Where did you find these?"

"Look harder. Smell."

"Smell?" Maggie frowned.

"Yes. Like that cologne Hank used to wear."

Maggie took up the yellow cloth and held it to her face as if her brother Hank could speak through it.

"What else, Maggie."

Eve waited.

"My dream," Maggie said all at once. "The yellow cloth and blue beads. I dream about these items all the time."

"And so do I," said Eve. "I found them in Suncloud's possession, among his things in his tipi."

Eve couldn't bring herself to say McCloud or Steven; perhaps she would never say these names again.

"Eve," Maggie said, hurriedly piling her body with baggage, "let's get out of here."

"What do you think I've been trying to do all this time!" Eve shouted.

Maggie looked over her shoulder at Eve. "Talk me into something!"

"Right!"

With a somewhat sad and regretful expression, Maggie said, "I've been with you all this time, Eve."

Thinking of the influence Tames Wild Horses had held over Maggie, Eve turned to stare hard at Maggie.

Eve said, "Not really, Maggie, dear."

Chapter Twenty-seven

"You are right, Suncloud," Tames Wild Horses said to his friend. "They are nowhere to be found. It is as if they have disappeared into the air." A strongly muscled arm swooped against the sky.

McCloud nodded and headed back toward his mount.

Tames laughed.

Before mounting Wind, McCloud looked back at Tames Wild Horses. "What can be so funny at a time like this? They are gone, escaped. They could be in danger."

Standing near his own warrior horse, Tames said, "Maggie has no clothes. I hid them. The women will not be hard to find. The going will be slow."

"Why?" McCloud looked down from his horse. "What do you mean?"

"Shining Eyes wears only a blanket."

McCloud looked surprised as his friend whirled his horse in preparation to mount.

McCloud sucked in his breath. "This Maggie of yours—she is naked?"

Leaping onto his horse, Tames said, "She is."

Frustrated and angry, McCloud growled, "We must go. The sun will be setting soon."

By nightfall Eve and Maggie had made camp. They sat before a low fire, chewing jerked meat and looking up at the stars.

Maggie swallowed, then gulped. "It's dark up here high in the mountains, and all these trees and huge rocks—who knows what lurks behind them. I'm afraid, Eve."

Eve pulled her own blanket around her. The real danger, Maggie, is that murdering Indians may be coming after us."

"I know you mean Tames and Suncloud. Yet I felt so safe with Tames Wild Horses, and now I do not feel all that safe."

"Why won't you put on a dress, Maggie? I've an extra one in my bag."

"I shall stay as I am, the way Tames meant me to be."

"Naked?" Eve blinked at Maggie's incredible statement.

"Hmmm." After a moment Maggie asked, "Do you believe what the storyteller said about two people coming together in another life?"

"I didn't hear him say anything about that. Tell me what he said."

Eve settled back to listen. Night had come with a rush of soft mauve, and before the deep green of trees and gray rock had completely changed into black, they had built a sputtering fire and were roasting the few rabbits they had snared during the day.

"He, Norman Tallfeather, said that when lovers

can't get together in one life, they do in the next. They search for each other, feeling lost because they cannot be with the one they love. Then, when they do at last see and touch, it's like two halves coming together. They know they are meant for each other."

Eve was quiet for so long that Maggie thought she hadn't been listening.

"Maggie?" Eve finally asked, staring up at the wilderness moon, shining stars, and black sky.

"Yes?" Maggie, who had been gazing at the cooking rabbits, now looked up at Eve. "What is it?"

"I wonder if—"

"Yes?" Maggie leaned forward in her blanket.

"Maybe they didn't do it."

Maggie looked up. "You are thinking the same thing I am."

Maggie looked very beautiful and innocent with the campfire glowing on her face. Eve looked wild, so womanly with her loose hair, dark eyes and brows, lean cheekbones, and pale doeskin dress. Her knee-high leggings and beaded moccasins made the picture complete; she looked like an Indian princess.

This is what Huivi saw as he watched them from his hiding place in the rock bluffs. No wonder Scar-Face would like to get this woman back, this Eve, the Dark Hair. The other one was lovely also, but his interest was in capturing the Dark Hair and bringing her to War Shirt. This would not be as easy as he'd thought. He would have to use care and cunning.

Huivi smelled something burning and groaned

softly, hoping the women were not ruining the food. He licked his lips as his stomach growled.

Huivi had been trailing them for miles as they trudged into the mountains. He could not just pounce on them. He knew the Dark Hair would put up a fight, and who knew what weapons she carried?

He could always tell them they were going the wrong way, deeper into the wilderness instead of toward civilization, which was true. Yes, that is what he would say to them when he got up enough nerve to approach them.

His mouth watered as he stared at the food they'd prepared. He had had no time to hunt or cook, and had brought nothing with him but a little pemmican. He had been so busy trailing them, he'd not thought of nourishment. He sniffed the air again and feared the food was close to overdone.

Swallowing his nerve, Huivi moved slowly and stealthfully closer. He was just stepping from between the boulders when a woman emerged from behind a stand of pines and surprised him into a frozen stance.

"What are you doing here?" he asked in a fierce low voice.

The woman with the laughing voice said, "I thought I would tag along and see what mischief you were up to." She tossed her head as she neared.

"Go back!" Huivi ordered, waving a hand frantically.

"Go back to where?" Chara asked, then grinned, showing him what she had. "I brought food. My bags are full of good things to eat."

Huivi's eyes lit up as he beckoned her closer. "Ah, good. You can help, then."

"They look hungry," she said, stifling her jealousy.

"Their food is burning as they stare into the dark," Huivi said.

"That is what I meant. And," she said, winking at him, "women always know when men need their help."

"Maggie, did you hear something?" Eve asked, spinning around to look at the tall boulders.

"No. But I smell something burning," Maggie said.

Ignoring her comment, Eve asked, "Did you hear a sound like footsteps or rustling?"

"No," Maggie said sadly. "All I can think of is Tames Wild Horses."

"Well, stop thinking of him. He's a murderer. Just like . . . McCloud."

Maggie snatched her blanket closer. "Remember, I don't know about that. Neither do you. Think about it. Wouldn't they have killed us by now?"

Eve thought for a moment, then said, "No. Maybe they had something else in mind."

"What, Eve, sacrifice?" Maggie frowned into the night. "I believe Suncloud is in love with you. You are his wife. Everything seemed so wonderful between you."

Eve grabbed her stick from the fire, unaware that the meat was burnt, she was so engrossed in their talk. "No."

"No?"

Poking the stick back, she said angrily, "He has had other wives. I am not the first, you know. He divorces women as if they didn't matter at all. He does not take care with them. He loves children, huh! He has enough of them—Whispering Bells, Feather . . . yes"—Eve nodded—"Feather is his daughter. He did not even know this. How many more children does he have running around Wild Thunder, do you think?"

Maggie shrugged.

"And Chara. What about her? I have a feeling he did not love Morning Moon. He never talks about her. The poor woman, she must have run away from him and Wild Thunder."

"But maybe to him you are different. Did you ever stop to think of that? Maybe he has never been in love before. They were all just women, someone to cook their meals, tend to their clothes, like an Indian squaw. Maybe they were good on the mats." She laughed. "For a time. Then he tired of them. Or they became nasty to him and wouldn't cook or clean for him."

Eve whirled to face Maggie. "How do you know? You are younger than I."

"By only one year." Maggie shrugged in her blanket. "You are really beginning to sound like an angry Indian woman, Eve."

"My God. You don't mean that." She saw the serious look on Maggie's face. "You do." Eve looked down at herself, saw the pale doeskin she was wearing, fingered the fringe. "I do feel like a squaw at times. You are right, I even talk like one lately, and walk like one. Oh! This really does make me angry, this talk. He is *so* Indian. He seems to hate whites. But why do you think he murdered our brothers?"

"You are just angry, Eve."

"How so?" Eve poked the stick back, not noticing the black rabbit meat.

"It has something to do with that child Feather. You are angry because he has had babies with other women."

Her eyes wide, Eve looked at Maggie. "I was angry before I discovered the other child. When I found the material and blue beads, that's when it began, when I knew he was a murderer."

Maggie did not believe what Eve was saying.

The discussion deepened as the food blackened.

"Men possess women, Eve. When they love us, they want to own us, they want to keep us. I know more about Suncloud than you can imagine. Tames has told me things. He does have Indian blood, true, but Suncloud's stepmother was a white woman; Brian "Spotted Horse" McCloud married her long after Many Stars, his sister, was abducted by Comanches. Tames said that his white parent was worse than the one who had Indian blood. She was what Tames calls the European white, and Suncloud did not love this second mother. After Spotted Horse took her for his wife, Suncloud hardly looked at her, as he saw how white she was. Suncloud put their marriage and her image from his mind. Their real mother was called Slender Arrow. It was not as if a chief took him to replace his lost son. Suncloud denies his white blood with vehemence, and mostly because of the wagging tongues."

"What?"

"Tames Wild Horses said that white men used to call Suncloud . . . Big Buck."

"What does that mean?"

"That is a white man's name for a male Indian:

Buck. But Suncloud is bigger than most men. The trappers can be so cruel, even the traders. Maybe this is why he hates the whites so much. And he hates the full-blood Spaniards *only* because his sister was captured by Scar-Face and used so badly."

"What else, Maggie? Did Tames say any more about . . . my husband?"

Eve took the stick from the fire and just then noticed how horribly burnt their supper was. Just as her stomach began to growl, Maggie saw their charred pile of meat. She stared, wondering where they would get other food.

"Maggie? Is there more?"

Eve was waiting, already reaching for the bags that contained the cold fare.

"Yes. Tames says McCloud even has a drop of Spanish blood and was sent to Cheyenne under Spotted Horse's orders to become educated by a man called Fitzsimmons."

Now Eve did not know what to think. Before she could dwell on this further, she heard another sound coming from the rocks.

"Maggie. There are people here!"

Maggie looked hopeful. "At last. We are not alone. Tames and—"

Eve stuck out her hand, pointing.

"No. Look. A man and a woman."

"What?" Maggie's mouth fell wide.

"Exactly."

Just then the couple stepped into the ember-lit clearing, looking at each other, pausing, then walking closer to Maggie and Eve.

Chapter Twenty-eight

Eve looked down at the beautiful object the dark-haired man held in his hand. Her gaze dragged slowly at first from the thing, then flew to the woman's face framed by moonlight; Eve could even make out the green of her eyes glowing like a cat's.

"Chara!" Eve gasped as Chara stepped closer.

Eve stepped back, frowning.

"Laughing Voice to you," purred Chara, holding a full bag of what looked like food.

Eve threw out her arm, asking, "What are you doing here? And who is this man?"

The silver in the moonlight shone down and illuminated their surroundings. Everything spun in Eve's side vision. What was happening? That object that man was holding, what was it?

Eve felt as if she might swoon. Her arm swept out and grabbed the nearest thing to steady her, which happened to be Chara's shoulder.

"Eyyy!" Chara screeched, and tried to step away, but she was held fast, as if Eve were drowning and needed a lifeline.

"What is *that?*"

Eve's other hand flew out and pointed at the

object which she could now see was a beaded bag in the shape of a turtle with a smaller creature on its back.

The man said, "Here, Dark Hair, look at it."

Huivi thrust the bag out at Eve and she danced back, taking Chara with her since her grip was strong on the woman's shoulder.

"Eyyy!" Chara screeched again, trying to get away from the Dark Hair.

"It is yours," said Huivi, trying to make her hold it. "Do you not recognize it?"

"What is he saying?" Eve asked Chara as Maggie stepped forward to look down on the beaded amulet. Eve looked at Maggie over her shoulder. "What does this look like to you, Maggie? Has Tames shown you anything like this?"

Suddenly Chara lurched forward, reaching for the red, gold, and blue object. "I will have it if she does not want it. It is very pretty, Huivi. I would like to own it. Why do you not give it to your sweetheart, eh, Huivi? Could this be part of the treasure you spoke so mysteriously about?"

Treasure?

Eve frowned. Maggie looked at Eve, noticing that she flinched at the word. What did *treasure* mean to Eve, she wondered.

Somewhat sadly Huivi said, "It is not mine to give to you, Chara. I will have for you another gift, the Golden Tears. But not this one. This belongs to the Dark Hair. You must listen and behave."

Chara pouted, then watched what was going on.

Maggie stepped up to Huivi and, looking into the dark eyes and seeing no danger or mischief there, she took the very lovely object into her hands.

"I will show it to my friend," Maggie softly said,

handling it as if it would fall to pieces. She faced Eve.

"It's an amulet, Eve, an Indian amulet and this one's very large, very heavy. I will not look inside because that wouldn't be right. I believe it contains some child's umbilical cord."

"What?" Eve cringed, stepping back. "Maggie—what?"

"Tames has told me something about these charms." Maggie looked up at Huivi, seeing the moon in his black eyes. "It is Sioux, Teton Dakota?" Her eyes passed over Chara.

Huivi saw that Chara did not look happy. She did not understand, he thought, because she was still pouting.

Huivi looked back at the young woman with the dark blond hair. How does she know so much about these things, he wondered. And who was Tames?

"Yes. How did you know?" Huivi asked the pretty young woman named Maggie; he'd spotted her briefly while sneaking about Wild Thunder.

Maggie explained, "I have a friend who has told me much about these things, these amulets; his name is Tames Wild Horses. This bag in the shape of a turtle could have been attached to a cradle-board or worn around a child's neck to bring him or her good fortune. The turtle and the lizard are both symbols of longevity." Maggie peered closer, trying to see it better in the pale moonlight sifting down. She smiled. "This turtle has a butterfly on its back. How beautiful."

Chara felt Eve slipping away from her and reached out to catch her before she fell. "Help me, Huivi. She is going down like the winter sun. She is not light; she is all muscle."

"Aiii!" Chara screeched and leapt sideways, only bumping harder into Eve.

Huivi jumped, reached them, and caught them both before Eve could drag Chara down with her to the ground.

Moments passed while Huivi and Chara wondered what to do next.

On the ground where she'd been placed, Eve opened her eyes and looked up. "What happened?" She licked her lips as Huivi knelt to pour water from a skin onto them. "Where am I? Suncloud?"

"Who?"

Huivi, Maggie, and Chara whirled to see Suncloud towering above them from his brown and white paint, Wind.

"Hide it," Huivi ordered Chara. "He must not find this. He will know what it means and what it contains." Then he shoved the beaded amulet under her arm.

Not understanding what was happening, Chara took the turtle, slipped it across her stomach and to her other side, where Suncloud and Tames Wild Horses would not see it. From there she slipped it into the folds of her serape, which was on the ground, and whirled the red and black length over her shoulders.

The amulet was safe now.

Suspiciously, Suncloud glared down at Chara.

"What is wrong with you? Why do you move like that? Are you cold?"

"Yes," Chara said at once. "The mountain air grows cooler. Do you not think?" She nudged Huivi hard in the ribs.

Huivi mumbled and then said out loud, "Oh. Yes. It grows much cooler."

"So," Suncloud said, his voice deeply menacing as he studied all their faces. "What is going on? Are you all here for a secret meeting of some sort?" He looked down at Eve and snorted. "And what is she fainting for? Is she ill from trying to escape me too fast?"

Chara looked at Huivi, saw that she'd better think fast, and did.

"She has fainted because . . . *she is with child,*" Chara said in her laughing voice.

Suncloud, his face painted in fierce colors, frowned at Chara as if he wanted to murder her.

"Whose child?" he ground out, staring down at Eve and then whipping his gaze back to Chara.

Whose?

Chara was sure that Suncloud and the Dark Hair had gone to the blankets after the marriage ceremony, hadn't they?

Blinking wide and shrugging, Chara looked to Huivi for help. He shrugged, then watched as the handsome young Tames Wild Horses pulled the shining-eyed girl with the light hair into the bushes.

All Huivi heard was "We must talk."

Then Tames and Maggie vanished into the wood and rock.

"Who else could be the father but you?" Chara snapped at Suncloud, her question ringing in her own ears.

Chara was remembering something that had been uttered by One-Arm. . . . Suncloud had been kicked by a horse and couldn't have more children. . . .

"You know why I say whose child." Suncloud glowered at Chara. "Or have you forgotten?"

Chara shrugged it off. "She is not with child, then."

Huivi slapped his forehead and fell back. The woman was incredible: How stupid could she be!

Recovering, Huivi looked at Chara again, hoping she was hiding that beaded turtle amulet well. Otherwise they—or she—would have to explain what it all meant, and reveal that she had no knowledge of what was really going on.

"Who are you?" Suncloud asked the dark-skinned man, his eyes boring into the stranger.

Taking Suncloud by the arm, Chara said sweetly, "He is my lover, Huivi. Do you not recall? I told you his name before I ran off with him. You saw him once before—briefly."

Suncloud peeled Chara's hand from his arm. "You did not say that name. It was another man's name you gave me." He pinched her cheek. "Laughing Voice." He patted her face hard then, almost a slap, and moved away from her.

"What has been going on?" Suncloud questioned fiercely, going to stand directly in front of Huivi. "You tell me. The women are too confused when they try to tell the truth and tell only little white lies."

McCloud shook his head as a sigh, a breath he could not identify, passed over him. He felt light-headed.

Huivi swallowed. He had never been confronted by an angry half-breed, not like this one at least. If Suncloud knew what he was up to . . . where he was going to bring the Dark Hair . . .

Suncloud now appeared more Indian than white. He looked fierce, the red and white paint zigzagging across his handsome face like lightning, his brows like storm clouds, his chest, muscled and bronze, just visible above the ivory-beaded breastplate he wore. His legs were clad in leggings with colorful designs; a dark breechclout could be seen on his behind. A section of long, loose hair was formed into a long braid, and from that two feathers dangled upside down.

Eve opened her eyes again and shut them, knowing that McCloud was standing there talking to Chara's friend.

No, not McCloud. Suncloud. Eve blinked and felt around for the object they had been showing her. She saw nothing of it now. And she did not wish to see it again. Just looking at the beaded object made her dizzy, and she saw things that had almost a nightmarish appearance. All this had to do with her dreams. She had seen the colorful object in her dreams before and she was frightened of it. This boded something she did not wish to face.

You must forget, Eve. Do not think of the past. It hurts too much. You must not remember that which hurts so much . . . Winter . . . Winter . . . Buffalo . . . Who is Great Eagle? What was she seeing? In her mind's eye it looked to be an Indian village where . . . she couldn't think with *him* so near.

Her eyes shifted, and Eve looked upon Suncloud's horse, Wind. The animal wore an eagle's plume in its forelock, and both Wind and Suncloud wore the mourning marks on them.

Who has died? Eve looked at Suncloud as he turned to her after speaking to the dark man in an unfamiliar Indian language.

As he walked toward her, Suncloud looked none too happy. "Why did you go?" he asked her, not touching her, not looking into her eyes.

Eve wondered if he was angry. Of course. He has to be, she told herself.

"What did Chara's man tell you?" Eve wanted to know before she said anything. Suncloud frightened her. He had never frightened her before as he was doing now.

"I've asked you," he said, still not looking at her. "You tell me."

"Why?"

He jerked his gaze to her. "You ask me why?"

"Why did you come after me?" Eve wanted to know, stalling for time, hoping she could tire him out with talk. He had ridden a long way, after all. "Why do you want me? *For a sacrifice?*" she asked.

"Why?" He peered down into her face as if she'd lost her mind. "You ask why? And what's this about a sacrifice? You are my wife. I thought you might have been in danger. At first. Then I learned that you walked right out of Wild Thunder with your bags and your friend Maggie in tow. Boldly, like nothing else counted in the world but that you walk out of my life. You left Whispering Bells crying and Many Stars worrying her head off. Even Feather was crying. And One-Arm held her as she cried; he cried also. Where did you think you were going?" He looked at her harder, more fiercely. "And who were you planning to meet?"

Eve slowly swept her arm out, saying, "You sent searchers out for us before you and Tames Wild Horses came along. They found us."

"Chara and her lover, Huivi? Don't talk around me, Dark Hair. I want answers and I want them fast."

Eve looked down at her bag. Then she jerked her eyes back up at his so he would not see where her eyes had rested ever so briefly.

But he had already seen.

"What is in the bag?" he asked as he walked over to pick it up.

Just as he was bending over, Eve took a dive and grabbed for the bag before he could reach it. Again, not fast enough. They collided and the struggle began.

Huivi and Chara took that time to melt into the shadows beyond the campfire. "What did you say to him?" Chara was hissing at Huivi. She couldn't hear his answer until reaching the other side of the rocks. He said, "I want nothing more to do with this. You keep it; I am going where no one will know me."

"Huivi!"

Eve tugged at the bag and McCloud yanked. He jerked her up to his chest, right along with the bag. His face was so close to hers, she could see the angry lines of his war paint. His huge, wise eyes studied her, and Eve's knees began to grow weak.

"You are so handsome and fierce, Suncloud," Eve breathed, closing her hand over his, still clutching the bag. "Maybe we can go off and be alone. Would you like that?"

Looking into her beautiful face, seeing her hair spread wildly about her neck and shoulders, Suncloud began to melt. He let go of the bag and ran his hand up and down her hip, feeling her shiver and move closer.

"What is in . . . ?" Suncloud began to ask, then he was making love to her as he smelled her womanly perfume, leaning closer to her throat.

"Only some, er, personal items, Suncloud." She panted and purred against him, letting him feel her womanly curves. "Let's you and I go into those bushes over there. We are alone. Maggie is with

Tames Wild Horses. Chara went off with her man.
We can be alone too. I will change into something,
hmm, something nice and pretty."

He looked her up and down. "You are already
wearing something pretty, Eve. Drop the bag. We
will go into those trees. You have worried and
frightened me. I want you badly."

Eve did as he asked. She dropped the bag, threw
her arms around his neck, pressed closer yet, then
kicked the bag behind some deadwood.

"We will go. Over there."

She walked ahead of him, enticing him with the
sway of her hips clad in soft doeskin, her lips
pursed, promising delights, her slim arms beckon-
ing him in the soft spill of moonlight.

She stopped to face him, kissed his eager lips,
and, crying out as they touched, put her mouth
against his ear.

"Suncloud, my warrior." A breath as soft as
dawn.

His hands moved down her back, caressing her
spine. Her eyes closed. They kissed again, their bodies touching, and then they moved on, slowly, then
more eagerly, hand in hand, laughing breathlessly,
like happy children.

Suncloud was so eager that once they were in the
deepest shadows, he pulled her up to his chest and
thighs, letting her feel the need in his loins.

"Oh, Suncloud, you are such a big man," she
cooed, already beginning to remove her doeskin
dress provocatively.

"Too slow, woman."

He yanked her dress down over her hips and
looked down, his eyes widening at the glorious sight

of her breasts bared, full, and inviting, begging him to taste the pink crests.

He watched as she lifted her face to the moonlight shining down into the trees. Her eyes were the palest violet with gold speckled around the rims of the large irises. In the night she looked primitive, like an Indian princess stealing into the wood to meet her lover. He saw no white in her now. He continued to stare in awe, transfixed, almost asking, Who are you?

It was as if he had never seen her before.

Then he said his thoughts out loud, *"Who are you?"*

She kissed him tenderly and he closed his lids to his moonlit reflection in her eyes. Her lips were incredibly soft. His long arms swooped about her body and he leaned to kiss her again.

"Who?" he repeated against her lips.

Her mouth broke away and she looked up at him. "How can you ask that?" Her slender hands roamed his body, exploring. She was a delightful child. "There is no telling, really. I don't remember who I used to be. Though I know who I am now."

His strong fingers twined in her long, silky hair made black by the shadows of the moon. It fell unbound to her shoulders, adorned with delicate turquoise feathers.

"How can I leave you?" she said softly.

"Must you?" His jaw hardened imperceptibly.

When he had her down on the dewy grass, he blew against her throat, asking the question still raging foremost in his mind.

"Why?"

She purred against his throat and pushed herself up into his grinding hips. "I was angry," she said.

"Why were you angry?" He kissed her chin and nibbled up to her ear. "Ah. You were perhaps jealous of Chara?"

"Oh, yes! Yes. That is the truth." Well, she thought, that was part of it. Chara's presence in Wild Thunder had not sat well with her, not then, not now.

"Why are you afraid of me, then?" He dragged his mouth away from a peaking pink nipple to look deeply into her dark eyes.

"What?" she squeaked. "I? Afraid?"

"Yes. There is a difference between being upset and being scared. You are quivering not as if you want me, which part of you does, but it is something more, like fear of a thing you wish not to tell me of."

"Oh, Suncloud, you do not know the half of it!" She tossed her arms around his neck. "I was so afraid of wild animals." Which was also true. "I thought something great and fierce would come along and eat us up, Maggie and me."

"Don't worry, Dark Hair. I am here now." He removed his breechclout in a flash and stood out like a hot and heavy stallion.

Looking away from the glistening rod, Eve blinked into the buckskin jacket he was still wearing over his breastplate. *Dark Hair.* He called her that only when he was angry with her or thought she was acting too much like a white woman.

When he entered her, he did so very hard, and the top of her head was thrust back into a tree trunk. *He is still angry,* Eve thought.

Then she forgot everything but the lusty pounding man as he made love to her like never before. He was a thrusting stallion, riding up and down her canyons, entering her valley of ecstasy and plunging deeply within the moist crevice.

Something glorious sparkled in the darkness of the cave at the end. The wild stallion plunged and thundered toward it.

Primitive sensations began in Eve as he rode into the valley of the sparkling waterfall, and as McCloud kept up the pounding, splashing through the rapids with rearing, thrashing hooves, she began to moan, then cry, groan again, and before long she was shouting his name.

Her eyes flew wide as his shoulders shifted.

When the greatest ecstasy took hold of her, she looked up into the sky, shaken to her very core. She became submerged in the sparkling waters, then surged upward to ride a shooting star into the sky.

She exploded into a million pieces of gold dust, tumbling, skyrocketing, plummeting, screaming his name with her release, hearing his own deeper voice melding with hers as shivers of joy shot from him to her.

After this tumultuous mating had ceased and peaceful bliss came with the afterglow, Eve lay like a wet rag.

Moments passed before she realized he was not with her any longer.

He had gotten up and left her.

She still lay there.

And then it hit her.

My *bag!*

Chapter Twenty-nine

It came to him, crying on the wild summer wind that whipped the slender pines atop the hill.

He held the objects of his vision dream in his hands as a smudge of saffron light showed in the sky.

Now his hands were steady, but when he'd opened the bag, they were unsteady as he pulled out the yellow material and the shiny blue beads.

Yellow material, exactly as it had been in his vision, bloodstained. But something was missing.

Eve came upon McCloud as he snatched up the bag and poured out the rest of its contents—buckskin dress, items of a woman's toilette, pemmican.

"Someone has invaded my dream; who is this intruder?" he snarled as Eve came to stand before him. "And where is the other object?"

"Other? There is no—" He could not mean the amulet!

With a strange look on her face Eve stared down at all her things on the ground, and then at the yellow material McCloud held clutched in his hands.

"What are you doing?" Eve asked, bending to pick up the blue beads.

"Where is it?" he demanded, dropping the cloth and shaking Eve by the shoulders. He snatched the blue beads from her hands and looked at her white face as the sun struck them both.

They were motionless. The sun was already sparkling along the granite and rock outcroppings. Birds called sweetly from the high treetops behind them on the slopes of the mountain. White clouds lazily floated across the blue sky.

"I don't understand," Eve said, shaking her head. "I should be angry with you." She looked over to a pile of rocks. "We must sit down and talk."

"Right here," he said, pulling her onto a fat log. "You are not going anywhere, not even over there. Sit," he growled.

At once she explained, "I found these things—the yellow material and the blue beads—in your tipi. Why are you angry at me? You are the thief, not I."

"Where did you say you got these things?"

She looked into his face, the smeared paint making him look grotesque in the morning light. She swiped the back of her hand across her face, then looked down to see that she wore some of his paint on her own face.

He saw it too, but did not smile. He did not feel like smiling at the moment.

"In your tipi, where you put them. They were found on the ground between my—no," she said, confused. "They were *not* found on the ground between my brothers. They . . . were missing."

"You speak in riddles. You never mentioned these items when we spoke of your brothers before."

"I did," she said in a shaking voice. "I believe I did. You were not listening."

"No. All we spoke of after your nightmare was if I would go searching for the ones who killed your brothers; I told you I did not know your brothers when they were alive and you became angry." He clenched his jaw, making his face look lean and hard, his mouth taut. "Please explain."

"I'm trying to. I had the dream about my brothers, and always in my dream was the yellow material and the blue beads."

"You must have also had a dream that you told me this. These items were in my vision dream, along with—"

"Yes?" She looked into his eyes deeply, waiting. "Why do you pause? What are you keeping from me?"

"Along with the turtle and the butterfly."

Eve thought long and hard, then looked up into his face. "Yes. I have heard about your vision where you saw the turtle. Someone has told me this. One-Arm. Or was it Many Stars or Whispering Bells. Maybe all of them said this."

"You do not remember very well," McCloud said. "Which makes me believe that you lie."

"You . . . you confuse me, that's why. It was One-Arm, now I remember. And—" She bit her lip and looked away.

"And?" He took her chin in his fingers. "I frighten you again. What is it, Eve? Why did you remove these things from my tipi, things that I had no knowledge were even in there."

She made a mewling sound.

"Tell me. Who has invaded my vision dream, Dark Hair? Who has put these things into my lodge? And why? There is a mission I must go on, but first I must have the turtle, blue beads, yellow material—they make a whole. This was seen in my vision quest. Who put these things, without the turtle, in my lodge?"

Her eyes closed, the long lashes jeweled in the damp morning.

"I am waiting. Please. What do you know?" His fingers fell away from her chin. "You must not be afraid of me. You sound to me to be innocent of any wrongdoing."

She did not try to wipe away the tears as she looked up at him. "I thought it was you," she murmured, touching his chest.

"What?" He leaned closer to her mouth. "It was I?" He shook his head. "Now I do not understand."

"I thought," she gulped, "you killed my . . . brothers"—she rushed on—"when I found the material and the blue beads in your tipi!"

"You thought I—" He heaved a deep sigh, turned, pulled her into his arms. "I have never killed without reason, Eve, and most of the times I had to, it was in battle."

She broke away. "My brothers were white. They were more . . . more white than I."

"What are you saying?" He looked at her strangely. "They were not your family, not entirely, but half?"

"Yes. John and Derek were my half brothers. I am"—she broke off with a shrug—"darker than they were. I believe my mother had some Spanish blood. My brothers were blond, not dark as I am. They had a different mother. They had blue eyes, light hair."

He studied her in the pink morning light. "Now

that I know you better and have looked at you every day in the light of sun, it seems to me that you are not Spanish at all."

"Really?" She smiled at once. "I did not want to be Spanish. My mother never told me what I am, not anything about my past. Oh, except that we lived in La Canadas. Way up north."

"Well then, perhaps you are French Canadian. Most of those people have Indian blood."

"And my brothers? What are they?"

He took her face in his hands. "I swear to you, Eve, I did not slay your brothers. Nor could I do such an evil deed to men I did not know."

She hugged him fiercely, then sat back. "I am so happy to hear this. I didn't think you could be guilty of such a horrible thing."

For a few moments they both stared at the delicate intruder—a dragonfly, lacy and purple, as it leapt into the air. The warm morning breeze crackled with the quick beats of its double wings, spread like shining fans in the sunlight.

Now McCloud turned to her face and spoke.

"Yes you did. For a while I think you did. Why else would you have run away from me?"

"Oh!" She looked at his handsome, streaked face. "You did tell me something about your vision dream. I saw the turtle amulet in reality, not in a dream. They have it!"

"Who?" McCloud shot to his feet, becoming the fierce Suncloud all over again.

"Chara's lover. I believe I heard her call him Huivi."

McCloud took her by the shoulders. "Yes. That is his name. He has the turtle amulet?"

"He showed it to me. He said it was mine." Eve

frowned, adding, "And I felt as if the thing belonged to me."

Eve followed McCloud as he ran to search the area. "Have they gone?" she asked.

"I believe they have. Come over here."

Pausing before a cold bit of long-forgotten charred rabbit, McCloud snatched up a leg and began eating. He handed her a piece and she ate ravenously, staring at him, waiting for what he would say. She faced him and almost laughed as she saw the burnt bits of rabbit circling his mouth, stuck to his chin.

He grimaced but kept eating. "We must eat to keep up our strength. Then we will keep searching for them." He looked over her shoulder. "Have you seen Tames and Shining Eyes?"

"Who?" Eve stopped chewing the tough black meat and licked her mouth. "Oh, you mean Maggie. No. I have not seen them since they ran off to be alone."

Eating as they walked, searching the area for clues to where the others had gone, Eve and McCloud both dwelled on their own thoughts.

McCloud needed the turtle amulet for his mission, to bring someone yet unnamed to the Dakota people.

Eve was afraid of the object she'd seen, and yet she knew this turtle had something to do with her past. She must remember, but it was still so painful to do.

McCloud stopped chewing, picked up a cloth to wipe the paint off his face, and Eve looked at him and screamed.

Dropping the cloth at once, he reached for his

Hawken rifle and spun about, ready to fire at the intruders that had frightened her.

"No," Eve said. "Put the rifle down, Suncloud." Why was she calling him that? "I mean McCloud. I—I didn't think. Look," she said, pointing down at the yellow cloth. "You wiped your face on the pretty material. We might need it."

Walking over to her, he cupped her face in his hands. "You may call me Suncloud, Eve. I like the sound of your voice when you say *Suncloud.* It sounds very beautiful."

"I—thank you, Suncloud."

He nuzzled her cheek as the dragonfly buzzed nearby and the two of them froze for a moment to watch the tiny creature up close; then McCloud said, "I have never told you that I love you, Eve."

"Do you?" She was shivering from head to foot. Waiting seemed like an eternity. *Well?*

Still cupping her face, he put his own next to hers. "I have loved you forever, even before we met. You were in my wild heart when I was born."

"That is nice, Suncloud." She pulled back to look up at him. "But shouldn't we find the others? Don't you want to know about the turtle amulet?" She sighed. "I do."

"Be serious, Eve. *Do you love me?"*

"Oh, yes." Her voice was soft and breathless. She placed her palm on his cheek, letting it rest there for several moments.

Before they could utter more endearments, Maggie and Tames Wild Horses walked into the clearing. Maggie was wearing her old dress and Tames was smiling from ear to ear. They were holding hands.

With a grin Tames said, "I love her too." He was looking down at Maggie.

Maggie ducked her head, her face red. "The others have gone," she said shyly. "We looked, but we couldn't find them."

"Hello, there, in camp!"

McCloud and Tames swiftly put their rifles to the ready and spun about, making turf fly beneath their moccasins.

"Who comes?" McCloud shouted.

"Me. Joe."

"Pawnee Joe," Eve whispered. "I know his voice."

"You hear well," said McCloud, unshouldering his rifle and standing straight once again.

"It's me," said Joe as he walked into the clearing. "Hey, watch it with those rifles. Don't shoot me. I ain't lookin' for no trouble."

From behind Joe stepped two Indian girls. Their eyes were very big and they looked scared. "This here's Yellow Mare and Sweet Water." He tossed down the packs he'd been carrying. "Scar-Face was holding them, making whores out of them, so I went back to the Teton Forks, where they were makin' race horses out of them, and took them outta there. Think Scar-Face had more in mind for Yellow Mare, though."

"Horses?" Eve looked at Maggie. "How awful. Joe, there's a bit of rabbit left at the cookfire. Maybe they are hungry."

"We just had ourselves some fresh meat. Cooked it back aways."

"Wait." McCloud said. "You mentioned Scar-Face. Where is he now? I have been looking for him."

Eve blinked up at McCloud. *He has? For how long?*

Joe told McCloud, "He went south with Pierre Dessine. That's why I got the girls outta that town, before he could come back, get 'em from Teton Taggart, and maybe kill them. The son of a bitch likes to kill women after he's used them a bit. He put a yellow dress on her and was goin' ta take her somewheres. Don't know where, can't get it outta her."

Yellow dress . . . yellow dress. Suncloud frowned, feeling a sighing breath pass through him like a ghost again.

"Many Stars," Eve said, hearing about the yellow dress but thinking of her friend. "She just escaped him not long ago. I believe he would have killed her too if we had not escaped from Fort Robidoux when we did. As it was, she lost a finger. I wonder if he would have dressed her up in a yellow dress and taken her somewhere too."

"Don't know who makes the yellow dresses; he must have some squaw sewing them up for him," Pawnee Joe said.

The Indian girls understood a little of the French Eve was speaking. And their eyes were very wide and frightened.

"You do not have to be afraid of us," Eve told them, speaking French and the Dakota that One-Arm had taught her.

"Tell me again what happened," Suncloud asked Joe.

"Well, I went to Taggart's on the day of the race to make sure the girls wouldn't be harmed by all those drunken mountain men. And I wanted to see if the rumors about Scar-Face and Dessine being in the area held some truth. Then I saw these here girls running in a race against each other."

Eve said something in French having to do with Scar-Face and everyone agreed with a nod, that that man was truly a bastard.

When McCloud was alone with Eve again, he said, "You speak good French, Dark Hair."

"I know. You have told me."

He had his arms wrapped around her body and she smiled as he cupped and caressed her backside. Before long they were alone in the trees, under their long purple shadows.

Eve felt her heart thudding beneath her dress, and for a moment she kissed him, on top of him, as he lay gazing up into her face.

He saw her expression change from one of passion to one of distress.

"What is it?" he almost shouted, fastening his breechcloth and leggings.

Straightening her clothes, Eve said, "Those poor girls, being used in a race like horses. They are human beings. How can men be so cruel?"

She had no idea that Suncloud had sat down hard next to her, idly picking grass as she went on about the mistreatment of the Indian girls.

Suddenly Eve slapped her face with both hands. "Oh!" she exclaimed, realizing what she had just seen Yellow Mare wearing, and leapt to her feet. "Oh!"

With his legs spread wide, hands braced on the ground, Suncloud asked himself if he should get himself all worked up and alarmed, or wait for what she had to say. He looked up at her, waiting for the dam to burst, or the fluffy white cloud to just go on sailing by.

"Sun—*McCloud!* That one Joe called Yellow Mare. Did you see what she had on?"

"I . . . really did not—"

"She had on a dirty yellow dress. And blue beads too!"

He shot to his feet and grabbed her hand.

Now, this was something to become excited and alarmed over!

"Joe!" Eve shouted to Joe, who was cooking some bread over a high fire. "Joe!" she repeated when he seemed not to hear her.

"Hey, Joe!" Suncloud's voice joined Eve's on the last note.

"You calling me?" Joe asked, turning to face the couple as they looked at him as if he'd gone deaf. "What is it? Wanta eat? You both look like you're really hungry. I'm making some Indian fry bread here."

"Joe, we don't want to eat right now. We have something to ask you about Yellow Mare."

"Oh. She's a real nice girl, ain't she? I'd like to marry both her and Sweet Water someday. But I'm findin' out that Sweet Water seems to have other things on her mind and—"

"Joe." Eve touched his arm and he looked down, then up. "Where did Yellow Mare get that dirty yellow dress?"

"I was tellin' you guys, but you wasn't listening. Scar-Face likes to dress some of his captives up in yellow cloth and put blue beads around their necks. Don't know why. They always get away before he can finish what he'd set out to do." Joe added grease to the pan and it sizzled. He picked up the can of batter next and a hand grabbed his wrist.

"Joe. Is this the truth?" Eve asked, ready to

mount the nearest horse and go after Scar-Face herself.

" 'Course. I wouldn'ta said it if it wasn't the God's truth. What's wrong? Why you guys lookin' at me like that?"

Suncloud fetched the yellow cloth and blue beads and then held them up for Joe to see. "Eve found these things in my tipi. Do you have any idea how they got there?"

Joe gulped as he saw the yellow cloth. "That's a lot of cloth. You could make curtains for a whole cabin with that bolt."

"Some of it has been taken," Eve said, looking over to where Yellow Mare was staring across to them with a dumbstruck expression. "So, Scar-Face likes to dress his victims in yellow dresses. I suppose this was meant for me? And when did he start this practice, I wonder. Many Stars was not dressed in a yellow—"

Suncloud touched her elbow. "How do you know if she was or was not? It was many years Scar-Face held my Honna captive." He watched as Eve went to sit beside Yellow Mare, then resumed his talk with Joe.

"Yellow Mare," Eve said. She bit her lip. "Oh, that is not your real name, I know."

Joe shouted over to Eve, "She'll never tell anyone her name. She hardly ever says anything. There's a secret she's keepin' and she's not letting anyone in on it."

Ignoring Joe's explanation, Eve kept on trying. "You are very pretty," she said in halting Dakota. "You are the same as Sweet Water?" She was going to ask if the girl was the same kind of Indian, but the Dakota words did not come easily.

Sweet Water leaned forward from behind Yellow Mare to look at Eve.

"She is same as Sweet Water," she said in English, startling Eve. "We both Teton Dakota Sioux. Some of her family from Cheyenne River Sioux. But I know Yellow Mare from Teton Dakota. She has mark of her family."

"What is the mark?" Eve wanted to know, looking at Yellow Mare but seeing nothing that could be a mark.

"On neck, ghost mark some call mist or smoke," Sweet Water said. "She is like Dakota princess."

Sweet Water reached over and flipped Yellow Mare's braid upward. At once Yellow Mare reacted by slapping Sweet Water's hand aside.

The movement was sufficient to see. Eve had looked upon the mark—a perfect Indian arrow on the nape.

"She has more," said Sweet Water.

"Where?" Eve asked, excited now at this new revelation. She felt this mark had something to do with the turtle amulet—and how it seemed to intertwine all their lives together, even Suncloud's and Many Stars's. "Where does she have more?" Eve looked at Yellow Mare this time as she asked this.

Pulling up the hem of her dress to her knee, Yellow Mare showed Eve a bow, one that fitted with the arrowhead. A slender bow.

"Do you know what your name is?" Eve asked, this time employing McCloud's knowledge of the Sioux language as he came to stand between them. "Ask her if she knows. Or has she forgotten?"

Yellow Mare looked up at Suncloud, seeing the handsome warrior in his smeared paint. She looked over at the Dark Hair, then back at him, and laughed. She saw the eyes of the man grow huge.

"Why do you laugh?" Suncloud asked the one temporarily named Yellow Mare. He looked at Eve and she held up her hand for quiet.

"I laugh," the Indian girl finally said, "because the lady with the Indian skin wears your paint."

Eve gasped. "Indian skin? What does that mean?" She looked at Yellow Mare, who was already nodding her head into silence. "Oh, please," Eve said. "At least tell us your name?"

"Beau Arrow," said the lovely Indian girl who was no longer Yellow Mare.

The truth was out.

"Beautiful Arrow," said Eve in a low voice. She has the ghost mark, mist mark, smoke mark.

Why do I feel like this has something to do with my own past? Eve mused, walking away to be by herself.

"Joe and I will take the women back to Wild Thunder," Tames was telling Suncloud. "I think you wish to be alone with your woman a bit longer. You have things that have to be said and done."

"How did you know?" Suncloud asked his friend, a twinkle in his eye.

Chapter Thirty

"Ugh," Eve said as she sat before a blaze, watching Suncloud work over the animal. "That looks awful. I don't think I could do that. I've skinned other smaller game, but it's *so* big." She frowned. "And such a beautiful animal. She must have been a doe."

"She was." Suncloud kept right on cutting up the red flesh. "Some Nez Perce have been trailing us from afar. When they come closer, I will give them some meat. Maybe we might even run across some Oglala or Teton Dakota."

She grinned. "Then they will find us later and give us some pemmican?"

"Yes. How did you know?"

"I guessed." She shrugged. "This is how all friendly Indians act." At least, she hoped the Dakota Indians would be happy to see them.

Eve stood and walked a distance. She found herself constantly standing still just to listen to nothing. And she never got enough of looking at the mountains, which changed every hour, yet they were always there, constant and strong and serene. She looked over her shoulder to Suncloud; he was still working.

So beautiful, handsome, and strong. Just like the mountains.

With a sigh Eve came back to sit across from McCloud, or Suncloud. She called him both nowadays. It depended on her mood. Suncloud was a great warrior, more fierce, more the savage. McCloud was more loving and giving and somewhat white. She decided he loved this white part of him as surely as he loved the Indian.

She was learning many things she did not know about McCloud—and Suncloud—before. He was relating more, of his history and life to her.

There were so many Indians in Suncloud's past that he did not know exactly what kind he was. He knew how to speak the many languages of the different nations spread across the territories. One-Arm was related to both the Cheyenne River Sioux and the Teton Dakota Sioux. So that made Suncloud a little of both tribes which were commonly called the Oglala Tetons. He loved the Shoshoni and had had an "uncle" who was from that nation, a man who had helped Suncloud grow up and learn how to fight defensively when One-Arm couldn't be around to show him.

Suncloud had been a leader when he was younger. He could have regained that leadership by going to war, but the treaties pledged him and other leaders not to engage in hostilities with either the white men or other tribes.

"Why is it that Americans talk so much of peace between themselves and the Indians, and between Indians and Indians, when they themselves wage such savage wars with their own kind?" McCloud had asked her one night as they sat before a comforting campfire.

"You mean whites fighting whites here and in other countries?" she asked, munching some bannock and raisins.

"Yes," he answered. "We are all the same when it comes to fighting. We all lust after land and wealth. The Indians just do it in a more careful way and with more honor. Like with the buffalo and the elk; we use all parts of those animals. The buffalo are a source of food, clothing, tools, and shelter; the elk the same, only with slight variation."

Eve tilted her head. "How is the buffalo used so widely?"

He directed her gaze to a few things in their camp. "There are the buffalo-hide parfleches you see there. The buffalo's paunch, you have seen me cook with it."

She laughed, asking, "How?"

"How?" He chuckled merrily. "It is that thing, that paunch, that is held over the fire with four poles. You have seen Whispering Bells doing this."

"Yes. And Many Stars. I have even cooked with the buffalo paunch when making stew. I dropped hot stones into the water to bring it to a boil. They soften, these paunches, after a few times cooking with them and have to be replaced. Now I know where that comes from. How interesting. What else? Meat?"

"Yes. Strips of drying buffalo meat are exposed to the sun; they are pounded into bits and mixed with berries to make the nourishing dried food—"

"Pemmican." She touched the pouch with that food in it, then turned to say, "Things are made from deerskin also." She laughed. "Do men really gamble with buffalo-bone dice?"

He grinned. "You know more than you let on, woman."

She shrugged. "I just like to hear you talk. You have a nice speaking voice, husband."

He looked her up and down, grunting.

Eve looked over to Suncloud's belongings next to a tree, his horse not far away. She saw his rawhide parfleches; they were the carryall of the Plains Indians. While in use, each of these containers held food, clothing, and other personal items. She saw the colorful geometric designs, traditionally painted by a woman. Women in camp, after the buffalo were brought in, had many tasks, she'd learned. Like the tanning of the hides that would be used for lodge coverings, blankets, and robes. In general, it was the men who killed the buffalo but the women who processed the carcasses. They turned almost every portion of the beasts into food, clothing, or shelter.

Now they resumed the conversation they had started many nights before, on the day that they had begun to search for the departed Huivi and Chara. The valley around them had darkened, but the mountaintops, bathed in sun, still shone on as they now sat before another campfire, eating some left-over pemmican.

"I knew some Cherokees too, cousins," Suncloud was saying as he poked at the fire and the stew cooking over it. "This was a bad time for the eastern tribes. The great Cherokee Nation had survived more than a hundred years of the white man's wars, diseases, and whiskey, but now it was to be blotted out. Because the Cherokees' numbers were many, their removal to the West was planned to be in gradual stages."

"Then what happened?" Eve asked, tucking her blanket around her legs so that the spiders could not crawl over her.

"Discovery of Appalachian gold within their territory brought on a haste for their immediate large-scale departure."

"Do you think gold will be discovered again out west?"

"Not all that much has been found, you are right," Suncloud said. "But I do think it will not be hard to find. The Teton Oglalas have found some. I believe Scar-Face was after some of their gold."

Her eyes brightened. "Do you think that my half brothers had discovered something that had to do with the finding of gold. That would have been a reason to kill them and take the yellow material and blue beads; their rawhide bags were also taken."

"Why do you see it that way?" Suncloud asked, his brow furrowed. "Just because the material is yellow? Gold is yellow. And what is *blue* like the blue beads?"

"The sky," she said. "Above the gold."

"Or water," he said. "The water can be just like the sky, only more blue, I think. Certain lakes are very blue. But the Indians don't enthuse over beauty all that much." He tossed some wild vegetables into their aging stew pot.

Eve sat staring at the stream of steam rising from the paunch. She looked up at him. "But you do?"

"No. Not really." He chuckled, then laughed out loud. "Any old hag will do."

She slapped him several times across the shoulders and back and head. "Hag, am I?" Then she jumped on his back, and as he stood suddenly, she gave out a squeal and held on for dear life. "Stop that. You will drop me. Stop spinning, I will get dizzy . . . *McCloud!*"

"Call me my Indian name," he ordered her, holding her by her plumped-up skirts and rump. "Say it. Suncloud is a great and noble warrior. Come on. I want to hear my squaw tell the earth, the sky, and the mountains how wonderful Suncloud is. How handsome, brave, and good-looking."

"Silly," she laughed. "Handsome and good-looking are the same thing."

He kept spinning, walking, spinning, ducking under tree limbs. He laughed as she squealed louder and louder.

"Stop it! Someone will hear us. Like a big old bear. He will come and eat us." She giggled so hard that her ribs against his back began to ache. "Suncloud . . . great and noble . . ." She laughed and choked. "Suncloud. *Oh, mighty Suncloud!*"

"Yes? What else?"

"This . . . this lowly squaw begs that you put her down. Before I split a seam!"

Down, down, she went, and Suncloud followed, lying right on top. She wriggled to get out from beneath him, but he held her down, his hands over her head, elbows outspread, lean hips pushing her into the ground until her legs opened and he fell between. He began to push up her skirts while undoing his breechcloth and leggings.

"I am going to have you, beautiful white squaw."

"Maybe," she said, trying not to giggle. "But you will have to fight hard to get me."

Then he stopped, his manhood at her moist and

willing valley entrance, stopped to gaze down into her wildly excited and laughing eyes.

Then they both heard a laughing voice.

Chara appeared in the tiny clearing, hands on her generous hips. "You two make me sick," Chara said with a sneer. "Is that all you do, make love? Suncloud never made those kind of eyes at me. I doubt if he even makes love the same to you."

Eve looked up into Suncloud's eyes as he turned back to say he was sorry. They had been interrupted again.

"Let me up, McCloud. Wait! Push down my skirts. There. Yes. Thank you for your help," she said in a cool voice, coming to her feet after she'd rolled out from beneath him.

"We have seen Scar-Face," Chara said.

Then Chara surprised them both when she sat down and began crying.

At once Suncloud walked through the grass and was at her side. "What is it?" He touched her head. "Why do you cry?"

Eve just looked on, feeling helpless—and somewhat piqued. What is she trying to do? Get Suncloud to come back to her? Why is she here alone? Oh, no, you don't, thought Eve as she stepped closer.

"Where is Huivi?" She shook her head. "Did I say his name right?"

"Y-yes!" Chara wailed. "I do not know. We became separated. He went the other way after we made out the form of Scar-Face and his friend from a distance. I thought he was going to come back to get me. He does not want Chara anymore, I can tell. He is tired of me."

Eve rolled her eyes heavenward as Chara wailed

again, sobbing, "Oh, I bet he has joined his c-c-c-"

Chara ground to a halt, realizing she was overdoing it a bit. She peeked up from between her fingers.

"His ka-ka-ka? What is that?" asked Suncloud, trying to get Chara to stand, but she kept falling back onto the pile of deadfall. "And where was Scar-Face when you spotted him?"

This part was true; they *had* seen Scar-Face. Chara pointed in the direction they'd seen Scar-Face heading, when he'd stopped to turn and look back at them. They'd been quite a way from him, but she still thought he might have spotted them. Huivi had gone out to look, then he had returned, saying Scar-Face and his friend had vanished. Then he too disappeared.

She went on, saying she walked and walked, had finally spotted Suncloud and his woman. Chara wished that Huivi would have given her instructions as to what she was supposed to do now. But he had left her; what was she going to do with this ugly beaded thing in her serape? Give it to Eve? No. She did not think so. Not yet. Huivi had turned coward, but she would not. She would wait until seeing Scar-Face and then join him.

Suncloud looked at Eve, where she stood looking off into the distance. He felt he should do something, perhaps go off alone for a time and seek a new vision.

"Eve, you stay with Chara. I will go looking for them. When I find them, you know what I must do, don't you?"

She looked across to him, where he stood with Chara, the woman who'd once shared his bed, borne him his child—and cheated on him!

"If you want to find them, Suncloud, then you

will. You will find Scar-Face and bring him down if
he's out there." She called him Suncloud now because she knew as he went to his parfleche that he
was going to put on fresh war paint. "You must
look very fierce," she called to him. "Be sure to put
lots of the black around the eyes. You look very
frightening that way."

Then she turned away, walked into the overhanging trees and pines. She wished to be alone for a few
moments.

Chara followed, looking over her shoulder at
Suncloud, a man she'd never really known at all. He
had never loved her. She shrugged to herself. Ah, it
is so, for she'd never loved him back though she'd
tried. He was hard to love, like most men, but this
one was the hardest.

Chara shrugged again. *Perhaps I should try with
Suncloud once more and see if we can find love.*

Suncloud's first wife followed the Dark Hair into
the trees. She was thinking, *If only I could do away
with her. But I cannot. I am afraid. The Dark Hair
has some strange power over all of us.* It seemed to
Chara that the Dark Hair had learned some things
that Chara had not.

Chara wondered if Suncloud knew this about the
Dark Hair. Perhaps he did, and this was why he had
left.

"Is Suncloud thinking to slay Scar-Face?" Chara
asked once they had entered another clearing, one
with horses standing in its center next to two lone
pines. "Tell me. Is he?"

Eve turned to look at Chara. "I believe he is.
Scar-Face is nothing but a murderer. And he likes
to dress women up in yellow dresses and blue beads

and then . . . I'm not sure what he does with them after that."

"He dresses them in yellow and then takes them like a sacrifice to some Spanish gods or something like that?" Chara asked, her eyes wide with excitement.

"I really do not know, Chara," was all Eve would say.

Suncloud was gone a long time. Eve began to worry that he had come to harm. Their meat supply was high, but she could not cook. Not wanting to attract unwanted visitors, she had put the fires out and the half-cooked deer meat they'd been cooking would spoil.

Another reason to keep fires out was—Scar-Face could have doubled back. And then what good would she be if she became his captive? He would lure Suncloud, slay him, and then kill her and Chara, or take them both for his women. Eve shook her head, thinking it sounded too unbelievable.

"Chara, do you know this man Scar-Face?" Eve did not say that she had been with him at Fort Robidoux.

"I know him," she said, feeling very weary. She was hungry too. "He is Huivi's c-c-c-" She again ground to a halt.

"Scar-Face is Huivi's ka-ka-ka?" Eve blinked. What is that? "His cousin!" Eve shot to her feet. "Huivi and Scar-Face are cousins! Why didn't you say so before?"

Chara slapped her face with both hands. She let them fall to her sides. "What is the difference? So they are cousins. Who cares?" She shrugged. "It changes nothing."

Turning her back on Chara as if she cared not about this either, Eve began to contemplate. And the more she thought, the harder she frowned, and the deeper her nails dug into her hands, the less she came up with for answers.

Eve let her whole body relax as she lay down on her blanket. Chara was already snoring, and Eve remembered how easily this woman could fall asleep.

Huivi and Scar-Face were cousins. They were both after something, then. One dressed women—certain women—in yellow dresses and blue beads. Derek and John had been coming back home with the yellow material and the beads when they had been slain. For those things, then? *Just* for their things? Or was there something to do with gold—or a map—that they'd been slain for?

Greed? Indian attack? Just plain hatred? Someone who liked yellow cloth? What?

Again she thought: What if my brothers had discovered something that had to do with the finding of gold. Did they know that if they dressed Indian girls up in yellow dresses, they would be offered gold as a treasure? To bring someone back, a woman, or child, who had been lost? She had to have Indian blood, then.

That sounds more like it, Eve decided. And seemed to tie in with what Scar-Face was trying to accomplish.

Wait! Many Stars had not been dressed in a yellow dress with blue beads.

I wanted them to bring back the yellow material and blue beads from the trading post.

Why? Eve asked herself. *Why did I say those words specifying those colors? Think, Eve. Why? Why!*

Eve shot up from her blanket, now knowing why.

I had a dream. In that dream I was wearing a yellow dress with blue beads. I was . . . I was much younger than I am now. In fact, in my dream I was a little girl.

What does Yellow Mare, Beau Arrow, have to do with my dream? My yellow material and blue beads?

Someone dressed me up like this, Eve told herself calmly. *Who was it and why was I put in a yellow dress with blue beads when I was a little girl?*

Eve ran to her bags and dropped onto her knees. She had seen Beau Arrow riding away wearing a rust-colored buckskin dress. Then where is . . .

Eve gasped as she pulled the yellow dress, the blue beads, and the remaining yellow material from her bags.

She left the material and carried the dress and the beads into the dark trees. Moving around inside the copse of pines, she tossed out her doeskin dress, her rawhide ties. She let down her hair and walked out from the trees.

Eve looked like a different person. Not a child, but a woman. A beautiful woman in a plain yellow dress and blue beads.

She walked over to where Chara slept, moving the sleeping, snoring form carefully—and there, lying beneath Chara, was the heavy amulet. It had spilled from her pocket as she slept.

The turtle with the butterfly on its back.

"They have been hiding this from me."

She picked it up, felt the polished beads against

her sensitive fingertips, and was flung back in time.
She stared, knowing it was hers.

When she opened the beaded amulet, she looked
at the strange yellow rocks, knowing this was not
what was supposed to be inside.

What *should* be inside? she asked herself, searching her memory. A child's toy? Grooming tools?
What had Maggie said?

Lifting one of the rough-hewn rocks, she stared at
the substance of yellow-gold. The stuff sparkled in
the dull light.

"Why do I feel so strange when I hold this old
turtle bag? It is as if my hands burn with a strange
light. Does this have something to do with my childhood?"

Holding the bag made her feel young and old at
the same time.

Stuffing the rocks back inside, Eve fastened the
bag and placed it on her horse with her other things.
Then she began to walk her horse.

Hours later, still wearing the yellow dress, Eve
walked into a strange, misty landscape. Something
seemed to call to her. Softly, softly, she could hear
the sound of drums in the distance.

Or was it thunder?

Eve wondered if she was asleep or awake.

Chapter Thirty-one

"There she is," said War Shirt. "My eyes at last behold her in the flesh."

"Who?" asked Red Buck, seeing nothing as he scanned the area up ahead. "I hear only the ghost bird. Listen."

"Ohhhh, ohhh, ooh-ooh."

That ghostly, haunting wailing was like a woman crying endlessly, hopelessly, or the mournful sigh of wind in the pines.

"Is this what you mean?" Red Buck asked War Shirt, hearing the ghost bird but seeing no one.

"No. You do not see her. She is there, the *winyan.* The true vision princess."

"I tell you," Red Buck said. "I see no woman, or this "she" you speak of. You say she is the princess, the one Great Eagle would look upon once more before he dies, the same one he has not seen since she was a small child?"

"Hetchetu aloh!" War Shirt said. "It is so indeed." He pressed Red Buck. "Look. You must look hard. She rides the painted horse. She wears the yellow dress and blue beads of her child-person, just as Winter Woman made these for her."

Red Buck argued, "How can she wear the yellow dress of her child-person. It would not fit her."

War Shirt growled impatiently, "She is grown now; the dress is bigger."

When Red Buck would have argued his point further, War Shirt cut him off abruptly with a slicing gesture of his hand.

"The woman we seek for years now?" Red Buck squinted and peered around but still could see nothing of what War Shirt was seeing.

"It is her. She is very beautiful and I feel—" War Shirt could not say how he felt. It was as if a breath of wind were sighing through his soul, touching his imagination. "A spirit," he added softly.

"You see visions again, War Shirt. You get old in your prime. I see only mist and shadows that move across the land like colored beasts."

"No beast," argued War Shirt. This man of the Teton Oglala was beginning to wonder about this himself, wonder if he was seeing the visions of her—Mist Smoke. The legendary lost child, the child who had never returned to Winter Woman. The child who would have become a woman herself by now, the one Great Eagle must look upon before the Spirits of the Deep Sleep come to visit him.

War Shirt sighed. "Perhaps only my soul does see this. Great Eagle will soon pass and meet the Shepherd Chief in the mountains of the sky, where he will go to live in the Big Tipi and sit down with the Shepherd Chief forever. He will never look upon his granddaughter before his passing."

"Come, we are weary. We will sit and eat."

Red Buck was about to dismount, when he looked up and blinked. He rubbed his eyes, wondering if he too was seeing what War Shirt had seen: a vision.

Riding through the mists and lights and shadows was a lone female mounted on a spotted mare. The sun shone with a watery light, and close to the ground, around the woman and her horse, mists wove and swirled.

"I see," said Red Buck, glimpsing the woman and looking from the glossy dark hair to the yellow dress to the moccasined feet, and then back to the spirited mare she rode. "Are we both experiencing the same vision?"

War Shirt knew he could never have imagined such a sight.

Red Buck blinked again and opened his eyes wider. It was all unbelievable, the sort of thing that happens only in childhood stories of the very old— or a vision quest.

The warriors of the Teton Oglala were wildly excited at this remarkable visitor from the Spirit World. A golden eagle appeared, swooping down and up in great wide arcs, sailing against the late July sun, then vanished. And with it went the woman on the spotted mare, into the watery sun's light.

"Great Eagle's vision. This is a sign. We must be close," War Shirt said. "Did you see the dress the beauteous vision wore? It was like the sun."

"*Ai.* Around her throat she wore beads the color of the summer sky." Red Buck shook his head, blue-black hair stirring on bronze shoulders. "Do you believe as I do?" Red Buck asked the older man. "That she, Mist Smoke, is near?"

"We must follow the vision," said War Shirt.

"There. Behind those rocks. She and the spotted mare went that way."

"Her spirit leads and we must follow the true vision princess. She might be in trouble."

"Han," War Shirt said. "Yes."

Carrying the yellow dress and blue beads, Eve walked to Zeena, tucked the things in her rawhide bags, the turtle amulet at the bottom, then mounted the spotted mare by taking a handful of the thick mane and hurling her body up onto Zeena's back.

Turning the horse, Eve looked back one last time at the sleeping Chara, then quickly urged Zeena into a canter. She rode off in the direction Suncloud had taken, her loose dark hair wearing two white feathers, black tips hanging down.

She was wearing a buckskin dress. And she didn't feel sleepy anymore, not at all. She had passed through a strange mist and found herself awakening in the tallgrasses beside a huge boulder.

Now she was wide awake.

Chapter Thirty-two

Eve drew a long, shaky breath.

She was alone. She did not like being alone in hostile country. There was no sign of Suncloud. He had ridden Wind in the direction away from the lowering sun; she rode that way now, away from the sunset and the hogback ridges.

The land sparkled in sunset tones that shot rays before her as she rode toward the hillier regions. She sent up a prayer for Suncloud's safety and kept riding over the hilly terrain slowly, carefully, to reserve her mount's strength in the event she would need to ride like the wind in the face of danger.

Scar-Face was angry and frantic. Astride his mount, he turned to Pierre and snarled, "Yellow Mare could have passed for her, the dark-haired one, Eve Michaels, in that yellow dress and blue beads. Eve Michaels, or Mist Smoke, as the Sioux call her. We could have gotten the Golden Tears by now."

"You are right, she does resemble Yellow Mare.

Although I have not seen Eve Michaels since she got away from us at Fort Robidoux."

"She did not get away. Suncloud took her," Scar-Face said with his nose in the air.

"I only meant—the dark-haired one is sly and swift. She got away from us because we did not have Kicking Wolf with us at the time."

"What has Kicking Wolf to do with it?" Scar-Face snarled into Pierre's face. "That one has deserted me and my plans." The handsome Spaniard rubbed his chin. "Hmm. I wonder if he even put the yellow cloth and blue beads in Suncloud's tipi. What became of that, do you think?"

"Well, we saw the Dark Hair, that was her, wasn't it? She was with that luscious Spanish tart Suncloud was married to at one time."

"How do we know it was her? Why take the chance to go back and see? I am looking for Yellow Mare now. Eve Michaels is too much like Suncloud by now. Kicking Wolf told us when Suncloud and the Dark Hair first arrived at Wild Thunder, he'd never let her out of his sight. He was thoroughly smitten with her."

"Smitten?"

"Yes, you know—enamored."

Pierre chuckled and slapped his thigh, making his mount dance sideways. "You cannot say the word love, can you?"

"That word does not mean much, if you ask me."

"There are those who believe otherwise, oh great, evil, nasty, dirty Scar-Face. Hate—that's what makes the world go round, eh?"

"Now you make sense, man."

* * *

"Someone is trailing us," said Pierre suddenly. "I have spotted a fierce face. He is painted in the war colors of the Shoshoni."

"Why did you see him and not I?" asked Scar-Face.

"You were not looking when I said for you to look. All you can do is lust after the Golden Tears. Listen, someone is coming."

"It is a woman." He groaned. "Not her."

"Who?"

"The Spanish woman."

"You are Spanish. Why don't you like her?"

"I have met Chara only once before. She has given me eyes, looked me up and down."

Pierre chuckled. "She does not know how dangerous and cruel you are with your women."

"We shall see what she wants. Perhaps she can give us some information and tell us who that woman was that we saw her with. She is not with her now." Scar-Face rubbed his chin. "I wonder where she's gone off to."

Chara rode up, and all she said was "Where is Huivi? Is he with the Dark Hair? I cannot find her."

The Dark Hair, hmm, Scar-Face thought as his eyes lit up with a hundred scintillating lights. Now, this is interesting. "Whom do you mean by Dark Hair?"

"Why, Eve Michaels, who else?" Chara was put off by his question. Always her, always the dark-haired one.

"Come, Chara, we will stop for something to eat. You will make a bite for us."

Chara looked Scar-Face up and down. What a man, she thought, and he has Spanish blood too.

"Good," she said. "I am very hungry. Eve left without a morsel to spare for me."

Eve!

Scar-Face's eyes glowed like a hungry wolf's.

After they had eaten and Scar-Face had questioned the Spanish woman fiercely, they rested for a while. As Pierre napped, Scar-Face took Chara behind a low hill and had his way with her. Chara was all too willing.

Pierre was shouting when they returned to the camp. He swore in French, then said, "Someone has taken our yellow cloth and blue beads!"

All of a sudden Scar-Face lashed out at Chara. "Bitch. You have stolen the items. That was our last resort. We would have had a fortune once we brought the woman Eve Michaels to the Dakota camp and received the Golden Tears. All we had to do was show our goods to Great Eagle and he would have believed any superstitious nonsense we might have told him. If not Eve Michaels, then Yellow Mare, with her dark hair the same shade of shiny beaver-brown as Eve's."

Scar-Face lashed out at Chara, striking her to the ground. "Now there is to be no Golden Tears. No Eve Michaels. Where did you hide the pouch?"

Chara gaped up at him from where he'd tossed her. "What gold? And what is this about Eve Michaels? Why does everyone want her? Even Huivi. What is the strange power she has over us all? That *puta.*" Chara spat. "She has put a spell on Suncloud also. Now you."

"Tell me what else you know?" Scar-Face ground out. "Where are all your friends?"

Chara gulped. "I thought you found me desirable. We just made love." She pouted, and Pierre looked at Scar-Face, but Scar-Face was looking only at Chara. "Now you accuse me of theft. What will you do with me now? If you harm me, Suncloud will come after you. He will kill you."

Scar-Face laughed. "But not so your lover Huivi. Hah! He is my relative."

She would not tell this pig that Huivi had run off and deserted her. "Huivi will kill you too, cousin or not. He loves me. We would have gone far away after . . . after he got that—"

"Got what?" Scar-Face wanted to know. "The Golden Tears?"

"I know nothing of these Golden Tears." She lied, for Huivi did say something about a treasure that would bring them much wealth. They could have gone far away to a golden land where the sun shone forever and there was white sand to lie upon.

As Pierre and Scar-Face took themselves aside for a private conversation, Chara muttered to herself: "I do not have that thing Huivi left me with. It was a silly old bag, a pouch of some kind with beads all over it. I hardly looked at it." She shrugged, unaware someone was sneaking up on her. "Eve must have taken it. Perhaps it meant something."

Chara never knew what hit her as something hard struck her head and she was given the death blow.

Scar-Face smiled and turned away, tossing the bloodied rock aside.

"There she is. I see her again," said War Shirt.

"No. This is not her, not the lost one we seek. Look, she does not wear the yellow dress, but a doeskin one with beads and fringes."

Red Buck then blinked and looked at War Shirt.

"The horse is the same. And look, the hair of the woman. It also is the same, shining with dark fires in the strands. And the dress is buckskin, War Shirt."

"What tricks are these?" muttered War Shirt.

"No tricks," Red Buck said as he slowed his war horse. "The only tricks were in our minds."

"Ah, this I do not believe," War Shirt said to Red Buck. "We looked upon her in our visions and knew she would come."

"The visions of two men who have not closed their eyes for the night? But see these visions in the full light of day?"

"I have done this," said War Shirt. "I am older than you, have seen more. Spirits come to us under many circumstances, Red Buck."

"I have gone out to a lonely spot in order to obtain a revelation. One has never come to me while unsought."

The normal procedure was to go into solitude, fast and thirst for four days, and supplicate the spirits to take pity on the sufferer.

"You lived with the Arapaho too long, Red Buck. You do not cherish the waking dreams as the Dakota do."

"You have obtained exceptional power from the spirits," Red Buck asked War Shirt. "Are you *wakan?*"

"No, Red Buck. I am not medicine man. I am only Dakota, as you. Now you too are with us once again, as I knew you would be when you walked back into our village ten summers back, just as Mist Smoke shall be."

"Woksapa. You have much wisdom, War Shirt."

"See her, then, as I. We will approach soon. Quietly, carefully, so we do not frighten and alarm her. She might flee like a swift doe. She must not run from us."

"Ho." Red Buck was ready.

Before they could ride toward her, a fierce horse and rider appeared before them. He unshouldered his rifle and warned them to go no farther.

"Forks of the River Man," said War Shirt.

"He is also part Teton Oglala. I know of him. He is the legendary Suncloud, Long Knife of the Shoshoni, and his grandfather is One-Arm, of the Cheyenne River branch. He is not Shoshoni, as many have come to believe. He has white blood also."

"Yes." War Shirt smiled. "This is why I must bring them both to our camp."

"Both?" Red Buck wondered out loud. "What about the woman? She does not wear the yellow dress and blue beads now."

War Shirt said, "I believe it is she. But I will know for sure when I see the ghost mark on her neck. Just as Beau Arrow, the lost princess of the Hunkpapa, has them—not one, but three of the ghost marks."

"The mist-smoke mark. Eve Michaels has this. And her child's name is Mist Smoke." He grinned.

"That is the real name of it," said War Shirt. "Suncloud has brought her to us,   less of the spirits tugging him."

"She has very long dark hair. How will you find this mark—if this is true?"

War Shirt looked at Red Buck as if he were stupid. "You lift her hair and I will look." He nodded.

"Ah—no. I will look. You lift her hair."

War Shirt screwed up his mouth. "We will tell her there is a bug on her neck."

"Bug?" Red Buck blinked.

"Yes." He nodded once quickly. "A bug."

"Ahhh. I do not know. She is rumored to be smart, not dumb. So is the Long Knife she is with."

"Forks of the Green River Man? He is in love with her. You can see it. They have stopped to stare into the eyes of the other. You can see love in their eyes. He will do what she wants." He shrugged. "Whatever that will be."

"You ask for trouble. Our brothers have been warring with the Wind River Shoshoni."

"Ah. It is such a small 'warring,' " War Shirt said, pinching his fingers together. "Small bands. Foolishness. They fight over the antelope in the hills. *Hoh.* This will never be recorded in stories of the past."

"Waśte, good," said Red Buck.

From a distance Suncloud saw Eve riding toward him. He knew there were those who were watching her. He would have to act quickly if he was to save her. The Dakota warriors looked strong, and although one was in his prime, older than the other, they would put up a good fight.

"I see him coming to us," said War Shirt. "Do you think he knows what we are up to?"

"What are we up to?" Red Buck asked, and War Shirt snorted.

"Maybe he will talk."

"I think he wants to fight to protect the woman." He looked at War Shirt. "Do you think he will give us a chance to explain why we have come this far from our lands?"

"No, not when I look at his face. He looks fierce, like a true warrior bent on revenge."

"Han. Something close to that. He believes we would kill him and take the woman captive."

War Shirt looked among the hills behind Suncloud, scanning the area quickly. "Do you think he has come with others?"

"We should have the turtle amulet now," Red Buck said. "To show to him."

"And to her, Eve Michaels. She might have recognized her own belonging from her childhood. Why did we trust Huivi and give it to him to show to her, believing he would bring her to us?"

"Ah. He said he knew where to find Eve Michaels. I believe this is why they have come, this Suncloud and Eve Michaels. Huivi must have gotten them out of Wild Thunder, at least."

"At least," War Shirt agreed. "This is true. He is perhaps a better storyteller than Scar-Face?"

"No one tells lies like that one," Red Buck hissed.

"Listen. He speaks." Red Buck leaned over his horse to nudge War Shirt.

"Why have you come for us?" asked Suncloud, surprising himself with his own question.

"It is not you so much we seek." War Shirt nodded toward Eve, slowly coming closer. *"Ai.* She is beautiful. Just as Great Eagle said she would be."

"Who is this Great Eagle?" Suncloud demanded, the black and red paint banding his cheekbones making him look fierce. "What does he want of the Dark Hair?"

War Shirt felt Red Buck's elbow as he paused too long. "Great Eagle would look upon his granddaughter's face before the Dove Spirit comes to take him to paradise."

"Granddaughter?" asked Suncloud. "Eve Michaels is his granddaughter? How can you prove this?"

War Shirt was nudged again when he lagged. "Her mother was Narcissa Roussillon LeBleau, relative of Winter Woman's. The child, Eve Michaels, had a turtle amulet"—he cleared his throat—"with a butterfly riding the back of the turtle."

"Riding?" Suncloud asked, still looking fierce.

"Beads," War Shirt explained. "The butterfly was beaded onto the back of the turtle." He cleared his throat again. "Silly things women do."

"I don't think it is silly at all," Eve said as she rode up to them, halting her spotted mare. She dug into her bags and showed them what she had. "This is the turtle amulet."

War Shirt and Red Buck lurched backward on their mounts.

Suncloud reached out and snatched it away, holding it high. It was very heavy. "This was in my vision."

"You had a vision?" War Shirt grinned, his turn to nudge Red Buck. "This is good. You are the one who must guard Eve Michaels all the way to camp."

Suncloud's gaze swung to Eve. "You are saying she has the blood of the Dakota? How?" He shook his head then as he recalled his visions.

"Come to our village. Great Eagle does not have much time left in this world. He wants to see the child Winter Woman greatly cherished in her younger days. He was too busy to spend much time with her—this adopted child—and would look upon her now before his time has vanished like—"

"Mist smoke," said Red Buck, nudging War Shirt.

"Winter Woman," Eve said with wonder and awe.

With astonishment on his face, Suncloud went to ride beside Eve. "I am to guard you," he said with a sudden sheepish expression, not looking at her.

"Why so gloomy, Suncloud?" Eve fell in behind War Shirt and Red Buck. Suncloud was still hanging on to the turtle amulet; it was growing heavier all the time.

"It is nothing." He hefted the pouch and almost broke his wrist. "What is in this turtle bag?"

"Heavy rocks. Pretty ones. They are a yellow-gold color. I have never seen anything like them. They shine like the summer sun."

Suncloud jerked his head to look at Eve. "Rocks? Pretty yellow ones, you say?"

"Yes. Very pretty. Shaped like tears."

"Gold."

She laughed. "Gold never looked like that; not the jewelry I've seen." A frown etched her brows. "When it is melted down and becomes gold pieces, does it resemble the beauty of these rocks?"

"It does."

Eve said no more.

War Shirt, Red Buck, Suncloud, and Eve were riding into Dakota Indian territory. No one trailed them, War Shirt said.

Suncloud said, "Scar-Face and his companion are not too far behind. I have spotted strange shadows back there."

"Scar-Face." War Shirt grimaced. "That one is after the Golden Tears. He has brought many women to us, saying each one is the Lost Child—

Mist Smoke. He already has much sparkling rock; he is greedy for the rest, the most precious of them."

"Were they all wearing yellow dresses and blue beads, these women Scar-Face brought into your village?"

"Han, yes. This is what they wore. Great Eagle said he would know the true Eve Michaels when he saw her face. He will be able to *feel* it is her also. She, Eve, always wore a yellow dress with blue beads about her neck. This is the way her mother Narcissa wanted her dressed, like a pretty white doll. Winter Woman made the clothes for the child, and the beads. She also made the turtle bag from colorful beads, like yellow and blue ones for the butterfly. Mist Smoke wanted to be fully Indian; she would run into the woods with the other children and she would borrow a Dakota dress to put on."

Eve looked at Suncloud. "I did?" She frowned downward and then looked up at War Shirt. "Maybe it was not me after all. I feel like the turtle amulet is mine. I had always dreamed of the yellow material and blue beads. I had my brothers John and Derek promise to bring these things back for me from the trading post. Do you know what?" she asked Suncloud.

"What?" he asked, still gazing at her as if she were a long-lost princess.

"When I was a grown woman living in that cabin with my brothers and Maggie, I wanted to make a yellow dress. My brothers looked at me as if I were crazy when I begged them to bring the material and beads from the trading post; I had seen these items the week before at the trading post. I knew they had a secret, the both of them, my brothers did. Do you suppose they knew about my life in the Dakota village?"

"They might have even been there with you themselves. I have no idea of the truth, Eve. You will learn much when we arrive at the village of the Teton Oglala." He caressed her cheek, then pressed a finger to her lips. Leaning over, he kissed her tenderly. "Beautiful white squaw. We will find all there is to know about you."

Later in the day, as they trudged their tired horses along, War Shirt glanced over at the amorous couple. His eyes fell to the turtle amulet and he frowned. He wondered why it appeared larger than before; it looked like an animal that had eaten voraciously and gotten larger in the belly.

"Her amulet bulges, looks bigger," said War Shirt to Red Buck. "There must be more in there than the cord of her birth; what do you think?"

"Maybe she herself has put some of her own belongings in there. It is hers and has only come back into her possession. She can do with it what she wishes."

"We are not sure. We have not seen the mist smoke mark."

"The ghost mark."

"If you say. Great Eagle will know. And then we will see."

"Are you going to tell her she has a bug on her neck?"

"No. You are."

War Shirt smiled as they rode on toward the Dakota encampment.

Chapter Thirty-three

War Shirt, Red Buck, Eve, and Suncloud jour-
neyed for many days across the hills and plains,
frequently encountering bands of the other Dakota—Mdewakanton, Wahpekute, Sisseton, Yank-
ton, and Yanktonai.

Once a raiding band of Arikara, savage warriors
with buffalo horns woven into their long hair and
wolfskin breechclouts swooped down upon War
Shirt's small party from the north. They had been
looking for an undefended village to yield them the
elk meat they had been denied because of a battle
that had taken place earlier, between the Bad Faces
and men of Wild Thunder. The Arikara sheared off
at the discharge of Suncloud's rifles, carrying their
dead with them.

War Shirt blew at the bore of the still-smoking
rifle. "Nice firestick, Sun Cloud."

"Suncloud; say it fast, not slow."

Nodding, War Shirt asked, "Can I keep the firestick, Sun—Suncloud?"

"You can carry it for me."

War Shirt beamed, hoisting it over his shoulder

as a soldier would. He beamed from ear to ear as he looked over at Suncloud.

"Suncloud," he said all in one breath this time.

At the end of a week's traveling, they met a wandering band of Yanktonai, who told them the Teton bands had crossed the nearest river and headed north.

"We have to go north again," Suncloud said, squinting up at the sun.

War Shirt and Red Buck agreed.

These Yanktonai were of leaner build than the Eastern Dakota, with keen, predatory faces and a harsher-sounding speech. Their mounts, which they stole from the southern tribes—who in turn stole from still other tribes—or bred from stolen stock, were small, clean-limbed horses with the Arabian strain.

The Yanktonai insisted upon accompanying them and, the truth was, as they penetrated deeper into the Plains, Eve appreciated as she had not before the advantage of the Yanktonai's knowledge and protection. She told them so, Suncloud translating. War Shirt and Red Buck only smiled a secret smile.

After the Yanktonai had ridden off, Suncloud told Eve, "I am sure the Yanktonai would have murdered us cheerfully if not for War Shirt's presence."

Eve's swallow went down hard.

They continued up the Valley of the River, having, to their discomfort, to pass over many tributaries, large and small.

The country, it seemed to Eve, sloped upward

slowly again, as though climbing toward the High Shining. They saw no people for days, but passed a number of deserted village sites, which War Shirt asserted to represent the course taken by the Teton in their westward journey, probably in search of better grazing conditions for their horse herds.

This proved to be exactly the case, War Shirt said. His people had moved on to another summer camp.

Their first glimpse of a man after they'd parted from the Yanktonai came as they surmounted a hill that shouldered abruptly above the level of the plains. As noiseless as a figure in a dream, a boy rode over its summit and peered down at them with startled eyes. A yelp rose from his lips, and he heeled his mount up and down as if not knowing which way to turn, then, shaking his hand happily in their direction, galloped off down the opposite slope.

"The Teton keep good watch," Suncloud commented. "But why did the boy wait to run?"

"He was signaling," explained War Shirt. "When we reach the hilltop, you will see what he has accomplished."

From the brow of the hill Eve and Suncloud looked down upon a broad stretch of level grasslands. In the midst of it, hundreds of tipis clustered in concentric circles with an opening to the east.

"Look," Eve said, feeling warm and wonderful, as if she'd just come home. She felt she had been at this Dakota camp before.

Smoke curled up between the lodge poles, and men, women, and children swarmed the many paths, all staring up at War Shirt and the others.

A body of warriors was running from the village toward the river, where several thousand horses were being rounded up by the boy they still watched. His shrill cries came faintly to Eve's ears, as they were a considerable distance away.

Now the herd was in motion toward the village, and an imposing troop of warriors galloped up to meet them. Eve was captivated as sunlight glinted on feather headdresses and lance points and the bright beadwork of sheaths and quivers.

Such color abounded. Eve blinked, catching her breath. *Tuwe miye he?* Who am I? The words from her dream.

"Ah," Suncloud exclaimed. "The Tetons have their eyes open."

"So they do," said Eve with a bright grin at the boy who had ridden along the hilltop.

Suncloud went on. "They do well to watch from the hilltop, but if I were choosing a place to pitch my people's tipis, I would not put them under a hill which I couldn't see through in the night."

"I suppose they have protection for their horses from the cold north winds here." Eve looked at Suncloud as she said this.

He snorted. "Wise Dakota woman."

"You say that too soon. I'm still not sure they will accept me as the Lost Child. Especially this fierce Great Eagle."

"He is not so fierce at the time, Eve. He is passing away and fades in and out of illness, War Shirt says."

"Yes, I heard. I remember a man who was fierce and brave here among these people."

Suncloud took his gaze from her tears and said, "And here beneath the hill they have fine grazing grounds and water for the taking."

"Thank you, Suncloud," said Eve.

"You thank me?" He stared at her beautiful face, bronze from the sun. *She colors easily from the late summer winds and sunlight,* he mused.

Suncloud and Eve halted at the foot of the hill to await the coming of the warriors. They stormed up as though they would ride Eve and Suncloud down. A once-tall, once-strong old man rode in advance, flung out a hand with a single word of command. The warriors yanked their horses to an abrupt halt, scattering the sods right and left and flowing around War Shirt's company in a circle that barred all chance of retreat.

"Ah!" War Shirt exclaimed with calm. "Have the Teton left the Council of the Seven Fires? Does Great Eagle forget the face of War Shirt?"

The shriveled-up chief eyed War Shirt and his company grimly from the back of his big horse. Great Eagle spoke with a hiss because of the loss of several front teeth. He was sudden in his actions, and his warriors plainly feared him, although any one of them could have tucked him under one arm.

This is the great Great Eagle? Eve wondered.

Great Eagle spoke. "Why did not War Shirt send one in advance to tell Great Eagle he was coming?"

"War Shirt knew not where the Teton were camped," replied Great Eagle's best warrior.

Then War Shirt saw that Great Eagle's mind was wandering from his body; he would come back to himself soon and be aware of what was happening. Great Eagle had done this often before War Shirt rode out several months earlier.

Suncloud rode up, his strong, mellow voice in strange contrast to the rasping tones of the old chief.

"I am Suncloud, leader of the people of Wild

Thunder, where the Wind River meets the High Shining in the Sky," he told Great Eagle.

"No chief? *Hai,*" Great Eagle said. "You are a long way from your lodge, young warrior."

Eve thought that the Dakota chief had said that rather disdainfully. She looked to Suncloud to see what his retort was going to be.

"Suncloud has honor in his own country."

Eve wanted to cheer, and then her face fell as she heard the great chief's words follow after Suncloud's.

"That may be," returned Great Eagle ungraciously. "Here you are unknown."

Suddenly Great Eagle turned in his saddle and scowled at his warriors, and the fear that showed in every eye was amusing to Suncloud, as it was to War Shirt and Red Cloud.

"Squaws! They were afraid to leave their tipis. The One-with-Scar-on-Face has left his bad medicine, his firewater."

Great Eagle turned on Suncloud now, adding to his tirade.

"That is why we will have nothing to do with any white men," he concluded, glancing back and forth between them. He scowled at War Shirt, one of his best, younger friends, though he could not recall this at the moment. "They might be friends of the one who bewitched my young warriors with firewater."

"And I, Suncloud, am also known in my country as the friend of the white man," he told Great Eagle, his eyes on Eve, who was smiling from ear to ear at his noble and generous words. "I am not a friend to One-with-Scar-on-Face," he concluded.

"If you are friends of the Spaniard who bewitched my young men, you shall go from here," snapped Great Eagle, "or I will take scalps and hang them from my lodge pole."

"Scar-Face," Eve said. "We do not like him. Believe us when we say this, old man. He is the enemy."

Blinking, Great Eagle slowly turned his head to face the Dark Hair.

"Why do you speak when not spoken to?" Great Eagle questioned her fiercely.

"You wanted to see me," she answered softly in the Dakota language. "I have my amulet." She searched her bags, came up with nothing. Looking at Suncloud, she asked, "You have the turtle bag, do you not?"

"I do not. You have it."

"No. You were holding it last."

"And then you took it from me."

"You never gave it back. You still have it."

"No."

"Yes."

"I tell you—"

Great Eagle's head had been going from side to side, and now he yelled, "Be still."

Turning his attention to the young woman, Great Eagle said, "Who are you?"

"Tuwe miye he?" Who am I? Eve asked. She wondered this herself. Great Eagle had not recognized her, and why should he? If she was the Lost Child, he would not recognize her now. This man was as senile as a hundred-year-old bear.

"I—I meant nothing. Forget—"

Starting to turn her mount, Eve was brought up short by the sound of his raspy voice.

"Say the words again," Great Eagle commanded.

"Words?" Eve looked back at him, trying to comprehend his command.

"Tuwe miye he?" Great Eagle said. "You say again, Dark Hair."

"Tuwe—"

"Hoh." Great Eagle expressed the word for wonder.

Eve repeated, *"Hoh."*

Suncloud cleared his throat as he touched Eve's arm. "No. That Dakota expression is used by men only."

"She is Mist Smoke," tried War Shirt, telling Great Eagle.

The old chief felt suddenly very weak. He looked at the Dark Hair with a strange glassiness in his eyes.

"I have known it would come to pass."

Hands reached out to catch him in case he would fall, for Great Eagle appeared very weak at the moment.

Great Eagle pushed the arms of his warriors aside. "I am not a *cinca,* baby," he said in a raspy growl.

Once again Suncloud turned to gaze at Eve with wonder in his eyes.

"Suncloud," Great Eagle said. "You and your friends are welcome. There are seats in my lodge awaiting you."

Eve stared with wide eyes as Great Eagle came to her side, putting his mount in line with her horse to return to the village.

"Come, Mist Smoke, and tell this old man of your wanderings. For soon it will be winter." He looked up into the sky. "We will sit around a cook-fire and talk of what has been."

Eve looked around for Suncloud but could not see him. Great Eagle had said winter. Did he mean Winter Woman? Was she there?

Answering her deepest thoughts, Great Eagle said, "Winter Woman has gone to the Land of the Sky People." He faced her for only a moment, asking, "Do you know of the Dove Spirit?"

"Yes," Eve told him truthfully.

"We must talk of this. For soon I will go with the Dove Spirit."

Eve frowned, looked to returning Suncloud. He translated this bit, and Eve answered Great Eagle.

"Yes," she said.

She was sad.

Winter Woman was gone.

She heard Great Eagle's words: *What is past and cannot be prevented should not be grieved for.*

But Eve had been watching his face, and his mouth had not moved.

When she finally looked away, Great Eagle smiled to himself.

His smile was one of sweet peace as he looked to the sky again.

Very soon and you will not be alone, Winter Woman . . . soon we shall walk the Land of the Sky People together. . . .

Chapter Thirty-four

The evening fires were blazing as the weary party rode into the Dakota village. War Shirt and Red Buck were greeted warmly and with excitement by women, children, and handsome warriors.

But where was the one called Suncloud?

Eve scanned the hilltop and surrounding area, that same question running in her mind. *Where is he? Why did he leave me now when I most need him?* She reined her horse around a pile of deadfall, made sure the way was clear up ahead, and then glanced back once, quickly, but still no sign of McCloud.

Great Eagle saw Eve's concern over her man, who had ridden back onto the open plains; Great Eagle said nothing as she dismounted and stood, looking disoriented. He sent her with a young maiden to see to her needs before she was to come to Great Eagle's lodge. Eve understood only some of the maiden's words.

As they entered the tipi, Eve asked, "Can you speak English?"

"Han!" Tacincala exclaimed, then caught herself and said "yes" in English.

"Great Eagle failing fast. He very sick before you

come. Been very sick from time Moon of the Snow-blind. He does not eat his favorite food: tall-ears."

Eve shook her head as Tacincala was pouring water for her that another woman had brought quietly.

"Tall-ears?" Eve asked as she turned her attention back to Tacincala.

"The rabbit. His favorite food, but no can eat. Great Eagle will go to lie down on his mats now. He will share the meal with you if his strength has come back after rest."

Looking around, hearing these people, seeing how they lived, their dwellings, their foodstuffs, showed Eve how much more primitive the Dakota lived than the people of Wild Thunder. No houses here; no stores like the trading post and the furnishings therein, but there was something here she'd not witnessed in Wild Thunder: her past.

Eve was reliving feelings she'd shoved back inside herself as she bathed with the water Tacincala had poured for her. After she'd used the cloth for drying off, Tacincala brought her a small tray and a skin of fresh drinking water.

"You eat prairie turnip now, good appetizer before you sit to eat with Chief Great Eagle."

Tacincala did not add that her chief might very well be lying down already, unable to eat, unable to sit up without being propped; he might not want his visiting friends to see him that way.

After Tacincala had closed the flap, Eve sat staring at the tipi wall. The words of Many Stars came back to her: Everything changes, nothing stays the same as it was the day before. Tomorrow we will be different than we were today.

"Oh, Suncloud . . . McCloud . . . where are you?

I miss you. Where have you gone? Why don't you come back and be with me now. I need you. You are my life. I want you."

She could not admit that she was afraid of something. Was it the past?

She was here now, among Winter Woman's people.

Tacincala stepped in for a moment, startling Eve. Then she quickly left, closing the flap.

Eve looked over near the entrance. Tacincala had left something; standing there was Eve's puffy deerskin bag with all her things inside it.

For a second, as Eve was walking to the entrance, she thought she saw a shining presence.

She felt it and knew what—or who—was there.

And then she could make out the frame of a small woman standing in the center of the tipi.

Eve was aware of the wild thumping of her heart, and, as she continued to stare, she saw more of the apparition when the figure cleared and became more visible. A woman in a doeskin dress. Kindly features. Small, thin hands. Her hair hung in a thick, dark braid down her back, hair with white in its strands, and her eyes had a fixed, concentrated look.

Eve swallowed.

"Winter Woman. I feel your presence now as I felt your presence in my dream. Why did you have to go before I could come here to see you, to hold your hand and walk the land with you as we did long ago. We could have relived memories. I love you, Winter Woman, you were like a true mother to me when my own had no time for me, except to dress me in pretty dresses and bows—and beads."

Eve stepped back as the silver light in the room

brightened considerably for a moment and the figure wavered like a watery shadow.

Eve's eyes fluttered at the bright flash before she saw what looked to be the golden rocks that she'd found in her turtle amulet.

The words breathed in and out of Eve's imagination: He is waiting. Great Eagle might not have much longer, Mist Smoke. The ancient Golden Tears . . . they belong to you and your love . . . Mist Smoke. They will remain in your care until another loved one takes them.

But he already took them. Eve almost spoke out loud, but did not in case the woman would vanish.

The haunting sound of the ghost voice uttering the words "Mist Smoke" called to her, and suddenly she was the child of her vision, remembering picking blueberries and bullberries with—Winter Woman.

Buffalo summer.

Wearing the yellow dress and blue beads. The bright green grass and windy hills, sapphire skies and cotton clouds, butterflies and hummingbirds, the fairy gold of wildflowers, and wood smoke in the air. Laughter in the air and good times in the camp.

I am awake; I am not sleeping. I can remember now. Suddenly it does not hurt to do this. Thank you, Winter Woman. I will go to Great Eagle soon, but first there are some things I must do.

Going to her bags, Eve took out the yellow dress and the blue beads. She stopped what she was doing, wishing again that Suncloud could be with her.

"Oh, Suncloud, where have you gone? Have you taken the Golden Tears, never to return to me? Is this what is going to be? I will see you never again?"

In the back of her mind she knew he had ridden off with her amulet. Was that all she'd been to him—a pile of golden rocks?

Golden Tears. That is how my own tears will be, frozen in time, always there; *I will always be crying, dejected, always sad that he went away and never wanted to see me again.*

Lovers do not reject lovers, she told herself.

The haunting words came again:

He is waiting for you.

"I know, Winter Woman, I hear you," Eve said to the voice within as she went from the tipi and closed the flap, a heavy red blanket wrapped around her head and shoulders.

Chapter Thirty-five

"Great Eagle is failing fast," War Shirt told Eve as she sat on the fluffy pile of buffalo robes where the chief lay.

Tacincala had come along to Great Eagle's lodge as interpreter for Eve.

"He just spoke to me a moment ago; I believe he understood my halting Dakota," Eve told Tacincala. "He was—he seemed aware of what we were talking about. I do not think he wants to die just yet."

Tacincala just stared at Eve. "He drifts in and out of—"

"Awareness?" Eve furnished, then, using simpler words, Eve told Tacincala to tell the chief that she wished to speak to him more. "We have unfinished business," Eve added.

Again Tacincala stared. Then she said, "Oh, Great Chief, Mist Smoke"—she looked at Eve and Eve nodded—"Mist Smoke would like to talk. Are you ready to do this?"

With a shove onto his elbows Great Eagle tried to sit up, grumbling that he'd like to be propped up.

Eve smiled as he sat up and faced her with a big, happy grin.

War Shirt said, "I will go for a time." He looked at Eve with a nod. "I will be back."

Peering down at Eve's neck, he smiled and nodded to himself. There had been no need to say that there was a bug on her neck since she was wearing her hair in a braid and he could make out the mist mark very easily.

As Eve watched War Shirt walk from the lodge, she thought of something, and with a word to Tacincala she went out behind War Shirt.

Eve caught up with War Shirt. Tacincala was right behind Eve, and Eve turned to look at her.

With a sweet smile Tacincala said, "You might need my voice."

Eve nodded. This was good.

"War Shirt, wait." Eve looked to Tacincala, and she translated what words Eve could not understand as War Shirt spoke.

"You wish to know what Winter Woman told the man who went to look for you?" War Shirt asked, meaning Huivi.

"*Han,* yes," Eve said, blinking wide. Can they all read minds around here? she wondered.

"Winter Woman told him: 'Find her, War Shirt, if Mist Smoke is still alive, find her and bring her back to show her where she learned to love, laugh, walk as a child. She will not remember, she was taken away at too young an age. Her white father did not care that her people wanted her to stay until she was older. Her mother cares only for the white ways; we do not know if Narcissa and her child are yet alive. If the girl-child is, she must be told of her grandmother's passing and that her grandfather

Great Eagle is now passing and he would see her before he goes. She, this Eve Michaels, Mist Smoke, has been in his dream.' "

War Shirt went on. Huivi's mission was to bring this beautiful Indian maiden to War Shirt. If he failed, it was Suncloud's duty to bring Eve Michaels to Great Eagle. Suncloud, leader of the Wind River Shoshoni and Basin Utes, had also been seen in Great Eagle's dream.

"This Huivi wanted the Golden Tears," War Shirt ended.

"Where are the Golden Tears now?" asked Eve. Then she breathed a loud gasp. "Suncloud has them. They are the heavy rocks, the pretty ones of a yellow-gold color."

"They shine like the summer sun," War Shirt said.

"Yes! Shaped like tears: He has them. Suncloud said Scar-Face was after them. No," she corrected herself. "You said that." She looked closely at War Shirt. "Do you know he has them?"

"They belong to him, to Suncloud. For bringing you here."

"What?" Eve looked at War Shirt. Her face fell. "He left with them? Suncloud wanted only the Golden Tears?"

Eve was looking sad.

War Shirt looked at Eve and smiled. "You wear the yellow dress and the blue beads." As if he hadn't noticed this before. "You also have the ghost—"

Eve turned abruptly to Tacincala. "Tell him there is no need for the dress and beads."

"She is right," said Great Eagle from behind them. "I knew Mist Smoke the moment she spoke the words *Tuwe miye he?* Who am I?"

Eve whirled. "You spoke English!"

"Han, yes. We will go inside and talk more now, Eve Michaels. Mist Smoke."

"Tell me again of the Dove Spirit," asked Great Eagle, lifting tranquil eyes to Eve from his seat on the buffalo robes.

"You tell me," Eve shot back, aware that his "spirit" was returning, as well as his strength. She would give him a good argument. . . .

With a stronger voice Great Eagle said, "It is true that the missionaries taught me. It is true that I have read the Bible. The missionaries are good men. The Bible is a good book. There is wisdom in it. But the men who wrote it did not even know that the Indians existed. They had never heard of this country. How then, daughter, could they know what the Great Spirit devised for the Indian? No, sweet Mist Smoke, I think that the Great Spirit who made the world, who put the saltwater in the ocean, which men use only for travel, and fresh water in the rivers, where thirsty men go to drink, may well have created a different afterworld for the Indian than for the white man."

"No," Eve insisted, "the soul that leaves the body is bodiless. It cannot be touched or seen. Remember, Great Eagle, the Great Spirit sent His Son to dwell awhile with the white men, to give his life for the saving of mankind. Yet he said nothing of this belief of yours."

Great Eagle smiled scornfully. "You are truly white, Eve Michaels." He waved his hand. "You may go now. Go, meet your man. He has taken the

Golden Tears. He brought you to me and I have seen you. Now I may die in peace."

"Life, Great Eagle, is a search," Eve went on despite his dismissal. "I seek for what I love. And I believe that the Great Spirit thinks of the Indian as often as he does of the white man."

Now Great Eagle grinned his toothless grin. "You think so?"

"I do."

"Tell me something from this black book, then."

Eve thought for a moment then said, " 'And God saw all the things that he had made, and they were very good.' "

"What is this?" Great Eagle asked.

"Genesis, Great Eagle, from the good book."

"The black book?"

"Han, yes." She grinned. "Black but good. It should have been a white book. And I do not mean that as insult."

Great Eagle thought for a moment, then said, "You must seek for what you love. Go, then, Suncloud's woman, and find your man."

"Wait," she said. "I have another question that I might ask."

"What is it?" Great Eagle inquired. "I grow weary and would go to meet Winter Woman; she awaits my coming among the Sky People."

"My brothers. Were they here with me? I mean, when I was a child, were they at the village, wherever that might have been at the time? I have a feeling it was here, where we are at this moment."

"Here, yes. This same place."

"That is all I wanted to know."

Everything else, all she'd thought of in the past, was falling into place.

"Warrior woman," Great Eagle said. "Go. Do what you must."

With a shy grin Eve said, "I'm very hungry. I believe I will have to eat"—she held up an arm and a muscle popped up—"to keep my strength, otherwise I might faint or drag my feet when I go to search for my love."

Following a delicious meal of buffalo ribs, Great Eagle handed a pouch, a very heavy one, to her, saying she would need it, he'd been shown that in his visions, and said, as Many Stars had told her before, "You will be different tomorrow than you were today—everything changes."

Eve was ready to go in search of Suncloud, mounted on her mare, Zeena, carrying the heavy pouch Great Eagle had given her, waving good-bye to everyone and everything she'd known.

And loved.

Great Eagle watched as Mist Smoke rode out of camp, and then he turned, giving orders as strongly as he had in the past. He stood straight and tall, looking to the sky.

"I am sorry. It seems that my life is not yet over, Winter Woman. My men—the 'squaws'—need to learn more of life and what comes after among the Sky People."

All Great Eagle heard was the pleasant sighing of the wind across the plains as he smiled, knowing Suncloud's woman would do with the pouch what had to be done.

He was happy now. As was Winter Woman.

She could wait. Great women do.

Chapter Thirty-six

Silently gliding onto Wind's high back, Suncloud rode after the Indian who had been sneaking about his camp, not showing himself, and then running when Suncloud went to see who was out there.

He had heard a sneeze, Suncloud knew that.

Catching up to the man on the piebald horse, Suncloud gave a leap and jumped onto the Indian's back. "Who are you and why are you tracking me?" He had the Indian pinned to the ground. "What is—Kicking Wolf, it is you. What are you doing? Why do you sneak around me?"

Suncloud was about to let Kicking Wolf get up from the ground where he'd tossed him, when he looked up to see the mounted figures riding through his camp.

"Who are they?" Suncloud demanded in a low voice. "Men you know?"

Still, Kicking Wolf said nothing, and as he was about to sneeze again, Suncloud reached out and clamped his hand over Kicking Wolf's mouth.

"Arrghhh!" Kicking Wolf's face began to turn a mottled red.

Grabbing the first bit of cloth he contacted on the

ground, Suncloud slapped it over Kicking Wolf's mouth. Kicking Wolf then sneezed into the cloth. . . .

Suncloud looked down.

The yellow cloth.

Now, grabbing Kicking Wolf by his breastplate fashioned from long-beads, Suncloud hissed another question into Kicking Wolf's face.

"What are you doing sneaking around my camp?" Suncloud shook Kicking Wolf so hard that the beaver cap the man wore was knocked off. "Who are those men? And why do you have this length of yellow cloth? What are you planning to do, Kicking Wolf?"

Lifting Kicking Wolf's head from the ground, Suncloud wrapped the length of cloth around his neck and began to twist the ends together.

"Talk," Suncloud demanded, his face furious.

Kicking Wolf squeaked like a mouse. "Scar-Face . . . and the Frenchie. That is who they are. I bring them . . . more yellow cloth."

"You have been following me. You lie. And you placed the yellow material and the blue beads in my lodge, where Eve would find them."

"Eve?" Kicking Wolf croaked.

"Eve, the Dark Hair. You know who I mean," Suncloud snarled into Kicking Wolf's face. "You have tried to make trouble between us. You wanted the Dark Hair to leave Wild Thunder so that it would be easier for you to take her to Great Eagle. You were going to get the Golden Tears for yourself. You carry the yellow cloth to make sure if you met up with Scar-Face that you would have an excuse: that you bring the cloth to Scar-Face. You would capture the Dark Hair for yourself and bring her to Great Eagle."

When Suncloud released him, Kicking Wolf fell back to the ground with a loud thud.

Watching those snooping around his camp, Suncloud was glad he'd hidden his things in an old thick stump miles away.

"It is too late for your evil deeds, Kicking Wolf. You gave yourself away with your sneeze; the material with the yellow dye makes you sneeze. I heard you sneaking around outside my lodge right before the morning Eve discovered the material and beads. I say again, it is too late. Great Eagle has seen and spoken to the Dark Hair."

"The Golden Tears?" Kicking Wolf wanted to know, holding his throat as if it were very sore.

"You will never know who has them, now, will you?"

Kicking Wolf shook his head. Suncloud pushed away from him and stood, catching his horse as Wind brushed by and halted, great hooves flashing.

"They could be buried somewhere" were Suncloud's parting words as he nodded in the direction of the camp.

As Suncloud rode away, Kicking Wolf watched him until he was gone, then scurried to his feet and ran all the way to the camp where Scar-Face and Pierre were still snooping and scratching about.

"Dumb men," Kicking Wolf grumbled, making the two whirl about to see him standing there.

"Why do you say that?" Scar-Face said with a sneer as he rode over to Kicking Wolf. "Do you know something we do not?" He looked the Indian up and down. "What has happened to you? You look as if you've been in a fight with a panther."

"I have," said Kicking Wolf. "Suncloud. He has gotten the Golden Tears."

"How do you know this?"

"He says they are buried somewhere."

"Fool," yelled Scar-Face, kicking his mount. "Come, Pierre, after him!"

"Who?"

"Suncloud. You idiot!"

As the two thundered out of Suncloud's camp, Kicking Wolf began searching the area, rooting in the grasses and weeds like a wild pig.

"Hoh!" he exclaimed as he found the pouch buried beneath a very visible pile of deadfall. "The treasure!"

Trembling, Kicking Wolf poured out the shiny rocks onto the ground. He scooped them into his palms and poured them over himself as he lay on the ground, rolling about in his riches.

Through the trees, Suncloud watched Kicking Wolf greedily sucking up the glory of his riches. Then he saw Kicking Wolf go still, reach into his pouch, dig around frantically and look up angrily, as if he'd lost something. *Like a folded piece of parchment?* Suncloud chuckled to himself as he patted his parfleche.

Knowing that the other two would return and a greedy contest over the Golden Tears would ensue, Suncloud kicked his mount and rode off in the direction of Great Eagle's village.

He rode for hours, and when he finally dismounted, a boy ran for his horse, the same boy who had spotted him from the hill before.

The boy shook his head, looking back over his

shoulder as he led the big horse, Wind, to the rope corral and Suncloud frowned, wondering at the boy's sad mood.

Suncloud went into Great Eagle's lodge, and for a long time he spoke with the old chief, who was alert, alive, and well.

They ate food, smoked, and then talked for several more hours. One topic of conversation was the Golden Tears. Getting up from his place by the chief, Suncloud stretched and looked down at Great Eagle.

"I would see Eve now."

"Mist Smoke," Great Eagle said quietly. "Eve Michaels."

"*Han.* Where is she? She must be waiting for Suncloud, yes?"

"No."

Quietly again.

"No?" Suncloud could not believe what he'd heard. "Where is she?" He remembered the boy's sad face.

"You have been gone for many days, Suncloud. You left her here alone. She was sad. She went in search of you, thinking you took the Golden Tears, that this was all you wanted. I think she wished to give you a woman-lecture. She returned days later, with two of my men that I had sent out to make sure of her safety. Five of my men went with her and now she is long gone. You have the Golden Tears."

"I do not want them. It was not my mission," Suncloud said, close to yelling.

"It was."

Something welled up in Suncloud's throat and closed it so that he had trouble speaking.

All he had to do was find the turtle and butterfly,

then the circle would be complete and Eve would be at home, where she belonged. Suncloud had thought that that home would have been Great Eagle's village, among the people of her childhood. After all, she did have some Oglala blood. He was planning to visit her often if she would have told him that she must stay there.

"She did not go north" was all Great Eagle would say, one eyebrow in the air, for he had promised to keep his lips sealed.

Astride Wind, Suncloud looked back at Great Eagle's encampment one last time, seeing the boy wave and the blessing of his smile, then he rode north.

I am Suncloud. I must go where my People are. My family . . . my heart.

He rode for miles. He reached a friendly Ute camp, took on an extra horse, food, and blankets. And then he chose another path, taking a different direction. Toward a river.

South.

Eve was just about to step onto the riverboat that would take her to St. Louis, when she heard a great commotion from where she had come.

She was wearing the yellow dress, blue beads, and moccasins, everyone staring at the strange sight. She carried her deerskin bags.

"Let me through," a man was saying. "You must allow me to get through to my wife. She has fainted. She is with child—part and let me pass."

Eve could see a man carrying a black bag—a doctor?

Nathan Adams? Was it? Could it be?

Eve waited while the doctor saw to his wife, held smelling salts under her nose, and then carried her to a waiting carriage.

"Nathan, Nathan Adams."

"Doctor, someone is calling your name. A woman in the crowd," a younger man told him.

Nathan turned, cocked his head, then dropped his bag. "Eve? Eve Michaels, is that you? The girl who almost killed me on the front steps of her father's mansion?"

Eve blushed. She nodded.

"Lord." He walked up to her and took her into the warm circle of his arms. Then he held her away from him. "I was such a cad. Can you ever forgive me?"

Her nose was filled with the scent of manly cologne. "Of course, Nathan." *My, has he changed,* she thought. *It must have to do with the pretty woman waiting for him in the carriage, staring out the window and smiling sweetly at him.*

Nathan's stare rose from Eve's moccasined feet to rest on her very tan face. "Where in God's name have you been, Eve Michaels? You look like a—well, to tell the truth, you look part Indian or something close to it."

"I am."

"You are what?" He looked about to drop his jaw.

"I am part Indian—Dakota Sioux, as the white people call them. Teton Oglala, to be exact."

He took her arm and tucked it into his. "You must come with me, Eve. I am writing a story about missionaries and doctors traveling into Indian territory. What a find. Do you have a place to stay?"

"No. I was going to look for a position upon arrival in St. Louis."

"Say, how in the world did you get here?"

"A few of my Dakota friends rode with me this far and then took my horse," she said tearfully.

He whistled. "That's quite a journey on horseback. Just like a squaw, hmm?"

"Well, almost." Eve laughed nervously. *"Squaw* is not a very likable word among the Indians, I'm afraid. Not in Wild Thunder, it is not."

"Come on, Eve. I want you to meet Olivia. She's the loveliest angel this side of heaven."

Eve glanced over her shoulder toward the hill, and then smiled when she saw the Dakotas who had accompanied her waving farewell. There was one horse that was riderless. Zeena whinnied and tossed her head, her beautiful black and white mane blowing in the wind.

Eve tried to swallow past the lump in her throat, but it stuck there and seemed to travel down to her lonely heart.

She turned and followed Dr. Adams to the waiting carriage.

Olivia Adams was a gracious hostess. She showed Eve all around the Adamses' beautiful white frame house. In fact, the woman showed her everything in that house, down to the drawers full of fine linen, white lace gloves, handkerchiefs, table napkins, on and on. Eve had never seen so much lace. There was an *A* embroidered on most of the fine linens.

There was not only the linen collection; there was

the silverware and all the beautiful delicately painted dishes. Olivia boasted that the Adams family held many dinner parties.

Olivia's nose wrinkled as she added, "For *our* many many *many* friends."

"You mean, of course, yourself and Nathan."

"Of course, darling, we are all that's left of the Adams family this side of Louie," Olivia purred. "Nathan's parents are both deceased. So are his brother and sister; they perished in a riverboat accident."

"How sad," Eve said as they left one room and went into another, where there were yet *more* treasures to be seen.

Eve ooohed and ahhhed at all the right times, but her heart was not in pleasuring her eyes with any of this fine stuff.

All she could see, as she continued to look at Olivia's possessions, were beautiful little Indian children playing in the dirt, their only toys cornhusk dolls, sticks, stones, and cactuses.

"Wait until you see my crystal," Olivia crooned.

Eve tried not to yawn.

Eve stayed with the Adamses for two weeks, and in that time she played hostess at five dinner parties and eight luncheons; she also polished tons of silverware, crystal, and dusted the many expensive vases that sat around the house, polished those very carefully, for her room and board, one of the maids called it.

Eve herself was a bit of a novelty to those who attended the parties, because they had never seen "such a beautiful Indian maiden." "But she has unusual eyes for an Indian woman." "She's not full Indian." "Where did she come from?" "What tribe?" "Does she have a 'brave' husband?" "Is he a chief or something?" "Oh, perhaps she's husband-hunting and wants to become some white man's squaw."

At one of the parties a man got quite drunk and yanked Eve around the waist, pulling her toward him. "How about a kiss, pretty little squaw."

Not one to argue with drunk rich men, Eve let him kiss her. His black beard was scratchy and his lips were moist and mushy. His breath was bad, not sweet with mint as was Suncloud's.

The man, William, pulled her down on a nearby satin sofa and gave her more kisses. She let him. She wanted to know if he would make her feel as wonderful as Suncloud could.

After a few more kisses the man grew bored and began to yawn. Two beautiful black and white dogs entered the room, and William ordered the dogs to "get her." Eve was up off the sofa in a flash.

She looked down at the man, William, and he was really yawning now, as if quite bored.

"The dogs could have bitten me," Eve told William. "Why did you do that? Look, they are still watching me as if they'd like to bite me."

"Get out, girls!" William spat out at the dogs.

"What do you know about gold?" Eve asked, seated on the edge of the sofa once again.

"Gold?" William's eyebrows rose. "Why? Are you planning to steal some?" He chuckled, then studied her face, every corner of it, as if he considered doing a painting of her. "Why do you want to know?"

"I had some, er, nuggets once."

"Nuggets!"

"Yes. They were not really mine." She looked up and saw he was frowning. "Never mind. Just tell me what you know about gold."

With his arms folded behind his head, looking relaxed and at home in his neighbor's study, William began. "Gold is an extremely dense, valuable, bright yellow metal with a resplendent luster." He was warming to his subject now, even though he did throw in a yawn every now and then. He looked up at the books on the shelves, tapped his head, then began again. "Gold can be drawn into extremely fine wire and beaten into thin leaf. Gold has been the symbol of wealth in all the great civilizations of which there is any record. Throughout history men have fought over and toiled for this beautiful and enduring metal. There is a wealth of ornaments, jewelry, and other artifacts throughout the world fashioned from this substance. No other possession in all time has been so zealously and effectively guarded. And fool's gold, now—"

Her eyes lit up as Eve asked, "What is fool's gold? What does it look and feel like?"

"Well, fool's gold flakes. It is iron pyrites or copper pyrites, and it is like real gold in its color somewhat. Gold, I believe, in its raw form, still sparkles in the sun."

"Sparkles?" Eve felt her excitement grow. "I thought only jewels sparkle."

"All right, then, you have me there. Gold . . . shines."

"Ah."

William yawned again, as if the conversation had been very taxing on every part of his body.

"You really do need some oxygen, William," Eve was saying. "Are you tired?"

"Not really. I just feel the need to yawn."

"Then what you need is air and exercise. That is why you yawn so much. You need to fill your lungs with fresh air. You are overweight in the belly, I see, and—do you ride horses?"

"Who is that?" William asked, sitting up on the silky red sofa all at once.

"Where?" Eve turned, at first seeing no one. Then she exclaimed, "Oh!"

"Why oh?" asked William, standing now, his beady blue eyes looking into the hall. "Do you know him?"

He looked her up and down and then at the tall man talking with the Adamses. William stared at the shiny hall floor for a moment; he lifted his eyes to the darkly handsome stranger again, and then looked at Eve.

Eve asked. "Why do you look at me like that?"

"I've never seen him before. He has dark hair, just as you do. He must be your brother . . . there seems to be a resemblance."

"No." Eve bit her lip, seeing those out in the hall turn to stare at her. "He's not my brother. Steven McCloud is my husband."

Chapter Thirty-seven

The same thing was happening that used to happen in Wild Thunder when she had been falling in love with McCloud. Warm rivers of excitement flooded Eve as she heard his deep, sensual voice.

She could hear the heartbeat of the drum.

Turning to look into his eyes, she felt their warmth like that of the summer sun. He made her think of the power and majesty of a vast, untamed land; mountains that melt in soft morning sunlight and change from violet to purple, seemingly translucent; forests of fir and spruce and bristlecones; a land of Guardian Spirits, where the game is plentiful, where the mountain lion roams, and the vast dome of savage blue spreads above skin lodges and cooking fires.

Eve used to think she'd feel excitement coming back to her old home, St. Louis. She had. But now it was gone.

She had wanted to be part of the civilization there. To walk the streets and nod at people while carrying a pretty parasol over her head. A warm house. A big white house with plush furniture, pretty pillows and lace, and candlesticks of silver.

Delicious hot foods and cakes. Strolling in a fragrant garden beneath the moon.

Now she had seen it all.

And didn't want it.

"There she is," cooed Olivia, her eyes traveling reluctantly from the tall form of Steven McCloud to Eve. "Come here, Eve. Someone has come to the party to be with you. Won't you join us? I'm sure William has had you to himself long enough."

McCloud's eyebrow hoisted over the name William and he glanced at Eve, as he smiled down at Olivia and nodded at something Nathan had said.

Eve used to think McCloud wouldn't fit into a setting such as this one, but he did, to her surprise.

He looked ruggedly handsome, dressed for the evening in dark trousers and white linen, no lace showing at the wrists.

Eve smiled to herself as she glanced at the rows of lace on Nathan's cuffs, just like William's.

Coming before the trio, Eve said with a half-grin, "William is, er, he is playing with the 'girls.'" Her eyes rested on McCloud's mouth. "They almost bit me."

McCloud coughed.

"William wouldn't do that with the dogs, would he?" Nathan asked Olivia, giving side glances to McCloud, still not sure about the man's sudden appearance at their dinner party and the savage look in his eyes.

Olivia said sweetly, "William might. If he's had more than his share to drink. Then he does become obnoxious."

The couple continued to chatter about such inane subjects that Eve began to think she might pull a "William" and start yawning.

Eve and McCloud silently decided they had stared hungrily at each other long enough. He walked over to her, his dark pants brushing her yellow skirt, hauled her up against his tall frame, and began kissing her right in front of all the Adamses' company.

With a purring sound Eve stood on the balls of her feet and put her arms around McCloud's neck. He kept kissing her devouringly as she spread her fingers and ran them through his swinging, shiny shoulder-length hair.

McCloud ran his hands up and down Eve's body, clutching her buttocks and lifting her, kneading her firm flesh as eyes fell to gawk.

Shocked murmurs ran through the room. The butler accidentally slid a few drinks off his silver tray as he paused to take in the romantic spectacle. Nathan and Olivia were clutching wrists, holding on to each other as if watching a tragedy instead of a wildly in love husband and wife.

"James." Olivia summoned the butler as quietly as she could manage. "See that *Mrs.* McCloud's things are put outside the door. *Outside.* I do believe the McClouds shall be leaving any minute now."

Breathlessly, Eve broke away from her husband, walked up to Olivia, tried to take her hand, and got a cold nose in the air instead.

"Thank you for everything, Olivia." She turned to Nathan, but he was hiding under the fingers he'd spread over his face, elbow resting on his forearm as he rolled his eyes heavenward. "You too, Nathan. I will not forget your hospitality. *Pilamaye,* thank you," she told him in Dakota.

Olivia smiled as sweetly as she could, but underlying the sweetness was a bushel of summer's first green apples. "You do not have to thank us, Eve. In fact"—Olivia slyly glanced at Nathan—"Nathan has a whole journal full of interesting items that you've told him about Wild Thunder and the people there—"

With a jerk of her head Eve turned to look at McCloud. He had been helping the butler with her things at the door, but now he stood straight, and when Eve's eyes ran up the hall and flew to the door on the right, he understood.

"And not only that," Olivia went on with a self-satisfied expression, "he has written down your little story about the yellow dress and the blue beads. Someday people all over the world will want to read that story. You have given us something worth a fortune." Her arm looped in Nathan's, she asked with a deep purr, "Don't you want anything to take with you?"

Pressing her lips, walking leisurely about the room, Eve picked up an objet d'art here and there while Olivia jerked forward and back each time. Eve hummed and tapped her chin, stared up at the ceiling often.

"Hmm, maybe this. No. Maybe that. Just do not know . . ."

All eyes were glued to the "legendary" Oglala princess whose story, written and edited by Nathan Adams, was going to become famous, with worldwide fame going to the author.

"Is there some little bitty thing you want, Eve?" Olivia asked again, flinching each time Eve touched one of her precious objects. "I will . . . see what I can do . . . and try to give you what you want. It does not have to be much . . . right, Nathan?"

"Whatever you say, dear Olivia." Nathan was

thinking of the "book" he wanted to show to his friends—after the "Indian" couple left his house and after they'd had a few more drinks.

All of a sudden Steven McCloud appeared at the end of the hall. Eve smiled at him and he at her. With a wink.

The Adamses gawked as Eve spoke in a delightful singsong voice:

"I do believe we have everything, Olivia. Nathan." Graciously, Eve nodded to each one of them. "We, Steven and I, have each other—and Wild Thunder—that's all that counts." She patted over his jacket where they couldn't see, ah, yes, tickling all the way down to her toes.

"Good-bye," Olivia and Nathan chimed as the front door closed on Eve and McCloud.

McCloud was already walking up the lane, bags slung across his shoulders, some in his hands. Eve followed, glancing behind her every few minutes.

"Did you get it? The big green book? I hope it's the right one," Eve said, feeling like giggling.

"I got it," he said. "And every note he made besides. While you were talking to 'Willy' in the study, there was a young man taking notes. Here, there's something"—he patted his jacket awkwardly—"about gold and what you wanted to know about it. The nuggets you mentioned."

Eve gasped. "You mean there was some young man trailing me around the house, taking notes, hearing every conversation I was having with everyone? Eavesdropping like I was some poor fool who did not have a brain?"

McCloud grinned in the dark. "He must have

been awfully quiet, and not sneezed or anything like that."

"Sneezed?" Eve asked. "What do you mean?"

"Kicking Wolf sneezed. That is how I found him out. He planted the yellow dress and blue beads in my tipi. So you would get angry and want to leave me."

"Thinking you were my brother's murderer. That man has a very shrewd mind. He is like some of Nathan's friends." Casting another glance over her shoulder, Eve said, "Do you think they will come after us when Nathan notices his journals and papers missing?"

"We will be far from here if they do start coming."

"What do you mean?" Eve asked, taking one of the bags from him when he handed it to her.

McCloud leaned close for a kiss. Eve welcomed his mouth and tasted, murmuring in his mouth, letting him know how good it was to be with him again. She pulled back suddenly.

"You left me at Great Eagle's camp. And you took the Golden Tears. I thought I would never see you again."

"No need to be upset, Dark Hair. You see me here, don't you? Does this not mean that I love you? That I have come for you, my wife?"

"Y-yes."

"Here are the horses. Get on. We have to fly like the eagles."

"Zeena!"

"Yes. I thought you would be happy to see her. She missed you also."

"We will have to ride far." Eve frowned, worrying. "How can we make it?"

"Up farther there is a change of horses. Guess who waits with strong mounts for us?"

"Hmm." Eve rolled her eyes, leaned over for another kiss, then said against his mouth, "Tames Wild Horses."

"Yes. And your white friend, Shining Eyes."

Wild Thunder. They were going back. Home to the blue waters. Tears misted under Eve's eyelashes. McCloud gave a whoop and a holler, a low, slightly savage one. And then they rode like the wind.

One-Arm had known the secret of the turtle amulet all the while; he'd just been awaiting the day when they'd discover their own paths of truth.

Kicking Wolf had been jealous of Suncloud's position and desired to destroy him and his love. Kicking Wolf had followed Eve Michaels for months, wanting her for a second wife. One-Arm told Eve when she returned how badly Kicking Wolf wanted those Golden Tears.

Many had coveted the Golden Tears, Suncloud had been telling her as they lay on blankets spread near the beautiful blue lake.

"Kicking Wolf had been carrying a map leading to the ancient artifacts."

"More than one?" Eve asked, lounging on her side, staring into McCloud's eyes while sipping Indian tea.

The last breath of summer had left the air. It was crisp outside during this Moon of Falling Leaves. Eve had gathered dry greasewood to make a fire. She had cut willow branches, stripped the bark, and set it to steep in the kettle over the fire to make willow-bark tea.

"More," said McCloud. "The original beads—
the blue ones which you have now—are lapis lazuli
and date back to the time of the Aztecs. The map is
very old parchment. I believe Kicking Wolf stole it
from your brother John. He was carrying it. When
and how he came by it and who gave it to John
Michaels still remains a mystery."

"Could it be that some old Indian man came up
to him and said: 'Here. This map leads to the mystery of your sister's past. There will be much wealth
to the one who brings her back to see Great Eagle,
Winter Woman's husband. The Golden Tears will
be your reward.' "

As she said this, McCloud shrugged, opened the
pouch, and spilled the gold onto the blanket.

"Tell me again how you tricked the Bad Faces
with fool's gold." Eve gave him her undivided attention.

"I took the amulet with the Golden Tears and
filled it with fool's gold. I'm sorry, your beaded bag
is lost to you."

"Maybe it will turn up again someday. What do
you suppose the three of them, Scar-Face, Kicking
Wolf, and Pierre did when they discovered the cord
of my birth in there with the fool's gold?"

"I do not know," he said. "But do you know why
Kicking Wolf brought all that yellow material to
Scar-Face? And what he was doing with it all?"

"No. I do not know."

McCloud explained. "Great Eagle has told me
that Scar-Face brought many maidens to him all at
once one day. He lined them up before the great
chief . . . and you guess."

"They were all very pretty and, hmm, each one

had the ghost mark and an amulet in the shape of a turtle or a lizard?"

"Nope."

"Well," Eve said, shrugging, "what, then?"

"All the maidens were wearing yellow dresses and cheap blue beads. Great Eagle had laughed at Scar-Face, telling the greedy man that he must have stopped at Fort Bridger and stripped every white girl of yellow material."

"Were there white girls at Fort Bridger?" Eve asked, already laughing at the sight of Scar-Face and all those maidens in yellow dresses and blue beads.

"Could have been. I don't think Scar-Face had any knowledge of the ghost mark, otherwise he would have known he'd been making a fool of himself all that time."

"Beau Arrow has the ghost mark. So does Many Stars." Eve gasped, adding, "Scar-Face held Many Stars captive for all those years. If he would have known about the ghost mark, he might have brought Many Stars to Great Eagle. Think what could have happened to Many Stars after Great Eagle denied Scar-Face's claim of Many Stars being Eve, me."

"I should go find the bastard and kill him. But I have visions of Scar-Face running off, crazy as the ghost bird."

"The ghost bird is not crazy; she is very beautiful with her black and white feathers. She has a haunting sound to her voice. I stop whatever I am doing just to listen to her—or his—call."

Eve lay on her back as McCloud shifted and came to lean above her face. He kissed her long and hard, soft and gentle. Like morning rain. Like wild thunder. Like the early morning sun.

"So the Golden Tears are ancient Aztec artifacts, just like the blue beads. I think John's journal is a treasure trove too, Steven. It tells all about our stay at the Dakota encampment when I was but a child and Winter Woman's Aztec relatives from long ago. Who do you think was with Kicking Wolf when he killed my brothers and Maggie's?"

"I have no idea, Eve. What happened there cannot be known. Dead men do not tell. Kicking Wolf is with Scar-Face and Pierre. I believe Scar-Face will go crazy and kill the other two if he has not done so by now. I have visions of Scar-Face with your cord of birth wrapped around his neck, choking him to death."

Eve shuddered.

"I have one question, Steven. Who do you think placed the Golden Tears in my amulet the first time?"

"That is a good question, my love. I have lately thought Beau Arrow was carrying the artifacts and put them in there. Where she got them from, you cannot ask me. That remains a mystery. She does have the ghost mark, just as you do. She is Dakota also, of a 'brother' tribe to the Teton Oglala."

"She will go back to her people, the Hunkpapa division of Sioux, or she will marry Joe, even though he is older, far older, than she." Eve looked down at the beautiful gold. "Then half of the Golden Tears belong to Beau Arrow," Eve said as she started to her feet. "They shouldn't all be in my possession."

Pulling her back down to him, McCloud said, "She is here in Wild Thunder. You can give her the other half in a while. First, I want you to make love with me."

"Yes," Eve said. "Do make love to me again, Suncloud."

And he did. Long and leisurely and lustily.

Beau Arrow had a surprise for Eve and McCloud. She carried another pouch; in it was the other "half" of the Golden Tears.

"You mean there are more? And you have them?" Eve asked, blinking at Beau Arrow.

Beau Arrow nodded.

"How did you get them?" Eve wanted to know. "And why do we both have the ghost mark?"

"Runs in the family," Beau Arrow explained. "Only ones who have blood of the ancients, Aztec blood."

"But that is from the Shoshonean line," McCloud argued.

"You live with Shoshoni," Beau Arrow went on. "Yet you have the Dakota blood of your elders. Why do you live with Shoshoni and not Dakota? Why do we mix our bloods sometimes and turn out half-breeds?"

"You mean the Aztec blood just crept in there somewhere along the line?" McCloud asked Beau Arrow.

"*Han*, yes." Beau Arrow nodded. "You and Mist Smoke have your half of the Golden Tears; I have my half. I am happy. You are happy. Pawnee Joe will take me to my people to visit and then I will return to live here with Joe; we be man and wife. Maybe he marry my friend Sweet Water too. Have two women. Life easy for Joe."

McCloud rubbed his chin. "Not a bad idea."

Slapping his arm, Eve said, "You are full of ideas and pretty visions, my husband. If you take another wife, you will have only one."

"How do you come up with that? If I have two wives, there will be two, not one."

"No. You and her. No *me.*"

Grabbing her around the waist, he carried her through Wild Thunder while she squealed. "Better put me down, McCloud." She lifted the journal, Nathan Adams's heavy journal—and threatened him.

Many Stars stood with Shining Eyes, laughing as the couple walked through town, going to the little log house he'd built for her. Whispering Bells was holding Feather on her hip, and they both laughed and shouted as the couple disappeared into the woods on the edge of town.

There was a little house there with a tipi out back, where he'd moved it to. Eve went to her dwelling and Suncloud to his.

Eve changed into her new, roomier doeskin dress, and in her hair were two feathers, black-tipped, upside down, when she stepped back outside.

Skunk Cabbage's flute music floated on the air and drifted lazily to the little house in the evergreen woods.

When McCloud saw her in that dress, he smiled proudly and held out his strong, dark hand.

Eve walked to him and wrapped her arms around his neck. He put a hand to her ripe, full breasts and moved down to her belly.

"Now you must wear the new dress," he said.

"Yes. Now I'm getting fat. Whoever said

McCloud can't have any more children?" Eve asked, rubbing a knee along his muscled thigh.

"Everyone thought so," he told her. "I was kicked by a horse."

"Well, they all thought wrong. They have to be, because you are the only man for me. Have been and will always be."

"Maybe it was Suncloud," her husband said.

"You think so?"

"Uhm, yes. He is very fierce and virile."

She laughed. "Especially with war paint on."

"You do remember that night."

"Of course."

Together they looked up, held hands, walked silently, knowing the blue in the sky was theirs.

Indian Version of the 23rd Psalm

The Great Father above a Shepherd Chief is. I am His and with Him I want not. He throws out to me a rope and the name of the rope is Love and He draws me to where the grass is green and the water not dangerous and I eat and lie down and am satisfied. Sometimes my heart is very weak and falls down but he lifts me up again and draws me into a good road. His name is Wonderful.

Sometime, and it may be very soon, it may be a very long, long time He will draw me into a valley. It is dark there, but I'll be afraid not, for it is in between those mountains that the Shepherd Christ will meet me and the hunger that I have in my heart all through this life will be satisfied. He gives me a staff to lean upon. He spreads a table before me with all kinds of foods. He puts His hand upon my head and all the "tired" is gone. My cup He fills till it runs over. What I tell is true. I lie not. These roads that are "away ahead" will stay with me through life and after, and afterwards I will go to live in the Big Tepee and sit down with the Shepherd Chief forever.

So be it.

TODAY'S HOTTEST READS
ARE TOMORROW'S SUPERSTARS